PRAISE FOR *Bloom Again*

"If you love the world, if you fear for its future, you must read *Bloom Again*. Its beautifully told story lifted me, inspired me, moved me to tears, and gave me ideas, energy, determination, and—yes, I'll say it—hope."
—KATHLEEN DEAN MOORE, author of *Great Tide Rising*

"Marybeth Holleman's novel ventures vividly and tenderly into beautiful and despairing ecosystems where life yet teeters on. Reminiscent, in warmth and charm, of novels by Ali Smith and Ann Patchett, *Bloom Again* asks the toughest possible questions. Are we asking the wrong questions about climate collapse? With extinction glaring us in the face, dare we hope for anything from life?"
—MANDY-SUZANNE WONG, author of
A Daughter of Mother-of-Pearl

"A feminist fictional account of current climate science, *Bloom Again* is an important book that marvelously captures the current science of climate change. Its appeal is both timely and lasting."
—MARTHA AMORE, author of *In the Quiet Season and Other Stories*

"Overwhelmingly compelling, beautifully crafted with lyrical descriptions."
—MEI MEI EVANS, author of *Oil and Water*

BLOOM AGAIN

Bloom Again

Marybeth Holleman

University of Alaska Press

FAIRBANKS

Published by University of Alaska Press

An imprint of University Press of Colorado
1580 North Logan Street, Suite 660
PMB 39883
Denver, Colorado 80203-1942

Printed in the United States of America

The University Press of Colorado is a proud member of
Association of University Presses.

The University Press of Colorado is a cooperative publishing enterprise supported, in part, by Adams State University, Colorado School of Mines, Colorado State University, Fort Lewis College, Metropolitan State University of Denver, University of Alaska Fairbanks, University of Colorado, University of Denver, University of Northern Colorado, University of Wyoming, Utah State University, and Western Colorado University.

∞ This paper meets the requirements of the ANSI/NISO Z39.48-1992 (Permanence of Paper).

ISBN: 978-1-64642-705-5 (hardcover)
ISBN: 978-1-64642-706-2 (paperback)
ISBN: 978-1-64642-707-9 (ebook)
https://doi.org/10.5876/9781646427079

Library of Congress Cataloging-in-Publication Data

Names: Holleman, Marybeth, author.
Title: Bloom again / Marybeth Holleman.
Description: Fairbanks : University of Alaska Press, 2025. |
Series: Alaska literary series
Identifiers: LCCN 2024035229 (print) | LCCN 2024035230 (ebook) |
ISBN 9781646427055 (hardcover) | ISBN 9781646427062 (paperback) |
ISBN 9781646427079 (ebook)
Subjects: LCGFT: Ecofiction. | Novels.
Classification: LCC PS3608.O4845665 B56 2025 (print) |
LCC PS3608.O4845665 (ebook) | DDC 813/.6—dc23/eng/20240802
LC record available at https://lccn.loc.gov/2024035229
LC ebook record available at https://lccn.loc.gov/2024035230

Cover illustrations by Kristin Link (www.kristinlink.com)

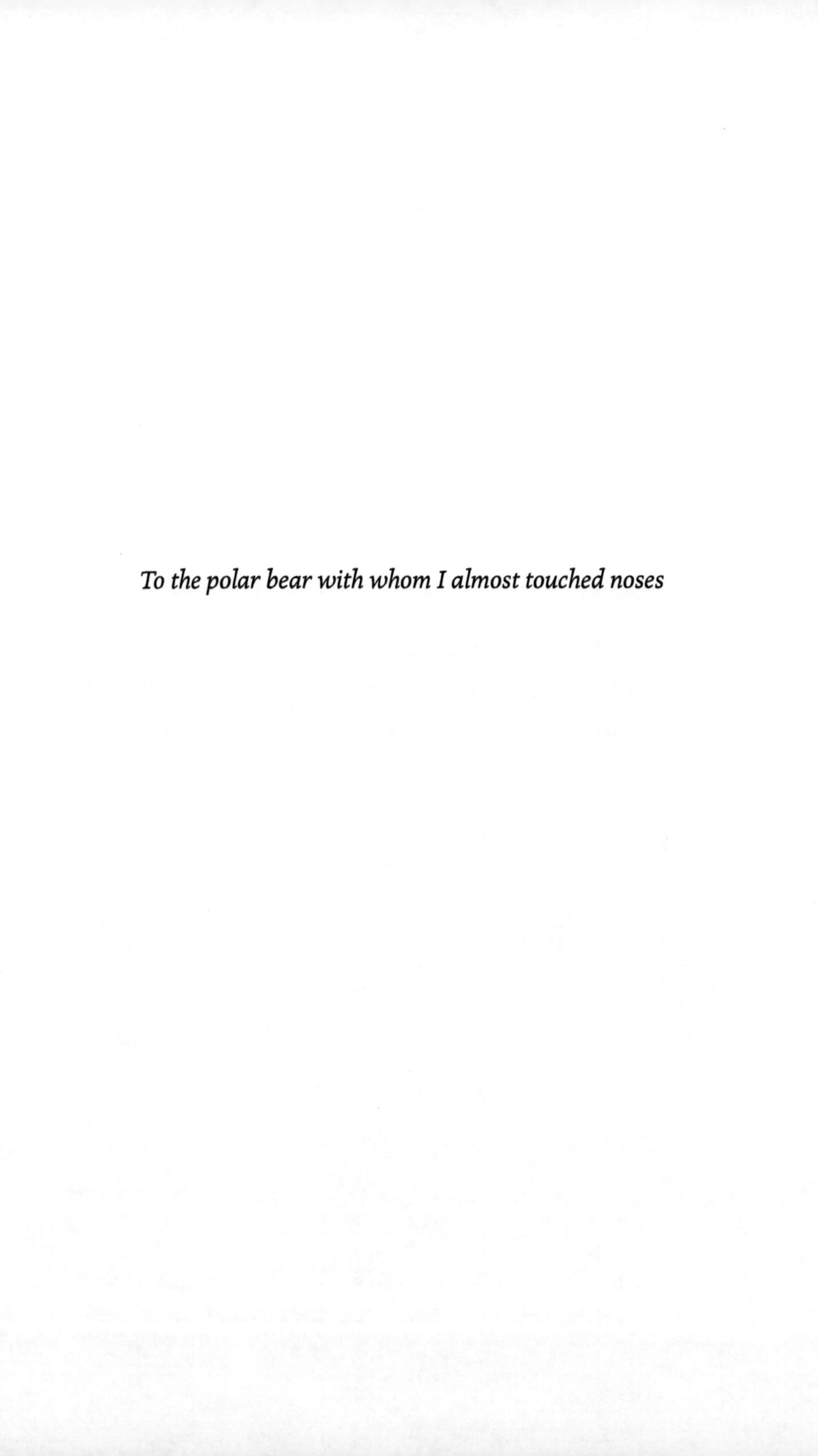

To the polar bear with whom I almost touched noses

BLOOM AGAIN

We may have come on different ships, but we're all
in the same boat now.
   —MARTIN LUTHER KING JR.

If you can believe in what you are and keep to your
line—that is the most one can do with life.
   —GEORGIA O'KEEFE

The next buddha will be a sangha.
   —THICH NHAT HANH

I want to stand as close to the edge as I can
without going over. Out on the edge you see
all kinds of things you can't see from the center.
   —KURT VONNEGUT

Tell me, what is it you plan to do
with your one wild and precious life?
   —MARY OLIVER

Section 1

Chapter 1

Elyse lifts the second half gallon of milk from the cart, her thoughts scattered like seeds in the wind until she sees a single image. Then she'll recall what she has managed to forget—except this time, the shifting winds of memory will not abate.

But for now, relentlessly, the conveyor moves faster than she, causing her to feel, once more, behind. She jams milk between orange juice and rice. It seems excessive, all this milk, but with her husband just back from another tour with Doctors Without Borders and their two sons visiting from college, she'll need it. Elyse sighs as she picks up a bag of oranges. She loves having them home, but she's already missing mornings spent alone with tea and sketch pad. She'd intended to finish that painting of James Lake before Dan returned, but has only succeeded in a series of drawings. She hasn't cracked open a single paint tube. Her show is six months off; she'd better get to it, or she'll have to display paintings done before her boys were born.

She drifts to James Lake in June: blue sky with wisps of cirrus clouds, cumulus row of lime-green birch trees, dark spikes of spruce flanked by a frothy line of willow, all mirrored in the azure lake. She wants to capture those bands of texture and light, show the perfect symmetry wedded to the tangle of cloud and forest.

She winces. Once again, inspiration arrives when she's far from her brushes. This morning is about groceries, not painting. Eggs.

Does she have enough eggs? Glancing up, she sees the cover of *Alaska* magazine. It's a full head shot of a polar bear, with that look of submission she loves to see on her Siberian huskies. She's about to smile when she reads the headline: *Bound for Extinction?*

The winds, and Elyse remembers, years ago, her friend Amy telling her about a colleague's experience. Flying over the Beaufort Sea for his biannual whale survey, he saw something neither he nor any other scientist had ever seen: facedown in the dark blue sea, thick limbs outstretched, floated four drowned polar bears.

It was just after a major storm, said Amy, and with shrinking sea ice, storm waves were stronger; polar bears, though excellent swimmers, can't endure the widening distances between icepacks and the increasing power of the storms. "But," Amy continued, as Elyse stood still as stone, "don't tell anyone yet, not until after he publishes his paper."

How well Elyse remembers this now, staring at the face of this polar bear. And how quickly she'd forgotten. She'd been so busy with—with what? Raising two sons. Sam was getting braces and resisting it with all his teenage-angst self, and Justin, in jazz band, was needing to be driven from one side of town to the other. Dan was off somewhere, some country on the opposite side of the moon, and she was juggling it all, so the ball that was drowned polar bears—and everything that meant—was easily dropped, rolling under the bed to join the gathering dust bunnies.

Something catches in her throat. She reaches for the magazine, tosses it onto the pile of groceries, and trains her gaze on the cartons of milk. It's her turn. She pastes on a smile for the checker, a young man who's quick and friendly. It's his speed she appreciates now, as the lump in her throat threatens to erupt.

Alone in her car, save for two sleeping huskies, she reaches for the magazine and skims the story. The polar bears' ice is shrinking. They're losing their habitat—the icepack they use for every aspect of their lives, from birthing cubs to hunting food. A warming climate is melting the ice, and even if every human on the planet immediately stopped emitting carbon, there's already so much in the atmosphere that the bears are likely doomed. This year's cubs, scientists predict, will be the last generation of Alaska polar bears.

Elyse stares at the words on the page, willing them to say something different. She looks out the front windshield, eyes fixed on the solid slopes of the Chugach Mountains. Can this be true? Just as she is reminded that polar bears are in trouble, she learns it's too late to save them. No. This she cannot, will not, believe. Of course we can save polar bears! Hadn't we saved bald eagles, gray whales, California condors, and all the birds of *Silent Spring*?

She jams her car into gear and heads for home.

**

Astrid's husband is late for lunch again. She stares out the window at another bluebird-sky day, trying but failing to distract herself from something that happened earlier. It just stuck in her craw, as her grandmaw used to say. She squeezes each of one hand's fingers between the opposite thumb and forefinger. Dean Thorn had been adamant about her taking this grant. Yes, she knows that half a million dollars would fund a dozen grad students. But the grant is for applied research. She doesn't do applied research, never has, not once in her twenty-three years with the university. She's built her career on basic research, on knowledge for knowledge's sake. And this one, well, it's clear as a bell that the funder knows the results they want. When an oil company offers to fund climate change research, any self-respecting scientist runs screaming in the other direction.

"Hi, dear," a soft voice says, as her husband touches her back with his hand. "Sorry to be late, but one of my students had the most interesting idea for a tomato sauce for braised zucchini."

Gareth's gushing enthusiasm is, for most people, contagious, especially paired with his singing southern drawl. It had been so for Astrid at first.

"That's nice, but I've got a meeting in an hour."

"Oh, yes, sorry!" he says, cheerily but forced, brown eyes blinking behind wire-rimmed glasses.

Not that she expects much from the meal. Because he teaches in culinary arts, Gareth often picks the restaurant for their weekly lunch date. And because Chapel Hill is a college town, there are endless quirky choices. Usually he chooses food over ambiance, and this time is no different: a small hole-in-the-wall in a rundown strip mall near the interstate, a Filipino restaurant called Angeline's. Astrid would have preferred The Last Taco on Franklin Street, where her friend Charlotte's art is on exhibition. She finds Charlotte's paintings gaudy, but likes to support her work, and she likes the ambiance: professors and students mingling over intellectual discussions and margaritas—what one chemistry colleague calls his weekly seminar on liquid dynamics.

"So, how was the meeting with Dean Thorn?" asks Gareth.

"Tedious," she says. "A big ExxonMobil grant they want me to run."

"Oh! That sounds fraught."

"Yes. It's obviously applied research. I was appalled that he'd even ask me, after all these years. But it's money the department needs, apparently."

"Maybe you could take it and just farm it out to grad students."

"That's what Dean Thorn said. He said they'd just put my name on as lead researcher."

"Right! So do that!"

"Except I won't have my name on applied research, Gareth. You know that."

"Yes, of course," he says, staring at her. "Just trying to find a good compromise; you know me."

Yes, she does know him: a people-pleaser, always ready to compromise. Not like her father, who taught her to stand her ground. It's just as well her father never met her husband.

She straightens her back, smiles at Gareth, and asks, "So, a braised zucchini sauce? Will you try it for the reception tomorrow night?"

Evening, and Astrid walks home through the arboretum. They live twenty minutes by foot from campus, and she takes pleasure in the few extra minutes of walking the circuitous paths through trees rather than the straight line of the street sidewalk.

She enters by the pergola, a lush green tunnel that drips with the sweet grape-juice scent of wisteria. She brushes at a bee who nearly catches in her brown curls, then watches as he disappears into a pale purple blossom above her head. Nearby another bee stumbles out, legs fat with yellow pollen, flying like a drunken sailor to another bundle of sweet nectar. Astrid sighs. Would that her days could be as clearly focused.

Exiting the pergola, she looks up, green eyes to the trees. The broad leaves of the tulip poplar are tinged yellow, bright dapple against blue sky. Foreshadowing fall, she knows, yet it seems early. Or maybe it's the drought. The last couple of years, summer rain has eluded them, and trees are showing signs of water stress, no matter how much the grounds crew waters and mulches. Astrid has given up washing her hair every day, even if it frizzes, just to save water for these trees.

A gray squirrel hops across her path, leading her to her favorite bench. She sits, dumping books and student papers beside her, and leans back against the weathered wood. She replays her conversation with Dean Thorn, feeling exhaustion wash over her.

She drops her head back to gaze up into the white pine's long lacy needles and dark scrolling branches. The needles, frothing from every twig tip, are like a carpet of clouds. As a child, she'd loved the story of the magic carpet and had dreamed, like many children, of flying. But for Astrid, the dream was not the flying sensation itself, or what new places she might find, so much as what she would get to leave behind.

Tears spring to her eyes. She doesn't raise a hand to wipe them away. She just keeps her eyes on the pine arcing above her, needles swaying almost imperceptibly, her skin warmed by the giving wood, the scent of wisteria pulsing in and out of her awareness. Fatigue drains from her, replaced by a surge of unheralded astonishment at this unadorned moment, as the boundaries between her, the pine, and the sky dissolve like wisps of a magician's smoke.

Two students walk by, chattering about a party Saturday night. "Three DJs," one says. "It's gonna be lit."

Astrid starts, as if from sleep. Both hands flutter to her cheeks and brush them dry, the exhaustion descending again as she pulls back into herself. She stands, smooths her tan knee-length skirt, pushes frizzing hair from her face, lifts her bag, and strides toward home.

**

Elyse does not go home right away. She's too upset to face her family, especially Dan, who would not understand her tears. And the thought of trying to explain it to him, of withstanding his volley of rational questions, knots her stomach. Instead, she drives to a trailhead parking lot that few people use, save teens on a Saturday night. The lot is empty, sheltered from passing cars by spruce and willow. She pulls a bottle of strawberry milk from the bag—one she bought for Justin, who loved it as a boy—and opens it, then flips the magazine's pages to find the article. She quickly starts to argue with it, as Dan would do, looking for flaws in the science, holes in the data. But it's a clear equation: no ice, no polar bears. She's trying to argue with reality. Lord only knows how many times she's done that, and to no avail.

Twirling a strand of thin hair, she lingers over a photograph of a sow with two cubs. Sitting on a blue-white expanse, the mother stretches her long neck out over her cubs. They both lean into her, one with head bent, forehead against the mother's sturdy leg, the other with chin resting on the sibling's back, mother's chin on the cub's head. It's a serene image of love and caring, of trust. A reminder of what so many species have in common with humans. Little do the bears know that their seemingly solid and endless ice home is melting away beneath their feet; little do they know that these cubs may never have the chance to raise cubs of their own.

The pulsing ache in her throat erupts. She throws down the magazine and grips the steering wheel, a sudden volley of sobs filling the car. Heat rushes through her body, the rising panic an unquenchable fire. Her bones, her muscles, melt, deflated, her throat dry as a desert. Then she falls silent and still. She is shocked at her own outburst but calm in the aftermath of it, empty and light. She steps from the car, opens the back door to let her dogs surge out, then swings back and grabs the strawberry milk as she would the hand of a child. She walks to the edge of the woods, slipping her thin frame between two spruce, needles pricking pale arms. Pushing through a bramble of elderberry, she keeps moving, eyes straight ahead, deeper into the forest.

Late summer, the grasses are chest-high, the fireweed banners of cotton tufted with fuchsia flames. Elyse has shouldered through alder thickets and high-stepped patches of wild roses, slender thorns scratching bare legs, to stand in a clearing where a giant spruce lies broken. The trunk is riddled with the drill holes of the spruce bark beetle, the pattern of the tree's demise. She leans against the fallen trunk, fingering loose bark. A shower of needles from a branch above tumbles down, dusting her head and shoulders in the leached green bits of a dead tree.

She crumples to the ground. She's watched this forest come apart over the last two decades, watched towering stands of spruce hundreds of years old turn dull green, then reddish brown, then topple in a fall windstorm. The spruce bark beetle infestation raged like wildfire through the Kenai Peninsula, laying waste to more than half the forested lands, then spread its tentacles to the Anchorage bowl. Below this ridgeline on which she sits, the mountainside looks like a giant game of pick-up sticks, littered with blown-over dead spruce.

And now, without spruce as wind protection, the big birches are falling as well. From pick-up sticks to dominos. These trees that grew up surrounded by the others, their shapes determined by close neighbors, can no longer stand without them. Even the forest floor is transforming, from tiny-leaved twinflowers and heathers to meadows of tall grass and fireweed.

Eventually spruce will return, thinks Elyse. Maybe. Or maybe the climate here will be too warm. The treeline will move north, spruce trees on tundra, forests where polar bears once denned.

She sits still, staring at the pockmarked tree trunk, tracing the scrolling lines of the beetle's hunger, as if they hold a code that explains the destruction. A pair of black-capped chickadees flit to a branch above her, floating down the trunk and closer to her tangle of straw blonde hair in small, quiet flights. A varied thrush scratches in the grasses nearby. Campbell Creek rumbles along far below through a narrow canyon, clear water bouncing off dark granite on a rushing bolt to Cook Inlet. Upstream, the Chugach Range rises, the jagged ridgeline to O'Malley Peak still limned with pockets of last winter's snow.

Leaning into a curve in the tree, she lets her head drop back, training her soft gaze upon the ridges, each scalloped dip and chiseled rise comforting in its familiarity. The water, flowing far below, hums steadily. Waves of sunlight wash the forest, limb and leaf, and the high notes of birds chime in the soft breeze. What if she just stayed here? What if she just slept right here, curled into this grass like a moose, woke to the symphony of kinglets and warblers, walked to the creek and knelt, drinking the clear water, scrounged a few berries and roots, and lived, for a while, like the animals?

A flare of sunlight crosses her face, and she squints, reaches for sunglasses. How did she get here? How did one magazine article, some words on a page, strike her down? She has a fortunate life, brimming with what she's chosen. She knows that's not a given, not even an option for most people. A life that would be called tidy except she's a scatterbrain. That's what Dan calls her—laughingly, of course, he never means to be cruel. It's a good life; she knows it; she remembers to be grateful for it. Lately, though, there are brief moments when she feels like the cottonwood by her favorite bend in the stream—the one who looked so strong and healthy until a storm snapped the tree in two and revealed the hollow core.

She sighs, puts one hand on her belly. Sips the strawberry milk, and remembers. When her boys were little, one of their favorite bedtime books was *Alaska's Three Bears*, about a black bear, a brown bear, and a polar bear roaming together across the state as each found the ideal environment to call home. Her boys loved that book so much that its corners were tattered, its cover stippled with grape juice and baby drool.

After reading it umpteen times, Elyse started reciting sequels. Every night the stories appeared, pulled from between waking and sleeping, where the edges of what's possible blurs to let in the light of creativity. The stories flowed, words falling one after another from her mouth, though she had no preconception of what she'd say next. She created an entire world, an intricate and safe world where the bears always found home. She talked until her sons were both asleep, drifting off beside them before returning to her own bed. And when Dan was on one of his DWB missions, they all slept together in the big bed, the three of them snuggled together, safe and warm in the stories and each other. Like the polar bear and her cubs. She tilts her head to the sunlight, closes her eyes.

By the time she rises, the chickadees have all but landed in her hair, so still has she been for so long. She calls her dogs, who have risen to this off-trail romp with their usual unbridled joy. Sophie returns first, obedient girl that she is, but Elyse has to wait another half hour for Darlene. As her calls mingle with the creek's tumbling, her hand on Sophie's sun-warmed fur, two juvenile gray jays light nearby, trying out new voicings on this curious stranger who has ventured from the trails. Finally Darlene comes leaping through alder, blue eyes blazing that wild husky gaze. Elyse laughs, "Where have you been?" and ruffles the soft fur of her head. Sorrow lightened, she turns back the way she came.

**

At the dinner reception for a visiting scholar, Astrid brightens when she sees the slight figure of Professor Strilay, shock of white hair like a halo, come through her front door. A physics professor, he'd been her mentor when she first joined the faculty. At twenty-six, she had been one of the youngest ever hired, and his guidance through the political and administrative maze of the state's largest university had saved her more than once, even as his own star kept rising. Since, they'd remained close, routinely meeting for lunch every Thursday at the Carolina Coffee Shop. She appreciates his dry wit and sharp intellect, his fearlessness in speaking his mind. His is a mind that matches hers.

"Ah, you've extracted yourself from piles of papers long enough to join us," she says, holding out her hand.

"Yes, yes, wouldn't miss one of Gareth's feasts for the world," he says, laughing, enclosing her hand in both of his.

Astrid's husband is renowned in the university community for his innovative cooking, so theirs is often the house of choice for gatherings. The old stone house, though small, seems roomy—open spaces and sparsely furnished, save houseplants crowding the windowsills. Figs, bromeliads, orchids, cactus—so many that guests often remark over them. One even counted the plants, announcing the results—forty-three—over Astrid's self-conscious objections.

"Well, I hope you won't mind greeting our guest in between bites," Astrid says.

Dr. Charles Lamont is visiting the university to speak to classes and give a public lecture on the effects of climate change on biodiversity. From the University of Cambridge, he spent two years on sabbatical, traveling the world to learn about changes in plant and animal life, as recorded not just by scientists but also by Indigenous communities and others who've lived in these places for generations. From Papua New Guinea to Siberia to Antarctica, he's had a remarkable journey to what remains of wilderness across the globe.

"I am looking forward to hearing about his work," says Professor Strilay. "I'm most interested in what he's learned about polar bears. I've a soft spot for them, I must confess."

"Well," says Astrid, "everyone knows that polar bears are toast."

"Whatever do you mean?" says Strilay, taking a step back, blue eyes widening.

"Well, you know," replies Astrid, "even if we stopped all carbon emissions now, what's already in the atmosphere will melt the polar ice pack, and without that, polar bears just aren't going to survive. It's too late to save them."

"I can't accept that," he replies, his voice taking on a sudden sharp edge, "and I can't believe you would so easily assume they're, as you say, toast. It's a surprisingly quick move to fatalism, especially from you."

"I'm just being realistic," says Astrid, her words slowing as she watches his face darken into one she does not recognize. "I didn't mean to sound flippant."

"Indeed," he replies, "that is exactly how you did sound, my dear. And I must say, it would do you good to take a look into your heart, what remains of it, and ask yourself why you have turned a cold shoulder to an entire species. As a paleobotanist, you should know better."

With this, Strilay turns and walks off. Astrid is stunned. She knows Strilay is an activist as well as an intellectual, a side of him that has often confounded her. He had, as a young professor, been involved in UNC's anti-war movement in the late 1960s. He was one of only a few professors who'd been arrested, for which he was nearly denied tenure. That's how he learned university politics so well. Still, to take such offense at her statement, especially one fairly well accepted by the scientific community, seems, well, almost anti-intellectual. And the look on his face chills her to her bones.

For the rest of the evening, he avoids her, stepping out the back door to the herb garden when she enters the kitchen, staying engaged in conversation with faculty members she knows he finds tedious. She can't catch his glance, not even when they're separated only by the red couch. And rather than being the last to leave, his usual practice, Strilay makes a quick departure soon after dinner. Even Gareth notices the chill between them and asks Astrid about it later.

"Oh, it's nothing," she tells him. "Just a difference of opinion. We'll work it out."

But she isn't convinced herself. For the rest of the night—as she shelves plates and wine glasses, as she straightens the rugs, as she releases her unruly hair from a bun—his words ring in her ears. What remains of her heart. Such condemnation from the one person she thought understood her.

Chapter 2

Late getting home, Elyse walks through the door to smell pizza and hear laughter from the den. Dan meets her in the doorway and asks where she's been. She smiles, says, "Nowhere important," gives him a quick hug, and slips past him, arms laden with groceries. Then she grabs a piece of pizza and sits down to a comedy with her three favorite men. Justin and Sam are on either side of the couch, their long legs stretched out in front of them. She sandwiches between them, and Justin drapes his arm around her, giving her shoulder a squeeze. She pecks him on the cheek and lets the science-fiction farce push images of drowned polar bears and fallen forests from her thoughts.

The next morning, Dan asks again where she was, deep-set eyes holding hers in such a piercing gaze that Elyse does, reluctantly, tell him about the magazine article. Reluctantly, because she knows he'll think it's trivial.

"I don't know why it upset me so," she says, cupping her tea close to her face. "I'm so sorry to have missed dinner with you three."

"Well," he says, "we're used to you being late. It's your trademark move. But it did give me a chance to talk to Justin."

"Oh, no, did you have another fight?"

"Not a fight, a conversation," he says, tone rising. "That boy just does not want to grow up."

"What happened? What'd he say?"

"Well I just asked about college, you know, what he's studying, what he's thinking he'll do with that degree. History of Consciousness, what does that even mean?"

"It's, well, it's, I know it's not a medical degree, like you have, like Sam is getting, but Justin has a different sensibility. He'll be okay."

"Right. Sure. There it is. He's sensitive. He's different. He's twenty-two, Elyse. Twenty-two. You need to stop making excuses for him. I still think . . ." his voice trails off, and he glances out the window.

"Think what?" she says, sharply, a heat rising within her.

"Think . . . that you coddled him too much when he was young. I mean, you nursed him until he was four, for chrissakes, and . . ."

"Stop right there. I am not having this conversation again." Elyse slams her cup onto the table, shoves back her chair, rises, and stomps from the room.

But Dan follows her. "You need to hear this," he says. "He said he might drop out of school. Because of climate change."

"What?" she stops in the living room, heat flipped to cold, and turns to face her husband. "What?"

"He said college is a waste of time when the planet's dying. He threw some quote from Thoreau in my face, about civil disobedience. He said rationalism isn't working, so we've got to use our bodies."

"Use our bodies? Whatever does he mean?" asks Elyse.

"I have no idea. He wouldn't say. He probably doesn't know himself. Just trying to get a rise out of me, I'll bet."

Elyse sits on the couch. Climate change. Justin. She sees the image of the polar bear sow with her two cubs, leaning into each other. She tastes the strawberry milk in her mouth. Sour.

*****

Dr. Lamont's public lecture is riveting. Not only has he compiled an impressive amount of information, he delivers it with such passion that no one in the room can possibly remain impervious to the plight of the warming planet.

Afterward, Astrid finds herself standing next to him, listening to praise and questions from colleagues. Something about it, she doesn't know what, annoys her. As a paleobotanist, she knows the Earth has sustained warming periods before—as well as cooling periods, known as the ice ages. She also recognizes that this warming is happening much faster than the others and does not doubt that the burning of fossil fuels is the primary cause. Still, she's irritated.

"Maybe there are just too many scientists now, doing too much research," she finds herself saying. "Maybe things seem so bad because we're just recording every single data point, and we can know what's happening in every corner of the globe instantaneously."

"Interesting perspective," Lamont replies, turning to look straight at her. "Interesting, indeed. Given your field, perhaps you can shed a little light. I'm assuming our new technologies are used to learn more about the past as well. What, in your opinion, are the main differences between our knowledge bases of past and present?"

Astrid stands still. She has spoken without first thinking it through, going against all of her formal training as a scientist. And now she has no reply.

"Yes, well, that sounds like a fruitful field of study, perhaps I'll suggest it to a graduate student," she says, hoping that her thin application of makeup—something she only does for these events—is at least sufficient to hide the blush she feels rising. It's one of those moments when she's glad for her olive skin.

"Yes, good idea," he says, as she sidesteps the question.

He turns from her to another colleague, leaving her grateful he doesn't pursue his line of questioning. She's grateful as well that Strilay wasn't there to hear her; he would not have let her off so easily.

She remains in place a few more minutes, trying her best to look casually interested as her colleagues continue to pepper Lamont with questions and comments, one after the other, as if they are trying to win an award for most intelligent member of the audience. Astrid finally slips away without, she hopes, anyone noticing, as the chair of her department is telling Lamont that he's the most engaging speaker they've had in years.

At home later, removing the makeup, which made her skin itch all evening, she laments feeling so distanced from colleagues she's known for decades. She also laments her most unfortunate remarks.

Whether or not she has a valid point does not always matter, not when it comes to university politics, and especially not if she can't back it up. She sighs, washing her face clear. No doubt, she decides, her irritation and unfortunate comment are simply a result of Strilay's surprising anger toward her at the reception. His reaction has unbalanced her. That's all. Tomorrow she will be fine, just fine.

**

When Maggie calls, Elyse is staring at a blank canvas, dry brush in one hand, palette of paints in the other. In her usual breathless rush, Maggie says, "Girlfriend, I need a favor. My kid's class is going to the zoo today—don't say no yet, I know you hate the zoo—but I have to teach a class and can't find a sub, and I had promised to chaperone I guess about a month ago and just completely forgot, and now they'll have to cancel the whole field trip if I can't go! Can you, please? It's so close to your house, and it's just for two hours, promise."

"Mags, I . . ." Elyse starts to say she's painting, but one look at the canvas reveals the lie. She wants to but hasn't, not yet. She's thinking about polar bears. So the last thing she wants to do is go see polar bears in concrete compounds. "Surely there's another parent who can do it," she says instead. "I can help you call a couple of them, but I'm in the middle of something."

"Oh, Elyse, you know I already tried that," Maggie wails. "Really, you're my Hail Mary."

Elyse sighs. Maggie, for all her chaos, is her best friend. How can she say no? "Okay," she says, "but I better not have to wipe any snotty noses."

For two hours Elyse walks the mulched zoo trails with six- and seven-year-olds alternately clinging to her like gum on her shoe and flitting away from her like butterflies. She knows all these kids; through the artist-in-the-schools program, she's taught volunteer art classes to them. They even have a nickname for her: Paint-Head, because she once showed up for story time with paint in her hair.

The child-swarm makes it to the polar bear enclosure last. She's the star, Binky the polar bear, the star of the zoo. And she is a handsome, winsome animal, with that thick white fur, those giant paws and sturdy legs, not to mention the way she rolls around on the cement pad as if scratching her back or plunges into the icy water to retrieve and then roll with a giant beach ball.

But she also embodies the reason Elyse dislikes the zoo. A polar bear with no ice. A polar bear stuck in a cage. The bears and wolves and all the animals of the zoo, captive, made to live in tiny enclosures just so this group of rambunctious kids can see them. What's more, she knows that what kids see at the zoo is not how these animals behave in the wild. She's read that zoo animals have smaller brains than their wild counterparts; they don't need much knowledge to survive life in a zoo. This gives her some solace—perhaps these captives, like dementia patients, don't suffer as much because they don't know what they're missing.

Still, she only visited the zoo with her sons' classes, and even then tried to avoid it. She never told her sons how she felt; she just got them out where they'd see animals in the wild. And when they encountered a moose on a bike ride, or a bear in the backyard, she'd remind them how lucky they were to live where wild animals were still relatively abundant.

Growing up, she rarely saw any wildlife other than squirrels and chipmunks and the occasional box turtle or garter snake—unless they had wings. Both her parents were bird-watchers; their backyard in Elizabethtown was a bird's paradise of feeders, birdbaths, and flowers planted especially for them. She'd grown up watching hummingbirds zip around cardinal flowers, woodpeckers tap at suet, warblers flit from feeder to branch. Once, though, she'd seen a family of coyotes.

Her father had finally taken her with him on one of his canoe trips into the Great Dismal Swamp. He'd been telling her stories of this place, spinning it into a mystical land of water black as night from which any sort of creature might emerge. A place of trees whose roots rose like gnarled fists above the water and whose limbs dripped with pale green plants that lived off the moisture in the air. She'd glimpsed these trees in Albemarle Sound, zipping by in a motorboat with friends. But Elyse wanted to slip into that dimly lit world of hushed water. For years he'd said, *When you're old enough.*

At ten, she finally was, and so, her belongings for a week tucked into an army duffle with her dad's name on it, she was in the hushed forest, only strange insect noises and the occasional rapping of a woodpecker rising to her ears. Her father slipped the paddle through water with such rhythmic ease that it made no sound, save the drip of water droplets. He did not speak, and neither did she. It was a condition of the trip. She was to leave her "Chatty Cathy self" at home. It was the only way they'd see wildlife.

And on their fourth day, they did. At first it seemed that the forest itself moved. Then it revealed shapes, like dogs who moved on wind, coyotes, five of them, slipping in and out of the shadows. They slid silently, every now and then one turning to her, amber eyes ablaze, piercing gaze lodging in her lungs.

That night in the tent she was awakened by their howling. Her father hugged her. "It's just the pups, trying out their new voices," he said. But what she felt wasn't fear—it was a longing that made her throat hurt. "I want to live like this," she told her father. "I want to spend my life outside, where coyotes live. Where wild things are."

That was her draw to Alaska: the wildlife. Dark as the winters could be and hard as it was to step outside when temperatures dipped into single digits, she still prefers living with wilderness all around. So the zoo seemed not only cruel but also a poor substitute for the real thing, and she worried that too many Alaska kids were growing up without any direct, unmediated experience with wild animals.

And yet, after this field trip, Elyse does start coming to the zoo. She comes to see Binky. She's not sure why. If asked, she'll say it's because she wants to paint the bear; she wants to learn how to paint the white fur that seems to emanate all the other colors of the spectrum, colors that shift with changing light and mood. It's as if the northern lights, the scattering and pulsing of color waves, were trapped in the bear's fur. So she brings sketchpad and watercolors, but mostly Elyse just sits with the bear. After a while, she begins to believe that Binky recognizes her and appreciates her visits, like an aging parent in a nursing home.

✶✶

It's because the sky is blue and the air less humid today, and not because she's dragging her feet about facing Strilay, that Astrid doesn't take a direct route to his office. Instead, she stops beneath a southern magnolia, shining leaves harboring fragrant blossoms. Nearby is the Natchez crepe myrtle, whose trunk reminds her of a childhood friend who said it looked as though tiny skaters had rolled up and down the tree trunk, patterning lines and grooves. How a girl from coastal North Carolina imagined ice skaters on a tree trunk Astrid never could fathom; surely that girl became an artist or writer.

Astrid bends a crepe myrtle branch heavy with flowers to her face and inhales. Such a sweet, clean scent. Natchez—she had walked the Natchez Trace Trail once, when she and Gareth were first married and attending the jazz festival in New Orleans. She had loved the ancient path depressed into a gully by all the feet that had come before them, from wildlife to Indigenous Americans to explorers, boatmen, post riders, fugitive slaves.

That was the first time Gareth had asked about her family's origins. He'd made some vague comment about how many southern families have interracial roots but don't know it. "Your mother," he continued, "her . . . features and skin tone. And the stories you tell about your grandmother using plants. How when one of you was sick, she'd go find some roots, make a tea. Sassafras, didn't you say she used it for colds? It just all . . . makes me wonder if you've got some Gullah in your family tree."

"I have no idea, nor any way of finding out," Astrid had replied, in a tone that also added, "Don't ask again." And he hadn't, mostly, though more than once he'd brought home some article or document about the Gullah Geechees and their traditions—a melding of African ethnic groups and American Indigenous Peoples—traditions that survived because of the community's isolation on the sea islands and the low country of the South.

Astrid never has told Gareth everything: that her grandmaw's skin was darker than Astrid's, and that she had a strange vocabulary, one she only spoke to her mother; that her mother rarely spoke about the rest of her family and had only once let slip something about relatives on St. Helena Island, one time, when Astrid's father was gone. He tried so hard, her father, to pull them up from their poverty and leave behind their past, that any mention of it was like "jumpin' into quicksand," he'd say, "when there's already plenty others ready to push you in."

Astrid straightens her back, just like her father always told her to. She lets go of the crepe myrtle and walks on, slowly, pulling her thoughts back to the present, as she reaches her favorite campus tree—not a big one, and not really old, but old in her own way.

She's a ginkgo tree, planted right in front of the psychology building. She's only about twenty feet high, but what Astrid loves are those fan-shaped leaves, and the way they chatter like a thousand cymbals in the slightest breeze. What she likes is that the gingko is among the oldest plant species still in existence, right up there with the tree fern and lycopodium: ginkgos are found in fossils dating back to the Permian, 270 million years ago. Individual trees can live a long time too. This one, probably younger than she, can live for, well, the oldest temple ginkgos in China are over twenty-five hundred years old.

She imagines that, just for a moment: this tree in twenty-five hundred years. What else around her on campus would remain? New East? The Old Well? Any of the knowledge, theories, ideas that are all the reason for the existence of this university?

Buttressed by a few moments standing beneath a tree so ancient, having put humanity firmly back in its proper scale, she walks straight to the physics building. She appreciates the scent of these old buildings; musty, yes, but filled with hundreds of years of minds all thinking, learning, trying to improve upon what humans know of the world and their place in it. She takes the stairs to the third floor, pausing one last time to gaze out a window at a pin oak.

Strilay's door is open, as always, and he sits hunched over his desk, surrounded by stacks of papers and books that make his already diminutive form appear almost vulnerable. Almost. He looks up when she enters, and smiles. Those blue eyes sunk deep into thick white eyebrows disarm her once again. "Well, now," he says, "if it isn't Miss Know-It-All."

She smiles, thinly. It's an endearing term he's called her ever since her first semester. Of all the professors she corrected from her student's seat, he was the only one not offended. But today the nickname feels like a slight—judgment that she would claim to know the fate of polar bears.

"I just," she starts, "I just wanted to apologize for upsetting you—"

"Oh, please, water under the bridge," he laughs, sweeping his hands wide. "I shouldn't have reacted so strongly. I'd read Lamont's articles, so I already knew what he would say, and frankly, the situation just seems so hopeless that I was looking to anyone—including you, m'dear—for a ray of hope."

"And I am sorry I didn't—"

"Please, really, enough! I know you, my dear Astrid. You'll always stick to the facts. Flights of fancy just aren't in your repertoire. Right?" And here he pauses, just for a second. "Me, the older I get, the more I want to escape into flights of fancy. Plus, as a physicist, I'm trained in them."

And they both laugh, a relief settling into the air between them, mingling with the dust that covers all the books on countless shelves lining the old walls of the campus.

Still, as Astrid walks by her ginkgo tree again, the sky tinted orange toward sunset, she feels a slight throb in her chest. A small wish that the relief would have felt, instead, like a brisk sweep of wind, or like ginkgo leaves falling in autumn: sudden, quick, complete. A tiny wish that she could have been, for Strilay, a ray of hope.

Chapter 3

Strilay had wanted Astrid to follow in his footsteps and study theoretical physics ever since that undergraduate class in which she'd correctly challenged one of his assertions. But physics, especially theoretical physics, made her feel squirrely inside; she couldn't quite believe any of it, regardless of how watertight the long strings of mathematical equations. It reminded her of religion, full of rules but made entirely from thin air. Astrid needed something more concrete.

Plants vined through her life. She was named both for the group of flowering plants called *Asterids*, and for the first Swedish woman to achieve a PhD in science, Astrid Cleve—whom her mother had found in a textbook she'd pulled from the public library's discards. No matter where they lived, and they moved often, Macey always transformed some small bit of soil into a vegetable garden. Astrid's best memories of her mother were of afternoons after school in the garden together: Macey, with more patience than usual, showing Astrid how to till the soil, form the rows, place each seed at the proper depth, and lightly cover them over, patting the soil down with bare hands. How many years had Astrid watched tiny green seedlings pop up among her handprints, like living jewelry on her fingers?

But it wasn't just the garden that drew Astrid to plants. It was all of her escape routes from the noisy, chaotic mess of her family. Her parents were poor—"dirt farmers" was what she heard them called—so they never had a house big enough for Astrid to have her own room. Except for one with the tiny attic, which Astrid immediately claimed. It was hot, so hot that summer, nights she lay on her back naked in bed, her whole body glistening with sweat, but alone, blessedly alone. Only for two months, though, until the eviction. Then when she was thirteen, and her father disappeared—Astrid never once doubting that her mother's chaos drove him away—her mother brought home a string of men with hopes one would stick around to help her raise three kids. All those men only added to the noise and drove Astrid more deeply into her own world, one rooted and blossoming in small woodlands within walking distance of their every dwelling.

Of all the places they'd lived, her favorite was the little house with the empty lot just behind it. The lot had been cleared years before, but no house had ever materialized; instead it was reclaimed by a succession of fast-growing plants, among them kudzu, the scourge of the South. Astrid learned in elementary school that kudzu was brought to this country for soil erosion, but in the southern states the plants grew so quickly—up to a foot a day—that they became noxious weeds, climbing over and covering and smothering everything in their path—other shrubs and trees, telephone poles, untended yards, and buildings. Even, claimed some old-timers, lazy children.

Her father despised kudzu. Hated it with the full force of his rage, as if the plants were to blame for everything that had ever gone wrong in his life. He'd tell and retell the story about the brick schoolhouse in Delway, one his grandpaw helped build, that was covered and then collapsed under what he called "that mean, awful, terrible, hateful plant."

Astrid, though she'd never admit to her father, though it shamed her to disagree with him, loved kudzu. Loved the plant's tenacity and relentlessness. Loved most of all the way the vines created leafy green caves into which she could disappear. Her mother swore a green streak every summer over having to hack back "that weed" to keep them from taking over her garden, but Astrid simply couldn't have survived those tumultuous years without their safe haven.

So when, in college, she took her first botany class, she was smitten. What could be more fun than a career spent doing what she already loved? And in her junior year, when she learned about plant fossils, about the geologic history contained there, she was elated. She still remembers that day: she nearly flew home on winged feet, stopping only at the gingko near the psychology building, before telling her boyfriend she knew what she would spend her life doing.

Still, because she cares so much for Strilay, because he has been more than mentor or friend, Astrid sometimes wonders whether she ought to have given physics a chance. Maybe it would have provided more—something—to her life. Something for which she has no name. Something to fill the hollowness that she sometimes, increasingly, feels. Here she is at fifty-two, tenured and set for life, but she feels as if she has taken a wrong turn in a kudzu-draped forest.

After her unsatisfying apology to Strilay, she busies herself all evening grading student papers. Still, it's a sleepless night. She stares up at the ceiling, one hand on her queasy stomach, searching memory for distraction. She recalls the kudzu cave behind the little house and the one time, just once, she had shared that place with someone, another child.

She'd met the girl in preschool. Astrid's parents were given money by the local church to send her, even though Astrid was a year younger than the others. Macey didn't want her to go, but her father thought it a good idea. "Give her some discipline, some backbone," he bellowed across the house. At first, Macey whispered every morning, "You can stay home if you want, sweet pea." But Astrid never did. She loved making her father proud, and she craved the clean order and discipline of the little classroom in the basement of the church.

Neither Astrid's nor Elyse's parents were churchgoers, something rare in a town tucked along the quiet backwaters of the southern coast. On the first day, the teacher asked how many had been in the building before. She wanted the children to find comfort in familiarity. Astrid and Elyse were the only ones who didn't raise their hands. They looked at each other, a smile flashing on Elyse's face.

After introductions, the teacher quickly moved the restless flurry of children into finger painting. Within minutes, Elyse herself was a canvas, with paint on her face, hands, smock, and a swirling mass of colors on the big white paper.

Astrid, meanwhile, was as neat and clean as when she walked in that morning. She was painstakingly sketching with the tips of her fingers a small building by the Albemarle Sound, a little shed out back where her father kept tools and which she had only once entered, to be surprised by cobwebs as big as she draping the corners. Later, when she told Elyse about it, Elyse said it sounded like *Charlotte's Web*, maybe it was where Charlotte lived. When Astrid quickly countered that Charlotte, if she ever existed, couldn't still be alive, Elyse said that maybe it was her kids, or grandkids, great-great-grandspiders.

Astrid's painting was the muted gray of the storm-weathered shed, even the lazy waters of the Pasquotank on the gray side of blue—until Elyse exuberantly swiped her own painting with a handful of purple, and bits of it splattered the sky above Astrid's cabin. "Stars!" said Elyse, "They look like stars!"

Astrid was simmering. She was used to this behavior from her two siblings, both wild as river rats. She started to dab off the purple, but it only smeared. Her painting was ruined.

The teacher moved slowly around the room, asking each child to tell her about their painting—a clever way of not asking, *What is that?* thought Astrid, who, even at five, was not fooled. At Astrid's, she paused and said, "Oh, my, what a sweet little cabin under the stars. The stars are a great touch; look how they add color. Great job, Astrid."

Astrid, surprised, nonetheless bloomed with the praise. After the teacher left, she turned to Elyse, "I'm sorry. I should have told her the stars were a mistake."

"Oh, it's okay," said Elyse. "Next time you mistak'ly paint a little cabin on mine!"

And with that, they became friends. Astrid found someone she could trust, and Elyse found someone to ground her. They were such complete opposites that they fit, like two pieces of a puzzle. Until they didn't.

Lying awake in the dark, Astrid presses her index finger hard, willing the memory to fade—and wondering why it rose. Wondering why this memory floods her with sadness. Wondering why, nearly every time she allows herself to trust another person enough to let down her guard, she's left feeling like a seedling yanked from the ground, torn roots exposed to harsh light.

**

Elyse is daydreaming in front of Binky's enclosure. It's a sunny October day, but there's still a nearly constant crowd watching the polar bear, what with fall field trips for elementary schools, an increasing number of shoulder-season tourists, and the fall season becoming longer, more mild, colors changing later and later. She's looking forward to winter, when she could be the only visitor in the entire zoo.

Winter, when she used to bring her two wild boys to the park near the zoo. So many days, no matter the weather, she'd pick them up from school and head straight for the park, carrying hot chocolate and peanut butter sandwiches. On those quiet snow-soft days, the boys had the swingset all to themselves; they'd swing higher than their teachers let them, stop to grab a bite of sandwich, rush to the creek, reveling in its icy shapeshifting. Justin, always the daredevil, jumped between ice chunks, relishing the challenge as much as his brother's laughter and his mother's anxious yells to stop. The pent-up energy from school finally dissipated, they sat and drank hot chocolate. Sometimes they raised up and howled toward the zoo, and waited, silent, bright blue eyes ringed by frosted lashes. Sometimes the wolves answered, their beautiful mourning for freedom ringing through Elyse's very skin. If only she could paint that, she now thinks, that howling, and its bodily reverberations.

Her reverie is broken by a group of foreign visitors clapping their hands and speaking in the winding syllables of an Eastern language. Binky is sleeping, curled up, black nose tucked into her belly, looking as harmless as the chickadees that flit overhead, winging from branch to branch. Elyse loves to watch Binky sleep; at least in dreams, she hopes, she can pad free across endless tundra and sea ice, those black eyes seeking the slightest darkening from a seal's breathing hole in the solid ice pack. But tourists don't like sleeping animals. So they clap and yell, trying to get the animal to react.

Just as she's about to take her eyes from Binky and down to her sketch pad splayed across her lap, she sees something out of place. At the far corner of one of two six-foot fences that surround Binky's enclosure, a man is climbing over. Her first thought is that he's a zoo employee, come to do maintenance or feeding. But why would he climb the fence? She jerks her head up as the man clambers over the second fence. He's a tourist, yes, she can tell by his plump fleece jacket, zip-off khaki-colored pants, bright blue tennis shoes that look like they just came out of the box. What is he doing?

The man approaches the cage, sidling right next to the sleeping bear. He raises his camera with the heavy black lens and—incredibly, who would do this?—sticks the lens through the bars to snap a shot.

That does it. The bear wakes up, jumps to her feet, and lunges, one giant front paw surging through the bars to grab the brightest, closest thing: a leg sporting the blue tennis shoe. The man pulls, but now Binky has his calf firmly in her jaws. People scream and yell at Binky to let go. A baby cries piercingly.

Two people climb the fences, break off some willow branches, and begin beating Binky with them. Everyone is yelling, screaming, crying, and then Binky drops the leg, bites the blue shoe, tears it off. The man falls to the ground, lying on his back and grasping at his leg. Binky tosses the tennis shoe in the air, and it lands in the pool. She leaps in after her new toy. The man is carried out by zoo attendants and two visitors.

The crowd stands silent, aghast, as does Elyse. Then they chuckle, point, and snap photos of the white bear playing with the blue shoe. Not Elyse. A heat rises from her legs to her face. Why in the hell would anyone in their right mind do such a stupid thing? What rises in that blood-boiling place is this: my bear. How could that stupid tourist mess around with *my* bear? And what will become of Binky? A river of fear through her chest: will they have to kill her now that she's attacked a visitor, even if that visitor was the one who put them both in danger?

On the front page of the paper the next morning, there's Binky with a tennis shoe in her mouth. That photo circles the globe like wildfire, making Binky as famous as Annabelle the elephant, who learned to draw with her trunk and whose paintings sold at the gift shop and auctions around the state. Binky, meanwhile, tosses and tears that shoe to shreds, while letters pour in to the zoo and newspapers, all with the same message: the bear is blameless, let her be. Some people send more shoes for Binky. Even the fence-climber, whose leg is on the mend, agrees that the bear is not at fault. "Just a stupid tourist," he's quoted as saying. So Binky is safe. But her enclosure has new and higher fencing, along with signs every few feet stating the obvious: *Do not climb the fence.*

The signs, the fence, the entire spectacle all make Elyse feel even farther away from the polar bear, farther away from finding whatever she is looking for. After a few more attempts to paint that luminescent fur, she gives up. Instead, she begins to sit and wonder what she can possibly do for all the wild polar bears who are also, thanks to climate change and their disappearing ice, moving farther away from her.

Chapter 4

Elyse dreams of Binky. She dreams the bear is sleeping in a snow cave, deep in darkness, and all that's illuminated is her white fur and the bright blue tennis shoe tucked beneath one of her great paws. There's a giant crunching sound, like the hull of a large ship hitting some immoveable object, ice or rock, a loud, long booming that wanes to a high-pitched scraping screech. The great white head rises; the great white bear lumbers to her feet and shakes out her luxurious coat. Then she picks up the blue shoe and pads down a long dark corridor and out into light—but a green, not white, light, so green it's blinding. A plant with big wide leaves covers everything like a blanket, leaving only the barest shapes in relief: a house, a lawnmower, a ship the size of the *Titanic*, and two tricycles, side by side.

Gasping, Elyse sits straight up in bed, eyes wide open. She looks around, locking her eyes on first one, then another familiar thing: the night-blooming cereus, the jewelry box Dan brought her from Thailand, the soft mound beside her, chest rising and falling—her husband, asleep. She turns to the clock: 3 a.m. Middle of the night, when things seem ungraspable and unsolvable. And even though she knows that in the light of day these things will resume normal proportions, still, at 3 a.m., they loom large. She sighs, slides back under the covers, and stares up at the ceiling.

By 8 a.m., after two cups of Earl Grey, the cobwebs begin to loosen, and Elyse is able to tell her husband about the dream. Often she won't share her dreams with him, because they sound so mundane next to his dreams of grand adventure and rescue. But this one is about the polar bear, and that persistent thread gnaws at her. Dan laughs, shakes his head, tells her it sounds like a fun dream.

"But there was something so menacing about that plant," she says. "It was kudzu. Kudzu. Did I ever show you that in North Carolina?"

Dan and Elyse met after they'd both moved to Alaska, Elyse to teach in the bush and Dan to be a traveling doctor for villages throughout western Alaska. At first it seemed so trite, that the only two outsiders in the Indigenous village of Quinhagak would fall in love. Wasn't it, after all, merely a union of familiarity?

After three years, Elyse moved to Anchorage to teach art at a public middle school. She assumed their love affair would fade in the light of the big city full of eligible men. Instead, she found herself missing everything about him, even his goofy loping gait, long legs and arms swinging. There was a certainty about him, a way in which he seemed to know his place in the world, and she was drawn to it if for no other reason than that she wished for all the world to feel that way herself. In contrast, she felt like a tumbleweed, blown this way and that by a fickle wind.

Alone with her third cup of tea, Elyse obsesses about the dream. Despite Dan dismissing it, Elyse can't shake the feeling that there's more to it.

It makes sense she dreamed of Binky, given all her time with the bear. And that Binky was threatened in the dream. She's been reading about polar bears and climate change, learning all she can about what's known of their status and the threats; she's quizzed her friend Amy, who sent her a series of links to government reports and scientific papers. She's pored over them, digesting all her scientifically untrained mind could handle: that sea ice is not just retreating but also thinning, not only making it harder for bears to hunt seals but also reducing the population of those seals. That little is known about the life that exists on the ice's underside, but it is likely important to the food chain on which seals, and therefore polar bears, rely. That some populations are struggling more than others, depending on the extent of the continental shelf. That polar bears are roaming farther inland, spending more time in villages, scavenging for dog food and garbage.

But she has yet to find what she's looking for: a way out. A way out for polar bears. A way that the science might be in error, that polar bears might survive, that climate change might not be as bad as expected. That it's not too late to save them, to turn this runaway train around.

She sets down her tea. Kudzu. Why would she dream of kudzu? It's been decades since she's lived in North Carolina, decades since she's been around that plant. There was the time in college when she and her roommate had taken LSD and were walking into town through a kudzu-covered vacant lot. It was a late summer evening after a scorching hot day. Entering the kudzu forest had felt like walking into an air-conditioned room. That's where the LSD hit them full on. They stopped and sat on some cool cement steps; they watched for hours as the kudzu danced around them; they never made it to town. She only tried LSD a few times, but she could remember every moment of those trips more clearly than nearly any other moment in her life, even the first time she had sex, even the birth of each of her sons.

So maybe that's where it came from: just that clarity of memory. Kudzu dancing above her in cool evening light. But then another, older memory rises, her earliest memory. She was four, maybe five, at a friend's, in their backyard, the two girls leaving the tightly tended lawn and gardens to step into another world—a bramble cluster, a lair, and beyond to a kudzu-covered wonderland. In her friend's arms, baby-bundled, was a stuffed white bear with blue eyes.

The memory is fleeting, but what bothers Elyse is that she cannot remember the girl's name, nor can she remember ever seeing her again. She has a sense that something happened there, something memory will not admit.

**

"It just feels like a lose-lose situation," says Astrid, putting down her glass.

Gareth looks at his wife across the table. He forks another bite of eggplant parmesan into his mouth, takes a sip of the cabernet, and smiles broadly. They're out to dinner at his favorite Italian restaurant, sitting at Astrid's preferred table, a quiet corner booth.

"Maybe you have it upside down," he says. "Maybe it's a win-win for you. Either you take the grant and farm out the work to students, or you turn down the grant and they'll find someone else to do it."

"Well, you know I don't want to take it. But Dean Thorn has been so adamant that I do," she says. "I've always had a good relationship with him, but I've never said no to something like this, either. Money always changes things."

"Not always," says Gareth, still smiling, and sipping more wine. "You're overthinking it. You're tenured, you're a world leader in your field . . . you're safe."

"Maybe," she says, "but I had to claw my way up from white trash, you know. It didn't fall into my lap."

Gareth laughs, shakes his head. "I know, I know. But it'll be okay. Trust me. Now, let's enjoy our food!"

Astrid smiles weakly and takes a small bite of her pasta primavera. Gareth is so trusting. He doesn't know, hasn't experienced, how vindictive even those who say they're your friends can be. She wishes, once again, that Gareth was more like her father: stronger, less gullible, ready to stand up for himself no matter how large the forces stacked against him.

Sometimes Astrid thinks she married Gareth just to have someone to make her laugh. It was all Strilay's fault; he'd told her she needed someone to make her laugh, and for some reason his words tended to carry weight. Maybe it was because he was world-renowned in his field; maybe it had to do with Astrid's own ambitions.

Astrid and Gareth met just after her graduation, when she was ensconced in the library researching graduate school options. The first two places she'd applied had both—to her surprise—turned her down. She was demoralized and sank into a depression for weeks. Now it was early summer, the heat of a Carolina June already slowing the limbs and the brain. Time to get on the stick about graduate school.

Leaving the Wilson Library, struggling down the marble steps with a load of papers and books, she'd nearly been run over by a long-haired boy with broad shoulders chasing a Frisbee.

"Oops, sorry," he yelled, leaping to catch the blue spiraling disk as it sailed by her head.

"Right," she simmered, shifting her load.

"No, really," he said, running to her side. "I'm an idiot when it comes to Frisbees. I'll slam into a brick wall, just to make the catch."

And then he grinned, a big wide grin with perfectly spaced teeth—except for the front two, a space between them like a small dark secret. She smiled back, involuntarily, surprisingly.

"Hey, wanna catch a cuppa?" he said, tossing the Frisbee back behind him to his waiting friend. "Celebrate the beginning of another great Carolina summer?"

She felt her head nod yes, again involuntarily. And that was that.

After coffee, they walked through the blossoming dogwoods. He stooped down and picked up a fallen flower and tucked it behind her ear. "There," he said, "now you look like a Hawaiian princess. Liliuokalani."

He wooed her with plants. Not bouquets, for he heard her say she didn't like the cut-flower business. No, he showered her with live plants, exotic live plants: hibiscus, plumeria, orchid cactus, and another that he didn't know the name of, and neither did she, an iris of some sort that grew like a spider plant, whose fragrant blue and white flowers bloomed only one day each. A year later, she was working on her masters at UNC, he was working as a cook at Le Residence, and they were planning their wedding. When he proposed, he offered her a jade plant, because, he said, jade signifies longevity.

Increasingly, now, there are times, like this dinner conversation, or hours in her lab, on a weekend when it's quiet and she can get some real work done, that she finds herself wondering how, exactly, she ended up with someone so different from herself. She wonders when her marriage will cease to work.

**

The kudzu dream does not leave Elyse alone, not even the next morning, her scheduled time to paint. Her sacred time. When the boys were little and she was trying to find time to paint, she heard about a mother who had set aside three hours on Wednesday morning as her designated writing time—and wrote an entire novel that way. So Elyse began to set aside Friday mornings. Now it's such a routine that, even with the boys in college, it's the only consistent time Elyse paints.

So here it is, then, that time, and a blank canvas. Her show at Sidestreet Espresso is two months away, and she has only three new paintings, just one that she likes. Her painting of James Lake rests on another easel drying and staring at her as if to say, *Okay, top this.* It is beautiful, the way the greens and blues seem to mirror and fade into each other and yet remain so distinctly themselves. Much like a good marriage, she thinks. It's a subtle, calming painting, like the place itself, so constantly seeming immune to the busyness and chaos and disintegration of the world of which it is, nonetheless, a part.

Elyse blinks. It's true: the warming must be affecting James Lake too. But how? Nothing she can see, at least not yet. Effects there may be so gradual and invisible that she could go there every year until she died and never notice any difference.

And that, of course, she realizes with another start, is why people ignore climate change, why politicians instead focus on the economy or foreign policy. A warming planet is easy to ignore. Until it isn't, as with Hurricane Katrina or Sandy or Helene. And then it's too late. And within the safe confines of that fatalism—it's too late—everyone, including her, goes back to the somnambulant state of ignoring it.

She shakes her head, trying to loosen the spiderweb of dark thoughts that threaten to immobilize her. Quickly, without thinking, she picks up cadmium green and yellow, sap green and cobalt and sienna and white, one after the other, smearing them on her palette. She reaches for her favorite big brush and blends colors, and then paints in big sweeping strokes, her anger and frustration turning to a soaring feeling of delight in creation. Before she knows it, her three hours are up, and it's time to meet a friend for lunch.

She steps back. The canvas is covered in green, except for one white hole in the lower right quadrant. The green is wild and virile, so full of energy it might just spread beyond the canvas and down the easel to the floor, the walls, the other paintings perched in various stages of completion, the canvas stretcher, her paint-splattered stool and her long wooden table cluttered with brushes, paint tubes, thinners, cleaners, palette knives, and sketches. It might even, left long enough, find a crack in one of her blue-trimmed windows to push through. She has a sudden image of her entire artist shed covered in this green, this kudzu, melting the snow outside as the vines continue on their rampage across the gardens and to the house.

But what is with that white hole? Why is it not covered? What is it? She can't wait to find out. Can't wait until next Friday, or even tomorrow. It's as if she's in labor, and it's time to push. She's never done an alla prima painting before, never completed a painting all in one sitting, except for her plein air sessions. But this one is getting done now, right now.

She wipes the paint from her hands, crosses the room, picks up her phone, and texts her friend: *Sorry, something came up, can we try again for next week?* Then she lays down the phone, covers it again with a cloth, and returns to the canvas. She picks up her palette, reaches for a few tubes of paint, and begins again.

Of course it is a bear, a white bear, a polar bear, Binky. She just doesn't expect the bear to be so small, so surrounded by kudzu, almost covered, in fact. It leaves her feeling dizzy. She steps back from the painting, farther, farther. Still the dizziness, still the sense of disorientation. But she also feels, somewhere beneath the groundlessness, that it is a good painting, maybe even a great painting. The kudzu swirls around the canvas like waves of the ocean, and the bear is so still, so solitary, staring out of the painting with such small black eyes that she looks as shocked as Elyse feels. But it is done, that much Elyse knows.

When she gets to the zoo that afternoon, it's crowded, with a church group and families getting out in the few short hours of winter sunlight, herding small children bursting with pre-Christmas excitement. Binky, the star as usual, is so surrounded that Elyse can hardly see her through the bobbing heads and children on the shoulders of adults. Discouraged, she doesn't stay long, but on her way out, she sees a notice for a meeting at the education center: The Wildlife Protection Organization is sponsoring a talk by visiting scientists and hunters from Siberia. Polar bears and walrus, says the copy, are converging on the town of Cape Vankarem.

The talk is a few weeks away, right in the dead of winter. She scribbles a note about it on her drawing pad and feels a tingling bolt up her spine.

**

Astrid opens the box on her desk. Postmarked Sydney, it contains fossils from the oldest known lycopodium species, a plant that has been extinct for 400 million years. Astrid studies the relationship between extinct arborescent lycopods that once dominated the eastern United States, and the extant recumbent species remaining. Now she's comparing local fossils to samples from around the world, particularly Australia and China, where lycopods first appear in fossil records. She is working on their family tree, contributing a branch from the ancient forests of North Carolina. She wants to make evolution visible.

Sometimes she feels like Charles Darwin, holed up in her small laboratory, as solitary as a hermit, studying things that fly in from the farthest reaches of the planet. Except she didn't start out her career with years aboard the *Beagle*, discovering new places and plants. She's never had that wandering spirit, not after the forced wandering of her childhood.

She gently peels back the wrappings, places one under her scope, and examines the veins feathering across pale limestone. These tiny bristles lining Y-shaped branching stems are the first examples of leaves in fossil records. This plant was supine, like today's lycopodium, but at some point evolved into giant woody trees that dominated the Carboniferous forests through which dinosaurs roamed. When did that happen, and how? What are the clues?

And what did the air smell like? She imagines it was sweeter. Lycopodiums can't grow in dirty air. They're different from ginkgos, popular city trees because they can thrive in pollution, where their leaves scrub the air cleaner. But lycopodium needs clean air. She remembers forest floors carpeted with their lacing, forests now fallen to housing developments and strip malls. They're still out there, finding small refuges; she sees them in Uwharrie National Forest, along the Haw and Eno Rivers. There are few places left in this part of the state that aren't paved or grazed, but she knows them all.

She stares at the venation, noting the faint mark of sporangia in the leaf axils that changed at some evolutionary point. The thought of air quality brings her back to some nagging thought: Dr. Lamont's response to her remark about climate change. It's not that she doesn't think all the carbon dioxide being poured into the air by human industry isn't a problem; she'd never doubt overwhelming scientific proof. She's just not convinced it's the planet's most dire situation. If her research into the past lives of plants has taught her anything, it's that human knowledge has barely scratched the surface.

She believes in basic research, of a kind that seems to be going the way of this plant whose fossil she examines. But funding for basic research is shrinking. Indulgent, some call it, given all the ills of the world. Just a bunch of grownups playing around in a lab like kids.

She takes a deep breath and returns to the study of the small piece of rock under her scope. This is where she belongs, where she is happiest. It's why she gave up being chair of the department. She had always wanted to continue rising in the ranks, to eventually become chancellor or even president. But being chair, she learned just how much she could not bear the politicking that went on, the false smiles and backstabbing, the oversized egos. The kind of behavior her father always railed against. Not to mention all the ways a university was now run like a corporation, with more focus on filling a classroom than what goes on in that classroom.

When she stepped down, at first everyone pried for some reason, some scandal. Maybe—there were whispers in hallways, Astrid knew—maybe she'd slept with a student, or had accepted research money under the table, or had stolen another scientist's work. No, there was only her disgust with the little dramas people create to make themselves feel important. She'd rather be in the lab, alone with her samples, or in the forest with lycopodium, watching her plant quietly spread generous tendrils over the earth.

Stepping down, however, signaled a sudden career stagnation and surprised colleagues around the world who knew Dr. Astrid Baldwin as one of the most fiercely devoted and competitive researchers they'd ever met. She was renowned not only for her work but also for her ability to keep research funds flowing in a field where women get, on average, 40 percent less money for their labs, not to mention lower salaries across the board.

Gareth, bless his cheerful heart, had been nothing but supportive, as had Strilay. They both told her the same thing: you will rise to far greater heights now that you're free of that busywork. Strilay has been chair of the physics department twice—the second time only because his colleagues pulled him in kicking and screaming after a period of low enrollment. He'd just won another award from the American Institute of Physics, and that, plus the vein of notoriety from his war protest days, convinced his colleagues he'd bring in more students—and they were right.

Gareth has since been tapped to run the culinary arts program, but for him it's a good fit: he loves people and people love him. He has a natural ease in any social situation that is a complete wonderment to Astrid. It's made her life easier, that much she knows. He deflects attention from her, provides a buffer. But it's also made her life more social than she'd choose, for Gareth likes to go to more events and stay later, not to mention hosting gatherings at their house—like Lamont's reception. All Astrid really wants, she thinks, as she follows lines in rock, is time and space and funding to do her research.

******

Elyse enters the vestibule, stomps snow from her boots, and walks into the big, warm, brightly lit room. On the back wall sits a table with a few brochures and two coffee pots, the sour scent of stale coffee sifting from them. Before her are rows of chairs, the room empty save a handful of people, and of those, she can tell, most are presenters. She wishes she'd been able to convince friends to join her. But it's a Tuesday evening in December, and it's hard for Alaskans to rally from their hibernation mode once they've gotten home from work, fed the kids, and settled into the yellow light of their living rooms.

She remembers a winter's eve when her two boys were driving her crazy with their excess tween energy, until she loaded them in the car and took them to the only thing she knew was happening: a lecture on quantum mechanics and space time. Justin had expressed interest in black holes, so she hoped it would engage them. And it did, Justin at least. She'd never seen him scribble so many notes, never seen his eyes light up in quite that way. On the walk back to the car, he leaned back at the night sky, a crescent moon glowing with Earthshine. "We're so lucky to have a moon," he said in a soft voice. "I mean, it would be way cool to have more than one, like Jupiter, but I'm glad we've got one."

In her chest, a familiar ache starts up. She misses her boys in ways she can't share with anyone. Not who they are now, but who they were then, as kids. Sometimes she'll pass a family photo hanging in the hall and cry, wishing for one more day with them at three, or six, or ten. Just one more hour at the playground, one more bedtime story. Sometimes the yearning is even stronger when she spends time with who they are now, two young men who no longer tell her every little wish. Sam, now so quiet and serious. And Justin—still reckless, with these ideas about dropping out of school, but increasingly distant. The son who was always so communicative, so demonstrative, falling silent.

A rush of cold air sweeps her back to the present as someone opens the door. The room is like a small school auditorium, and lit as harshly. There's a big screen at the front, and behind it through the plate glass windows is Alaska's dark winter, snow and streetlights. A few people—clearly the presenters—talk in hushed voices up front.

All four are men. One is tall and skinny, wearing a suit that drapes his lanky frame like a father's overcoat. The other three are short; one white and rotund, with a thick gray beard and thinning hair, and the other two stocky and standing with legs wide apart, arms folded across their chests. Shiny dark hair trimmed neatly, one with some salt and pepper; skin the color of toasted almonds, and eyes that same almond shape: these must be the two Yup'ik Siberians.

Slowly, thankfully, the room fills, and the tall scarecrow man moves to the front, clears his throat, looks out over the audience. "Thanks for coming," he says in a voice so booming it could wake the zoo bears from hibernation. "My name's Jim Monaghan, I'm the director of the Wildlife Protection Organization, and we're delighted to sponsor tonight's program."

Scarecrow Jim talks awhile, per usual at these events, where the introducer seems to want to be the presenter. But still, WPO did bring these Siberians to Alaska—one is a marine mammal biologist, and the others are Indigenous marine mammal hunters. The trio has already traveled north to Utqiagvik and Point Hope, talking with those Alaska Indigenous communities about how they are responding to changing wildlife movements brought on by shrinking sea ice.

Change, respond, adapt. All these words we use, thinks Elyse, to insulate ourselves from what we're really talking about. Seals, walrus, polar bears desperately trying to survive as their ice shifts and leaves, as shores that were once firmed by ice for eight months of the year are now exposed to surging fall and winter storm waves. The ice disappearing, the shores eroding, the animals losing their home ground foot by foot, trying to find food, trying to find a place to rest and to birth their young. They are desperate, scrambling, and just behind them, scrambling, the few remaining Indigenous communities that subsist on these animals, in this place. Communities whose shores are eroding, entire villages faced with relocating or watching their houses fall into the sea. But the rest of humans, well, they just keep pouring the stuff that has created this whole mess into the atmosphere.

Elyse has now read enough to know that most everyone is focused only on adaptation, on dealing with the current situation. Hardly anyone talks about curtailing it or, heaven forbid, reversing it. Nope. It's like sitting in a tub with the faucet on, with the water rising around your neck, and instead of reaching over and turning the faucet off, which would involve some exertion and a slight change of position, instead you just sit there and try to figure out how you're going to learn to breathe under water.

Elyse's internal rant ends abruptly when Scarecrow Jim finally turns the floor over to the Siberian biologist. He speaks halting English with that beautifully harsh accent that all northern speakers have—as if their very language was born of the crunch of ice against shore, the blast of cold air on a face, the brief sliver of sunlight slipping over the horizon on spring's return.

With maps and charts, he shows what Elyse already knows: the ice pack is leaving us. Especially those of us in Alaska and Russia. And as it shrinks, there's less ice to reflect, and more dark water to absorb, the sun's heat—which then accelerates the melting. Models show that ice will cling to the far north of Canada and to Greenland, and biologists predict that will be the polar bear's last stand.

Elyse is slumped in her seat, her pen by her side, her eyes staring at her sodden snow boots by the time the biologist is done giving his grim news. She'd started to sketch one of the images he'd shown, of a polar bear leaping across cerulean waters from one white iceberg to another, limbs fully extended, long neck reaching forward. But she gave up, despair settling in like the windless night outside the windows.

The biologist finishes, his head hanging low as if all the terrible knowledge he's just shared is bending his body in half. The two marine mammal hunters are a marked contrast: they stand before the crowd, side by side, muscular arms folded across wide chests, stocky legs spread wide, smiles spread even wider.

They know little English, already having two languages under their belts: Yup'ik and Russian. So Scarecrow Jim interprets; his Russian seems surprisingly good. The hunters dive right in to what they're doing—not what's wrong, how humans have screwed up, no wallowing in dire news. Just direct action.

In their coastal town of Cape Vankarem, sea ice loss has brought a strange phenomenon. Walrus have begun to congregate just east of town on a long, broad beach. These walrus typically use ice packs for their haulouts, but with those shrinking, they're increasingly congregating on land. Because little of the coast has the wide, low terrain they need to haul themselves out and shuffle above tideline, the ample beach east of Cape Vankarem has drawn not just a few hundred but tens of thousands of walrus, all crowding together in a teeming mass.

The younger Yup'ik speaks rapidly, then stretches his arms wide as if to hug the room.

"A super haulout of massive proportions," interprets Jim. "More than they've ever seen in one place, let alone so near their village."

This is not, however, the problem. The problem is what the massive haulout attracts: tourists and polar bears. Here the older Yup'ik shakes his head, slowly, like a parent at a wayward child. Tourists and polar bears make for a deadly combination, and not just because hungry polar bears might snatch a tourist. No, it's a reason closer to the heart—and belly—of a marine mammal subsistence community: tourists and polar bears are causing walrus to stampede, and the massive stampeding is killing walrus, mostly pups and yearlings, the future of the herd.

The hunters, worried about the continuation of the walrus population, can't just stand by watching the walrus die. Inaction is not in their vocabulary. The younger man's face brightens as he explains what they are doing. The community's marine mammal hunters have become self-appointed marine mammal protectors, the Umka Patrol. They police tourists, keeping the shutter-clicking crowd far enough away to avoid disturbing the walrus. And they police the polar bears too. Whenever a bear comes near, the hunters approach the bear, waving big sticks.

"That's right," says Jim, a grin spreading across his face. "No guns. Just sticks."

Elyse gasps, and then smiles. She's heard that Alaska Indigenous Peoples have been killing more polar bears in defense of life and property as the bears come closer to their villages looking for food. She's wondered if there was a nonlethal alternative. And here it is. Armed with nothing but big sticks, these men are chasing off hungry polar bears. No PowerPoint presentation is necessary for her to visualize this scene.

But there's more. The hunters know the polar bears are starving, and they know the stampede-caused walrus deaths are leaving more meat than the village can use. So after a stampede, less frequent now with the Umka Patrol, the hunters gather the bodies and carry them far away, west along the coastline, in the direction from which the polar bears come. There they pile them up, these walrus carcasses, as food for the polar bears.

Elyse's smile grows. She picks up her pen and, still watching them, listening to them, begins to sketch, rapidly.

Chapter 5

After the talk, Elyse approaches the two Siberians to thank them. Though they don't understand a word, they give her their full attention. In their silence, she tells them she'd love to see the haulout, the walrus and polar bears; she'd love to paint that scene. Jim, overhearing, says there are no organized tours from the U.S.; the tourists are mostly Russian. So she is surprised when, just three weeks later, she gets a call from Jim.

"Listen," he says, "we're thinking of organizing an expedition of scientists and artists to Cape Vankarem. Something to highlight what climate change is doing right now, how it's affecting these people and the wildlife they depend upon. It'd be modeled after the Harriman Alaska Expedition, are you familiar with that?"

Elyse is not, but while Jim tells her of his plan, she jumps on the internet. The Harriman Expedition of 1899 started out as a rich railroad magnate's pleasure cruise to Alaska, but Edward Harriman invited a cadre of well-known scientists, artists, writers, naturalists, and photographers, including Edward S. Curtis and John Muir. During their two-month voyage from Seattle to Siberia and back again, they documented hundreds of previously unknown species and created a rich resource of artistic, cultural, and scientific information.

As she listens, her heart sinks. Jim isn't interested in Elyse applying; he just wants her help reaching the best artists in the nation.

"You know," he says, "some top New York artist, wouldn't that be something? City artist in Siberia."

After the call, Elyse stares at the Edward S. Curtis photographs on her screen, black-and-white images from the Harriman Expedition, the weathered face of an elder Tlingit woman, angled high cheekbones and deep-set eyes that look up and away from the camera. She sighs, deflated, even as she feels a heat rising in her face. Jim didn't say it, but she has no doubt that she seeded his idea with her comments after the presentation.

She may not like it, but she does understand why he didn't ask her to apply. She's a barely known Alaska artist far from the national scene; a famous New York artist will bring more media attention. It's for the place, she thinks, for the polar bears. For a cause larger than her small desires for her own work. All she can do is support the effort.

She closes her laptop, grabs a cup of tea, heads to her studio. Dan is home in a week from a three-month stint in Nigeria, and her Sidestreet show looms. She can't waste time feeling sorry for herself. Besides, she realizes, as she takes off her snowboots and breathes in the scent of her studio—a grounding admixture of oil paints, thinners, canvas, wood—Jim didn't tell her *not* to apply.

A week later, Dan is barely settled in the car with his seatbelt on when Elyse begins to tell him about the talk, about these marine mammal hunters armed with nothing but sticks protecting walrus and feeding polar bears, taking the situation into their own hands, literally, and not waiting for some government funding or intervention or world consensus.

"Just imagine," she says, "nothing between you and a hungry polar bear except a stick! And they don't even want to kill the bears but instead feed them walrus carcasses! What an incredible culture. What incredible practical intelligence. What courage, compassion."

Dan, who is, to be fair, jet-lagged and exhausted from a harrowing assignment, replies curtly, "Well, maybe they just don't have enough guns. Or maybe their walls are already covered in polar bear skins.

Anyhow, they can't hunt polar bears for subsistence like they can here in our fair state."

Elyse drops it, not wanting Dan's lack of enthusiasm to dampen her own. That has happened enough times for her to know better. Instead, she asks about his flight and focuses on the drive home. But there's a now-familiar shiver running up her spine, the one that comes whenever she thinks of Cape Vankarem. As Dan describes the clawing humidity of the Niger Delta, she makes a decision: she'll apply for the expedition. So what if she has about as much chance as getting invited on a lunar expedition?

She uses the polar bear and kudzu painting for her Cape Vankarem application but doesn't even consider including it in her Sidestreet show. Instead, she fills the coffee shop's walls with the James Lake painting and others like it—soft, almost dreamy Alaska landscapes. Only five, rather than the eight she'd intended.

At the opening, she surveys the space: five is fine. They're large paintings, and this place is tiny, crowded with tables and chairs. It doesn't take many people to fill it, and the nearly constant buzz of the espresso machine gives a bustling sensation regardless of how full the room is. Elyse drops into enjoying the nice mix of friends and strangers, with the jubilant air of First Friday on the cusp of springtime.

Near the end of the opening of her Sidestreet show, Maggie bounds in, big eyes wider and wavy brown hair more disheveled than usual. She rushes to hug Elyse, whispers, "You'll never guess what my crazy dog got into!" and then surveys the room, hands on ample hips. "Ni-ice!" she says. "Can't wait to see where your work takes you next!"

"Well, about that," says Elyse, "you know how you're always telling me to take more chances?"

"Yep! Sure do! Girlfriend, you've got so much light needs shining! What's up?"

Sitting at a small table in the back corner, Elyse tells her everything: about the zoo talk, Jim's expedition, Elyse's decision to apply—and Dan's pessimism.

"I'm just, well, I don't know . . . I've been so obsessed with polar bears lately, all thanks to you making me go to the zoo, you know."

"Well, glad to help!" says Maggie, "That's my gift to the world. I stir things up, keep the sludge from forming around our feet!"

**

Astrid is busily grading midterms when her phone rings. Normally she wouldn't answer; she abhors interruption when she's grading. A stickler for fairness, she knows that an interruption might change her mood—for better or worse—which might then be reflected in papers graded afterward. But the call is from Strilay, so she picks up.

"I'm going to Churchill!" he nearly crows, all hint of his soft old-man voice momentarily gone, like fog lifted. "To see polar bears! Real, wild polar bears, in their natural habitat. Not just zoo bears. No, the real animals, in all their glory. Isn't that wonderful?"

"What?" says Astrid, trying to pull her thoughts away from a student's answer. "Are you—how? when? with whom?"

"Next October," he says. "Less than six months away. I'll be on sabbatical, my last one, and what a fitting way to go out."

"Out?" she says, "What do you mean?" She puts down her pen.

"Well, my dear, I think it's time for a change. Who knows, maybe I'll just move to Churchill, be around those bears all the time."

"Wait a minute. One shocking news flash at a time. Who are you going with?" asks Astrid.

"You remember Joe," he says. "He's in Churchill, working for the city on polar bear determent. What a job. Trying to keep the bears away from the town dumps. They even have a bear jail for the worst offenders. Imagine that!"

Yes, Strilay had told her stories of Joe over the years. He was the first student Strilay took fully under his ample wing, in the same way he did Astrid. But rather than follow the academic life, Joe veered off in his junior year, taking a semester break to "find his groove," as he told Strilay. He remained in Chapel Hill, working at a dairy farm and meeting Strilay for long, rambling intellectual immersions at the Carolina Coffee Shop.

"But they don't kill the bears," Strilay continues, his voice full of pride. "That's all thanks to Joe. In keeping with his pacifist beliefs, m'dear, same reason he wouldn't go to Vietnam."

Joe was, like Strilay, a true-blue pacifist, and he marched alongside Strilay down Franklin Street many times in the late 1960s. No doubt he'd have joined the student strike if he'd still been enrolled. He disappeared days after his draft notice arrived, and then resurfaced in Canada, where he has remained, staying in touch with his favorite professor.

Joe has been bugging Strilay to visit for decades. But Strilay isn't a traveler, except in his mind. He's always claimed that Chapel Hill, despite its flaws, is as good a place to live as anywhere. Astrid knows nothing about his childhood growing up in Boston, except one rumor about a sister lost in the Korean War. He doesn't talk about it, and whenever a question is asked, he deftly changes the subject. He's never left the United States, not even to visit cousins in Great Britain; he's never owned a passport. So, a trip to Canada is more than just a surprise—it's a reorientation of his solar system. And it's a black-hole-sized jolt to Astrid's.

"Well, I'm speechless, professor. And so happy for you," Astrid says finally. "It sounds absolutely wonderful. You'll have some fine stories to tell when you return."

"*If* I return," he chuckles. "Well, back to your grading, m'dear. Thank you for letting me interrupt you. And don't worry, I won't tell the polar bears that you've decided they're toast."

"Oh, wait, I thought we'd let that go," she says, feeling a sudden weight in her chest, a stone in her throat, lead-filled limbs.

"Of course, of course, I'm just joking. Cheerio!"

Though Astrid immediately returns to grading, her arms remain leaden, the stone lodged tight in her throat. It lingers, hanging like a shroud in the room, this small misunderstanding grown into a festering wound. She's known it wasn't yet mended, but has expected that, over their weeklies at the Carolina Coffee Shop, it would scar over and slowly fade. Time heals. But how can it if he's way up north in Churchill?

******

Elyse returns from the grocery store to a message on the landline. It's from Jim, and his voice is so even she's certain he's delivering the bad news she's been expecting since applying months ago. Instead, he says, after thanking her for helping them reach nationally recognized artists, "We've made our selections, and you've been chosen to be one of three artists on the expedition. Congratulations!"

Elyse jumps up in the air, groceries jostling in her arms, an avocado thunking to the floor. The tingling rises from her spine to her head as she puts the groceries on the counter, picks up the avocado, and listens to the rest of the message: details about visas, health checkups, all the forms they'll be emailing once they get her acceptance.

"Well," she says, letting out a sigh that fills the house, "evidently the moon is not out of my reach."

Hands shaking, head buzzing, she texts Maggie, who immediately calls.

"Oh. My. God." she says, "I cannot believe it. Well, of course I can, your work is amazing. But what a fucking adventure this will be. Damn, girl. Damn. I'm so proud of you."

"Thanks, I can't really believe it. I keep expecting him to call back and say, whoops, so sorry, my bad . . ."

"Nah. They're lucky to have you. Hey, so what are you going to do about the husband? Won't this upset his apple cart?"

"Dan? He'll be fine with it, I'm sure. I mean, this is Wonder Bread compared to his trips."

She calls Jim to accept, trying to sound professional even as her feet do a little jig.

"Your paintings," he says, "are so surprising. Kudzu and polar bears. But what really sold us was what you wrote about how art can reach people in ways that science can't. That it bypasses the analytical mind and goes straight to emotion and imagination, creating understanding and empathy. It's just what we want. To change minds *and* hearts."

"Oh," she says, trying to keep her words from erupting into the breathless speech of a beauty pageant winner. "Well, that's wonderful. And I'm just honored to be a member of such an innovative expedition."

"Yes, and we also found it intriguing that you say, let's see: 'In the same way traditional ecological knowledge is another way of knowing, art is another way of knowing.'"

"Well, I think the more ways we can look at something, the more complete a picture we have, right?"

"Precisely!" he says. "Well, we'll be in touch. Lots of work between now and then!"

The cloud-slippers she wears for the rest of the day fall off as soon as she tells Dan. She'd forgotten about his trip planned for that same period, and he doesn't like the idea of the house being left empty for that long. Then he asks questions she didn't think to ask: How much does it pay? Does it pay? Does it at least cover expenses? Where will you stay? How are they planning on using the art once the expedition is over? "Doesn't sound very well planned," he says. "These kinds of ventures take a lot of logistical and strategic planning. Are you sure this is right for you?"

"Well, yes, I . . ." Elyse starts. "I was so inspired by their talk, and..."

"Of course you were. But that doesn't mean you'll follow them off a cliff, right?" he says, his voice getting louder. "Look. This is precisely the kind of thoughtless leaping that our youngest son is known for. You don't need to keep modeling it for him."

"That seems a reach, Dan," she says, even as the undercurrent of worry she carries for Justin rises.

Then Dan throws the big punch. "Aren't you afraid this will pigeonhole you as an environmental activist instead of a professional artist? If you're a serious painter, doesn't that mean you don't take sides politically, that you have an independent view? Art for art's sake, right?"

"Well," she replies, plopping down on the bottom step, "I haven't thought about that." As doubts roll in like a bore tide, she realizes that in her excitement to see wild polar bears, see the walrus haulout, see those hunters with sticks keeping polar bears away, she didn't ask Jim a single question.

**

Astrid sits in the living room, shades pulled against slanting sunlight, reading the *Journal of Paleontology*. Increasingly, every single research article links the work to climate change. It irritates her. Not just the retreat of basic science, but also the repeated chorus claiming their research is relevant to the day's most pressing issue. Such obvious politicking for funds, such narrow-minded self-interest, and in one of the world's most influential journals.

Gareth pushes the door open, letting in a blast of sunlight, and exclaims, "My god, is this my house or the underworld?" And then laughs. When she doesn't laugh back, he puts his hand on her shoulder, and peers into her face. "Hmmm … bad day? Well, howzabout we go out for a late dinner? Joel and Ernesto have invited us to The Last Taco, and I know you've been wanting to see Charlotte's installation."

"No, thanks. You're right, bad day."

"All the more reason," he says, pushing a curl from her face, still bent over the journal. "Really. Do it as a favor to me. I'm famished."

And once more, against her wishes, she says yes to Gareth.

The Last Taco is bustling, and the foursome have to wait for a table. But they immediately order a bottle of wine, Joel and Ernesto toasting their one-year anniversary and Gareth's dinner party where they first met. "It's all thanks to you two," says Joel.

"And the magic potion Gareth puts in the pie, no doubt something you've concocted in your plant lab, Astrid," laughs Ernesto.

Astrid sighs. Most of their friends don't understand what she does all those long hours in her lab, staring at etchings in rock. It's not as evident as Gareth's fine cuisine, so, she supposes, they have to make up some outrageous stories to explain it.

Not Charlotte. As an artist, she knows better than to expect some concrete product from hours and years of sitting in the lab, or the studio. And just as Astrid thinks of her, Charlotte's familiar voice rings out. "Astrid!" she cries, her tall form moving like water between the crowded tables. "It's about damn time you got in here to see my new stuff! What were you waiting for, for it to become fossilized?"

Astrid's foul mood dissipates—for if Gareth can make Astrid say yes, Charlotte knows how to lighten her mood. Charlotte gives her a hug, then gives one to Gareth. With him, she lingers. "Mmmmm . . . the boy's been making cookies. I smell vanilla."

She releases him, but their faces are still an inch apart as he stammers, "Well, yes, no, yes, I was using vanilla, but not cookies. A new kind of sauce for salmon, actually. Can't you smell the fish on my breath?"

"I'd have to get a closer taste of that," she says, and makes as if to kiss him, then pulls back and laughs, making the beads on the ends of her long cornrows sing.

Gareth, his face reddening, smiles wide, showing that gap in his front teeth.

"Well, Astrid, let me show you my latest creation!" Charlotte says. "Then I'll let the four of you get back to dinner."

"Why don't you join us?" says Astrid. "We've got room."

"Oh, yes," says Joel and Ernesto in unison.

Charlotte glances at Gareth before she says, "Alrighty, then. But first, Astrid, come."

Charlotte's work is big and bright and strong, a feisty combination of metal, glass, and oil paint that shimmies and stretches across the walls, around corners, overhead of the small restaurant. Astrid's first impression is of a vine, of kudzu, but then faces appear. Wild faces, human, but not quite.

"So," Astrid finally asks, "what do you call it?"

"Oh, girl, that's just your polite way of asking, what the he-ell is going on here, sistah?" Charlotte laughs. "It's actually quite a serious subject, sweetie, you'll appreciate it. It's called *The Return to the Garden of Eden*."

Astrid looks closer. Yes, a raucous fecundity, yes. The vines looping and stretching, the leaves big and broad. But the faces don't look so pleased to be in Eden. They look, well, surprised. Some are almost entirely obscured by the plants, only eyes round as pennies, the whites stark against the darker shine of greens and reds. In some, the features are completely in view, but the smiles seem more like grimaces. Not at all like the Green Man of European lore, whose countenance is serene, as if he feels at home in the woods, at one with the wild.

"You see, shug," Charlotte continues, her words rushing out like water burst from a dam, "thing is, we've been away so long, we've reshaped the world so completely, that if we were to return to the original garden, well, I'm not sure we'd fit in, you know?"

"Well," Astrid says slowly, "it would be an adjustment, certainly."

"And," Charlotte continues, "I don't think we'd be welcomed either."

The two friends stand in the crowded restaurant and stare at Charlotte's creation, the cacophony of voices and deep bass of music so loud that Astrid's head rings. Simultaneously, they turn to each other, neither smiling. For a moment, Astrid sees how much more there is to Charlotte than the wildly charming, outspoken art teacher she's known so long. She sees beyond to some aspect of her character that initially drew the two seemingly opposites together. For a moment, she almost expects them to communicate telepathically—the way some scientists seem to listen to plants. Then she thinks, well, given how loud it is, that's probably the only way we *could* communicate. And with that, the moment is broken, and Charlotte, as if sensing it at precisely the same instant as Astrid, breaks into a grin.

"Enough of this art stuff," she says, "let's go flirt with those three handsome men over there. Lookie, one of them's waving us over."

Chapter 6

Elyse is in her studio. She's painting entirely with palette knives. Filling the canvas with sharp edges and jagged lines. Her forearms ache from scraping up mounds of paint and slicing it onto the canvas. But the ache feels right.

She is conflicted: Dan doesn't want her to go to Cape Vankarem, but she—ardently—does. He had apologized for his harsh response, but then, in that even tone he always used on the boys, he asked even more questions she couldn't answer. Now she wonders: should she call Jim and ask these questions? Or would asking him about money and liability make him reconsider her invitation?

So easy, when her kids were young, to know what she wanted, because it was wrapped up in what was best for them. They were her first priority, a fact of which she always felt certain and defended to anyone, including her husband. She'd known the empty nest period could be challenging, but she'd expected to fill that with a return to her painting. What she hadn't expected was that by giving all those years to parenting she'd lost any certainty about what she, all by herself, wanted.

She only knows that she's felt something like—sap rising—ever since reading that article on polar bears. There's something going on, and she doesn't want to miss it. It's not what she'd expected her path to look like after her boys fledged, and it's certainly not what Dan expected. She feels a twinge of guilt. But the sap-rise is strong.

Painting. She paints. It's something to do while her mind mills around in the darkness of not knowing. Painting with palette knives is especially satisfying when she feels this upsurging of aimless energy—she can throw that energy into scraping and slathering. She's working that kudzu form again, only this time it's blue, all the shades of water, the light tips looking like kudzu leaves. It's an almost violent image, though it's nothing more than shades of the most calming of colors.

An hour later, Elyse is ready to stop. Her arms are tired, and her mind has calmed. Maggie calls, wanting to meet for tea. Perfect. Of course they talk about Dan's reaction, and Maggie is not surprised.

"It's way easier," Maggie says, inhaling the sweet steam of chai, "to be agreeable when it doesn't cost a thing. Dan's got that kind of agreeable down. But, girlfriend, you have got to go. If you don't, you'll just resent hell out of him. And it'll be good for Dan. He's been top dog all these years, with you as his lovely assistant. Every life needs a big shake-up now and again."

On the drive home, Elyse wonders if Maggie's advice is right. Maggie has been a single parent for as long as they've known each other, since their boys were in third grade. Pregnant and newly separated, Maggie had seemed a friend in need. But as Elyse got to know her, she realized just what strength her friend had. Had the strength been there all along, or had it grown out of the necessity of her life? If your mate walks out the door when you've got one clinging to your legs and another kicking inside your belly, doesn't strength grow?

Strength, and more. The way Elyse feels about Cape Vankarem is the way she felt about all the decisions she made on behalf of her boys. Decisions she alone made: with Dan gone so much, she was, in many ways, a single mother. And then there are all the decisions he's made over the years, continually choosing dangerous missions without once asking her first. Choices she has, nonetheless, always supported. As she steps into the house, she feels the sap-rise growing.

**

"But he's throwing away a lifetime of dedicated, ground-breaking research! He's tanking his legacy!" says Astrid, throwing up her arms.

"Maybe he doesn't care about his legacy," says Gareth, standing calmly before his wife.

On the drive home from dinner, Gareth, who had tuned himself to his wife for nearly three decades, asked Astrid what had been troubling her all night. "Strilay," she said, and launched into a tirade about him shirking his responsibilities to go off and see polar bears.

"It's just," she says now, standing in their living room, "what do polar bears have to do with physics? And what if—he *is* nearly eighty now, Gareth—what if he's starting to lose control of his—mental faculties?"

"Oh, horseshit," says Gareth. "He's as lucid as ever. And as compulsive. It's that daring, that lack of concern for what others think, that's made him so successful as a physicist. This is just another leap, from a man whose life has been full of winning leaps."

"But Churchill! So far away! He's never even left the East Coast. He's leaping to the edge of the world. And leaving the university too!"

"Well, you know this, Astrid, I really think you do: sometimes you've got to go out on the edge to find your own center." He continues, his shoulders sagging, "I think what's really bothering you is that you'll miss him and worry about him. He's like a father to you, sweetie pie. So of course you're unhappy he seems to be abandoning you, just like your father. But he's not. And I'll still be here," he says, holding out his arms.

Astrid only gives Gareth a searing look and blazes from the room. Alone in her study, she knows Gareth is right. She recognizes that feeling, as if she's just swallowed a cannonball. She just thought she'd left it behind with childhood. How enraging and embarrassing that it's back, that she's still weak enough to be consumed by it.

It's like her father all over again, her mother's boyfriends all over again. Saying they were going to be there forever, taking her little brother and sister to ballgames and out for pizza, treating them like their own kids, and then disappearing with no explanation. The first few times, she'd ask her mother where they went, but soon she'd stopped: the answers were always the same: *It's not your fault. You'll understand when you're older.*

Well, she's older, and she still doesn't understand. And this time she can't blame it on her mother. She feels childish, getting so upset over Strilay being gone for a few months, but she thought that Strilay understood her, thought this time would be different. And she worries, though she knows it makes no sense—she worries that Strilay is still disappointed in her, that he is, in a way, abandoning her. And worse, that this time it *is* her fault.

Her thoughts leap, as if escaping flames, to Charlotte's art installation, to the familiarity of the kudzu, to the backyard haven of it where she had once, and only once, brought a friend. She had thought carefully about inviting Elyse, since it was the only thing that was hers and hers alone. And then, with Elyse, there was abandonment, too, but it wasn't Elyse who abandoned her; it was she who abandoned—no, severed—the friendship.

**

In turmoil, Elyse visits Binky. Maybe, sitting in front of her enclosure, letting her eyes rest on the multicolored hue of fur, she'll figure out how to talk to Dan about Cape Vankarem. It's quiet at the zoo; few people visit in early spring. A sunny day, warm enough that the top layer of ice and snow softens, and the zoo has a certain odor to it: the smell of a winter's worth of defecation from dozens of animals. As much as the staff try to keep enclosures clean, winter's quick freeze makes it tough. Passing by the coyote pen, where three beautiful animals trot lightly along the back fence line, their cinnamon coats undulating like northern lights in the slant of sunlight, Elyse wonders how this smell affects the animals. Scent is so important for them—for everything from territory marking to finding prey to eluding predators—she wonders if this loud conglomeration of smells might make them, well, crazy.

Binky is sleeping, right by the pool, which this time of year is ice. Her right cheek rests on her paws, crossed in front of her, one on the other. Elyse sits, watches. The center of her body rises and falls, rises and falls.

So. What should she do? Well, when was the last time she and Dan disagreed, and how did they settle it? They disagreed many times over child-rearing decisions, but usually Elyse just did what she thought best since she was the stay-at-home parent. But outside of the children, when? Sure, his medical residency had required her to drop out of grad school, but they had come to that decision together. They'd laughed over how clichéd that was, the wife following the husband.

There was that two-month cross-country bike trip. After they'd married but before kids, a high school friend had asked Elyse to join her. Elyse said yes and then told Dan. He'd been surprised, then had his usual list of reasonable questions, but she'd answered them quickly and packed her bags. Years later, he told the story to a friend, framing it as "the time my new wife abandoned me," complete with several mournful looks in her direction. When she'd asked him about it later, he said, "Well, of course I didn't want you to go. We were married. We're supposed to do things together." That was the last time she'd done something that he didn't want her to do. Pre-kids. A quarter of a century ago.

Binky is dreaming: her ears twitch in rapid succession, as if her head is trying to take flight. Then first one, then the other, of her rear paws twitch too. Her breath quickens, black nostrils widening and narrowing. Then all movement stops, and she lets out a big sigh.

"What are you dreaming about, my love?" Elyse says, apparently out loud, because then she hears a response, not from the sleeping bear but from a woman's voice behind her. "Uncle dreams of the hunt."

Startled, Elyse turns to see a young woman with shining folds of long black hair. A woman she knows, but from where?

"I call her Uncle," says the woman, "because that's what my grandfather called polar bears."

"Oh," says Elyse, hesitating. Beverly, that's her name. From the sangha, where Elyse is a sporadic member. "Well it's certainly a better name than Binky. I mean, who named this poor creature? A three-year-old?"

"I know!" Beverly laughs. "It's funny, but it's also, well, disrespectful, too, you know?"

"Yes I do. You're Beverly, right? From Cottonwood Sangha?"

"Yes," she says. "And you are—Elyse, right? You jump-started my car that one time, after sangha?"

"Yes! That really cold stretch in January. So glad I had my jumper cables!"

They both fall silent, almost as habit, since most of their sangha interactions have been just a nod and smile as they sat to meditate or listened to dharma readings. But they've shared deep moments in the silence, so that now between them is an ease like that of two old friends. Beverly's voice now reminds Elyse of the few times Beverly spoke to the group about learning the traditions of her people through her grandmother, how she didn't understand why most people didn't listen to their elders, and how her grandmother's stories resonated with the teachings of the Buddha, especially what Thich Nhat Hanh called Interbeing. Elyse recalls feeling a surprising sorrow—that Elyse herself had not talked to, and learned from, her own grandparents, knowing only vaguely that her grandparents had fled turmoil, persecution, and war in what had been called Poland. She'd noticed how her father always cringed when anyone told a Polish joke, and had, too late, realized how her heritage was buried under the silence of cultural shame. Listening to Beverly in sangha, she had wished that would not be the case for her.

"So," she says, "it's nice to see you here."

"Yes," says Beverly, "I just started working here this month. Summer job, saving up to get back to college."

"Well, how interesting it must be, working around all these animals."

"Yeah. Especially when I'm done cleaning their enclosures, and I just sit for a while, hanging out with them. I'm weird that way, I guess," she says, glancing at Elyse.

She looks back at Binky. "My people, you know, we see them as food, as clothing, to be killed. When we were kids, we were always pretending to hunt caribou, moose, bears."

She pauses, glancing again at Elyse. Elyse feels heat on her neck. She doesn't, as a rule, condone hunting, except for Alaska Indigenous subsistence: it's part of their culture, she tells herself; I have no right to impose my values on them.

"But my grandfather," Beverly says, "his stories, they made me feel like the animals were so close to us, so much like us . . . sorry, that's probably TMI."

"No, it's not, I mean, I'm sitting here all the time with this one," says Elyse.

They both laugh. Elyse likes Beverly. She likes her apparent empathy, however culturally conflicted, with animals. She likes her candid responses. And she admires her initiative: Beverly is saving up to return to college at the University of Alaska, Anchorage, and from there to veterinary school. She's telling Elyse that she's from Kaktovik, a small village on the Arctic coast.

Elyse grabs onto this like a dog with a bone. "What's it like, living around polar bears?"

"Well," says Beverly, then she pauses, long enough for Elyse to recall something from teaching in Quinhagak: that Alaska Indigenous students tend to not make eye contact much and to have long pauses in conversation. "It's all I knew, up until a few years ago," says Beverly finally. "So it's hard to explain. It's like asking, what's it like to live where there are trees? I mean, we don't have trees in Kaktovik, you know? It was hard for me to feel comfortable living around all these tall ones," she sweeps her arms wide to the spruce and birch forest ringing the zoo, "and not being able to see very far in all directions. I guess, well, polar bears are different from brown or black bears. They take up space differently."

Her voice trails off, almost apologetically. Elyse fills in, almost too quickly, irritated with herself for asking such an stupid question. "Oh, that's a great analogy. Trees. Yes, of course, it must be impossible to explain! Silly of me to ask! I'm just, well, I've got this opportunity . . ."

And suddenly Elyse is telling Beverly everything. All in one long breath, like a child coming home from school and spilling everything to her mother. Then she finishes, and another long silence ensues. But this time, Beverly holds her gaze, and Elyse has her answer.

******

The next week at their usual lunchtime, Strilay is nearly jumping up and down with excitement over his trip. Astrid, resolved to act supportive, only smiles. She looks around the Carolina Coffee Shop at its dark leather seats and trim, shined by generations since it opened in 1922, still a welcome respite from the humidity that courses through life in this southern town. She turns back to Strilay with a bright smile.

"It's quite amazing, really," he says. "How these bears are adapting to changing conditions. That will to endure, you know, m'dear? It's one of life's great mysteries." Strilay smiles. "Joe says he can see it in their eyes, how they'll never give up. Of course, that's what makes them desperate enough to come into towns and eat dog food."

"Dog food?" says Astrid, feigning interest. This must be how mothers act when their children are about to do something stupid, she thinks, but they're too old to be told not to.

"Yes," he says. "All those dog teams, tied up and fed outside all the time, easy enough for a bear to steal a meal."

All in one rush, he tells her about a series of photographs of a polar bear playing with a sled dog. Instead of devouring the dog chained to a stake, the bear rolls on his back, and dog and bear start rolling and pouncing with each other. "I love it!" Strilay says. "If only we humans could get along with others that way!"

"Well, they don't always, you know," says Astrid, trying not to dampen his spirits but frustrated with how unscientific he sounds. "Not usually. Survival of the fittest, you know, tooth and claw."

"Yes, yes, of course, but we've misinterpreted that," he says, staring hard at her. "Remember, it wasn't Darwin that used the phrase *survival of the fittest*; it was that philosopher, Spencer."

He leans in, his voice low like he's letting her in on a secret. "That's where the whole social Darwinism fallacy began. Darwin said natural selection isn't as war-like as we humans think of it. I think that's why he wrote so much about cooperation in nature. We've just corrupted poor Darwin's brilliance to justify our own bad behavior, haven't we now?"

That's it, thinks Astrid, it's not about her: it's the old anti-war activist taking aim at the climate change war. And here they are in the Carolina Coffee Shop, where he'd led a sit-in during the Vietnam War—the sit-in that almost cost him his career. Astrid sighs, leans back into the worn leather. Strilay isn't Strilay if he doesn't have a wrong to be righted. This one's got everything: innocent victims, intolerance and injustice, intractable and uncaring institutions. And humanity's own greed, complacency, complicity. Bless his heart.

"Lamont says that coexistence is a much better descriptor than competition," says Strilay, slipping into lecture mode to list examples: wolves marking territories to avoid conflict, trees leaving room for neighbors in the canopy, microorganisms in human bodies aiding in digestion and immunity. "A human isn't an individual who's won some sort of survival competition but part of a system of cooperating species," he says, "just like healthy ecosystems."

"Lamont—" says Astrid. "Is this from a paper he wrote?"

"No," says Strilay, "it's something he told me last week. He'll also be in Churchill, researching his next book. It's on Lovejoy's model of how plants can save us, but he's slipping in something about polar bears."

"Plants can save us? Pray tell, what is that about?" says Astrid, ears burning as botany enters the conversation.

"You haven't read about this? Lovejoy's model of how global warming can be mitigated by regreening the planet?"

Astrid stares at him, wilting a little inside at her ignorance.

But Strilay doesn't miss a beat. "We could offset as much as a third of climate emissions simply by stopping deforestation and restoring forestlands. A third! It's one of the most hopeful things I've learned in years!"

He's beaming so brightly, his expression so open, that Astrid catches a glimpse of what he must have been like as a little boy. A wide-eyed exuberance.

"That, and the promise of reducing black carbon's effect on sea ice loss," he continues, switching rapidly back to polar bears and a recent study. "Black carbon—soot—is a major contributor to sea ice decline, but it's easier to reduce because it's short-lived. Reduce it, sea ice melt slows, and polar bears have a better chance of surviving. There's hope, m'dear," Strilay grins, "and with it, a call to action."

"Goodness, you're veering far away from theoretical physics, my dear professor," Astrid smiles playfully.

"No, not at all," he replies, his gaze intensifying. "I'm just looking to broaden our field of vision. That's what drew me to physics: the way it expands our ideas about this universe we're temporarily occupying."

"Well," says Astrid, trying to choose her words carefully, "it just seems like this is far afield of your own research, from QFT or ToE, from what you've spent your entire career doing."

The waiter appears at his elbow, refilling his coffee without asking, and then slips away. Even the staff recognizes the professor's prophetic tone.

"Oh, no, you're entirely wrong," he says, leaning across the table and lowering his voice almost to a growl. "All this *is* part of my research. That's why it's called the Theory of Everything. If physics has taught us anything, it's that everything is energy; everything is connected. We're not separate bundles of matter; we're energy waves. What we do to polar bears we do to ourselves. I don't want to get all mystical, m'dear, because that's the surest way to lose you, but this *is* what it's all about. Climate change is our latest lesson, the culmination of all our learning and mistakes. It's about energy and its effects. What we can see and what we can't."

Astrid's smile loosens its grip, and a certain dizziness sets in, one she hasn't felt in a long time.

"I have not forsaken my research. I've done what you do, Astrid. Pure, basic research. Following the hunches, not the money. Following where excitement leads, like Jim Hansen, who quit the Venus project because he found Earth more interesting. I'm listening to what the data says, not what I want it to say. Even if it leads to some edge with no funding, no academia, no one listening. Even there."

He sighs, sits back, sips some coffee. "Being at that edge is good news, m'dear. It means you're doing what no one else can do, following your work into something that the world has never before perceived. Then, bingo! The Nobel Prize lands in your lap. Hah!"

Strilay throws back his head, a single deep belly laugh, and then continues, but his voice is lighter, softer, sounding more like the

Strilay who has listened, advised, and soothed her all these years. "No, it may not happen until centuries after you're dead. But recognition isn't what motivates me, and you, either, Astrid. I knew that from the beginning. Did you think it was just your intellect and drive that led me to mentor you? No. It was the purity of your intentions. I knew you wouldn't be swayed by others' expectations. Otherwise you'd never have given up being chair of the department, never have turned down that grant from ExxonMobil. It wasn't just a distaste for management or politics, it was your inner compass, pointing you down the path only you can take."

Astrid is speechless. She feels like an undergraduate again, sitting in the first class she ever took from him, watching him up front pacing the stage, so energetic that she could almost see sparks emanating from his body. Sparks that ignited her own, and threaten to do so again, sending her off into somewhere new, somewhere she doesn't even know to go.

"Well," she says, trying to keep her tone even, "thank you for explaining that."

"You're welcome," he says. "Very. I'll always believe in you, m'dear, no matter where your path takes you. I'll always know you're doing what you're meant to do."

Section 2

Chapter 7

"You're kidding, right? You're kidding!"

"No," Elyse says. "No. I am not kidding. I am going."

"Well, that's just insane. I've a dozen questions right now you've given absolutely no answer to. Is this an empty nest thing? Have you talked this over with Atifah?"

Atifah is a therapist Elyse has seen over the years, most recently after Justin left for college.

"No, I have not talked with her because it is not a problem I need help figuring out. It is an opportunity I am going to take. I am very clear about it, Dan. And very excited."

She is talking to her husband the way she used to talk to her boys when they were teenagers. That firm and unemotional tone with clear enunciation and no contractions.

"Well," he says. "Well. This just seems very selfish, very thoughtless."

Elyse stares at him, her mind racing with all she could say but won't. All the years of her holding down the fort so that he had the freedom to go, to do the work that called to him. Hard work, worthy and risky, yes. But all his choice. Now this is her choice. Her turn.

"Okay. I'm speechless. Let's just take a time-out and discuss this again later."

"Sure," she says, "if you want. But please do not think that you will be changing my mind."

"Let's just . . . talk about it later," he says, pulling his phone from his pocket. "I've got to take this call."

The phone hasn't rung, at least not that she could hear—but that's fine by her. She lets out a long sigh, closes her eyes, and stands still. The armor slips off, and a lightness floods her, a buoyancy. Unbidden, she sees her kudzu and polar bear painting.

"I'll be in the studio," she says, turning to go. "If you need anything."

There are times in the following weeks that Elyse feels she is at a silent meditation retreat, the way she and Dan share the same space yet barely speak. She can feel him simmering, alternately between anger and something else she can't name—is it shame? But he doesn't bring it up, not once.

She begins to feel sorry for him, sorry that because she is setting out on a new course, he is having to reframe his reality. Sorry that she has to be so firm, even cold, toward her husband. Sorry she doesn't believe they can talk it through and come to agreement. But not sorry enough to give in. They are kind, so very kind to each other, though polite may be the better word. *Please* and *thank you* ring through the house like they did when they were teaching their boys manners.

To escape the tension in the house—and to make up for the time she'll be away from them—she spends more time out with the dogs. She wants to nurture that lightness she's felt about her decision to go. But now even these outings, usually joy-soaked, are fraught. It's a searing spring, so hot the snow melts too fast and floods streets, houses, forests. Many trails are closed, some look glacial, snowmelt on top of the bluish ice underneath a glimmering azure. But the sun will not let up. Every day is beautifully sunny, day after day, even after the last of the floods recede. Then it is budbreak, usually her favorite time of year, but because they haven't had any rain, she fears the trees won't make it. That's all anyone is talking about—the strange spring drought. Two months of it.

Walking a trail along Turnagain Arm, on a south-facing mountainside where wildflowers first appear in spring, Elyse finds the plants curled up, drying out, buds desiccated. She tries to cheer herself with what she'd learned in a wildflower class: that the plants are reducing the surface area exposed to the drying sun and will plump back up once it rains. If it rains. The plants can only wait so long. The trail is so dry that her dogs kick up dust in front of her, and runners that pass wear bandanas over their noses. She gazes across Turnagain to Hope and the Kenai Mountains. There's still snow on their highest peaks, slivers of white caught in their upper valleys. But the lower flanks are dry and brown, the greening of springtime paused.

A few days later, a wildfire explodes on the Kenai Peninsula, just a hundred miles south. It starts along a border of the Kenai National Wildlife Refuge, most likely from an adjacent homeowner's mishap, but with the drought spreads quickly. Firefighters from all over the country arrive to help protect the towns of Kenai, Soldotna, and Cooper Landing. One firefighter finds a wolf den with four pups in it. Two pups have porcupine quills in them, probably from a porcupine seeking refuge from the flames. The tiny blue-eyed pups become a national sensation in a matter of hours, with images of their small faces nuzzling firefighters and sucking from a bottle, of a vulnerable little fuzzball held in a fireman's burly, tattooed arms.

"Cute," texts Justin after she shares the photos with him, "but if those pups were six months older, Alaskans wouldn't be calling them cute. They'd call them vermin and shoot them from the air."

Elyse knows her son is right: Alaska is not kind to its predators. Wolves, bears, lynx are trapped and shot across state and federal lands, with liberal bag limits and lengthening seasons. Just the previous year, the pregnant alpha female of Denali National Park's most often seen wolf group was killed just across the wilderness boundary by a sport hunter from Arkansas.

She's often haunted by thoughts of all the beautiful Alaskan animals whose hides now hang on walls of living rooms and game rooms around the world. It's like the house she drives by on the way to a favorite trailhead: chalet-style big front windows, which would have a million-dollar view of the city and Cook Inlet and the Alaska Range beyond, are instead crowded with a taxidermied giraffe and zebra gazing glass-eyed out onto a world they can no longer see. Just as there must be an Alaskan polar bear staring out of the windows of a house in Germany or Texas.

After a sleepless night dreaming of their house filling with dead animals, of climbing over an elephant corpse to get to the bathroom, of pulling back the shower curtain to find a collapsed caribou, Elyse visits Binky. She wants to apologize, again, for the bear's captivity, for the myriad ways her species treats all the others with such cruelty, such thoughtlessness, treats them like everything except who they really are. But seeing her bear does not lighten Elyse's unnamed sorrow, for Binky is sleeping, her back turned, motionless.

**

On the days that she would have been meeting Strilay for lunch at Carolina Coffee Shop, Astrid feels untethered. The weekly talks had anchored her; all week she'd tuck away any problems or worries to tell him, sure he'd know what to say to put her at ease. At first she's determined that his absence will give her more time for her research. But the lab at lunchtime is a lonely place, and the fossils, for all the concentration she gives them, cannot replace Strilay's bushy white brows raised in amusement over her agitated replay of the last faculty meeting. So she tries going to the coffee shop alone, but that makes her feel more lonely. And awkward.

Finally, she packs a lunch and walks to the arboretum. To her favorite bench. At first her thoughts turn to the knots she wants to untie. To the conversation with Strilay, him lecturing her to follow her path. To Lamont influencing Strilay with his far-fetched ideas. Arguing in her head with a journal article that makes a link, one she finds thin, between the decline of Colorado birches and the decline of arboreal lycopods. Climate change, concluded the lead author, is creating warming and drying conditions similar to the middle Permian, so the fossil record can help us anticipate what's in store now. Just another rationalization for more funding, she thinks. We don't know squat about what caused the drying in the Permian.

Slowly, the arguments spin out, and she is just sitting, nibbling her sandwich, watching the trees around her find their way toward winter. Pink threads green on the sugar maple across the path, leaves upturned like palms of a hand, sunlight scattering across them. Maples are almost everyone's favorites in falltime, and they do make the mountains around Asheville look like a Persian carpet with their multi-hued reds and oranges and pinks. Those rolling Smokies fairly ring with color, and from certain points on the parkway, it's so overwhelming that one must check the impulse to leap into their waves.

Astrid still prefers the arboretum: for the singularity of each tree on their own, for the multitude of textures and more subtle color changes of the elms and beech and tulip poplar, of redbud and dogwood and sassafras, blended with the long green sprays of loblolly. It's a conversation, all these different trees brought here to grow together, their limbs and roots and leaves all navigating shared space.

By far her favorite tree in fall is the ginkgo. Not just for the brilliant sun yellow but for the way the leaves change all at once, and then, on a single day appointed by some combination of temperatures and day length and water levels in the cambium, all the leaves drop, and the tree stands bare, with a glowing corona encircling the base. Like an upside-down halo, a botany student had once commented, from a tree that originates on the other side of the planet.

Astrid leans back on her hands and looks up into the pinnated leaves of a red oak. The branches bend and twist in every direction, as if they keep changing their mind, knowing the thick trunk will remain upright regardless. Even the oaks, though all they do is turn brown, add to fall's conversation.

"Nothing prettier than a deciduous forest in the fall," her mother often said. "You'll never find a more beautiful sight."

Her mother, for all her faults, knew the names of every single tree and shrub and plant around her. And she talked to them too. A walk through the woods with her mother was like a walk down a crowded street: every plant was given a nod, a smile, a greeting. She much preferred plants to people, she said, because they were so much better at cooperation. "See how they get along," she'd say, stopping in the midst of a forest. "If only people could be like them." She even addressed her houseplants. "They're pets, same as the dog and cat," she'd tell Astrid. "You've got to listen; they'll tell you what they need."

Her mother could make anything grow, anything bloom. She was the only one Astrid had ever known who could coax orchids to bloom again and again. Visitors would look at the orchids, assume they were fake, rub a petal, then pull back in surprise. "Oh! Real! Well, imagine that! You must be doing all right, to be able to buy flowering orchids."

Astrid's mother would just smile thinly and reply, "Naw. These are all rejects, just like everyone else in my house. The flower shop just gives me the ones they're going to throw out, you know, ones damaged in shipping or knocked over in the shop. I get them to bloom again."

"You'll bloom again," she'd once told Astrid after a particularly bad experience with her sixth grade teacher, right after her father had left for good. The teacher was a complete imbecile, and Astrid had corrected him one too many times. She'd been sent, for the first time in her life, to the principal's office, and suspended for three days for disruptive conduct. Astrid, who was always the smartest kid in the class, always the teacher's favorite for her high scores, front-row seat, and rapt attention. But the teacher had been wrong, and too bull-headed to admit it. It's one of the few times Astrid had allowed herself tears in front of her mother. When her mother compared her to a plant, Astrid knew she loved her.

You'll bloom again. The words echo in her ears. A sudden breeze sets the oak leaves to trembling. A maple leaf floats into her lap, grazing her wrist. The pointed fingers are a soft rose color with lime green veins, the pigment transitioning before her eyes. She stares at it and looks up and across the path, as if the tree had spoken her mother's words.

"Stay." She says, out loud. "Stay." But of course it doesn't. That moment. That feeling she's experienced a few times before, but only fleetingly, always unbidden. The feeling of boundaries disappearing. The feeling of opening into something larger than herself. Of opening, of coming home.

"Stay!" she nearly shouts. Then catches herself.

"Absurd," she mutters. "Absurd. Trees don't talk. You're tired, or maybe it's menopause. Yes, that's it: menopause. You are not your mother. You are sensible and responsible, you don't take others' rejects, and you don't let other people make you veer from your path. Strilay included."

Astrid very nearly pounds the pavement all the way back to her lab. Head down, refusing to look at the fall colors, she doesn't even side-step the few colorful leaves that have fallen to the sidewalk. Once there, she swings the door shut, strides to her chair, and sits.

Before her are the latest samples sent from Australia and China. They represent two different possible genera of *Lycopsida*, and she is hoping they'll provide answers to the linkages with lycopods who once thrived here. With her scope and one of the samples, she drops down into that familiar place, where time becomes irrelevant and nothing exists except these small slabs of stone etched with ancient messages.

A tapping on her door, though quiet and tentative, nonetheless nearly makes her hit her head on the scope just above her bent gaze. She takes a deep breath, pulls herself back from the Devonian to the Holocene, and goes to the door. "Yes?" she says, opening it halfway.

A man stands outside, small, balding, eyes the color of greenstone. He smiles, quickly. "Hello, I'm Professor Sanders, here on sabbatical, working with a team on the ExxonMobil grant you passed up. Might I bother you with a few questions?"

The last thing Astrid wants to do is to help someone with a project that she had, much to her dean's dismay, turned down. "Well," she says, "I'm sure I can't be of help to you. After all, it's not a field of research that I've spent any time considering."

"Yes, but," he continues in a crisply formal British accent, "there's a reason ExxonMobil came to you first. Your background in this period of *Lycopsida* growth puts you on the top of the heap."

"Not fond of the heap reference," she says, "since I don't care for the competitive model in science. But I will give you five minutes."

He enters, surveying her lab as if he is the potential buyer of a new house. Astrid's lab is highly coveted: it's a large corner room in one of the university's oldest buildings. Plaster walls, a ridiculously high ceiling built to keep it cool in summer before there was air-conditioning, windows on both outside walls with generous sills, views into a wooded space, and an entire wall of glass cases where Astrid keeps all her specimens, carefully organized by region and labeled with source information.

"Nice," he says, rubbing his hands, "very modern equipment, and what a collection. This would make the Peabody envious."

"Yes, well, it works fine. So, what are your questions?"

"I'm wondering," he says, "mostly I'm wondering if you have any *Lycopsida* samples from the Guadalupian epoch that we might borrow, so as to better understand that warming period's effect on diversity."

"Oh," she replies, taken aback by how quickly he asks. "I would think you'd have the funds to acquire your own samples, rather than beg and borrow."

"Yes, well, we are generously funded," he replies, his unaverted gaze seeming to pin her down like a butterfly to a board. "But it's my understanding that your collection, in fact everything in here, belongs to the university and, as such, is at the disposal of any other university-sanctioned researcher who has a legitimate use for them."

"That's," she says, reeling, "that's true in theory, yes, but I maintain the right to, as a full professor and lead scientist in this field, I have the right to determine the legitimacy and the terms of such use, so I suggest you put your request in writing, and I will consider it."

"But of course," he replies, quickly. "I just wanted to start off on the right foot by asking in person, colleague to colleague. You know, just being friendly."

"Well, yes, thank you," she says, sitting in her chair. "And if that's all, I need to get back to my research. I have to finish this sample preparation before my seminar class."

"Of course," he smiles, stepping toward the door. "But of course."

⁎⁎

Two weeks before she leaves, and two days before he leaves, Dan brings Elyse a dozen roses. It's very out of character, as Dan has often held forth on the evils of the cut-flower business, and for the most part Elyse agrees: it's a big carbon footprint just to bring a dozen tulips to her table from Holland, or even stargazer lilies from California. Still, sometimes she indulges a few stargazers, just to have the color and scent of real blooming flowers in the middle of winter.

"Here," says Dan, thrusting the blood-red bouquet toward her. "Maybe they'll last until you leave."

"Well, thanks, dear," Elyse says, as she takes the flowers and turns to the sink to remove the wrapping, cut the stems, find a vase, and fill it. She's never particularly liked roses, thinking them overrated, like diamonds, too expensive and emblematic of blind consumerism. But since Dan so rarely does this, he probably doesn't know her favorites—or that she has any.

"I just," he says, coming up behind her and touching her shoulder tentatively, "I just want you to know that I hope your residency goes well. I hope it's all you want it to be."

Her back stiffens just as it had the night before, when he'd curved his body around hers in bed and cupped her breasts. She wasn't interested then, and she isn't now. This support was what she'd wanted to hear from him for months, but now it's so late she can't shake the steel armor she's developed to endure the tilt of the conversation whenever her trip comes up. Instead, she's bracing for the punch line.

"You okay?" he says, "You're not having second thoughts, are you?"

She turns, quickly. "No, I'm not, not at all. I'm just . . . I'm fine. Just . . . the flowers are beautiful, it's really so sweet of you."

His shoulders sag even as he pastes on a smile. "Great! You're off on your adventure, then."

"Yes, and you, yours. Will you be stationed with anyone you know this time?"

And with that, the tension eases, and they both enter into familiar conversation about his work. He's headed to Liberia, where he's been before, ten years earlier when the country was still in the throes of civil war. Now his assignment is much less dangerous and more administrative: he'll be helping DWB turn over the hospitals to the Liberian government.

"It'll be tricky," he says, his brow furrowing, "because not everyone believes the government will run them fairly. I have my doubts as well, but DWB is always making hard choices about limited resources."

"Yes, that's got to be tough," says Elyse.

"Well," he says, flashing a smile, "at least I won't have to worry about bullets flying overhead while I operate on a civilian caught in crossfire. I'll be able to travel the countryside a bit, make some old-fashioned house calls, even."

Elyse has always been impressed with Dan's ability to travel and live under difficult situations. Most often they have nothing but wall tents to live and work in, and in areas of conflict they are rarely allowed to leave the compound. But he seems to thrive with challenges, and to enjoy that feeling of being so desperately needed. She hopes that she can bring such cheerful adaptability to her time in Cape Vankarem.

She's always wanted to be more like him, selflessly being of use to the world. In the past, whenever she expressed this, Dan countered with the value of raising kids. She agreed, but now the boys are grown. She was a child herself when Doctors Without Borders first formed, in response to the war in Biafra. She sat in front of the TV watching images of children her age with stick-thin limbs and extended bellies. She wondered why they were so calm, until she learned that hunger drains energy.

Those images haunted her, so when she met a man determined to work for DWB, of course she was enamored. And when they were married with children, she never questioned that his work with DWB took priority, whether it was over her career or their family vacation, not even when they had to cancel the family trip to Hawaii, the one they'd promised the boys all semester in exchange for joining track, the one that was the beginning of what Dan referred to as Justin's rebellious phase, when Justin refused to believe anything they said or to do anything they asked.

"So," Dan asks one evening as they sit with glasses of wine, "have you heard from Justin lately?"

Elyse hesitates, fearing that talk about their youngest's floundering might lead them back to her trip, to her being unavailable should their sons need anything.

"I have not," she says slowly, "other than a brief text last week with a link to some story about the tar sands project in Canada. He didn't comment on it, just sent it to me."

"Yeah, I got it too. Same, no comment, and he didn't reply when I asked what he thought about it. Sure wish I knew what was going on with him."

"I know, me too," sighs Elyse. "But it's his life now, his decisions."

"You sure have mastered letting them go, Elyse. I'm surprised. Don't you worry about them, especially Justin? Aren't you worried that, with you gone . . ."

Elyse looks up from her wine glass. "Of course I worry about them, all the time," she replies, trying to keep her tone from sharpening. "But the days of active parenting are behind me. I have to trust that the work I did—we did—has prepared them well enough now for whatever they encounter."

As she says the words, she realizes that she isn't just parroting some how-to book: she really means it. And even as Dan glares at her, almost daring her to admit she's lying, she rises from the chair and feels that sap-rise again, clear and strong.

Not until Dan is safely on his flight does Elyse begin packing and getting the house ready. It's a lot of work, especially setting up for a house sitter, but she'd rather do it herself than have Dan moping about, finding more reasons why this isn't going to work. Besides, waiting until he's gone allows them to pretend it won't happen.

And for the space of an afternoon, she thinks the same: the day before her early morning flight, she takes Darlene and Sophie on a long hike up to Wolverine. She wants to wear them out before leaving. But then, as had happened years ago before a family kayaking trip, just minutes before getting back to the parking lot from the fourteen-mile hike, Darlene disappears. That's when Elyse remembers that fated kayak trip: how they'd had the kayaks on the car, bags packed, water taxi paid for and waiting; how they'd taken the dogs for one more walk before the kennel; how Darlene had disappeared; how they'd waited and waited and finally had to cancel.

Elyse could kick herself. Why did she forget Darlene's innate ability to know when she was going to be left behind? As Elyse paces the parking lot, calling for her and asking every person if they've seen her dog, she wonders what she'll do if Darlene doesn't show up in time for her to make her flight. Can she really board a plane to another country when her dog is missing? Or will she have to cancel the entire trip just to wait for her wild husky to get bored and come home?

Not that Darlene ever does come home on her own. Mostly Elyse has to wait for a call from whomever the husky has attached herself to, usually some incredibly nice people who take Darlene home, give her treats, let her snuggle on their couch with the kids or curl up on the bed with a bone. No wonder she never comes home on her own.

This time is no different. Hours later, after Elyse has gone home and finished packing and eaten a bird-food dinner, after she's checked the airlines for a later flight, after she's stared at the phone with her stomach in knots, she gets a call from a man whose children had found a dog and kept her in their backyard all afternoon, playing with her. Not until he got home from work did anyone think to—or maybe want to—call the number on the tag.

Still, as Dan said after every Darlene escapade, all's well that ends well.

The next morning, on the plane, Elyse takes a long breath. The plane is full, but she's got a window seat; she settles in with her book and earplugs. The takeoff is smooth, and she revels in the view of Fire Island, Cook Inlet, the broad flats of the Knik emptying into it, and the Alaska Range, which reveals new peaks and valleys no matter how many times she flies out of Anchorage. She strains to see Kennebuna Lake, where she and Dan had been dropped off with their inflatable kayak for a few days, and shared it with no one but bears, lots of them. She's wanted to return since, but between his work and her raising the boys, it hasn't happened, not yet.

As the small plane levels out, as the view out the window changes to tundra flecked orange and red, braided river snaking below her, things fall apart. The view out the window, the voices around her, the hard leather of the seat against her thighs and back, the pages of the book between her fingers, all sensations jumble, she can't make out what is sound and what is sight and what is touch, her senses have entered a cyclone. Rumble, voices, page, what are they? So loud, booming in her head, amplified, river and tundra outside inside pressing her chest. Chest heaving in and out pumping the river and talking, talking. Swirling all around the chattering, the weightless lift, pressing and pushing. Words flying with windrush overhead, a flailing, a falling. Breath. Breathe. She breathes, rapidly, counts, slows it, her breath, separate again, the voices, each belonging to a person, some closer than others, the river and tundra back outside the plane and far below, words back on the page, silent.

She puts her hand on her heart, feels it racing. Hand to forehead. Face flushed. But cooling. Cooling. She forces a hard look at her right hand, traces the lines on the palm, the ones a fortune teller once stared at and said she'd have four children and live a long life. She's had only two children. Two is enough. And she is still living. Right here. Now.

Her mind is reorganized, working again, everything in its place. An anxiety attack, that must be what it was. Traveling alone for the first time since before her kids were born, traveling to another country, to the far reaches of another land, another culture. All the doubts, some her own and some planted by Dan, all of them that she'd so successfully kept at bay as much to resist Dan as to keep herself upright, all of them burst to the surface at once.

A fifty-two-year-old woman, with two grown children, who's lived in the same house for twenty years and hasn't traveled alone since college: what is she thinking, heading off to the far reaches of another country, one only recently from which that Iron Curtain was lifted? What is she doing? And for what, to make a few paintings?

Why did they choose her? That's what really troubles her. Did they not have any other applications? Is Dan right? Is there something about the project that's suspect or underfunded or not entirely what it should be? Is this safe?

Well, she's on her way now. There's no turning back. *Best deal with it.* That's her father's voice, he who never looked back, only forward—something she admired in him, but could never quite do, instead constantly looking over her shoulder, doubting every choice. But not this time. She turns to the page that once more has organized itself into familiar words, sentences, ideas.

The man beside her rustles, and she looks up.

"Nice view," he says.

"Yes," she replies, feeling a pang of guilt that she's not making better use of her window seat.

"My home's down there somewhere, along that river," he says, nodding toward the window. "Just between the river and the lake."

"Really? What's the village?"

"Point Albright. Small place, but really pretty. The lake water is so clear you can see the salmon swimming by, and sometimes it's so calm that when a moose drinks from it on the other side, the ripples reach all the way across."

"Oh, sounds lovely, how I'd like to see it. Alaska's so big, though I've lived here twenty-five years, I've yet to see even half of it."

"Yes, it'd take several lifetimes, wouldn't it now? But it's a good way to spend the one."

She smiles, nods, takes a deep breath.

**

Astrid works late into the night, then walks back to their small stone house along Ransom Street. She opens the door to the savory scents of Gareth cooking dinner. Vegetable fricassee, and no one makes it better. Good food, a glass of wine, easy conversation, reading, then bed. A fine evening. So why does she find herself awake, tossing and turning and finally tiptoeing out to the living room couch to keep from waking Gareth?

She turns on a lamp and, in the yellow light, picks up the letter and reads it again. From Strilay, old-fashioned fool, using snail mail.

The bears, he writes, are everywhere. But they're a motley crew. White coats stained and muddy, thick fur hanging off thin frames. Too thin even for the end of summer. They stand on the banks of the bay, stretching their long necks, pointing their black snouts toward the open water as if sniffing for the ice, waiting for it to return.

Well, she thinks, now he's becoming a poet.

The captive ones, the bad bears in cement holdings, they still do the same thing—face that open water. They don't like being near town, he writes, they'd rather be out on the ice, hunting seals, but desperate times call for desperate measures.

Desperate times. She's feeling desperate about this grant she didn't take, and how it might damage her own flow of research money. Her late-night voice reminds her of a study showing women scientists face more hurdles in maintaining a steady stream of research funds. But what's even more troubling is that this grant may now take her precious collection of samples, using what she's built up over her twenty-three-year career to prove—what? What is it they're looking for?

She sighs. All the corporate funding in universities today flummoxes her. She understands that as government funding has shrunk, corporations have filled the gap. But it irks her no end to walk her esteemed campus, over two hundred years old, and come upon a building named for the corporation that paid for it. Bad enough naming things after people who funded it, but at least with something like, say, the Dean Dome, the structure was named for someone who was actually involved in the activity for which it was created—men's basketball, the famous coach Dean Smith. Or Coker Hall, the biology building named for the first chair of the botany department and founder of the arboretum. Better yet, why not name buildings after who once lived there, before they were razed to the ground. White Oak Hall. Galax Wing. Black Snake Auditorium.

The naming, she knows, is only the surface sign of change. These corporations are also dictating the research conducted in the buildings bearing their names. It's getting increasingly difficult to tell the difference between campus and Research Triangle Park, where corporations house their research teams. That's what really upsets her. She believes in the value of pure science, science for knowledge's sake, not to promote the goals of a corporation. It undermines the scientific process to do otherwise.

The apparent goal of this research project funded by Exxon-Mobil is to investigate the effects of previous warming periods on plant communities of the time. The implied questions: Is the current warming trend really so bad? Won't plants adjust just fine, as they have before? Isn't this just another natural occurrence, one that we're here to witness up close and personal, armed with all our science? Aren't we just making far too big a deal of this?

She'd naively thought that if she turned it down, the project wouldn't happen. She had hoped scientific integrity would win out over money. It's not that she has a position on the questions being asked; it's that she is opposed to the very nature of it: forced questions and applied research lead to suspect answers. She wishes she could meet Strilay for lunch and talk through all this. He'd know what to do, or at least how to put it in perspective, if only to just make light of it.

She picks up his letter again and takes in his broad slanting scrawl. The polar bears staring out to sea. He describes that so poignantly that she can almost see it herself. What do they do if the ice never comes?

Chapter 8

The turboprop touches down, bumping on the gravel runway, and the handful of passengers, hunched over in the small cabin so they don't bump their heads on the overhead bins and door hatch, disembark. A bitter wind hits Elyse in the face, whipping up dust from the runway. Her eyes tear up as grit lodges under one of her contacts. In the dim midday light, she sees before her an expanse of flat land, treeless and brown. To the right is the town, a rambling array of one-story buildings sprouting from the flatness, an awkward cluster on what looks like the edge of the moon.

A man, short and stocky and covered in a thick gray jumpsuit, waves to her. "Elyse Sowka?" he says. She nods, and he motions to the back seat of his four-wheeler with one hand, grabs her bag with the other and hefts it onto the flat platform over the rear wheels. He tosses her two boxes up on top, slings a rope over them, tugs it in place. Then he swings on and motions again for her to climb on behind him, and so she does, thigh to thigh with this stranger in a strange new land. He guns the engine and they fly off, the windchill slapping her face like a bowl of ice.

When they stop in front of a low-slung rusty red building, he helps her off, wordlessly. Trying for some light camaraderie, she laughs, "I can't feel my nose. Is it still there?" But he just looks at her in silence, then grabs her bag and heads for the door.

A blast of warmth pulls her into a small arctic entry, then a large room with table, chairs, and a fraying brown couch. The warm air carries the smell of burnt coffee and creamer and another pungent smell she does not yet know.

"You wait here," says her driver, dropping her boxes and motioning to a chair. Then he's gone, back out the door, the sound of his four-wheeler breaking the silence and slowly fading away.

Elyse sighs, reaches into her backpack for her eyedrops, and notices what looks like a large oil stain on the thin carpet. She puts in the drops and, as her sight clears, scans the room. It seems to be a classroom as well as a meeting hall. Whiteboards are scribbled with lists and diagrams; children's drawings are pinned like a paper quilt to one wall, some of them clacking in the breeze from the forced-air heater beneath them. A row of shelves is filled with a collection of phone books, children's books, and manuals. But everything, every word, is in Russian and incomprehensible to her.

What is comprehensible is how different this classroom is from anything her own sons had experienced. Not the language, but the room, the materials, the resources the children had for learning. She's reminded, again, of her own blind luck.

She pulls her water bottle from a side pocket and takes a sip. The water is so cold that it hurts her teeth, chilled from that short ride. She pulls off her hat, runs her fingers through her hair, wishes she had a mirror. Then, as if through the heating vent, she hears Dan's voice: *Are you sure this thing's legit?*

She didn't tell Dan, but Jim's initial idea of an expedition had been whittled down, from a lack of funds and deteriorating relations between the U.S. and Russia, to just a handful of people who would overlap with each other for a few days near the end of Elyse's month. Besides her, there'd be a photographer, a journalist, a poet, and two scientists—and except for the photographer, the others would only be here for a week. Permissions and funding, Jim told her, had thrown a wrench in the expedition plans. Still, he assured her, this would be a comprehensive effort, and they'd all have some time together. But Elyse is the first one here.

Surely they knew she was coming. The driver was waiting for the plane, and knew just where to take her. Surely someone will be along soon.

Outside, what remains of the light leaks away. Her stomach reminds her it's closing in on dinnertime. She resists grabbing one of her energy bars. She doesn't have many, and there may be other times she'll need them more. If right now is any indication, many more times.

She sinks onto the couch and leans her head back. At least she has arrived. At least all those months of resistance and doubt are behind her. It is what it is. Either it will work out or it won't. But at least she got herself here. At least she kept that promise to herself.

Promises. The promises we keep. If there's one thing Elyse cannot abide, it's broken promises. She had schooled her sons on that so hard that it had become a family joke: *Promise? Promise? You sure you want to say that word?* they'd say to her with a wicked grin. She grins now, thinking of their sweet boy faces turned up to her, and then feels that sudden catch in her throat. She wills the longing away, for in its shadow is a loneliness she can't afford right now. This trip is a promise to herself. Kept.

She is fastidious about keeping her own promises—like being a vegan. She can recall the precise moment she stopped eating chicken: driving out to her boyfriend's house after a day of classes at UNC, she got stuck behind a semi from which clouds of white feathers flew back and smattered her windshield. The truck carried chickens, hundreds of them, stacked twelve high in small crates. Afterward, when she learned how the beaks of chicks are burned so they won't peck each other to death in their crowded quarters, how the cages are so small they can't even stand up, and how they lived less than six months before falling to the blade, she stopped eating meat of any kind. Even though she still, too often to admit, craves meat, she won't budge—all she needs do is recall those images and remember her promise.

There's little else Elyse has stood firm on; she's always considered herself to be flexible. Sometimes too flexible, she thinks, hearing

Maggie's admonitions about Dan cancelling plans at the last minute. "He never promised," she always replies. "Right," Maggie always says. "He's so good at saying *maybe, tentatively, hopefully*. No way would I put up with it."

Pinkie promise. That's what she and her childhood friends would do. Curl their pinkies around each other's. But then, those pinkie promises weren't always kept. There was a best friend, in second or maybe third grade, a friend who was so close that Elyse called them "secret sisters"—and then suddenly not. A shunning. The friend breaking a promise and going silent, then disappearing from her life. The friendship erased as if blown away by a gale. And a pain in the pit of her stomach, a sharp aching, she still feels whenever she remembers. She doesn't remember anything beyond that; she doesn't know what happened, will never know, but she does know that promises should be kept.

A cold blast of air wakes her.

"You must be Elyse, welcome," she hears, starting from thin sleep to see a man striding toward her. His pale blue eyes smile above his thick, unkempt beard. "Very sorry to keep you waiting. I failed to hear the plane land. My apologies."

"Yes, hello," Elyse says, running her fingers over her eyes.

"You must be tired and hungry," he continues. "Let me take you by your house, and then my wife and I would be pleased to have you for dinner."

"Okay," she replies, still groggy.

A pickup truck, big and warm, carries her a few minutes to a small house perched on a corner street. A large red bucket sits outside, a weathered lean-to stacked with crates braces one side of the dwelling, and a blue tarp taps out time with the wind on a corner of the roof.

"This house is Mikhail's, but he is only here in summer, so now it is all yours," says her current escort, opening the door into a one-room house with vinyl floors, vinyl counters, a card table and two folding chairs, another worn brown couch, and a recliner facing a stand where she guesses a TV once sat.

"It is small but enough, no? And it just base camp. We set you up with studio space in school, tomorrow."

This man, whoever he is, speaks very good English, but she can still hear a Russian accent, that emphasis on the hard sound of consonants. Much like Iñupiat and Yup'ik, and most northern languages, really. The southern languages have all the vowel sounds, the melodious drawing out of each soft sound. Before she can ask anything about him, even his name, he heads out the door, promising to return in thirty minutes to bring her to dinner.

Her stomach grumbles. The energy bar in her pocket is warm and inviting. She takes another swig of water and crumples onto the recliner. Comfortable, yes, it is. If not for hunger, she could fall asleep right here. She tosses her bag in the corner, pulls out a hairbrush and toothbrush, and tries to make herself presentable. Eyes burning, she swipes out her contacts and reaches for her duffel to dig out glasses. Why can she never remember to find her glasses before she removes her contacts? Fumbling around in her duffel, she finds a slip of paper, a bright yellow sticky note with a red heart on it. Dan. She used to do that for him, hide love notes in his luggage for him to find on his trips.

Glasses on, she reads the note: all it says is *Be safe.*

**

The phone rings, insistent, shattering night into a thousand shards. Astrid bolts up from a dream. Gareth groans and mumbles, "Who could possibly be calling in the middle of the night?" She turns, checks the clock: 3 a.m. Then grabs her phone to silence it. The number is unfamiliar, is not, in fact, even in the U.S. She answers.

"This is Joe, in Canada."

Joe. Who is Joe? Canada. Strilay.

"Yes?"

"Yes, well, I'm sorry to call you in the middle of the night, but Strilay's had a heart attack. He's in hospital here, but they will probably be transferring him to Winnipeg. We're still waiting to see how bad it is. He listed you as emergency contact. I know you're not family, but ..."

"No, no, yes, that's right, I am the one to call, thank you, yes. I—shall I come?"

"It's up to you, of course, but like I said, I don't know how bad it is yet. I don't know if he's . . ."

"Going to make it? Going to survive it?"

"Yes, right."

"Okay, okay, let me, let me know where he will be, I will get there as soon as I can."

"Okay, thank you, and I'm sorry."

"Yes, yes, thank you."

Sitting in her bed. She's still sitting in her bed. Gareth is already up, the light on, he's in the kitchen making coffee and on the phone to the airlines. Her legs and arms feel sunk in concrete. Her stomach in her throat, her throat rising from her eyes into a silent scream. Her left ear rings, the one she heard the news through. Rings, like a scream, one long scream. She clasps hands over her ears, on top of her head, and rises, staggers to the living room, where Gareth is on the phone.

"No, two," he says, "two seats. You only have one?"

"It's okay," she whispers, "I can go alone."

So she does. She is not one to travel. Just one more thing she and Strilay have in common. The farthest she usually goes is to the Peabody in Connecticut or the Field in Chicago. Once she went as far as the Museum of Natural History in London.

Within twelve hours, she is in Canada. Joe has texted her that Strilay is still in Churchill, so that's where she goes. A bitter wind nearly blows her from the stairs as she gets off the plane, where one man, stocky, bearded, hairy as a bear and as broad-shouldered, waits.

"He's awake, he's jovial, you know how he can be," says Joe as he takes her small bag and opens the door for her. "They think it's better not to move him right now. You want to go see him?"

"Yes, right away," she says, surprised by Joe's thick southern drawl and thinking, suddenly, of her mother. Of when Astrid's grandfather fell ill and Macey's employer wouldn't let her off work, so Macey had quit to be by her father's side—only to arrive moments after he died.

Her mother, in grief so deep, never forgave herself. Not that, Astrid does not want that.

Dark already in Churchill, all she can see is what's lit. The town stands like a rim of candles in a vast darkness. The amber light beckons her to what could be warmth, but isn't. She has been cold since she picked up the phone. Bone cold. The rush of warm air, the bright lights of the hospital, the clean and awake nurse behind the gleaming counter—all a blur she moves through like ice water. To Strilay, white cloud of hair spread on the pillow, skin pale and wrinkles deeper, but those blue eyes open, shining, as if he'd had a vision.

"Oh, my dear," he says, struggling to rise to his elbows but then falling back, "so very good to see you again, but under such regrettable circumstances." He reaches out his hand, and she grasps it, staring at him, speechless. She is overcome with gratitude that he is still alive, that she made it in time, but she has enough sense left to not say that.

"I'm glad to see you too," she manages, smiling. His hand in hers is warm but thin and light as bird's bones.

The heart attack was a big one, but thanks to a quick response time, the damage isn't as bad as initially feared. Medications seem to be working, so surgery has been ruled out for now. The consensus is to keep him in Churchill for recovery, then, when he's able to fly, he can decide whether to go to Winnipeg or all the way to Chapel Hill.

"Or just stay here," he tells Astrid. "That's the third option, the one I'm aiming for. I just can't get enough of these polar bears. You'll get to see them now! So you'll see. What animals. What amazements."

"Sure, yes, I'll see them, yes," she stammers, "but it's you I'm here for."

"Yes, this is working out perfectly, my diabolical plan to wrest you away from that fetid university and unleash you onto the big world. I have great plans for you, m'dear."

"Oh, very funny," she replies, involuntarily smiling. "Very. You could have just faked it, you know. But no, you had to go and have a real heart attack."

"True, true, hadn't thought of that," he chuckles. "How I've missed our banter."

"I have too," she says, thinking of all the restless lunches in her lab.

Morning light finds her asleep on a cot in his hospital room. He snores like a freight train, but somehow she slept through it. Strilay's morning is booked with tests, so Joe steers her away, to breakfast, to his warm truck, to the edge of town where Hudson Bay spreads silver liquid northeast. Joe is calm and sweet, a southern gentleman who opens doors and offers his hand. They sit in his truck and look out at the bay. Ice forms along the edges, and on those thin ledges, white mounds that Astrid thinks are snowdrifts but are not.

"Those," says Joe, "are polar bears. Sleeping polar bears."

"What?" says Astrid, "Really? Right here in town?"

"Right here in town. Yes, ma'am," says Joe.

"But I didn't . . . I've never," Astrid stutters. "I've never seen a polar bear. They are so . . . big. And close."

"Yes, ma'am," Joe continues, "yes, they are. Big bears. And close. While they're waiting for the ice, they scavenge, and as good as we've gotten at containing trash and food, they still hang around us. Churchill's built on the migratory path for polar bears, so it's not just about us; they've been coming here to wait for the bay to freeze for who knows how many centuries."

Joe tells Astrid that in the late 1960s, there were as many as eighty bears in town in fall, half of them at the town dump. Bears considered a threat were simply shot. Then a series of dangerous encounters, including the fatal attack on a child, led Churchill to launch their Polar Bear Control Program. That was the same year Joe got his draft card and fled the States. Since he'd already had an affinity for bears and was, in fact, hoping to make research on Appalachian black bears his life's work, Joe hitchhiked to Churchill and has been here ever since.

"It was a rough start," he says, "because at first, the only change was that the government took over killing problem bears, as many as twenty-five a year. Well, that and cleaning up the dump." He shakes his head, sighs. "Now, here I'd left the U.S. to keep from killing the Viet Cong and found myself being told to kill polar bears. I was just about to throw in the towel when we got the go-ahead for the bear jail. Well, technically it's called a holding facility," he grins. "Now we hardly ever kill a bear; instead, we move them or hold them until the ice forms. Then we release them onto the ice. And y'know, they gallop away from us pretty dang fast."

Just what Strilay wrote, thinks Astrid, as she nods, dumbstruck at seeing polar bears—such massive, mythical beings—for the first time in the wild and, at the same time, basking in the familiarity of Joe's warm southern drawl.

But now, says Joe, the ice is forming later and melting sooner, so the bears are getting shortchanged on both ends. Fewer cubs are surviving, and those that do are smaller. The population is plummeting, and the ones that do survive to fall freeze-up are nearly starving. "It keeps things challenging for us, and, well, it's just heartbreaking," Joe sighs, "watching them struggle and not being able to do anything but try to keep them away from our food."

Joe's voice trails off and his head drops. But then he snaps it back up, shrugs his shoulders as if to shake off some heavy load, and turns to Astrid with a forced smile. "I'll take you to see the bear jail later, if you want. Right now I've got a staff meeting. You can join me or head to your room, or to the hospital. What d'you fancy?"

She opts for the hotel and some time alone to rest, to digest everything. Strilay's frail arms jutting from a hospital gown. Massive polar bears huddled by an iceless bay. Joe's soft drawl explaining this sharp land. Sitting on the hard single bed in a room whose heat wasn't turned on until the moment she stepped into it, she shivers. Everything in the room is like a block of ice. She pulls back the covers and lies down, trying to get warm. The cold, though, it emanates from her bones. She needs to move; she needs to walk.

She walks the town's few streets, not willing to venture far in any direction lest she meet up with a polar bear. But the haphazard array of industrial buildings, tourist shops, and assorted housing peters out quickly, and she is left to stand before a vast expanse of flat land punctuated by a few stunted spruce and bordered by the bay and the Hudson River. She walks the riverside, the flow of water rumbling through caverns of ice created from a melt-thaw cycle and the ebb-flow of tides. The edges are awash in lenses of ice so clear they shine blue; in places, bubbles are trapped like head-lights deep within.

Into her head pops a John Prine song about a carful of people careening into a lake with no bottom. Just falling and falling. How odd. She hasn't listened to "The Bottomless Lake" since, well, since Prine came to play one summer night during her college years. It's an upbeat, silly song, underlaid with a deep sorrow. A sorrow she didn't pay much attention to then, but now it seems to be the ice-water swimming in her bones.

She shakes herself like a polar bear shaking off frost in the morn-ing's light and walks more briskly. Strilay's heart attack has struck her to the roots, that much is clear, but she is still surprised by how offbalance she feels. After all, a man of his age—things are bound to happen. Maybe it's the excitement and weather and novelty of being here that brought on his heart attack. Or maybe not. Still, she's known too many people who died shortly after retirement to not feel that had something to do with it.

She kicks at some stones. It's deeper, this sorrow, than her fear for Strilay's health. It's an underground river that's been gaining speed, little feeder streams she hasn't even noticed adding to its flow every day. She feels so heavy. Feels the river powering her down into a bot-tomless lake of grief.

She looks down at the stones she's dislodged and wonders what fossils might be found around here. Oh, who cares, she thinks. Who cares what used to be here. Soon what's here will also be gone, all of them with it, and the polar bears first. It's all leaving. We're all leav-ing. Why study the past when I'm standing in the middle of it?

These are thoughts she has never had. These are doubts she has never felt. She turns back toward the cluster of buildings and nearly runs back to her room, clomping up the stairs to drown the sound of her thoughts. She opens the door to warmth, blessed warmth. She lies down on the bed and is instantly, gratefully, deeply asleep.

That night, at the hospital, Strilay seems his old self, as chipper as ever. It surprises her; she can't help but think of how birds, when sick, work so hard to feign wellness.

"Say, m'dear, I've a favor to ask. Lamont is arriving in a couple of days, and I was supposed to entertain the fellow while he's here. You know, stroll the town, take him to dinner, that kind of thing. I'm thinking I may not be done with this tomfoolery by then, so could you take my place?"

"I wasn't . . . I don't know how long I'm staying," says Astrid. "I'm really only here for you."

"Yes, of course, but while you are, I won't put up with you sitting by my bed all day. You'll bore me," he says, blue eyes twinkling with mischief.

"What's he here for?"

"That book he's working on. He's been here before, of course, and can find his own way, but at least a dinner or two, some intellectual conversation for the man."

Astrid agrees, but only because she knows Strilay can't fly for another ten days, and she's suddenly decided to stay until he comes back to Chapel Hill with her. She'll coordinate information exchange between the doctors here and those at Memorial Hospital and Duke Medical Center. She wants the absolute best care possible for him and is certain no one can manage it as well as she.

******

Thin sunlight awakens Elyse. She bolts upright. It must be late. Time to get to the studio. She had worked late the night before and had wanted to continue this morning before heading out to see the walrus. But now, if it's already light, she's missed her chance. No matter, she thinks, her head buzzing with all she's seen and done in just a week.

After the first couple of days, meeting people, getting to know the place, feeling her way with language and customs, Elyse has quickly—surprisingly quickly—found a rhythm. Mornings in her studio, midday accompanying a scientist or marine mammal hunter or watchman, dinner with one or another of her new friends, and then nights, back at the studio. She feels on fire, a rushing of energy, filling her with light, even though the place itself is cold and dark and still.

But the animals. The walrus, the seabirds, the polar bears. Polar bears, outside a zoo, roaming freely. And so many. Their regal stealth, those tree-trunk legs carrying them as graceful as a breeze across the tundra. Encountering each other, they back off or rise up on two legs. Nearing the walrus, their gaze intensifies. The smells and sounds and textures of these masses of walrus, one brown body melding into the next, a rolling wave of rounded shapes, each animal at first to Elyse indistinguishable, until the sizes and shades of brown, the movements of flippers and whiskered heads, reveal individuals. And the birds, swooping in and out of vision, smaller in number now than in summer, but still a few stragglers: black brants, eiders, and the small brown sandpipers nipping along the shoreline.

The more she watches, the more she sees: how smaller female walrus slip aside for larger ones; how the nursing pups shimmy to their mothers, their suckling sound mingling with the groans and bellows of others; how the sandpiper flits at her approach, flying in an arc to land ahead of her; how the smaller polar bears hang back and watch the larger ones, eyeing any scrap they miss; how the walrus let the lilting waves carry them to shore, lifting and depositing them on the beach. Elyse is absolutely enchanted with observing these wild animals so closely and for so long. She can't get enough. A deep thirst, one she didn't even know she had, is being quenched.

And yet there is the dread that runs like an underground river, an insistent rumble through every moment. The crystal knowledge that what she is experiencing is already not the norm, that even this is fast disappearing. This sharpens the thirst, makes it greedy, insatiable.

She is to meet Yurgyev at 9; he promised to show her the carcass pile today, the place miles from the town where they dump the bodies of walrus—mostly pups—found dead on the beach. Most of these deaths are caused by stampeding, and most of the stampeding is created by the increasing number of tourists swamping the town and swarming the haulout. Never before have so many walrus gathered in one spot; never before have walrus hauled out so close to a town. The visitors also hope to see polar bears migrating along the coast, waiting for the ice and lured closer by walrus.

Between the bears and the tourists, the walrus would be stampeding constantly but for the Umka Patrol. These men, armed, as she's now seen, with nothing but sticks, keep bears and people far enough away that stampeding has nearly ceased. Elyse has not seen a stampede, nor does she want to. It's clear that young walrus would not fare well if the teeming mass of animals were to suddenly bolt for the security of the water.

Over a cup of tea, she flips back in her sketchbook to her first drawing of the haulout. There's the cobbled beach crowded with walrus, huddled together so close it's hard to see where one leaves off and another begins, fanning out, growing smaller with distance, falling off one end of the page. Only around the biggest males is there any space. Between satiny brown females, the pups' darker fur sandwiches. Just offshore, dozens of walrus, heads bobbing in waves. In the foreground, standing wide-legged, wearing thick caps, two walrus guards. One holds his stick like a pole, tip firmly on the ground. The other holds his like a rifle across his chest. Both wear smiles so wide they threaten to erase any other facial feature in those broad, wind-weathered faces.

Every time she's seen any members of the Umka Patrol, she has been struck by their continuous smiles. Why? Why do they smile all the time? Surely they know that the climatic changes they face are overwhelming, that protecting walrus from stampedes is not going to bring the ice back or reduce the carbon dioxide warming the winds and the waters. And why do they smile when what they're doing is a far cry from what they would be doing had the ice returned as it had every other year of their lives? They would have been hunting walrus, not protecting them.

And yet they seem so cheerful, so full of confidence, in the face of what, to her, is hopeless. It buoys her, keeps her from dropping into a depression over all the loss she is witnessing. It reminds her of images of the Buddhist teacher Thich Nhat Hanh, how he was always smiling, he who endured such hardship and witnessed such horrors during the Vietnam War. Maybe, like he was, these guards are just happy to be alive, happy to be human, to have the opportunity to walk the Earth, to take action for that which they love. This cheerful confidence, she thinks, must be what carries them through hard times and uncertainties, the waxing and waning of hunting successes, dark winters and storms.

She's looking forward to having Yurgyev, the Russian scientist who has educated her in everything walrus, finally take her to the carcass site, where polar bears are more often seen. The pile is not only a way to remove the stench of rotting walrus but also to protect the townspeople from polar bears: if the bears are drawn to an easy feed at the carcass site, they're less likely to approach the town's beach. But if they do, they're met by an Umka patroller.

"No yell," one patroller told her. "Loud sounds only make them come close. Instead, make yourself big." The patroller raised his stick high overhead. "If bear doesn't back off, hit with stick between ears, right on top of head."

Elyse chuckled, thinking this a joke, but he went on to tell her how he did that, not once but twice, and the bear did finally run off. And then he threw back his head and laughed, the sound ringing in the crystal air.

When she arrives at the school that morning, however, it's not Yurgyev but Nicolaf, one of the patrollers, who waits with the scientist's white pickup. A bit taller than most of the men, but with the same stocky build and thick black hair, Nicolaf explains that Yurgyev has a conference call with his agency in Moscow and has asked him to take her instead.

She thought she'd gotten used to being around all these new people, but Nicolaf isn't one she's talked with much; he has seemed more quiet and reserved. That discomfort she felt her first few days here returns. English is spoken well only by a few residents, so she's had to pick up some Russian from a quick online course she took in preparation for this trip. Most of her conversations have leaned heavily on hand motions and context.

So she hesitates. The truck is warm, the heater blasting, and the road bumpy. Having awoken late, she could easily fall back asleep, were it not for that awkward responsibility she feels to make conversation. "So, how long have you lived here?"

"I have not lived in any other place since my birth," he replies, glancing her way, almond-shaped eyes expressionless.

"Oh, right, of course, I mean, yes," she stammers, glad at least that he speaks some English. "Well, this is quite the place, so very— wild—and remote. How lucky you are to live with all this wildlife."

Even as she talks, she remembers her question to Beverly and realizes how ridiculous her words must seem. This is all he knows; how could he consider it good fortune? How could he know how wild it is compared with where most people live?

"So, are you, do you have children? Family here?"

"I am not betrothed," he replies. "It was not in the favor."

With this line of questioning making things more awkward, she switches pathways. But even her questions about walrus and polar bears are so contrived that he likely guesses she already knows the answers. What does she not yet know that this stoic man with whom she will spend the day can tell her?

At the pile is blood all around, frozen now, and bones; there's not much besides skulls that the bears don't eat. Still, a few bears pace nearby, keeping their distance from the white pickup. They're thin, as they normally are at summer's end, but thinner than usual, he says. "That one," he says, pointing to the smallest, "she will not make, I do not think."

"Make? You mean, make it? You think she's starving?"

"Yes. Starving. Not enough fat left. You see how her skin hangs like too-big coat."

"Oh," says Elyse, at a loss, again, for words. But he continues, the focus on something other than his life allowing him to relax. His voice loosens, his broad shoulders drop. "She is not only one. We see this all the time now. It is death coming. We see so much death here, always. It is familiar. No hospitals for the hiding. We know in our families, our towns."

"So, you can tell when it's coming, then? Because your culture doesn't hide it like ours?"

"Yes, that is what I say, yes. And the polar bears, they are like family to us. Uncles, cousins. We have live together long time. And walrus and seals. They are neighbors. So we can see their death. But what we see now, it is different. This I cannot explain."

"You mean, how they're dying? You can't predict it?"

"No, we can predict, as you say. But it has different feeling. Before, death would be more easy to accept. There would be a seeing—in person or animal dying—it was their time. We do not feel that now with the polar bears and walrus."

"Yes, because so many of them are dying."

"Not so much numbers for us. But the way. The ice is dying. In our time here we never think the ice would die, would betray us by leaving. We have no stories from ancestors of ice leaving. It not thinkable. The ice is like father or mother, source of life for us. With it leaving, we cannot survive. The polar bears tell us, the walrus show us—first them, then us."

Elyse stands still in the icy air. This man who had seemed so recalcitrant has opened up once they stood before this scene; he's described feelings that she couldn't see in the guards but sensed must be there. She stands beside this man she has just met, witnessing what she has never before experienced, and feels the very ground beneath her feet tremble with grief's clear truth.

"This," she says, after a long but not uncomfortable silence, "this is what I want to reveal with my paintings."

"This place?" he asks.

"Yes, the place, but what's beneath that, what it means. I want to show the loss that you're feeling. This unnatural death. It is so hidden, so abstract, to the rest of the world. If I could make it more tangible, then the world might wake up and do something."

"That," he says, slowly, "that is something we would like. It hard for us to explain. We can keep bears from walrus, and people from bears and walrus, but we cannot make ice come back."

It is late, far past dark, when they return to Cape Vankarem. Elyse feels more tired than she has since arriving. Still, after dinner, she goes to the studio. For hours she simply stares at the white canvas. As she does the next morning. Until she lays down her brush, bundles up, and goes for a walk alone, out past the village, across the tundra and to the river, which at this time of year is in a freeze-thaw cycle that creates some of the most beautiful sculptures she's ever likely to see.

She stops and kneels before one that curls and breaks upward like a wave tectonically split. She takes off her glove and places her hand on the clearest part, where an array of tiny bubbles are trapped like stars. The surface is smooth, almost soft, and warms to melt beneath her bare palm. She runs her hand around the curve, pushes into an indentation that almost, but not quite, opens to the other side. Then she sighs, stands, puts her glove back on. Even the beauty of these transient sculptures will not cheer her today.

She walks, and walks, aware she is going farther than she has yet alone. The polar bears, though, stay closer to shore this time of year, and she is traveling inland, away from them. The sun hangs low on the horizon, lifting just enough to send shivers of gold across the tundra, lighting the backs of lowbush blueberry and sedges, making them appear taller. Nothing moves, nothing makes a sound, except her boots crunching morning frost. She stops and listens. The immensity. The power. She can hear the place thrumming, a low sound, a vibration. How is it possible that humans are causing the destruction of a place with such power?

She has not yet accepted it. She still holds tight to a hope that it's not as bad as they think, that there is still time to turn it around, that humans will suddenly wake up and do it. In time for polar bears, walrus, and sea ice; in time for Arctic villages and the atolls of the South Pacific. She cannot accept the alternative, not and keep breathing.

Open heart, broken heart, she whispers. Open heart, broken heart. Whatever happens, don't close down.

A rustling, and she turns swiftly. Nothing, only tundra, the tight smattering of buildings, and then the dark sea. Another rustle, in the grass, and she sees the sound's source: an arctic fox. Small and with a fur coat so thick that the fox looks rotund. The petite triangle of a face staring at her, that white face with perfectly pointed ears and those two bright amber eyes. There is a moment of shared gaze, as if fox is daring her to look away. A moment, so fleeting, when she is fox, fox is she. Her warm white fur, her hunger. Then, baring a small toothy grin, the fox snaps up a vole and lopes across the tundra, an undulating movement of absolute grace, the bushy tail following like a sine wave.

Chapter 9

Lamont is thinner than Astrid remembers, even with bulky arctic clothing. Yet he still carries himself with a certain grandeur, filling whatever room in which he finds himself. In this case, it's just the lobby of the Tundra Hotel, which isn't very large to begin with. Sitting by the fireplace in a big overstuffed plaid chair, surrounded by dark wood furniture, caribou antler chandelier, and matching antler table lamps, Lamont is flipping through outdated magazines on the coffee table. His thinning gray hair and gaunt look in such a lanky frame make him seem vulnerable, until he speaks.

Just as he greets her with annoying effusiveness, the shuttle to the polar bear tour arrives. At the tour office, no more than a tiny one-window shed on the edge of town, they and a couple dozen others board a large white vehicle with oversized wheels and four axles, like a schoolbus on steroids. And because it's just as packed as a schoolbus with excited, talkative tourists, Astrid and Lamont sit sandwiched next to each other. Astrid generally abhors group activities where people are herded about like cattle, but Strilay was adamant she go.

"You can't have come all this way without spending at least one day doing what people from all over the world flock here to do," he'd said.

As they bump across the tundra over the year's first dusting of snow, she stares out the window, pretending to look for polar bears while she sorts out the previous few days' overload. She's reviewing conversations with specialists at Memorial when Lamont's voice intrudes.

"You know, I did this nearly ten years ago, this tour," says Lamont. "So I'll be interested to see how it's changed, how the bears have changed, or whether I can even tell. I've got this card to help us determine the health of the bears we see." He pulls out a laminated sheet produced by Polar Bears International titled *Polar Bear Score Card: A Standardized Fatness Index.*

"It's kind of hilarious: it's just like the one my veterinarian gave me to make sure our old Lab wasn't getting obese. Same views above and sideways. Seems obvious, but truly, I can't imagine spotting a polar bear and deciding the bear is obese."

"Yes, that would be surprising."

"Especially this time of year when they're at their thinnest waiting for that ice to return," he continues, "and in this region around Churchill, well, Joe probably told you, the bears are already getting smaller and thinner. They're literally showing stunted growth from lack of food. And lower cub survival. Interesting how animals react to stress, isn't it? Reminds me of the male orcas whose dorsals go limp when they're stressed by lack of food or contaminants, like some males after the *Exxon Valdez* oil spill in Alaska."

Astrid thinks about her houseplants, how they adapt when water-stressed—how orchid leaves shrivel then droop. If she catches them before they droop, they'll come back. If not, that droop is permanent. She's seen it in grocery store orchids. Sometimes, if no one is looking, she pours a few drops of water from the cut-flower containers onto the orchids. In her opinion, grocery stores shouldn't be allowed to sell live plants. She can't pass them by without stopping to stand up fallen pots, tamp the dirt back down, spread them around so their flowers aren't breaking from overcrowding. More than once, customers have mistaken her for an employee and asked her questions she couldn't answer.

She's hoping Gareth waters her plants correctly, the steady rumbling of the engine and the wave-like action of lumping along across the tundra making her drowsy, when a woman at the front of the bus yells, "There! Is that a bear, there on the right?"

The brakes rub the bus to a stop, and binoculars appear before everyone's eyes.

"Oh, no," says the tour director, standing up front, "That's a rock. One that's been mistaken for a polar bear many times. But better we stop for a rock than not stop for a bear, so thanks for speaking up."

The bus shudders to a start and is just getting up to rolling speed when another passenger calls out, "Bear! On the left! Or is it another rock?"

"It *is* a bear, good job! A female, too, with a cub," says the tour director. "Let's meander over that way."

"There are rules about how close you can get to them in the U.S.," says Lamont, leaning in to whisper to Astrid, "but none that I know of in Canada. It will be interesting to see how they handle this."

Fortunately, according to Lamont, the bus doesn't drive directly toward the bears. It's close enough, though, for the bears to take notice. The sow rears up on hind legs, the cub scurries over and hides behind her, small furry head poking out between the pillars of her rear legs. Then the sow drops to all fours and noses dried grass stalks sticking out above the snow. The cub, still leery, stays safely hidden behind his mother.

"Sometimes they come closer," says the guide. "And then it's okay, we just stay where we are, we're not harassing them as long as they're the ones doing the approaching. We just don't want to stress them, particularly sows with cubs, by chasing them."

Lamont nods his head. "Excellent, excellent," he mumbles.

Minutes later, they come upon another bear, so close that no one questions whether it's rock or bear. They stop, brakes rubbing. This one, a large male, approaches.

"They're extremely curious fellows," says the guide. "Remember, they're top predators here, so they don't have anybody to fear."

"Well, except humans," says Lamont, continuing his side commentary, much to Astrid's dismay. "But they are fearless. I've seen a photograph of three polar bears approaching the USS *Honolulu* submarine after it partially emerged through sea ice. They just walked right up to it, onto it, checking it out. Absolutely fearless. Love it."

Lamont seems cheered by the big bear. "There we go, we've got a good view of his back now, I'd say he's a healthy bear, not thin at all."

The bear keeps approaching. Right up to the bus. Right to Astrid's window. The other passengers crowd around her, making her momentarily claustrophobic. The bear raises up, placing his two front paws right on the glass below Astrid's face. Giant black pads fringed by feathery white fur. Staring at her, she staring back. Just the two of them. All else recedes. There's no camera in front of her face; even the glass fades away. Boundaries fall away. Massive white head punctuated by coal-black eyes and aquiline snout. Bottomless black eyes holding her gaze, looking for something in her green ones. Black nose touches the glass, lightly, briefly—then he drops down and saunters away, wind and muscle rippling rivers of fur along his shoulders.

Lamont may or may not be talking to her; she doesn't hear him or anyone else. She is motionless, quiet, staring at the pawprints long after the others return to their seats, the bus begins to move, the bear becomes no more than a white spot on the flat treeless tundra. She sits still and watches the bear's receding image, listening to her breath, feeling her heartbeat slow, feeling a space grow inside her chest, something bright, something new but familiar, something right.

Over the next few hours, they see another dozen bears, some close and some far away. Lamont keeps score on their health, finding many that are thin and of concern, especially mothers with cubs. Astrid watches each bear intently, heartbeat racing whenever one is near, the brightness glowing like an inner sun, binoculars pressed to her eyes for so long that Lamont laughs at her raccoon face.

"Well, it's been a long day, but a good one, eh?" says the tour driver, and everyone on the bus sighs, claps, and settles back in their seats as the bus lumbers back toward town. Astrid, however, does not sit back with eyes closed. She watches as golden-light sun flattens on the horizon and the sky darkens, to red, to purple, watches the sunset kaleidoscope through the paw prints of the polar bear.

At dinner, Lamont asks about Astrid's work. She recoils; it's nearly impossible to explain what she does to someone outside the field. So much is lost in translation. Still, she takes a breath and gives her well-practiced elevator speech. "I'm studying the earliest lycopods, *Baragwanathia longifolia*, from fossil records of Australia and China, and relating them to the arborescent lycopods that were found in the Carboniferous forests of Euramerica—you know, the temperate forests where all our coal comes from now. And I'm also, well, I've got a few study plots where I'm working on how closely extinct lycopods relate to extant—still living—lycopods."

"Ah, so, you range the world and come back to your own backyard, eh?"

"Yes, well, something like that. Although I don't personally collect the fossils. I get them from colleagues around the world."

"Right. Of course, of course." Lamont grins, ever so slightly. "Have you ever collected your own?"

"Yes, as a graduate student, in Pennsylvania. But my work is mostly in the lab now. Spectrascopes, carbon dating, that sort of thing."

"Well, hmm . . . ," he says, smile widening. "Wouldn't it be fun to go collect your own? I mean, go to, say, China, and find them yourself?"

"Well, yes, no, not really," she says, growing uncomfortable talking about herself so much. "It takes too much time and money. Not very efficient. Even Darwin, you know, did a lot of his work, after the *Beagle*, from specimens sent to him from around the world. Others did the exploring and collecting; he did the research. I'm fine with how things are."

"Yes, of course you are. And you probably don't mind that all those specimens belong not to you but to the university, unlike ones you'd collect yourself."

Astrid inhales quickly, wondering how, or if, he knows about Sanders.

Lamont leans forward, chin on clasped hands. "I'm just thinking out loud. There's a project I'm involved with in India. Tree-planting project. Very large scale. First of its kind, but hopefully not the last.

We're attempting to regreen the planet to mitigate climate change. Have you heard of Lovejoy's theory?"

"Certainly, yes. I haven't yet read the research, but it sounds encouraging." Astrid, who does not want to get into another argument with Lamont over climate change research, vows to keep her answers upbeat. "And it couldn't hurt to reforest, for biodiversity, and for air quality, which in that part of the world is, I hear, atrocious. Assuming you're using native trees, of course. Can't hurt, certainly. Good for you."

"Yes, well, it's an ambitious project. It's part assisted migration and it's part afforestation. But we'd like to know more about the botanical pasts of these areas, so we're planting the right species. That's where you could help. Interested?"

"Oh, my, no, I mean, thank you for asking, I'm honored, but I've got a full plate with my own research."

What she thinks, but doesn't say, are two things simultaneously. The first is familiar: what Lamont proposes is applied work, not even science, and she is a scientist devoted to basic research. The second is not familiar: she cannot go off to the other side of the world and leave Strilay, not in his current condition.

She has never been considered a nurturing sort; whenever Gareth fell ill, he was better off if she just left him alone and went to work. Now, however, she very much does want to take care of Strilay.

Gareth has often claimed that Strilay is a father figure to her, and it's true, he did give her away at their wedding, but beyond that, Astrid sees little resemblance. Her father was a large man, filling a room the way Lamont often does, with a large personality he never tried to hide. For her father, the world was a battlefield, and when he came home, she always knew which way the battle was going: sometimes he was the happy, loving father who swept his children up in his arms, tickling them until their stomachs hurt from laughing, and sometimes the heavy-footed man who burst into anger at the slightest provocation—which her mother's chaos almost always provided.

Things didn't come easily for him, not like they have for Strilay, who, though she knows little, seems to have had a comfortable upbringing. It shows in his calm cheerfulness with everyone, from the most egotistical of colleagues to the most lazy of students. His feet are as confidently on the ground as a polar bear's wide paws, his sense of justice is legendary on campus, and he is generous, so much so that Astrid fears he may neglect his own health.

Fortunately, Lamont doesn't press her. "Of course, of course," he says quietly, sitting back. "Just another of my far-fetched ideas. But if you change your mind, do let me know."

That night in bed, Astrid's thoughts keep returning to her father, whom she hasn't seen since she was thirteen. She recalls a time that now sparkles like stars in her memory when she was trying, in the midst of yet another family drama, to slip away. Instead, she got their rowboat stuck in the mud, and tore a new shirt trying to free it; her father not only helped her pull out the boat but didn't tell her mother, just bought her another shirt like the one she'd torn. But that secrecy, she suddenly realizes, works both ways. That he was so willing to keep a secret from his wife: what else did he not tell her?

That is one of Astrid's last memories of him, for shortly after, it all came to a calamitous end when he lost his job. Officially, he was laid off from his job in city parks maintenance because of budget cuts—but he was smart enough to know that was just an excuse. She can still hear him crashing through their tiny house, yelling to furniture and children alike: "That city manager, he's always had it in for me. Stuck-up Ivy League bastard!"

Astrid had stood stock-still, then made a quick retreat to her kudzu haven. The city manager was Astrid's best friend's father. Elyse's father. This created no small amount of confusion and torn allegiances in her nine-year-old mind, a mind that leaned heavily on a belief in a rational world to keep her afloat in a chaotic household. It must be, she was certain of it, that her father was right—which meant Elyse's father was wrong, was lying. She knew what she had to do: she had to defend her father, and that meant her friendship with Elyse had to end. But it didn't matter: Astrid's father left for good just two years later.

Over four decades later, as she tosses in a narrow bed in a northern land, Astrid still wonders if there was anything else she could have done to keep her father from leaving. What she does recall with searing clarity is that it marked the end of the only two relationships on which she had depended: her father and her first true friend. And it taught her to be meticulously careful of whom she trusted.

After a night of dreams littered with odd juxtapositions—a polar bear approaching her school bus while her father chases the bear off with a kitchen chair; kudzu lining a bear den where Strilay and Elyse's father play poker—Astrid is relieved to be spending the morning with Lamont and Joe visiting the bear jail.

"Oh," says Astrid, as the three of them walk toward it, morning frost crunching beneath their feet, "look at that." She stops and crouches, fingering one of the tiny tundra plants still green in late fall. "It's a lycopod. Looks like—" She pulls up the loupe that hangs around her neck whenever she takes a walk, flips it open, and peers through it. "Looks like the genus *Huperzia*. Like the *H. lucidula* whose southern range is in North Carolina. Shining clubmoss. Wonderful! Do you want to see, Joe?"

Joe waves away the loupe. "No, ma'am, sorry. Without my glasses I'm afraid I can't see better than a groundhog. But y'know . . ." His voice drops as he recounts that a naturalist once told him about a local lycopodium being driven to extinction by other plants pushing north. "I guess," he says, "they'll still survive farther north until, like the polar bears, they just get shoved off the Earth entirely."

"Shoved off the Earth? Sounds like a flat-Earth statement! The original deniers," snorts Lamont.

"Well, you know what I mean—they'll run out of habitat," says Joe, hunching his shoulders, "like the pikas in the Rockies. Their winter blanket of snow, their alpine meadows are shrinking to only the highest elevations. They can keep moving their homes only so far up until they reach the tips of those mountains. Then there's nowhere left to go. Same for these little fellas. It's a shame, they evolved such cool adaptations to be here."

"Oh, now, I can hardly believe you're seeing them go. Unless we're talking a meteor strike, things don't happen so rapidly," says Astrid, a rush of heat rising to her neck.

"I'm afraid they do, now," says Lamont. "Pikas are already gone from parts of the Southwest, like Zion National Park. And botanists are recording alarming changes in plant communities just over the course of a decade. You might want to take a sample of this lycopod; this one may be joining your collection of extinct plants."

Astrid, still crouching down, peers through the loupe at the plant, letting the tiny magnifier expand her view of this plant's life and blur the unsettling conversation continuing overhead. She admires the bracted stems of lycopods, their sturdy scale-like leaves, their patterns of branching and spreading like the yellowed-lace table rounds her grandmaw made. She admires, too, their tenacity: the way they can, no matter how hot or cold, how light or dark their habitat, photosynthesize and stay that deep saturated green all year round. She stares a moment longer, her own sight blurring at the idea that this tenacious plant may succumb after all.

"Well," she says, straightening up, ignoring a sudden pain in her temples, "I'm fairly certain this is *lucidula*, and they're not in any danger. And I do believe we're all underestimating the staying power of lycopods. After all, they've been around for over 400 million years. They know what they're doing better than we do."

She folds her loupe, rubs her temples, and forces a smile. "Now, let's go see these polar bears. Tell me, again, Joe, what misdemeanors have they committed to end up so confined?"

As they enter the former airport hangar and walk by small cells housing polar bears, Joe recounts how each bear had repeatedly tried to obtain food from the town—finding a bowl of dog food left outside, stealing a piece of muktuk from a shed roof, or just repeatedly banging on food storage lockers and, though not successful, nonetheless causing enough damage, mayhem, and fear that the bear was deemed a nuisance.

"This one here," he says, stopping in front of a bear who sleeps curled up on the cement, the head tucked so far into the belly fur that only the tip of one ear sticks up, "was determined to get into a food locker outside the mayor's house. It's a good locker, new design, impenetrable. But this here fellow, he just couldn't let it be. We're guessing he's a three-year-old, a teenager." They stare at the sleeping bear, whose coat is muddied to brown, the lustrous fur matted and stained from confinement. "You've got to admire his persistence, at least."

He pauses, then goes on, "It's too bad you're leaving before the bay ices over. It should have right about now, but every year it's later. I'm guessing it'll be another three, maybe four weeks."

Astrid gazes across the water where the ice should be, her mind as choppy as the water's surface in rising winds. The polar bear's face at her window, the lycopodium tucked against a rock, the patterns and lifeforms of this landscape flash before her; they feed into that underground river, mixing with her fear of losing Strilay, just as she lost her father and her childhood friend, all of it sweeping her ever faster down the bottomless lake.

"It's surely a sight," Joe is saying, "when we let these bears out and they just make a beeline to the ice, not even a backward glance. They're hungry, no doubt about it, but instead of sniffing around for trash, they just head straight to that ice like they can smell the seals. Heading for the end of the Earth."

Chapter 10

We cannot make the ice come back. After her trip to the bone pile with Nicolaf, Elyse's residency shifts. Open heart, broken heart, she keeps telling herself, as reality digs in its heels. Fortunately, reality also finds new ways to keep her busy. Through Yurgyev, Elyse learns that Nicolaf is the son of the town's most respected marine mammal hunter. It was Nicolaf's father who had initiated the Umka Patrol, who had come to the United States, whom she heard speak at the Anchorage zoo. His father, however, no longer wants to travel, so they are hoping to convince Nicolaf to take his place.

"He *is* very articulate," says Elyse, "once you get him going."

"Yes," says Yurgyev, "but he is not willing, yet, to speak in public. He says his English is not very good. Perhaps you can help him, no?"

And so she does, spending evenings helping him practice English. At first, she tries to keep the lesson time brief, so that she can continue painting at night. She knows her time here is fleeting and precious, and she wants to get as much down on canvas as possible. But after a few evenings, she finds herself enjoying their time together. She realizes that the problem isn't his command of the language—he has that rare gift of being able to learn other languages with ease. Instead, his problem is stage fright. She assures him that everyone has it, and the only thing that cures it is practice. She shares her experiences teaching children and speaking at art conferences. "It gets easier," she assures him, "it's just like any exercise—the more you do it the better you are at it."

She suggests he tell her stories, about things he's done or seen, things he knows well and feels confident and excited about. Within a week, the English lessons become conversations, ones that Elyse, to her surprise, already fears she will miss.

One sunny afternoon, with wind racing across grasses and waves foaming shoreline, they walk south, away from town and the walrus haulout and the carcass pile. Pushing into chilling wind, Elyse pulls her coat tighter around her. Before them, land and sea fan out to the horizon. Pebbles clink and clatter against waves, and the wind plays high notes through dried grasses and sedges. She hasn't walked this way before, but Nicolaf wants to show her something, to thank her, he said, for the speaking lessons. He wouldn't say what, and she didn't ask; she's learning to talk less and listen more carefully to the few words spoken. Their conversation ranges wide, from her sons and life in the United States to the fossil-fuel industries' plans for northern Siberia.

"Some of my people," he says, "they want the development. They think it will bring jobs and wealth. They have heard about the Alaska Indigenous Peoples and their wealth."

"And you?" she asks, slowly, accepting the pause.

"I do not know. I hear what my father says he has seen in your villages. That more is not always better. More brings problems too. There," he says, pointing, "see that small hill?"

Elyse strains to see some undulation in the flatness, then, far toward the horizon, thinks she sees the faintest rise. Faint, so faint she could be imagining it. She blinks, crisp wind making her eyes tear, and looks again, seeing more clearly now across the seemingly unending flatness a gentle mounding.

"That is where a polar bear dens. We help with study on denning, and when we find one, like that, we want make sure no one home before we go up to it," he says. "And so we go close and listen for breathing, maybe smell. If nothing, then take a snowball, throw it in den, see if any moving or sound, do that many time, before looking in it."

He stops speaking, just for a moment, as if savoring something. "That one, though, bear sleeping so hard, we almost shine light in when see big white paw reaching out as if to swat fly. We run back, fast, everybody okay. Even that bear and cubs."

He laughs, throwing his head back into the wind. Elyse laughs, too, and watches him, surprised at so many words spilling out, and at the story itself—to approach a polar bear den, she cannot imagine. She admires, again, his complete comfort with this land and animals. And she notices once more how his voice harmonizes with the sounds of the place, the wind and waves, the keening of a hawk. How the grace of place flows out in language.

"Thank you," she says, "for showing that to me. It's a wonderful present."

"Oh, but that not it," he says, "we have farther to go."

They walk on, both falling silent. Elyse yields to the rhythm of her legs carrying her across the land, of wind whistling grasses, of water pulsing shore. A sliver of loose grass skitters across the sandy shoreline, and she attends it as she would dancers on a stage: the racing, lifting, diving choreography of wind. Now several miles from Cape Vankarem, they round a corner and come upon a rocky headland that juts above shore. It's only about fifty feet high, but in this flat expanse, it looms like a mountain.

"Shall we climb?" he says, offering his hand. She takes it, and feels a tingle, like static electricity. She looks at him, but his face remains serene.

"Is okay, this climb, you can do it?"

"Yes," she says, "it's no problem."

They scramble up the backside over a thin layer of grasses to the lichen-coated rock on top. Eccentric shapes of pale green and russet and gold cover every nook and cranny. And the view, with so little elevation, makes her gasp. Waves of water and grasses spread like a quilt in every direction, the low, cloud-filtered light playing across it like northern lights. Gazing out, she feels a sense that she has been here before, that she has never been away from here. Nicolaf turns from the shoreline to look inland, and she follows his lead.

He stares with the exacting eyes of a person who relies on his vision for life's essentials.

"Do you see it?" he says, almost in a whisper. "There, just before pingo."

Pingo. This is a word she knows now, having seen many of these mounds of earth-covered ice lenses as she flew over the Arctic. Each pingo, which may be centuries old, has a distinctive shape, forming like a frost heave above the wet tundra. This one sits on the horizon like a shield volcano, the perfectly spherical dome with broad slopes leading to a nearly flat top. And there, just in front of it, something glitters golden in afternoon sun.

"What is it?"

"Let me show you."

They climb down, careful not to brush off any lichen, and begin making their way across tundra, their movement quickly changing from easy walking to an awkward clamber over what looks, from a distance, like flat grassland, but is instead a deceptively uneven obstacle course of tussocks jutting up from wet bog. Twice Elyse stumbles, and twice Nicolaf's hand, warm and strong, is there to keep her upright. Finally, they stand before the unmistakably long arc of a wooly mammoth tusk. The fossilized ivory, multi-hued and varnished by time and weather, rises ten feet above tall grasses at the base of the pingo. It shines in thin afternoon light, glassed by time and weather. The protruding tip, sharp and unbroken, provides a perch for raptors, for at its base the tundra is littered with guano and small bones and shells.

"Snowy owl likes this," says Nicolaf, his voice soft. "She nests on pingo most years."

"Oh, it's gorgeous," says Elyse, "just gorgeous. Thank you for bringing me here."

"Yes, you are welcome."

"Have you, has no one wanted to dig this up? There could be an entire skeleton here."

"No, it is not for study. It belongs to this land. To snowy owl. And to help us remember."

Elyse has never seen mammoth remains outside of a museum, has never seen them in the place where the animal lived and died. She touches the tusk, the smoothness surprising her. But it's the colors that are most astonishing, as if every color that has ever existed is in that fossilized curl. Browns open to reds, blend to purples, fade to blues; hints of greens reveal yellows. They swirl together and apart in a patterned rhythm like some forgotten language. How many thousands of years has this lain here, undisturbed except by wind and snow and the talons of the owl, burnished ivory spiring from vast tundra, speaking of the tenuous hold of existence.

Especially here, in the farthest reaches of the north. This place, so unforgiving, and life here so fragile and tenacious at the same time. She remembers a term Amy told her: *extremophiles*: species that live in environments where most others cannot, species that live at the edge of what seems possible. That's here. Life at the edge. Polar bears and walrus and snowy owls, living at the edge.

On their walk back, Elyse keeps turning around, watching the spire grow smaller. "How," she asks, high-stepping over a tussock, "did you know it was here?"

"My father showed me when I was boy. It is known by many in town, but no one speaks of it to strangers. Even Yurgyev does not know. He is scientist; he would have to report. But you, you are artist, you can see it for more than just study."

"Yes, thank you, I do—I can—see that. And I am very honored you showed it to me," she says, face flushing. She rushes on, knowing how a focus on individual glory is avoided in Yup'ik culture. "And the owls, have they nested there long?"

"Just the past three years, I think. I think it is new pair, since they have not yet raised one to fledgling. I think they are still learning."

"Still learning, yes," she says, with a soft laugh, "aren't we all."

It's only later that night as she's drifting off to sleep, basking in the delight of such a surprising and beautiful gift, that she realizes she didn't ask Nicolaf what the mammoth tusk helps them remember.

She paints furiously. In the mornings, she paints the place. During the day, she fills notebooks and small canvases with quick sketches and plein air paintings—of the walrus haulout, the carcass pile, the town, tundra, sea. But at night, increasingly, she cannot sleep, so she returns to the studio and paints large, wild, unsettling images. Two canvasses pinned together across an entire wall, filled with waves big as the room, crashing, and the small wet head of an arctic fox. A disarray of feathers, flamenco pink, spread across the tundra, floating and catching on dwarf willow's upreaching arms. A tropical forest of vines climbing and covering the pile of walrus and whale bones, a huge male walrus sitting on top with his head turned to one side, hanging back, submissive. And a series of small paintings of that wooly mammoth tusk, rainbow-colored and reaching to blue. Her colors are saturated, her forms energized. The tropical forest is a swirl of greens and bright red swipes, yellow pistils disembodied and larger than the walrus's face. The bone pile spirals upward like a pyramid, an enlivened form that looks like the Easter Island Moai had awakened and were reaching to the sea.

Once she is home, in her familiar studio, all alone, the painting accelerates. The last week of her residency had been annoyingly filled with other fellows. Though she usually loves meeting such interesting people, she had wanted nothing more than to stay in the flow of painting, talking to Nicolaf, and being there—watching the walrus, walking the tundra, waiting for polar bears at the carcass pile. The bright new faces, filled with wearying expectations, were a rude interruption. She wonders how much more jarring it was for the people who live there, to have these new visitors taking up their time and asking all the same tone-deaf questions again. Had she, too, seemed noisy and greedy and oblivious when she first arrived?

All she wants now is quiet. She wants to stay in the experience, with no interruptions. No filtering of feeling through talking. The way she and Nicolaf could walk together without speaking, inhaling every single thing about the place, the moment. No obligations, no expectations, no limitations. She's glad Dan will be gone for several more weeks, glad she has time to integrate who she's become into her life at home. That's familiar, too: his absence.

A simple gladness persists. She's finally learned to love the tabula rasa moment: the blank canvas set before her, the possibilities endless, that space before creativity begins. Before, she'd found this moment terrifying; she'd find some excuse—washing dishes, making a phone call, getting tea, anything—to step back from the blank canvas. But since her residency, that's changed. The trip has freed her.

On the cork board where she pins ideas, pictures, inspiration, she's posted the first line from Twyla Tharp's book on creativity: *I walk into a large white room.* It's the choreographer entering an empty studio, knowing the dancers would come, knowing it is up to her to create their every movement. Through habit, says Tharp, the moment that terrifies can become the moment of bliss. Elyse now stands before a blank canvas electrified with anticipation.

A week before Dan arrives home, she meets Maggie for a walk. On the few rare removes from her solitude, she'd already told Maggie everything. Maggie gave her a hard look when Elyse mentioned Nicolaf. "Nothing happened, Mags," she'd said. "Nothing. Just conversation, and walks. Just friendship." Still, her heart leapt when Maggie suggested there was more, and now she feels again his electric touch when they climbed the headland, and she worries. What if Dan suspects something more in her friendship with Nicolaf? What if there *is* something more?

"I wouldn't worry about it," says Maggie now. "I mean, what are the chances of you ever seeing Nicolaf again? Even if you are crushing on him, so what? What I *would* worry about, girlfriend, is what it says about your marriage."

Snow crunches underfoot as they walk the familiar trail up through a hemlock forest. Ahead of them is Maggie's dog Arnold, who rarely strays from the trail. Elyse's two are off romping through the woods, Sophie letting out a yelp now and again as she finds the scent of snowshoe hare, moose, squirrel. Sophie's excitement is not discerning; she doesn't calibrate her response by the size or degree of danger the animal poses.

Up they climb, following the winding trail as the hemlocks grow shorter, trunks and limbs angled and sculpted by wind, star-shaped fans of needles bravely opening toward the light. The two women stop to shed layers even in the –10 temperature. From a pale blue sky, ice crystals fall with each breeze, and the hair around their faces is white with frost.

"Well," Elyse says finally, slowly, "you may have something there. But I don't know what. I mean," she says, rolling her neckwarmer into a headband, "I haven't even seen Dan for two months. Who knows how it will feel when we're together again."

They reach Hemlock Knob, a clearing above the forest that looks upvalley to the Chugach Range. Late-winter sun warms their faces and paints peaks and ragged ridgelines with gold. The U-shaped valley opens in a wide embrace, snow a deep blanket over the sinuous path of Campbell Creek. Elyse gazes at the spire of O'Malley Peak, which she and Dan climbed together several summers ago, without planning to, only because they were chasing after Darlene. From this angle it looks impossible; the backside, she now knows, is more gradual, sloping to hidden tarns couched deep in ancient cirques.

"So," says Maggie, sensing Elyse's need to change the topic, "tell me more about these wild-ass paintings. Are you still as on fire as you were at the residency?"

"Oh, yes," Elyse replies, brushing sun-melted frost from her eyelashes, "I am. It's so wonderful, to have the work flow so easily. I have no idea how good it is or whether I'll ever show any of it, but for now, I'm just getting it all down on canvas."

"Well, when you're ready, I sure would like to see them. I hold permanent dibs on first viewing of new work, remember?"

"Yes, yes, other than Sophie and Darlene, I trust you the most with my crazy stuff."

They turn and head back down the trail, glissading down steep parts with all three dogs bouncing beside them. The snow is softer now, warmed by sun, and bits of it plop from hemlock branches, causing small cascades of light, bright snowfalls. The branches, freed from the weight of snow, spring upward, small star-needles shimmering like a wet dog shaking off water.

"How about tomorrow evening?" Elyse says.

"For?"

"For coming by the studio. To see the new work. I'd like you to see it before Dan comes home, so you can tell me by just how much I've lost my mind."

The walls of Elyse's studio are crowded with the new work. One large canvas overlaps onto the next. Several more stand on easels. It's a riot of color and motion, a sensory overload for anyone coming in from the quiet, still monochrome of an Alaskan winter day. So when Maggie enters, she steps just inside the door and stops. Holds her breath. Doesn't move or speak for so long that Elyse begins to regret inviting her. Maybe the paintings aren't good. Maybe they're just gaudy representations of a confused mind. Maggie starts walking around the studio, slowly, pausing, looking at every image, reaching out a few times as if to touch the canvas. Finally, she draws in a sharp breath, lets out a slow exhale.

"Wow. Just, wow. These are—amazing. You have gone where you have never gone before. I don't see . . . you did these, right? I mean, these are totally different. Totally. Wow."

Elyse sighs. "Good, good, glad you like them, that's such a relief."

"Like? You kidding? Applying such a mundane word to something so . . . not mundane? I love these. *Love* them."

"Okay, okay, no need to get gushy, Mags. I know you're my biggest fan. My only fan."

Maggie strides over to Elyse and throws her arms around her. "I may be now," she laughs, "but you just wait until the rest of the world sees these."

But Elyse isn't ready. She isn't ready to show her paintings to anyone else. She isn't ready for Dan to come home. She isn't ready to lay down her brush to be a wife again. Dan will be home in two days, and Maggie is urging her to show her new work to some local gallery owners, at least to use them for the next show Elyse has scheduled, at the Fireweed Gallery. Elyse does trust Maggie's opinion to be more than that of a loyal friend: Maggie had been starting a PhD in art history when she got pregnant. But all Elyse wants to do is paint, walk the dogs, and have conversations with Nicolaf, if only in her head.

She would like to be done with the paintings, done figuring out her friendship with Nicolaf, done integrating her new self with her old life, before her husband returns. In between painting sessions, she visits the zoo and sits with Binky. The bear likes the cold; Elyse can tell. She seems more energetic, rolling on her back in the new snow, pushing her snout deep into it as if looking for a seal hole. She loves to see her playful, but mixed with joy is grief: there is no seal hole there, not ever, for Binky.

Maybe, she thinks, maybe her feelings for Nicolaf are just enmeshed in her feelings for Binky and all the other polar bears, and walrus, seals, all the animals, for the people of Cape Vankarem and all the villages throughout the Arctic whose lives are being threatened, upended, torn apart. Maybe it's all wrapped up in one big ball of unexpressed love and grief for the world. Love and grief: always a pair. Twins tugging at the same heartstrings. Tugging and pulling for reaction, for response, for reply. And maybe her paintings—all the flaring and rising of images poured onto canvas—are her attempts to reply.

Dan's flight from Liberia arrives at 1 a.m. Typical, for Alaska, this arriving and departing in the middle of the night. Still, Elyse assured Dan she would pick him up. After thirty-two hours en route, four plane changes, customs, and several long flights, Dan will be beyond exhausted, and she won't make him endure a taxi home just so she can have one normal night's sleep. Besides, the dogs are consistently up for a midnight ride. They seem to believe that, as long as they're in the car, they won't miss any fun. Darlene, especially, enjoys it: she sits up straight in the passenger seat, focused on peering out the front window as if it's her job.

Traffic is so light that Elyse arrives outside baggage claim before Dan's plane has touched down. She turns off the engine and slouches in her seat. Behind her, a large truck sits idling, a deep rumbling sound that shakes the very ground. Before her is another mammoth vehicle, a Suburban, also idling. Though the dogs would have liked to sniff their surroundings, she keeps the windows rolled up against exhaust fumes. The roar of a plane taking off rumbles the windowpanes.

Elyse sighs. All this fuel, burning up the atmosphere. She's just read a book describing how, in all energy sectors but one, existing technologies can reduce consumption to drop atmospheric carbon dioxide levels to below 350 parts per million—all without any change in lifestyles. The one that requires changed behavior is air transportation: everyone needs to fly less. This makes Elyse's heart sink. For Alaskans, air travel is almost a necessity. Dan, for example: he couldn't do what he does without flying. What about all those people he helps?

Sophie whines, and Elyse looks up to see Dan's wiry frame striding toward her car. As he opens the door, both dogs nearly jump out in excitement.

"Hello, hello," he says, nuzzling each dog to him, "I've missed all my girls!"

He plops in the passenger seat. His thick brown hair, tinged white, is tousled from airplane sleep. As he leans across to hug her, she smells coffee and the stale scent of airplanes.

"Hello, my beautiful wife. Thank you for coming to pick me up."

And just like that, they fall into the easy conversation of two people who have known each other so long that the walls between them are nearly transparent. Dan's reentry happens much more smoothly than Elyse expects. He's cheerful and full of riveting stories from the field and expresses appreciation at every turn. One night they go out to dinner, and over a bottle of wine, Dan tells Elyse about being stuck in a small Liberian village without any communication, waiting for the armed security guard to return. It's the kind of story he never tells her until he is home, safe and sound. Even with the civil war behind them, the country is still too dangerous for a Western doctor like him to travel without security.

Then he immediately lightens the mood by recalling their family trip to Costa Rica, when their flight unexpectedly landed in Venezuela for fuel. They had to spend the night, and the two tween-aged boys were too restless to stay in the internet-less hotel all evening, so the family had ventured out for dinner. And proceeded to get lost and end up in a part of town that resembled a shantytown. A man had approached them, wearing a long coat, and asked in very halting English if they needed assistance. It was a moment that could have gone either way. Elyse had made the call, sensing the man was sincere, and he'd led them all the way to their hotel. When Dan had offered money, he waved it away. "No, mi amigo," he said. "When I come to your Miami, you help me find my way."

"And that," Dan laughs, "is why I always listen to your intuition."

Elyse looks at her husband, hearing in his voice the man she fell in love with. She loves how dedicated he is to helping people and animals. She loves his sense of adventure. His contagious self-confidence. Maybe everything is okay. Maybe they just hit another rough patch, and now they'll be happy. She takes a sip of Malbec, a wine they discovered on a trip to Chile several years before, when he spoke at a conference in Santiago. So much history together, so many fine and lovely memories.

Still, when Dan heads off to work a few days later, Elyse sits at the kitchen table with a third cup of tea and watches the steam rise. The stillness of the house tugs at her, pulling something up from her gut, a discomfort beneath the glow of the last few days.

Dan hasn't noticed. He hasn't noticed a single thing about how she has changed. All her worries that he would suspect something about Nicolaf, or feel threatened by how she had grown, were for naught. He has listened to her stories about her adventures with the same attention that she listens to his. Why does this bother her?

"Maybe I haven't really changed at all," she says out loud.

Darlene, sleeping by the door, heaves a big sigh.

"Exactly," Elyse says, "exactly."

The deadline for her show at the Fireweed Gallery fast approaching, Elyse perches on the stool in her studio, staring at her new paintings. Should she show them, or should she show work she completed before Cape Vankarem? She sighs, and decides on the latter: it's safe, it's what the gallery had in mind.

Her phone rings; it's Jim. He's calling to ask if WPO might use her polar bear painting in a series of advertisements about climate change. "Polar bears," he says, "are climate change's poster child, but everyone glosses over the usual photos of them on melting sea ice."

They need something new, he says, to shake people up, and he thinks her pairing of polar bears with kudzu, a plant that is an everyday presence for so many Americans and that symbolizes unintended change, might just be that something new. "Besides," he continues, "There's the emotional weight of a work of art."

Elyse doesn't hesitate to say yes. She holds no illusions of being another Judy Chicago or Ai Weiwei. And she adheres to the mantra a professor drilled into all his students: art before politics. Great art can contain politics, but not vice versa. Focus on the art, and—if it's good enough—the emotional response will naturally arise. On that she has relied, all the while hoping her art will, someday, somehow, effect positive change—at least some subtle shifts, rippling effects she may never witness. What Jim now offers is a dream come true.

Dan, however, is less than enthused. His vehemence surprises Elyse, since this isn't about her taking another solo trip, and since always before he's treated her painting as nothing more than a pleasant little hobby.

"No," he says, "you need to think long and hard about letting your work be used for direct advocacy. It's bad enough you went on the WPO expedition. Now more than ever you need to distinguish yourself as a serious artist."

"Well, you do advocacy work, and it doesn't hurt your standing in the medical community."

"That's different. DWB is a mercy mission. We never take sides in political issues."

"Climate change isn't a political issue," she says, her face flushing. "It's a real problem that's affecting all of us, every day. It's killing people just as much as disease or war."

"Yes, but you can't compare WPO to DWB. WPO takes political stands, you know that." He lets go a big sigh and continues, his voice steely. "Okay, look. Remember that filmmaker who created the Berlin Olympics film for Hitler, Leni Riefenstahl? She was an artistic genius, but she used her genius to help Hitler's Germany continue genocide. And that's how she, and her work, are remembered. Do you want people to think of your work as propaganda, or as art?"

Dead silence, and then Elyse says, "I cannot believe you just said that. Comparing this with Hitler. Beyond absurd. Look, they're my paintings. I can do with them what I want."

"Well, that's true, but I think you should tell Jim you've changed your mind. I'm just looking out for your best interests here."

With that, the tension that had run between them before her residency returns, this time settling deeper. Like a tear deep inside a muscle, she thinks, it will not soon, if ever, heal.

Chapter 11

On the plane headed south, Strilay sleeps while Astrid stares into space, pressing her fingernails and wondering what awaits her back home. She's rarely been gone this long, especially so late in the semester. It's early December; finals week is just around the corner. But more important, she's felt uneasy leaving her collection ever since Dr. Sanders dropped by with his audacious request. She knows the university will support his demands—but she cannot imagine having to share what she's spent her entire adult life creating. She turns to the sleeping professor, wishing she could ask his advice, but knowing, already, what he'd say, he who so cheerfully leapt from his laurels and ran off to Churchill.

She studies his face, notices the faint smile. No doubt he's dreaming of his bears, the ones they saw just before their flight. Their departure had been delayed by a stormfront, and instead of staying in the warmth of the airport, they'd pushed against relentless winds to see more bears.

"This delay, it's a sign," Strilay had crowed. "I'm not supposed to leave before the bears are released."

"Right," said Astrid. "That's what this storm is about. Why don't we just take such good care of you that you'll be here for the release next year?"

"It won't be the same, m'dear. I've grown attached to these bears, the ones in jail right now. They're the ones I want to see released."

Then Lamont had appeared, red-faced from the wind and grinning, to tell them about a sow with cubs nearby, and Strilay, with Lamont booming agreement, persisted: "One more polar bear watch before we leave. You can at least allow me that, Nurse Astrid."

The bears were on the shoreline beside a thin ledge of ice that had formed in the night. Wan sunlight glinted off the ice ledge and traced an icy halo along the scene. The cubs, gold light threading their fur, tumbled over each other on a pile of driftwood stumps half buried in sand and ice. As the cubs played what looked for all the world like a game of king of the hill, their mother lay off to one side, keeping an eye on them while taking a break from their rambunctiousness.

"Ah," said Strilay, "a perfect moment, if ever there was one. This wind, they know it means winter is coming, and with it, their ice." He turned to the bears, crooning, "Yes, soon, my dears."

Astrid smiles now at the memory. It *was* a perfect moment, as long as one didn't think about what came before or what may come after. At least, she consoles herself, she and Strilay have moved far beyond her callous comment at Lamont's talk. She presses her fingernail, wishing Strilay could tell her the secret to his contentment.

The next morning, after a fitful sleep, Astrid wastes no time getting to her office, striding across a campus buzzing with students in their final dash to semester's end. There, in the pile of intercampus mail, is the formal request letter from Dr. Sanders for "full and unhampered access to all specimens in the University's collection currently residing in the office of Dr. Astrid Baldwin." The word *currently* sends a chill up her back. She lets the letter float to the desk and listens to her office phone voicemail. Three calls from Sanders. And another, from Dr. Tom Shank, who studies coastal plant communities. She stares at the phone, at the letter, at the phone again, and then calls Shank.

The sun shines high in the sky, even in late January, softening morning's cold air and silvering the threads and pools of still water lacing the meadow. In this bog the plants are all no more than six inches high and remind her, suddenly, of the tundra surrounding Churchill. But this is coastal North Carolina, her own home turf. These are the wetlands and scraggy storm-bit coastal forests in which she grew up. Beyond the sun-soaked meadow, the dark waters of the wide Alligator River saunter by, and beyond that jut the shaggy growth of pines and pin oaks, thick arms draped in Spanish moss that drips in long pale tentacles to the ground.

It feels good to be in the field, to be in a place that's so familiar. She is glad she agreed to help Tom Shank with his research, glad she listened to colleagues who extolled his reputation in basic science, even if she finds his motivations for this project questionable. She is glad to be doing nothing other than looking closely at every single plant, each leaf and blade and root, her mind completely engrossed with what is right before her eyes.

She stands in sunshine, taking it all in. The waters, the trees, the meadow, the pungent scent of wet peat rising as sunlight warms it. The great blue heron standing like a statue in an oval of water, staring intently at the mirrored surface. The snag on forest's edge where a woodpecker, heard but not seen, taps a syncopated rhythm that echoes off surrounding woods. The log in tannin-darkened waters of a narrow slough where a row of five green slider turtles bask with necks stretched out, exposing bright red neck stripes. The spongy ground beneath her feet, blanketed in tiny water-loving plants.

One bit of green catches her eye, and she drops to her knees, pulls out her loupe.

"Yes," says Dr. Shank, his drawl pouring over her head like the sun's own warmth, "that's the one. What do you think?"

"Oh, yes, this does seem different, but I'd have to take a sample back." She tucks a curl back into her unraveling bun and pulls a trowel from her pack.

"Only if it's absolutely necessary," he says. "We don't know how many are left, so we're going to follow protocol for endangered species."

"Of course," says Astrid, stashing her trowel and grabbing a pair of scissors. "I'll just take a sample branch."

For two decades, Tom Shank has studied coastal plants, identifying rare and endemic species like the dey's moon lichen, found only within several square miles of the Alligator. But with projected sea-level rise, these plants—including this newly discovered lycopod—will be inundated with saltwater and die within thirty years. Unwilling to simply document loss, Shank has made a sharp left career turn into applied research to save them.

But how? Do they build dikes to keep out seawater, or do they move the plants inland? Attempts to protect Outer Banks light-houses have proven that structures to hold back the sea ultimately fail, so he's focused instead on some fallow farmland several miles inland that could, if he can find funds, be reclaimed into new homes for these coastal plant communities.

"It's crazy," Astrid had told Strilay at lunch a month earlier, on one of his first outings since recovering, "to think Tom can re-create an ecosystem, especially one as fragile as a coastal wetland. It smacks of landscape architecture rather than botany."

"I see," said Strilay, brows steady with a look that meant he wasn't convinced.

"It's this whole assisted migration concept," she continued, "in which your friend Lamont is also embroiled. Moving species to climatically suitable habitats that they would, if not for habitat destruction and rapid warming, be migrating to anyhow. But it's full of guesswork and rife with risk."

Strilay took a sip of coffee, unperturbed, so Astrid soldiered on. "Haven't we learned enough from invasives to know this does not end well? And yet there's this group moving this endangered tree, the Torreya yew, from their last stand in Florida to the mountains of North Carolina. My cousin in Asheville has gone to see those trees, a scraggly little stand on private land, and she's worried they may do so well they'll edge out native species. Then what happens to every-thing that depends on that native species? It throws the entire eco-system into chaos."

"And is Dr. Shank in support of the Torreya yew transplant?"

"No, he's not, I did ask him about that. I would never agree to work with him if he was. All he wants to do is move plants inland onto old farmland, so there's no native species displacement. It's more of a land-reclamation project. But it's still, well, it's still tinkering with ecosystems."

"Well, m'dear, I'm sure he's thought it all through," said Strilay. "He's a smart man. I'm guessing he just couldn't stand by and do nothing. Just like the fans of the Torreya yew. Desperate times call for thinking outside the box, you know."

"Yes, desperate measures," she said, before Strilay can finish.

"Listen, Astrid," Strilay said, "how much data do you need before you can draw your own conclusion? Climate change is happening, and fast, and it's going to wipe out a large number of species, even if we suddenly wake up and arrest our fall tomorrow. That's just the fact of the matter."

"I suppose you're right," said Astrid, her voice trailing.

"You know I'm right. Heaven knows I wish I wasn't. I think it's time for you to leap. Not just to a conclusion, but to action. Time to step outside the box you've built around yourself."

"But I am not . . . I didn't take that ExxonMobil grant," she said, voice rising. "I am not following the status quo. I'm sticking to what I believe is my right career path; you know that."

"Yes, your integrity is very much intact, and that's just one more reason why your leap could make a big splash. With your impeccable reputation, anything you do will be regarded seriously by the entire academic world."

"Well, even if I were to follow your advice—which I'm not, just to be clear—what would you suggest I do?"

"I don't know," he said, quietly, blue eyes softening. "Only you can figure that out."

And so she has gone to the coast to help out Dr. Shank. It isn't a grand leap, not like traveling to India to help on Lamont's project, which is what she guessed Strilay wanted. But at least it gets her out of Chapel Hill, postpones her inevitable decision to turn over her collection to Dr. Sanders, and softens the latest blow of her National Science Foundation funds being cut. And with Strilay's heart condition stabilized, she feels comfortable being away, at least just the few hours' drive between Chapel Hill and the refuge.

Now she stares at the cutting in her hand, this small green piece of what may be a new species found on the verge of extinction. She hears Strilay's voice telling her, on the day she headed to the coast,

"Just promise me you'll keep your mind open. Your heart too." She looks over at Tom Shank, who kneels next to her, staring at the same piece of green in her hand. Then she rises, lifts her eyes to the lowlands spreading like fine lace all around them.

In the quiet of her lab, Astrid crouches over the scope, tracing again the venation on the lycopod sample, then turns again to the photographs of the plant. Again and again. Every time she comes to the same conclusion: this is a new species. She has corroborated with every lycopod expert she knows, and all agree. And yet, she cannot believe it. That she has discovered a new species. She should feel elation over this gift that few contemporary scientists receive. But what she feels is unmoored. She has discovered a new species just as the plant is on the brink of extinction.

Because this newly discovered plant will now be on the way to a federal endangered species listing, and because the endangered and popular Venus fly trap also grows in the area, Shank is able to get funding for his relocation project. Astrid is still uneasy with it. "Just look at kudzu," she tells Strilay. And as even Shank admits, it's temporary. The waters will keep rising, the land will continue to subside, increased storms will cause more erosion—and this lycopod will be threatened again, if not by rising waters then by air pollution or development as the human population grows.

"We're buying time, is all," says Dr. Shank in one of many interviews that follow the new plant discovery, "in hopes that humanity will wake up and smell the lack of roses before they're all gone. There's still a chance to make a change, to at least lessen environmental catastrophe. Maybe not in time for this little plant, but perhaps in time for the next. For roses and honeysuckles and, hell's bells, even the damn kudzu."

Astrid declines most interviews by telling them Tom is the wizard at quotable statements, but it's a quicksand feeling that keeps her from being able to talk to reporters. As a paleobotanist, she's no stranger to extinction. But this is happening now, on her watch, and it's because of the way her species is living on the Earth. She's haunted by them all: this newly threatened lycopod, the lycopod outside Churchill, the polar bears, the plants and animals disappearing before they've even been discovered.

Increasingly, she fears what their extinction might mean for the greater ecosystems. Shank shared research papers on what's now called the Wood Wide Web—forest trees are linked in communication and nutrient-sharing through a complex underground network of mycorrhiza. Given how intricately connected each tree is to another, some scientists now suggest a forest should be considered a single superorganism.

So, thinks Astrid, what happens to the rest of the organism when one species goes extinct? The more she learns, the more she tries to reason her way out of it, and the more she is thrown into a confusion so deep that her sleep, her research, even her ability to form articulate sentences is compromised.

One morning, after another restless night, Gareth tells her, "Charlotte and I think you should take a weekend and go to the beach with her." He's taken to sleeping on the couch for both their sakes. "She could keep you from spending too much time stuck in that big brain of yours."

Astrid's back stiffens at the mention of Charlotte. She'd pieced together, from comments they'd both made, that Gareth and Charlotte had spent significant time together while she was in Churchill and at the coast. So much time that a waiter at Cilantro's had seemed surprised to see Gareth there with Astrid. He was new, and so was to be forgiven, for asking Gareth whether his wife would also be joining them. Still, Astrid does wonder just how Gareth and Charlotte were acting to give this new waiter the idea that they were husband and wife.

Now she glances at the plant Gareth has given her for a homecoming present. This one is a red-leaved Hawaiian ti, known to bring good luck to a household. Why is there need for good luck?

"Well," Gareth says, "don't look at me like I've suggested a crime. Just a weekend at the beach with your best girlfriend. Take a break from all this mental heavy lifting."

Astrid sits at her desk, fingering the dark brown fossil imprint of a stem, the arboreal lycopods that once grew right where she now sits. *Lepidodendron.* This fossil was the first she ever found, in the hills of Pennsylvania when she was a graduate student. It was her professor's tradition—one not supported nor known by the university—that each of his grad students would be given, upon graduation, the first fossil they ever found. Astrid remembers unearthing this one, the split rock giving way, the shard falling into her open palm, revealing the perfectly preserved scale-like stem. She was the first human ever to set eyes on it, a fact that had filled her with an admixture of pride and humility that alchemized to gratitude. She still feels grateful every time she holds it. What a wise professor, to give his students that gift of wonder's source.

Whenever she is truly uncertain about something—and those times are rare—she holds that fossil, waiting for the solution to arise as the rock warms in her palm. As she does now. It's an absent-minded habit, really; she doesn't believe the fossil holds any magic power. It just grounds her. Should she continue helping Tom Shank? Should she tramp off to India to help Lamont? Or should she stay put, continue her research, despite having to share her collection with Sanders and his parade of grads, despite having to do most of her work unfunded? She still believes with all her mind in knowledge for knowledge's sake, but forces beyond her control are gathering to push her out of her comfortable office chair and dump her on unfamiliar ground.

Charlotte will be waiting. Astrid has promised her an afternoon coffee break. She puts the fossil away and sets off through the arboretum toward town. The blue sky sparkles, one of those spring days so full of new growth and brilliant cerulean warmth that one can't help but feel a bit of lightness. Perhaps she should take a jaunt to the beach with Charlotte.

She stops beneath the ginkgo, a gentle breeze playing among the tree's shiny new leaves. She touches a hand to the trunk. Solid, and cool. Steady. The coolness brings to mind last October, when she'd watched as, over the course of an hour, the tree went from fully leaved to absolutely bare—an astonishing concerted leaf-drop. As waves of students go by, their voices light with the coming of summertime, she leans against the sturdy trunk. This species rose to prominence in the middle Permian, under the same warming and drying conditions that signaled the end of the arboreal lycopods whose fossils she studies. Ginkgo reminds her that life will endure.

Charlotte sits at a table in the middle of the room, a group of art students gathered around her. She would have made a fine college professor, thinks Astrid, with her ability to captivate and energize a crowd. But Charlotte fans the students away when Astrid walks up.

"Come. Sit, stranger. Can you believe this day? Oh, springtime, when all the world's ablaze! Hey, why don't we sit outside on the patio? Have ourselves a warm summer beer."

Astrid grins. Charlotte's exuberance reminds her of Gareth. Her jaw tightens. Gareth. And Charlotte. Should she? No, ridiculous. And fretting is a waste of time. She shakes her head.

"No? You don't want to sit outside?"

"Oh, no, I mean, yes, let's. Sit outside."

Charlotte carries the conversation, telling Astrid about a conference she's speaking at in Washington, DC, in June. She's nervous because she's never spoken at a conference before. Does Astrid have any tips? It's an environmental art conference, she says, a collaboration between the American Arts Association and several environmental groups. Unusual, she says, since artists organizations are so heavily funded by corporations.

Astrid listens, but only half-heartedly. She recites her method of preparing for a presentation—writing it all out, condensing it to one page of bullet points, practicing the speech in front of the mirror; getting there early to check equipment; speaking more slowly than normal. But she speaks in monotone, distractedly, thoughts swimming with the choices before her, none of which she could have imagined a year ago.

"Oh, shug, just listen to me, rattling on!" says Charlotte, "I've got beaucoup time to work on this. I'll practice with you. But tell me, Astrid, what's new in your world? Are you going to keep on with Dr. Shank?"

"I don't know," replies Astrid. Slowly, over tacos and beer, then just beer and sunshine, Astrid fills Charlotte in on all that's changing, on all the choices before her. She doesn't confide fully just how untethered she's feeling about the entire direction of her life. She only describes the tangible choices as if they were a taxonomic key. As she starts to draw it out on a napkin, Charlotte places her hand on top of Astrid's, like a mother calming a child.

"Gareth is right," says Charlotte, quietly, dark eyes settling hard on Astrid's. "You need a break from that big brain of yours. A weekend at the beach. Next weekend. Before school's out and summer gets swinging. It'll be quiet and easy. We can stay at my cousin's place in Corolla."

"All right," says Astrid, quietly, "that sounds fine." But her thoughts keep spinning out, like fishing line unspooling and twisting back on itself, a mess that can never be untangled, only cut and tossed out.

The day before they are to leave for the coast, it happens. A sudden storm, record-breaking cold and high winds, a northern blast that closes schools and ices roads and topples the ginkgo. The trunk is broken off three feet from the ground, the branches breaking and splintering the length of the lawn, the new spring leaves torn, tattered, twisted.

Astrid stands before the waste, her hands clenching into fists, the spooling of her thoughts reaching the end, growing taut, and breaking. The final piece of what she thought she could count on, broken. She had known her lycopods were susceptible to humanity's progress, needing as they do clean air in order to survive. But the ginkgos, they are a species who owe their evolutionary survival to humans. Ginkgos are so resilient that they can come back from nothing but a stump, can endure droughts and searing heat, can flourish in the concrete jungles of the world's largest cities. And now even they are at risk from the chaos of a changing climate. Even her ginkgo. While she's been busy untangling the past, searching pieces of rock for clues to what once was, the future has been unraveling right before her eyes, fraying and thinning like the great ice pack of the far north.

Chapter 12

At the opening reception of her Fireweed Gallery show, Elyse walks through the crowd, smiling and accepting praise. It's a good turnout, with the jubilant air of First Friday on the cusp of springtime. So many friends and colleagues, some she hasn't seen for years: Sam's high school art teacher; Barbara, with whom she taught a feminist art class; a former student who went to Boston for college and just moved back; Beverly, from the zoo; friends from Valdez and Cordova; Alaskan artists whose work she has admired and encouraged.

The gallery owner, Ingritte, sidles up to her and says, "All these friends from years gone by. It's like a high school reunion, isn't it?"

Elyse grins, but then feels a small shudder inside. Was that a compliment or a critique? Is the room full because her work is interesting, or only because she has lived here long enough to know so many people who feel obliged to support her?

She shakes off doubt and scans the packed room. An older couple is gazing at the James Lake painting, a couple that she does not, reassuringly, know.

"Lovely," says the woman, her head tilting to touch the shoulder of the man with a cane. "It's just lovely. So calming."

Elyse takes in the familiar painting again. Yes, she thinks, it is calming. All the blues and greens, the soft melding of one line into another. It's a pleasing image. Nothing unsettling about it, not even the slightest ruffling of breeze on water. And then she gets a sudden gut feeling that she did not paint this painting. She flushes, and the room spins. She stares at the painting again. It was someone else who painted it; she is not that woman. Her eyes dart around the room at all the paintings: she's not connected to this work. She has left it behind. Pretending that this is her latest and greatest drains the blood from her face.

Maggie touches her elbow. "You okay? You look like you've seen a ghost. Here, have some super-sweet bright red punch."

Elyse emits a laugh, and takes a sip. "Wow, this tastes like something a hummingbird would love. Yeah, I'm fine. A bit overwhelmed, I guess. So many people here!"

"Yep, good job, girl. You deserve it. And you need the energy of a hummingbird to keep up with all the people who want to talk to you tonight."

Elyse wants to tell Maggie what she's feeling, but instead she takes another sip of the hummingbird drink and gives Maggie a quick hug.

A few weeks later, Elyse receives an invitation from the Alaska Museum for a solo show. She's ecstatic; to have a solo show there is to enter the rarified realm of the state's best artists. But her ecstasy is short-lived, for she immediately begins to fret about whether to debut her new paintings, the ones she's kept under cover to all but Maggie. Well, and to Jim, at least the kudzu one.

She's afraid to go out on a limb when she's finally getting a chance for something big-time: a solo show in a bona fide museum. This could affect her career as an artist from here on out. It is terrifying as much as thrilling. But then she remembers that moment of—disembodiment—at the Fireweed opening. She wonders if she can fake it again, wonders if she can create new work for the show that was like her old work. She'd have to remember how to be that person.

She could talk to Maggie, but she knows what she would say: show the new stuff. She could talk to Dan, but she knows what he would say too: show the old stuff.

So she takes the dogs for a walk, and then goes to visit Binky.

It's springtime again, with all the attendant smells. A lower snowfall the past winter has made breakup easier, though everyone is already talking about heightened fire danger. Here at the zoo, though, the birch and cottonwoods are beginning to leaf out, and ruby red fireweed fists through brown ground. She reaches for a cottonwood bud, rubs its sticky bracts, then inhales that clear summertime aroma. Feeling calmed, she settles on the bench and gazes upon the bear, sleeping.

"Well, old friend," she says to her, "I hope you don't mind, but I'm here again asking for your advice."

Now that winter is leaving, Binky has become more sedate. Or maybe she's just resting up for summer and the bright circus of people that parades by her small home. Elyse wonders whether the commotion of visitors creates stress or relieves boredom.

"What shall I do?" she asks the sleeping form. "Is Dan right, are these new paintings just propaganda, or do I have something here? Should I just do what they're expecting, or take a risk? Oh, bear," she says, sighing, "we humans make things so complicated."

And just after her sigh, the bear sighs, too, her whole body rising and falling, yellowed fur fanning and then pleating. One paw stretches out, flexing the toes to display the curve of black claws, then goes limp again.

A slight breeze moves through the trees, and she breathes in something familiar. It's that smell she first encountered in the little classroom in Cape Vankarem while she waited for her ride to Mikhail's house. A smell she later learned, while standing beside Nicolaf at the bone pile, is the distinctive musky scent of marine mammal blubber. Whale or seal or walrus, all have a very pungent, sea-strong, acrid odor. Which she smells now. Which must be Binky's breath, or something thawing in her enclosure. In any case, it is as overpowering as ever, only instead of holding her breath against it, she inhales it deeply. And smiles.

"Well, that," she says, chuckling, "is pretty darn clear. You're right. Why am I being such a wimp? It's not about what Dan or the museum wants. If my paintings are to mean anything, they have to mean something to me."

The paw stretches out again, reaching toward Elyse, and the bear gives another long, deep sigh.

The museum show is eight months away. At her first meeting with the curator, Aaron Weddell, a trim young man in a stylish suit, they walk together through the museum. They pass through the Exxon-Mobil Gallery, where she tries to focus on the exhibit of contemporary Alaska Indigenous art, rather than the naming of an art gallery after an oil company; she knows that the majority of the museum's funding comes from oil companies but wishes they'd at least not advertise it so blatantly.

They walk by the history exhibits, where she tries not to think about how much space is given to the earthquake and to the building of the pipeline versus the 1989 *Exxon Valdez* oil spill. Even though this oil spill was, at the time, the most destructive in U.S. history; even though it forever changed the coastal ecosystems and communities of Southcentral Alaska, it is still largely erased from Alaska history. Justin, ever the rebel, had written a history paper on this in high school. It had cost him a letter grade, the teacher saying it was "too opinionated" for a research project.

Elyse grimaces at the memory. She knows her son was right. Several walls of the history section are devoted to the pipeline, including a big heavy piece of it. For the *Exxon Valdez* oil spill, there's only one glass case, displaying an orange survival suit covered in crude oil. Even that focuses on the human element and not on the thousands of animals killed and miles of shoreline destroyed—as if the most significant thing about the oil spill was that some people got oil on their clothes.

Finally they reach the top floor, where her show will be. It's an artist's dream, all light and airy. Two skylights are centered on the ceiling, and along one wall, full-length windows give views of the city and Chugach Mountains, creating a work of art in itself.

"Some artists," Aaron says, "prefer not to compete with the view, so we lower these window coverings," and he pulls a cord that releases a translucent covering, light filtering through but view obscured.

"Oh, no, I love that view," says Elyse, "I love its expansiveness."

"And most of your work is based in scenes from Alaska, right?"

"Well," she replies, slowly, "my work has taken a new direction since I applied for this show, and it's quite different than what you've seen. So, well, it's not so . . . based in Alaska. It's all over the place, really."

"Different material? Form? Content?"

"Oh, still oil. Some different techniques, and content, yes."

"Wonderful, wonderful. Of course, we encourage artists to show their latest; it's exciting to be the first to show a significant advancement in an artist's oeuvre. But sometimes we do ask to see some of the new pieces first, just to verify they meet our . . . vision for a solo show."

Elyse hears what is not said: they want to make sure the new work is good. She knows that a new direction in an artist's work is not always judged to be better. Unless, until, the artist has reached untouchable status where anything they do is golden.

"I understand," she replies.

"Fabulous," he says, bringing his palms together in a silent clap. "Why don't we see one or two of those new pieces, then? When could you bring them by? Next Wednesday, 1 p.m.?"

Elyse fairly slinks out of the museum to her car, where Darlene and Sophie sit patiently waiting for their reward: a walk along the coastal trail.

"I feel like I just shot myself in the foot," she says to Darlene, stroking the silky fur behind her black ears.

The walk helps. Just moving along a familiar trail, one foot in front of the other, the rhythm of the body taking over, loosens her thoughts. The coastal trail is wide and paved and level, winding between Cook Inlet and the city. It's high tide, winter's ice gone from the inlet, and the slick mud shoreline greens with emerging sedges and grasses. A flock of dunlins dabs at the silty water's edge, darting around each other and flitting across rivulets of water that carve small canyons in fine mud. The wind turbines on Fire Island, like a field of giant white sunflowers, swing around slowly, catching a breeze so faint she can't feel it. Beyond them, the snow-clad peaks of Mount Susitna and the Alaska Range are washed in peach. A cloud on top of Mount Spurr wisps like smoke from the now-quiet volcano. A bird flits by in front of her, bright yellow, black cap, and disappears in a tangle of alder and willow beside the trail. It's a Wilson's warbler, returned for the summer, first one she's seen.

Of course she has no choice. There's no other choice but to show her new work and let the chips fall where they may. Anything else would be fraudulent.

It has to do with why she paints. The reasons arise from a place within her that she knows is true and right, but often the process gets hijacked by—well, she's not sure what to call it. She gets swept up in something outside herself and finds herself painting for all the wrong reasons. For reasons that arise from what others deem success. When what really feels like success is painting something that satisfies a yearning, an inner conversation or question. That yearning, for her, usually rises as a desire to express the beauty, the wonder, the incredible mystery of the living world.

It gets messy quick. As every teacher says, you paint for yourself. But you also want to communicate, and that succeeds only when the work is embraced by others. So you begin to paint not for yourself but for others. And are swept away from that original inner compulsion. And cling to the hope that, if you create work that pleases enough people, you'll become so well known that you can take the risk of doing the work that rises from within. Someday.

But Elyse is fifty-two, not twenty-five. She can no longer wait. She can no longer play it safe.

The next morning, she closes the door to her studio, sets down her tea, and looks around. Which of these paintings should she show Aaron? In short order, she's going from showing them to nobody but Maggie, to showing them to the curator of the state's most renowned museum. If only she'd taken a few middle steps, shown them to other artists or gallery owners. Or even Dan. No, not Dan. She's certain he won't like them, certain he'll lump them in with the polar bear painting. She could have at least shared them with Jim or Nicolaf. Nicolaf. What would he say? Do these paintings express what she said she wanted to when they took that walk? That walk, the residency, seems so long ago.

She shakes her head, sips her tea, and steps back, looking at the room full of paintings as if she were the curator. The flamingo feathers on tundra please her, with contrasts of colors and textures, the absurdity of dwarf willow drenched in pink feathers, like a boa tossed around a woman's neck. The bone pile one has so much going on, maybe too much. The wooly mammoth study, there's something there, but it's not yet done. What are those angular shapes behind it? The rocks didn't look like that. But the shapes articulate something she felt when seeing those giant bones rising from the Earth, all the colors in the spectrum flaring.

From behind the door, she grabs a large canvas, sets it on the easel in the center of the room. Paints, brushes, solvents, all gathered quickly. She stares once more at the mammoth study and picks up a brush.

The phone rings. She heaves a sigh, trades brush for phone, and looks at the number: no, not Maggie, so no need to answer. It's—Jim. Surprising, but even he can wait. Phone down, brush up, she dives into the canvas, a furious energy propelling her. Colors, so many colors, and angles everywhere. A cacophony of shapes and colors. In the center, branching out across the canvas, transecting the color shapes but also, oddly, subsumed by them, those mammoth bones. She blocks out the entire canvas, still not sure what it will be, and then stops. Cleans up, takes a sip of now-cold tea, picks up the phone.

"There you are!" says Jim, answering on the first ring. "Good news! Our ads featuring your painting will debut next Sunday. Full pagers in the *New York Times, Wall Street Journal*, and *Los Angeles Times. Seattle Times*, too, and *Miami Herald*. And online, of course."

"Well, great, that's great," says Elyse. Her thoughts are still with the new painting, the thrill of discovery. She should have waited to call him. "I'm just—honored you're using my painting for something so important."

"Well, we're honored to have it, Elyse. I do think it will shift people's thinking."

"I hope so, I really do," says Elyse.

Jim begins to tell her about island communities in the South Pacific, tiny islands already disappearing from rising seas. Elyse's mind swirls in several directions. She's thinking of her mammoth painting; she's listening to Jim; she's—the *New York Times*? Did he say the *Wall Street Journal*? Her heart skips. Elyse knew he was thinking big but didn't, doesn't, grasp it, even now. Can't. She focuses on her breathing, calming. She focuses on Jim's voice. He's saying that these island communities are buying land in other countries so they'll have somewhere to go.

She leaps to Noah's Ark, to boatloads of immigrants from Cuba to the U.S., from North Africa to Europe. Their desperate fleeing. How they leave everything behind, their homes and belongings, goats and chickens, banana trees and vegetable patches. The shade tree under which they'd sit while taking a break from plowing the fields. The flock of brightly colored birds that flew overhead, just as the sun set. The quiet bay where they moored their boat.

Permanent migrations, people have always done that. Make a mess of things, then flee to the next place. Leave behind the plants and animals to fend for themselves. Leave behind all that their ancestors valued. She watches the rows of royal palms that the woman's grandparents had planted at her birth, palms that grew to shade the path to the house her parents built, sink beneath rising seas. She sees the mammoth tusk rising from the tundra, the shapes looming over it.

"What do you think, Elyse?" Jim is saying.

"Oh, I'm sorry," she says. "Bad connection. What'd you say?"

"What do you think about joining us at the rally in DC? And at the environmental art conference? Can you come?"

"Oh! Well, that sounds wonderful, thank you for asking. Why don't you email me the details?"

"Okay, will do. We'd pay your travel, of course, and a speaking fee. Just let me know what your speaking fee is."

Elyse hangs up the phone and laughs, a whirlwind of emotions grounding out on Jim's last statement. Her speaking fee? Well, she'll just have to make something up. Something larger than zero, which is all she's ever gotten before. She'll ask Dan; he'll have some idea.

But though she reads the email that evening, she doesn't get around to asking Dan or to replying to Jim because she's busy with the wooly mammoth painting. It's the one she's bringing to the museum. It pairs well with the tundra flamingo, she thinks, as she shows them to Aaron.

"Wonderful," he says, as he steps back, hands folded beneath his chin. "Okay, yes, I can see that these are substantially different than your previous work, aren't they? Brighter, sharper, more movement, energy. And the contrasts of subject matter. Interesting."

Elyse stands quietly, waiting for his pronouncement, every cell in her body vibrating the way Darlene's body vibrates on the way to a trailhead.

"Yes," he says, and she exhales, trying not to make it too audible. "Yes, these will do just fine. I love the contrasting subjects, the hilarity of it all, the passage of time and stretches of space. Very bright and playful, yet there's a darkness to them, something I can't put my finger on. Adds a nice depth. Let's go for it."

"Oh, great! That's just great. Thank you. I'm very excited about them, but you're only the second person I've shown them to so I just didn't . . . yes, thank you."

The cloud on which Elyse is riding floats higher when the ad appears and her phone begins to ring with reporters who want to interview this new artist who has burst on the scene in such an unlikely way. At least, that's how they frame it in the messages they leave.

"So," says the reporter with the *New York Times* during their third phone interview, "how do you feel about the way your painting was used?"

"Oh, fine," she replies as she lets the dogs out the door and then follows behind to sit on the soft summer lawn. It's one of those rare days of 70° sunshine, with just enough of a breeze to keep mosquitoes and overheating at bay. The kind of day she dreams about in January. "Fine, it's great, I'm very honored that WPO thought it would help their cause."

"Yes, their cause, precisely," says the reporter, voice smooth as summer air. "That's what I'm wondering about: how do you feel about having your art associated with a cause? You don't consider it ad art, right? You made it without any intention of using it in an ad, correct?"

"Right, yes. And no, of course it's not ad art."

"Yes, that's what I'm getting at. As I'm sure you know, many artists wouldn't want their work shown that way, sort of—co-opted—or maybe—simplified—for lack of a better term."

"Oh." Elyse feels a chill at her back. She stares at the vegetable garden, where one particularly large bumblebee ruffles a borage flower before diving into a zucchini blossom. "Oh. Well. I didn't see it as co-opted. Or simplified. Though I'm not sure what you mean by that. Just—of use. I mean, I paint to express what I experience, and much of what I experience is the degradation of our natural world. I mean, it goes without saying that climate change is the defining issue of our times, and one we all have to face if we're to survive. Even us artists. I mean, no matter what we do for a living, we all have to face up to this. And I'm honored, like I said, that my painting captured something WPO thought would help."

"I see," the reporter says, her voice wavering not one bit. "That's very clear, thank you."

After she hangs up, Elyse sits perfectly still, watching the bright yellow blossom tremble and recalling the conversation she had with Dan when she was considering the artist residency. Advocacy. Being taken seriously as an artist. Is he right? Has she just . . . what has she done?

Soon enough, she finds out. Just days after the *New York Times* article sees print, she gets a call from Aaron at the museum. He tells her they're going to have to postpone her show. A San Francisco sculptor whose work they've been wanting to show has an opening in his schedule for a traveling exhibit, and to make space for it, her show will have to wait. He apologizes profusely, ticking down the list of other exhibits that can't be bumped: Lifted Light is an annual event that always opens the same month and always uses the Atrium; the Alaska exhibit must be up this year and takes up the regular gallery space.

On and on he continues, until Elyse finally interrupts. "Thanks, Aaron. I get it. I understand. It's okay. I don't mind more time to work on pieces for the show, anyhow. But, so, when is the new opening date?"

"Well, here's the thing," he says, pausing. "We don't have a new date right now. There are just . . . a lot of things up in the air, with reduced funding and other shows' schedules . . . so we don't know yet. This isn't a cancellation, it's just a delay, it's just, we can't give you a date yet."

"Okay," she says, slowly. "So, when will you?"

"I don't know. It's not up to me. It's the director's call, and he's not . . . he says he doesn't know, but not to hold your breath."

After he hangs up, she cradles the phone in one palm, thinking of movie scenes where people throw the phone across the room, or into a lake, or just onto the ground and then crush it under their heel. She won't, of course, it's not the phone's fault, and besides, the only outcome would be the time and money and hassle of buying a new phone. Instead she just stares at it, wonders what that conversation was about.

It's not a cancellation. That's what he'd said, but why say it? Why imply it may have been exactly that?

"Humans!" she says to Binky, sitting in front of her enclosure with throngs of summer visitors crowded around. "I mean, humans! What a crazy bunch of monkeys we are!" Then she apologizes to the real monkeys. There isn't a creature on Earth that deserves the insult of being compared to humans.

After not destroying her phone, Elyse had screamed, wept, called Maggie, who she then remembered was on a backpacking trip, wept some more, yelled about not being able to find a tissue, and then sat on the floor of her studio. That's where she was when Dan called. He was home, wondering about dinner, but didn't want to disturb her in the studio. She crawled up to a standing position, slumped into the house, and, before he could ask what was wrong, poured it all out.

He'd been soothing, giving her a hug and tissues, patient and kind. But he'd also confirmed her fear: that the postponement was because of the newspaper article, in which she'd been called "more activist than artist," and her paintings had been designated "a new style of propaganda." "Is this a signal of what's to come? Is the art world changing? Are the lines between art and advertising blurring?" The reporter had taken it to the extreme, and then some. And the Alaska Museum responded by stepping back, way back.

Now she sits in front of Binky, the only animal besides her dogs she can stand to be around, thinking about the museum's history exhibit, about all the galleries and university buildings and public spaces named for oil companies. The museum—hell, all of Alaska—is just one big oil company town, and climate change will never be addressed, except by a few outliers. Of which she now, evidently, is one. All she's ever wanted to do is to paint what she sees. How has she ended up so far from such a clear and simple desire?

Section 3

Chapter 13

For years, Astrid had charted the exact day on which, all at once, the ginkgo shed the golden crown. For years, she tried but failed to witness it, once arriving just in time to see the last dozen or so leaves disembark. But last October, finally, she was there for the entire spectacle.

Having asked several people whose office windows faced the tree, Astrid waited for a call. Finally, one morning just after 10, an administrative assistant to the psychology chair texted her that one leaf had fallen. Within minutes, Astrid arrived with a blanket and her book bag. She looked up into the tree and watched in silence as leaf after leaf fluttered to the ground, at first just two, and then increasing numbers, as if the leaves were encouraged to abscission by the fate of the first few brave volunteers. In just under two hours, ginkgo stood bare of leaves, golden corona at the tree's feet, a perfect circle on a sea of green.

Blissful moment turned bittersweet memory: she finally witnessed the graceful choreography of the ginkgo's leaf-fall to now learn it was the final performance. Not that her ginkgo was the only one to fall that spring. Climate weirding, as many now call it—as if finding the right name would fix things—is happening all over the world: too much rain or drought, stronger and more frequent storms, record snowfall, searing heat. And with this unpredictability, an unbearable dissonance—especially for someone who works so hard for solid ground beneath her feet.

But today, on their drive to the coast, Astrid and Charlotte have a warm sunny day, with typical springtime temperatures. Typical enough that Astrid begins to believe she overreacted; there must have been something wrong with her ginkgo, something that made the tree susceptible to high winds, perhaps some disease killing the cambium, some hollowness in the core. Typical and sunny enough, this day, that she can almost talk herself out of what she'd rather not know.

With Charlotte at the wheel, Astrid looks out the window at the familiar countryside. She always anticipates getting beyond Raleigh, racing around its beltway and through the jumble of strip malls and tight housing complexes, and then gradually seeing buildings thin out and the road narrow until all is a sea of fields punctuated here and there by a lone farmhouse or derelict barn. In that expanse, her breath lengthens, slows.

"So," says Astrid, turning to her friend, "how are your preparations going for the environmental art conference?"

"Oh, thanks for asking! I'm feeling pretty good about it, but let's, while we're at the beach, let me run through my talk with you."

"Yes, sure, let's do that."

"The main thing I'm gnawing on is how much to focus on art-making versus advocacy, y'know, since the conference is about that intersection."

"Yes," says Astrid, "well, I'd say, stick with what you know, talk about your process . . . and I guess, well, part of that is what inspires your work."

"Well, I'll be . . . you're right. That's it! I can bring in advocacy by saying what inspires each piece. Organically. Thanks, A. You're a gem."

"Always glad to help you, shug."

Astrid sits back in her seat, watches the world go by. This time of year, the fields are awash in bright promising green: the fuzzy-leaved cotton, the perky spikes of corn, and the shining leaves of sweet potatoes. They spring from dark soil in rows and clusters, waving their small new hands in the breeze, carrying memories. Astrid's mother grew sweet potatoes; wherever they lived, she'd find some patch of ground to grow a small plot. Her grandmaw always found a way, sometimes through the mail, to provide them with slips nestled in damp paper towels; Astrid always helped her mother plant these little two- or three-leaved tufts and keep them watered in the sandy peat.

Then every fall they'd have the treasure hunt: armed with small shovels, Astrid and her brother and sister would gingerly dig and shriek in delight as each shovelful held a tumble of dark orange tubers, like buried gold doubloons from Blackbeard himself. They'd carry their baskets of treasure to the hose, scrub them clean, then parade them in front of their mother, who sat like a queen on the old metal glider. She'd exclaim over their booty and grant each a wish, within reason, of course: a trip to the ice cream stand, an extra hour at the swimming hole, a new skirt. Astrid asked for the same thing every year: a trip to the botanical gardens in Chapel Hill. And every time, her mother said, maybe next year, and instead took her to the local greenhouses, where Astrid roamed the aisles, asking questions of the staff. Questions that, increasingly, they couldn't answer.

Astrid sighs, wishing her mother's flights of fancy could have, just once, materialized for her daughter. How fortunate that Astrid inherited her father's stubbornness, so she finally got herself to those botanical gardens—and found a way to stay. Stubbornly, she has done what her father wanted to do: remade herself into someone better. Pulled herself up from poverty, first in her family to graduate high school, not to mention earn a PhD. But, she thinks with a start, what good did it do? Everything is falling apart around her, and she can't fix it.

She stares out the window at the passing fields. She finds comfort knowing many of these farms have been in the same family for generations. She's grateful for the white clapboard and red brick houses, with long driveways lined by giant live oaks. She remembers learning how farmers in the old South would, upon their child's birth, plant two long rows of oak saplings to line the future driveway of the child's future house. By the time the child was grown, so would the saplings be, towering and giving blessed shade.

One home along the drive Astrid particularly anticipates. She met the owner, a state senator, at the Island Inn on Ocracoke one New Year's Eve when she and Gareth first started seeing each other, thirty-some years ago. Gareth had a motorcycle they'd ridden to the beach. In January, even in the mild winters of North Carolina, that was an unusual feat. In fact, for extra insulation, they had to stop and buy newspapers to line the insides of their coats.

At the Island Inn bar, this man, white-haired and round-bellied and red-faced, quizzed Gareth about the motorcycle ride. "Well, I'll be hornswoggled," he said. "Let me buy you some Southern Comfort to get that chill out of your bones!" He kept their glasses full all night.

On their ride home, a crisp day spilling with winter sunlight, they picked out his house, just as he'd described it, a grand white house set far from the road, with two rows of giant oaks lining the long driveway. As they passed, a flurry of white birds had lifted from the bright green lawn. The sight had lifted Astrid's heart right to her throat and had melded with the growing warmth she felt toward the man whose body she leaned against, arms around his waist.

So she always feels a particular leap of joy at seeing that place again on a drive to the beach. As they approach, she sits up straight. "Slow down, please," she tells Charlotte. "We're coming up on the senator's house."

And there it is. The grand bright white against expansive green. Only something is terribly wrong. The trees. The double lines. Broken. At least a third of the trees are down, lying on the ground like dead soldiers on a battlefield, massive limbs twisted and tangled into grotesque forms. The stately lines are now jagged, rent apart. A man with a chainsaw stands among the toppled giants, looking small as an ant. Not the senator; he probably died years ago.

"Oh. My. God. The storm," says Charlotte, pulling over to the side of the road. "Same one that took down your ginkgo. Gotta be. That wind tearing across these wide-open fields, wow. It's an amazement anything's left standing."

Astrid blinks once, twice. Sits very still, feeling something leak out of her, a certain brightness. Feels it pool away from her, threads to wisps of smoke. Drained, like the fields, dry, small green hands hanging limp. Then she shudders, shakes herself, a familiar frustration rising, heat replacing chill, frustrated that she can still be toppled by what is now the new normal.

"Well, they were old trees," she says, looking straight ahead down the highway that had been, several years ago, widened to four lanes.

"Oh, honey pie," says Charlotte, "I'm so sorry. And this trip was supposed to be a break!"

They drive on in silence, and for the next hour pass more destruction: an old barn crumpled under the weight of a broken loblolly pine; farmhouses left exposed to the summer sun by fallen trees in their yards; a stream, where Astrid once saw two river otters rolling and leaping in play, now swollen and backed up from a logjam of more downed trees.

It's dark by the time they arrive at the condo, so though they hear the reliable rhythm of waves, all Astrid wants to do is settle in her room, get the internet going, and check email.

"I guess it's grounding for you, that computer," Charlotte says. "Well, honey, I'm just going to walk down to the water, get my toes wet. You can greet the ocean in the morning."

"Yes," Astrid says, irritated already with the elaborate log-in process. "You go ahead and enjoy it. Soon enough this whole place will be under water. What's that password again?"

Steeled with anger over all the loss she'd seen on the drive, Astrid barely reacts when she reads the email from a colleague in China, a young paleobotanist who has been sending her samples. Her colleague tells her, "regrets to inform" her, that the Shukkei-en ginkgo in Japan has also, just the day before hers, been ripped down by an unusually strong storm.

The tree wasn't, by ginkgo standards, very old, having been planted in the Shukkei-en Japanese Garden around 1740. But the Shukkei-en ginkgo was perhaps one of the world's most famous and revered ginkgos for the travails he had endured. He was one of six ginkgoes that were among the few living things to survive the 1945 atomic bomb blast. The four-hundred-year-old gardens, and Shukkei-en, stood less than a mile from Hiroshima's ground zero.

The Shukkei-en ginkgo, with a nuclear-blast-charred trunk, measuring thirteen feet around, had stood as testament to tenacity and regrowth. A plaque nearby described his near-miraculous survival, and he was known throughout Japan as "the bearer of hope." Now, however, the massive symbol of hope and regeneration lay in a great broken heap, shattered limbs draped across an ancient stone bridge.

The ginkgos, the live oaks, all this fallen grandeur. These trees were cultural treasures. There are ginkgos all across the East who are revered, who stand like sentinels to culture and civilization; there are trees all over the world who hold human history in ancient limbs. The Major Oak in Sherwood Forest, who sheltered Robin Hood and his merry men; the Cotton Tree in Freetown, Sierra Leone, where former African American slaves found freedom; General Sherman in Sequoia National Park, world's largest and oldest individual tree; the Cedars of God, all that remains of the biblical Cedars of Lebanon. Even the Davie poplar on UNC's campus, propped up by cement and cables because, as legend tells, if this tree falls, the university will crumble. This isn't only the loss of big old trees, Astrid realizes, but the crumbling of culture itself. Climate change is eroding the foundations of human culture as well as the very Earth on which they rest.

The woman had done something terribly wrong, something for which there was no redemption, and if she lived then they were surely lost. The woman lay unconscious as they both looked down on her. The old man caught Astrid's eye, pulled a gun from his bag, and put it against the woman's throat. He looked up at Astrid again, and she may have nodded. The gun went off. The woman was dead. Blood pooled. Astrid leapt from paralysis to efficiency, helping him move the body, wiping and wiping all the blood away, all their fingerprints from the room, the doorknob, every place they might have touched. She does not know what he does with the body, but it is gone. She is walking, alone, thinking, confused. Did she nod? Did she want him to kill the woman? She didn't do it, but she is an accomplice, as guilty as he. A body is found in the lake, apparent accident, car going off the cliff. The body is decomposed, identification will be difficult. She is hoping it is the woman, and the matter will be closed, and she will no longer have to constantly look behind her, constantly worry about being discovered. But still she does not know. She wants to turn herself in. She wants to no longer carry this horrible feeling of guilt and fear, fear of waiting for the moment when they catch her and her life is over. Best to get it over with. Turn herself in. Release at least the fear; the remorse is hers for life.

Astrid wakes, trembling. Though she knows it's a dream, she can feel what it's like to be an accomplice to murder, to be on the run, racked with guilt and fear and lost to yourself. Even if there seemed no other choice. There are always other choices. She gets ups, stretches, moves her body, crawls back into bed.

She is falling, falling down a deep hole, a bottomless hole, falling, feeling the wind created by her speed, the flapping of a sleeve against her arm, her hair tugging the roots, lips pulled apart, eyes tearing, though there is nothing to see, nothing but total darkness.

She wakes again. She lies in bed, reminding herself, again, that it was a dream. She is not falling. She did not kill anyone. She did endure a long flight wondering if she'd see Strilay still alive. She did have to give Sanders use of her collection. She does have less support for her own research. She doesn't know what to think about Gareth and Charlotte. She does miss the ginkgo, and the giant oaks, and the Shukkei-en, though she never saw the tree. She does feel complicit and powerless. She does wonder what's next, what will be swept away from her, and when. She does feel her life shrinking to the size of a life ring, to which she clings.

Okay, enough, she mumbles. She gets up, throws on jeans and a sweatshirt, finds her way through dark rooms, steps out into the night. It's clear and moonless; the skies glimmer with starlight. She sighs, looks up. She hasn't seen constellations so clearly since—well, since she was a girl, standing on a beach, just like this. There's the summer triangle—Vega, Deneb, and Altair—glowing low on the horizon. Overhead arcs the Milky Way, spreading like the pages of a favorite childhood story.

She follows the wooden boardwalk across dunes, hearing the faint shushing of seagrass in the breeze. She descends steps, feels the cool giving sand on her bare feet, and draws closer to the steady drumbeat of waves. Eyes now attuned to the dark, she sees the white scrolls of breaking waves, the foam fanning over sand. She drifts closer, toes into the foam, feels the bubbles touch skin. Closer, just within their reach, and the waves race up to meet her. She stands still, letting each wave sink her feet deeper and deeper into the soft, warming sand.

Fifty-two bones. She wiggles her toes in deeper. Fifty-two tiny bones in my two feet, holding me up, holding me down, holding me here on this beach. She feels the pulsing, the weaving, as her weight shifts almost imperceptibly from heel to toes, from one foot to the other. She'd learned about this from a med student, this slight movement of muscle and blood. It's a figure eight, he'd said; when the body stands in balance, it naturally weaves in a figure eight. Or, she now realizes, the sign of infinity.

The waves curl to her, then retreat, pulling sand and leaving foam swirling around her ankles, appearing and dissolving, filling and emptying. Her feet become buried ever deeper in the settling sand, her body held more tightly to the Earth.

They tried to bury us. They didn't know we were seeds.

As if from the stars, or sand, or waves, into her mind pops a Mexican proverb her mother used to recite. She sees the sweet potato slips, the bomb-scarred ginkgo, the phytoplankton just now lighting the waves with their bioluminescence. Such power in a seed, in plants. So much more than we humans comprehend. Certainly more than we give plants credit for.

She knows what she will do. She wiggles her sand-covered toes, leans back to the star-shimmering sky, and laughs out loud, her voice keeping time with the sea.

They drive home over the arcing bridge across Roanoke Sound, leaving the long sand islands of the Outer Banks behind. Across

Roanoke Island, then over another bridge across the calm waters of the Croatan, and then the road drops into the swamps, the low forest of the coastline, and a small sign tells them they're entering the Alligator National Wildlife Refuge.

"Oh," says Astrid, "why don't we drive through part of the refuge? Who knows, maybe we'll luck out and see one of those elusive red wolves."

"You got it, shug," says Charlotte. "As long as we can stop at that barbeque place by the Scuppernong River."

They turn off onto a narrow road that quickly becomes a one-lane dirt passageway crowded with chain ferns and river cane. The scrub oak forest is so thick and matted that something would have to charge right out in the middle of the road for them to see it. They stop, get out, hear crickets and a far-off call of what might be a screech owl. A great heron passes overhead, long neck outstretched, wings silently fanning air. In the blackwater ditch beside the road, four small green slider turtles sunning on a log slip off as the heron's shadow passes.

"Well," says Charlotte, "growth this thick, we're lucky to have seen those turtles! But we'll keep going. I think it's a loop."

They drive slowly, Astrid lost in thought, in her mind already back in Chapel Hill. And that's when it happens. Less than forty feet in front of them, a shiver of undergrowth and then a large animal trotting across the road. The animal reaches the middle, stops, swivels the furred head, stares at them. Now they're only twenty feet away, close enough to see the rippling of cinnamon fur over haunches, the tents of ears pricking higher. They can almost feel yellow eyes sear their skin. No one moves. Stillness. Then the animal drops his head, sniffs the ground, and slips into the forest.

"So," says Charlotte, in a whisper, "what do you think, red wolf or coyote?"

"Hard to say," says Astrid, her voice low. "It's supposedly hard to tell the difference. That's part of the struggle with reintroduction efforts; hunters say they mistake them for coyotes. That, and sea-level rise will decimate these swamplands."

"Oh, you and your negative spin on everything!" says Charlotte, her voice rising.

"Okay, okay," says Astrid. "Let's say we just saw a red wolf. There's fewer than twenty left in the wild. And this is the only place on Earth where they still run free. The only place. So if that was … well, then, we're pretty damn lucky."

Then she turns to face Charlotte. "Shug. Listen. I've got something to tell you. I've decided to go to India, to help Lamont with the afforestation project. Leave the university for, I don't know, six months. Not much to leave anyhow, since Sanders has my collection and my funding has dried up, but—it's not about running away, I promise," she says hurriedly, seeing the flash in Charlotte's eyes. "It's about running toward. Strilay keeps telling me I've got to leap. Well, I'm going to leap."

"Wait just a minute now, hold your horses," says Charlotte, drawing each word out like a slow breath. "You su-ure this isn't about all these things falling apart? Your ginkgo, your funding . . . I mean, you've had a lot of shit hitting the fan lately."

"I'm sure of it, I am, Charlotte," says Astrid, her voice soft but steady.

"Well, hell almighty. My dear stodgy Astrid. I can't believe it!" Charlotte laughs. Then, in an accusing tone, "Why didn't you tell me? And Gareth. What does he think?"

"I just decided. Our first night at the beach. I woke in the middle of the night and went out to the waves. I'm sorry I didn't tell you, I just didn't know … if it would stick. But it has. And Gareth, he'll be fine. He'll probably be relieved to get me out of the house. I've been so morose."

"Yes, well," says Charlotte, "I hope so. It sure as hell is a big leap. I mean. Wow. Amazing. I can't believe you decided so suddenly. That's just not like you, Astrid, not at all."

"I know, it's not," sighs Astrid.

"I know you've been struggling, but … well," Charlotte continues, softly, "I'm just tickled for you, sweetie. Tickled pink. And a little bit green, too, with envy. Plus, I sure will miss you. Maybe I'll come visit."

"Yes," says Astrid, "Who knows? After all, we just saw a red wolf. Anything's possible."

As they drive the narrow road, each peering into dense thickets, each lost once more in thought, Astrid's wanders to Strilay: to all this time she's been worried he's leaving her, when instead he's been leading her, urging her down a new path. And then to Tom Shank's work, how she once thought it crazy but now sees its brilliance: why not try anything for that which we love?

Chapter 14

Elyse can feel the downward slope, feel herself slipping each day farther away from being a respected artist. She now dreads going to any event for fear she'll see that look in her friends' eyes: that mix of pity and aversion. No one wants to be associated with an outlier.

But she goes to Indira's opening; Indira is a longtime friend. Raised in New Delhi in a wealthy family, Indira moved to the U.S. for college and never left. Elyse often wonders why Indira's story hasn't found its way into her work: her career as an air force pilot, her struggle to hide her bisexuality within the military world, the hazing she endured after some peers discovered her secret visits to nightclubs. None of the rage or sorrow over having to give up flying jets once her "indiscretions" were reported.

Indira, Elyse thought, will not shun her. And some of her friends, artists she's known for decades—surely they will buoy her. Still she carries like a rock the story Maggie told her about a friend who'd written a book about child abuse: she became a popular speaker at educational and political events, but not with the literary community. She'd hoped her success, with her MFA, would secure her a university position. But it didn't, and she learned why when she attended a professor's book signing, where he'd written in her copy, "I admire your advocacy work." Only that. She was not considered a true Author, just an activist who'd written about her cause. Has Elyse now fallen from the pedestal of being a true Artist?

Ingritte, the owner of Fireweed Gallery, rushes up as she enters the crowded gallery. "Elyse," she says in her clipped Swedish accent, "so nice to see you! So very. Your work at the gallery has sold well, but sales have stalled, so, I think, perhaps you pick up the unsold paintings next week? We must make room for the new, you know!"

"Oh, course," says Elyse, heart sinking another notch. "Of course, next week."

"Wonderful!" Ingritte says, looking past Elyse. "Oh, Peter has arrived! I must go ask about the new baby!"

Alone in a crowded room, Elyse moves to the hors d'oeuvres, though she's not sure how she'll swallow anything. She can't locate any of her friends, and Indira remains surrounded by well-wishers. She at least wants to congratulate Indira before she makes an exit. With a few carrots and dip on her plate, she negotiates her way to the far wall where Indira's works hang. They are complex, as her work usually is, using surprising materials. In one, she has used only what she could find in her trash can that day. Coffee grounds, overripe raspberries, these she used to paint and drip and slash across the canvas. Nothing looks like what it is. Even the yogurt container and candy wrapper are in disguise. The overall impression is of chaos, with a surprising calm in the midst.

"So, what do you think?" says a man's voice to her left.

"Oh," she says, turning to see Vic, an art professor at the university, "I think it's magnificent."

But he wasn't talking to her. He was talking to a woman on his left, and at Elyse's comment, they both stare at her.

Then Vic says, "Oh, well, hello, Elyse. Imagine seeing you here. Well, enjoy!" And they move on, quickly, skipping over the next two pieces.

"It's about being a serious artist," she hears Vic saying later to his woman friend. "Some artists stay true to their art; others merely use it for advocacy. One must be careful to retain one's integrity and dignity now that art can so easily be co-opted."

She doesn't know if they are talking about her, or Indira, or someone else entirely. It doesn't matter. She drops her uneaten carrots in the trash and slips out the side door, inhaling the cool springtime air as if she'd been underwater too long. She looks up at the trees lining the street, their buds swelling with each day. She swallows the lump in her throat.

"Serious!" she croaks, her throat loosening. "Serious! Well, if being a serious artist means sacrificing everything else, even my own moral compass, well, then, well . . ."

Her shoulders sag. Well, what? She doesn't know. She only knows that there's a tear in the fabric she's so carefully woven, one she doesn't know how to repair. Over her head, a flock of cedar wax-wings lift from a birch, chattering among themselves as they rise and fall, rise and fall, sunshine illuminating the scarlet on their wingtips. They cloud and then settle onto a mountain ash to which a few overwintered berries still cling.

Elyse grabs pencil and pad. Charcoal, hard, 557-HB. She starts on the right edge of the paper and draws a line. A jagged, sharp line. This ridgeline, right outside her window. She wants to capture it as it is right now, with morning sun full on.

She has been watching the light return for three hours, watching since there was only the faintest glow in the sky, that pale yellow halo tracing the ridgeline, and gradations of black, with the darkest being the spruce outside her window. Slipping in between ski and tourist season, she's spending a couple of nights at the hotel in Girdwood, which, though just an hour from home, feels like another world. And after Indira's opening, she needs another world. She loves this upper-story room, feeling as if she is in the tops of these giant Sitka spruce. Last night a crow lit on top of one, and she felt as if they were seeing eye to eye.

She loves drawing, too, for this precise reason. Nothing else captures the form best. As much as she adores the rich colors of oil painting, she sometimes wants nothing more than to ignore color entirely and focus only on shape. Nothing does a jagged ridgeline better than to set color concerns aside and focus on that line etched between rock and sky. Only a few sections are smooth; the gentle curves of these snow saddles are a surprising contrast to the chiseled rock. From this distance all she can see is the curve, but she knows those snow cornices are actually shaped like frozen waves, white with hints of blue, gorgeous but deceptive.

Mountains are so stalwart. So impermeable. Whenever she feels discouraged by events in her own little life; whenever she descends to despair over yet another animal going extinct, another forest destroyed, another reef bleached, she pulls her thoughts to mountains: no matter what, they will be here: their rock-hard, solid selves.

But even these ridges are changing. The soft lines will disappear, are leaving. The glaciers receding, icefields shrinking, snow thinning. Still, the mountains, the rock, will remain. As long as they are not blasted for coal or gravel, they will remain. They will soften by the geologic forces of wind and rain and time, but those are as they've always been; mountain erosion is not her fault, not humanity's fault. She is weary of all these changes being her fault, weary of the burden of accountability. Weary, too, of trying to comprehend her own species, with its fickle and selfish fault lines. If only she could be a child again, small and unimportant and ignorant of all but what's right before her eyes.

She pulls her focus back to the lines before her, the way they sway and dip, the crescendo of peak after peak, a syncopation of finely etched points. Each one she wants to draw with an exact precision. A true rendition of form. Not what she sees there, but what *is* there. The hard trueness of it. That's all she wants to do. Her eyes and hand merely conduits.

The light continues to change, never stops changing. This is why plein air artists learn to paint fast. Otherwise, what they start with disappears before they can finish it. But to learn each minute shape in a ridgeline would take her whole life. Which she'd gladly give because it's when she feels that bliss: losing herself into the knob of dark rock, then the slope of white, the folds of dark and light.

The letter from Nicolaf is sitting on the kitchen counter when she returns home. They've written a few times, only letters, as Nicolaf rarely uses a computer. The letters take weeks to arrive, so she savors each one, reading it several times. In this one, he tells her about a polar bear raiding his father's stash of duck eggs. Collected in early summer, the eggs are buried in a type of root cellar to be used throughout the winter. But sometime last winter, when all the bears should have been out on the icepack far from town, this one found the stash, dug it up, and ate every single egg. "Just think," Nicolaf writes, "what happy bear!" She can't help but appreciate that they weren't upset with the bear for taking a winter's supply of eggs. "Another lesson on how to survive," he writes, "from Wise Teacher."

Elyse looks up from the page. Just yesterday she'd read about a man in the Canadian Arctic giving a whole salmon to an emaciated polar bear. And a week ago, another story about starving polar bears breaking into homes in the Siberian Arctic. They hadn't harmed anyone; they were just looking for food. She recalls the words of a biologist at a talk on climate change and polar bears: "They're not going to just lie down and die."

She goes back to reading, her heart both heavy and light. Nicolaf tells her he's going on the speaking circuit, coming to Alaska the following fall. "Thank you," he writes, "for giving me courage to trust my English. Our conversations were very important to me."

Elyse stares out the window where a pair of nuthatches take turns in the birdbath. Alaska. Nicolaf is coming to Alaska. He has overcome his public-speaking fears and is making the leap. She shakes herself, as if breaking loose of some old shell. Time to get over myself, she thinks, time to stop being so whiny about losing whatever respect I had in this small pond of the Alaska art scene. Life's too short. Time to leap into the flow.

It was time, then, to answer the email from Jim. He had sent her forms for her participation in the environmental art conference—something she'd agreed to in a rush, without much thought, back when she was brimming with confidence over the museum show. So much changed so quickly, though, that when she'd gotten the email a week ago, she had avoided it. She was too beset by self-doubt to make the commitment. Now, boosted by Nicolaf's letter, she is ready. All that's left is to tell Dan.

"Well," Dan says, "of course you know what I think. We've been over this. You've already seen what activism does to your standing as an artist. I thought you'd learned your lesson."

"Lesson," she replies. "Lesson. Well, the only lesson I've learned is that most of my so-called friends were only colleagues, and fair-weather ones at that. If my art is good, it stands on its own. Right? I mean, don't you agree?"

Elyse is counting on Dan's gift at cutting through to the root. She is hinging her news on his own pride in doing what he thinks is right rather than what society dictates. But she also knows the underbelly: he doesn't want her to change.

"No, I don't. You're being idealistic. You've got to face the facts of the world we live in. The way things work. Not how you want them to work. You're behaving just like Justin."

"Justin?"

"Yes. I was going to tell you. I got a call from Sam this morning telling me that Justin had dropped out of college and was joining some group called Turning the Tide."

"What?"

"I told you. He's letting his idealism trash his own future. Just like his mother."

"I didn't. He didn't tell me. What is this group?" Elyse stutters.

"I don't know. Neither does Sam. Unless he's not saying, protecting his little brother."

"Well, I'll call Justin, we'll sort this out."

"Sure you will. You both get led around by your hearts instead of your heads, that's what gets you into trouble. And that's why I'm telling you: do not go to this conference."

"He's . . . I'm . . ." Elyse says, a heat rising, her tone shifting as she realizes Dan chose this moment to tell her about Justin so that it might topple her own decision. "I'm going. And if you can't accept that, then maybe we need to rethink our marriage."

The words are out of her mouth before she even knows she's thinking them. She watches his face suddenly go blank. His skin ashen. A silence fills the kitchen, the hallway, the house. It spreads beyond the walls to the melting snow in the yard, to the birch branches with their swelling buds. It fills the very sky.

"I," he says, finally, his voice booming through the silence, "I am not sure what to do with that. I've got a, a conference call in a half hour. We'll talk again after that."

But they don't, not right away. Dan is adept at avoiding hard talks about their relationship, adept at finding some work project that takes precedence over anything having to do with intimate matters. And so Elyse isn't surprised when he leaves her a note the next morning saying that DWB needs him in Syria right away. The civil war there, fueled by the corruption oil extraction brings, has flared again. He spends the day finagling his visas and plane tickets, is up half the night packing, and leaves the next morning. There is the hurried kiss, the rushed I-love-yous, the quick hug. And there is a brief flash in his eyes of something she hasn't seen before.

Chapter 15

Astrid still has doubts. So many that she hasn't yet told anyone, save Charlotte, about her plans to go to India, and that only because the decision was so new it shone bright enough to cancel all shadow. Now shadows loom large. She is to meet Strilay in an hour for lunch at Carolina Coffee Shop, where she plans on telling him. But she knows that, once she does, backing out won't be an option.

She slips her fossil in her pocket and walks through the arboretum. Coker Arboretum was the brainchild of the university's first botany professor. In 1903 Dr. William Chambers Coker envisioned five boggy acres as an outdoor classroom, filled with trees from around the state, the nation, the world. Over four hundred species now thrive here, some of them as old as the arboretum itself. Astrid has often imagined what it was like before Coker's vision transformed it. She is not one to admire the ways in which humans transform natural landscapes, but she recognizes the arboretum as a living collection akin to her collection of fossils in their glass cases.

Here, every tree is known to her, every pathway worn. She holds the fossil in one hand, warm in her pocket, and strolls through stands of trees filled with the bright green of new leaves. It's one of the most electrifying of colors, the green of a new leaf. Melded in with it are the soft pastels of the flowering trees—dogwood, redbud, crepe myrtle. She fingers a fallen dogwood blossom, recalling her preschool teacher's words in the church basement. The dogwood tree, she told the children, used to grow very large and was used to make the cross that Jesus hung upon. The dogwood was so distressed at being used for such cruelty that from then on dogwood only grew small and twisted, so the tree could never again be used to make a cross. And dogwood flowers, said the preschool teacher, became a reminder of Christ's crucifixion.

Astrid stares at the flower. The white petals are in the form of a cross, with small holes at the end, a rusty red color, signifying the nails in Jesus's hands and feet. And the flower's center resembles the crown of thorns he wore. It's a good story, but of course Astrid knows the functions of the four white petal-like bracts and the tightly clustered flowers in the middle; knows the red drupes in fall are not to signify Christ's blood, but to attract birds to eat and then spread their seeds.

She lets the blossom fall. Science and religion have been duking it out for a long time. That's one reason she gravitated to basic science: no one can argue with the desire to understand something. Applied science, however, is an entirely different beast, and she does not relish entering that world—yet she cannot forget the fallen ginkgos and live oaks, the newly discovered lycopodium, the polar bears of Churchill.

A quarter of all terrestrial animals and plants are now threatened with extinction. A quarter. She looks around. Which of these trees will leave? The crepe myrtle, with their smooth curving trunks? The white oak, and those gently lobed leaves clustered in towering crowns? Sunlight filters among the spring green, a color that can only be uplifting. As she walks, the springtime green of every tree and shrub grows brighter. By the time she turns toward town, she has renewed her conviction to go to India.

He sits in the back booth, as always, white hair thick as ever, eyebrows more dense and wild every time she sees him. The hair on one brow curves down, while the other sweeps upward, so that he always looks like he's raising an eyebrow. Two students sit with him, perched on the seats as if only stopping by. But by the way they lean on their hands, she can tell they're enraptured by another one of the professor's stories, or maybe just his sheer excitement for life.

She knows one of the students; he's an economics major, but now, he tells her, he's thinking of taking a semester off to go help with the polar bears in Churchill.

"Ah," says Astrid, "you've been won over by Professor Strilay's impassioned stories? That's perfectly understandable. He's persuaded many of us to do what we might otherwise never have imagined."

The student grins, nods his head, slips away.

"So, have I persuaded you to do something you would not otherwise, Astrid, m'dear?"

She laughs. "Oh, very funny. Only every major decision in my life."

"Well," he says.

"Well," she says, "except for botany. That one I chose on my own."

"Yes. And you have regretted it ever since, no doubt. And now?"

"Now," she begins, but the waiter appears, refills Strilay's coffee, takes their order.

Strilay's gaze remains on Astrid, and as soon as the waiter leaves, he asks, "Now?"

Astrid looks out the window at the familiar alley, sunlight showering between the old brick buildings. She takes a deep breath, and in a rush, says, "Now, here I go again, following your advice against my own better judgment. I'm going to take a sabbatical and go to India, help Lamont with that afforestation project."

"Yes!" says Strilay, his body leaping up a bit in his seat. "Finally! Oh, you will not regret it, Astrid, not for even a moment. Why, this will be a life-changing experience for you. Not to mention that it might help save this old planet of ours."

"Yes, well, I have my doubts."

"Of course you do, m'dear," he interrupts. "You wouldn't be Astrid if you didn't have doubts."

"Well, it is afforestation, not reforestation. I do have some hesitation about that, especially since others have been less than successful. I don't want to get involved with something that wastes my time or the planet's resources."

"But of course. Wasting time is right up there with plant neglect in your book of sins," says Strilay, grinning.

"Right. Very funny. But seriously, take the Green Wall of China, in the Gobi Desert. To reverse desertification, they planted poplar. The first red flag was monoculture. The second red flag was a non-native species. It went well for a while, but then most of the trees died. Turns out the poplar, chosen because they don't use much water, just has deeper roots. When they used up the deeper water, they crashed—and put native vegetation even more at risk."

"Truly, a shame," says Strilay, shaking his head. "But since so much of previous forests are now lost to human development, afforestation makes more sense, does it not?"

"Yes, true, we don't have many good options. And Lamont's program is using native species, making it diverse, being careful about water. It's not perfect, but it's as good a place as any to try. And," she continues, with a halfsmile, "it will give me access to some interesting fossil sites. I'll get out in the field and collect my own samples, for the first time since, well, since grad school." Her hand moves almost instinctively to the pocket holding her fossil. "I could finally have a breakthrough in my research, find that missing link I know exists."

"Well, that is a very fine plan, m'dear," says Strilay, sitting back in his seat. "I am thrilled to see you stepping up to that edge, where things will no doubt surprise. I know uprooting your life does not come easily for you."

"No," says Astrid, and she suddenly recalls one of her family's moves when she was about eight. She is peering out the back window of their station wagon, its shocks straining under the load of household goods strapped to the roof, staring out the dust-covered window to the small house with the kudzu kingdom out back.

"No," she says again, "I do not like to uproot my life. But this is just a sabbatical. I'll come back in six months. With, I hope, some new data from which to get funding."

"That's good, m'dear, very good. It's not adding that you dislike, is it? It's losing."

Now that Strilay knows, Astrid needs to quickly tell her husband before he hears it from someone else. It doesn't take her long to find the right time. The next morning, he awakens her with a kiss on her neck, then runs his fingers down the length of her back. She arches, stretches, rolls over to face him. When they make love in the mornings, it is slow and sweet, her favorite kind, her mind uncluttered by all she went to bed with the night before. Lying in his arms afterwards, she looks up at his familiar smile, and says, "Love, I have something I want to tell you. Something I think you'll be happy about."

And he is. Gareth is nothing but supportive. He says he'll miss her, of course, but he has known she would need to do something dramatic to get out of the funk she'd been in for a while.

"It's perfect. Striley always does know what you need. Including," he says, with a light kiss on her nose, "me."

"You're right," she says, sliding both her arms around him, "I do need you."

"You'd better!" he says. "But it's good timing, because I've got plenty to keep me busy with the initiative on food waste."

He'd helped organize the "Feeding the 5,000" event at the campus cafeteria and was so happy with how much food was kept from waste heaps that he decided it shouldn't be just an annual event. So now it's monthly, with plans to bring local restaurants into the program. His students are equally jazzed, and he now teaches a class on food waste and security. "It's simply untenable," he's been widely quoted, "that a third of the world's food goes to waste. This is a problem we can fix, because it's edible."

"Charlotte," he now says, "is designing the logo for the initiative."

"Charlotte?" says Astrid, with a quick inbreath.

She hesitates. Questions, accusations rise up, but she does not speak them. Instead, she listens quietly, then unravels herself from his arms and slips from the bed, telling him she just remembered that she's got an early office meeting. She's still thinking about Charlotte and Gareth when she walks into her office and finds, kneeling on the floor in front of one of her collection cases, a young woman, riffling through Astrid's fossil specimens. Her head snaps up when the door opens.

"Oh," she says, nervously, "sorry, I didn't know . . ."

"It's okay," says Astrid, "these aren't my normal office hours. But I will need some time here, when you're done."

"Of course," she says, her short curly hair bobbing enthusiasti-cally. "Yes, I will . . . I'll come back later. I'll just be across the hall, in our research lab, just let me know." And with that, she dashes from the room.

Once Sanders had received permission to use her collection, Astrid was given a choice: either the collection would be moved from her office, or he and his graduate students would have open access to her office. She couldn't stand the thought of her collection moving, so with the assurance students would stay away during her research and office hours, she chose the latter, even though it meant she couldn't drop into her office any time she wanted without expecting just what she's come upon today. And she has to keep all her person-als locked in her desk. Not that she keeps anything obviously per-sonal in her office. There are no pictures of family, not even Gareth; no little collection of keepsakes. What is personal to her—like her grad research fossil or the loblolly pine cone—wouldn't appear that way to anyone else. Still, she tucks them all away.

As Astrid fumbles with the desk key, she smiles wanly at how quickly the young woman scurried from the room. It will be easier on everyone once she's gone to India. It's the right timing: Strilay, fully recovered, will be returning to Churchill in August; Gareth is busy with his new initiative; her fossil collection will be otherwise occupied. She stands up straight and looks around the room, at her collection, her books, her equipment, hoping nothing will change while she's gone, wondering if it will look the same to her when she returns.

Chapter 16

Elyse tries not to think about it. To think about her marriage, and whether or not it is over. She is angry at Dan for not supporting her, and even more so for not sticking around. It's nothing new. His pattern has always been to flee when they fight, but it's happened so rarely in recent years that she's forgotten just how tough it is to be the one left behind with all the emotions splayed across the living room.

Yes, she knows: the work he does is vital. The situation in Syria has heated up. The emergency need for doctors is real. But surely there are others who could fill the need. Just this once—if not for her, then for Justin. Sam is right: Justin has dropped out, has moved to Minnesota, has joined this Turning the Tide group. He was vague when he told her what they do, only that they're working on something new that gets to the root of our oil addiction. But talking to him assuages her fears; he promised he'll go back to school. Think of it as a gap year, he said. She's actually a little proud of him, for so bravely aiming to be of use in the world. Like his father, she thinks, even though Dan refuses to see it.

She does the journaling her therapist had suggested years ago. Unsent letters: write down the anger, get it onto the page, then destroy it. She writes, tears, throws pieces in the firepit, burns them. She stands in the promising sunlight of spring and watches the pages turn from white to red to ash, watches them become small bits so light that some are carried aloft in the flame's updraft and rise beyond the thin tips of the birch's highest twigs into the blue sky. She pokes at the pile, leaving not a single word unburnt.

She walks the dogs. Long hikes, now that snow and ice are disappeared, to Wolverine Peak, to Rabbit Lake, where they all three dip in the frigid clear waters. She takes them to Kincaid, and they run on the beach, play fetch in the silty high-tide waters, then relax on the sand, Sophie rolling on her back, Elyse leaning against sunbleached driftwood, listening to small waves clutter to shore.

And every time she returns to the house, or awakens in the morning, she imagines what it would be like if Dan never came back. She looks at the furniture, the artwork, all the knickknacks he's brought from his travels. The old couch she used to sleep on when he was jet-lagged and waking in the middle of the night; the painting of a tree on sheets of music that she bought on their trip to Barcelona; the scowling masks he brought back from somewhere in Asia that she has never liked—she inventories it all, deciding what she would keep, what he would take, what she would give or throw away. It soothes her to focus on furnishings.

Mostly, though, she soon falls into the way her days unfold when Dan is on one of his extended trips. She is surprised at how quickly she makes the shift this time, and relieved. She lets dishes pile up in the sink. She takes evening walks with the dogs, eats cereal for dinner. She hosts a girlfriends' night, filling the house with friends.

It helps that she must prepare for the conference. She's showing some of her work and talking about her process, focusing on her time in Cape Vankarem. Jotting down notes, she thinks about Nicolaf. She had written him back, said she'd love to see him if they come through Anchorage on the way to the Arctic.

The day Elyse leaves is brilliant with sunshine. She sits in her window seat, nose pressed to the small pane, gazing at the beaver shape of Fire Island, with its halfdozen windmills slowly spinning on the broad tail end. She stares down at the arc of the Point McKenzie mudflats where she once saw hundreds of harbor seals as she and a friend flew in a Super Cub on their way to a river trip in the Neacola Mountains. Then the plane turns, over Knik Arm, over the Chugach Range, rocky spires still covered in snow and laced with glaciers and icefields. There's Lake George, a pocket of radiant blue surrounded by crevassed and undulating ice. And then the crystal blue fjords of Prince William Sound. A catch in her throat, tears in her eyes. Tears of sorrow that she's leaving, if only for a week. Of joy, that she's lucky enough to live in such a spectacularly beautiful place. And twice now of sorrow, that all this snow and ice, the glaciers and all they create, are leaving. This view, such vast swaths of the planet that appear entirely untouched by human development—even these are not immune.

She arrives in DC a day early, to adjust to the time zone. She sleeps in, then heads to the U.S. Botanic Garden. She hasn't been to DC in nearly fifteen years, but what she most wants to revisit is the glass conservatory, that ornate and fecund greenhouse. She has fine memories of her boys in the Central Tropics Room, leaning over to watch fish in the pond, staring up through towering tree ferns and imagining dinosaurs nibbling their leaves, Justin shrieking with delight when a songbird flitted over his head, lyrical song filling the room.

Now she stands with her memories, reveling in the abundant green filling the prismed sunlit space to the high glass ceiling. She lingers in the World Deserts Room, where she and Justin had sketched the clean patterns of succulents. But in the Orchids Room, looking deeply into one that clings to a thick limb at eye level, she's struck by an even older memory. The dark purple flower, with a white rim and yellow center, looks both like some exotic insect and like a face—a face gazing as quizzically back at her. She wishes she could remember what she'd learned in botany class about flower parts and pollination.

She does remember staring into another orchid at a friend's house when she was a small girl. The living room window ledge was lined with orchid plants, but only one was in bloom. That flower, also dark colored, was the first orchid she'd ever seen outside a flower shop. It was such an extravagant thing, the blossom, so surprising in the otherwise spare little house. Her friend had showed the orchid to her proudly, and Elyse knew, in the way children know, that this plant was as cherished as gold.

Elyse does not have a chance to remember why the orchid was so important, because her solitude is interrupted by a guided tour. A man trailing the guide asks whether any of the plants in the Rare and Endangered Room are at risk because of climate change.

The guide answers quickly and smoothly, as if she's been asked that before. "Yes, the plants' labels tell why they're at risk. And there's a brochure, at the front desk. We'll get to that, but for now, let's enjoy the orchids, and next the Mediterranean Room, where we'll catch the scent of lemons…"

The way the tour guide so quickly turns attention away from the man's question reminds Elyse of an experience when she was an artist-in-residence in Southeast Alaska, tagging along with Forest Service rangers giving talks aboard tour ships. She'd noticed the rangers didn't bring up climate change. However, at least one visitor at every talk would ask about retreating glaciers and acidifying oceans. Later she asked one ranger why he didn't just incorporate it into the talk, and he said he didn't want to dampen their vacation time with bad news.

Elyse wades upstream of the tour group and returns to the Medicinal Plant Room. She's saddened by how ubiquitous climate change has become. We can't be on alert mode all the time, a friend had said to her, our adrenals just can't handle it. Yet it is increasingly impossible to ignore.

The rally is not well attended. Held on the National Mall near the National Gallery of Art, it's set up for thousands, but only a few hundred show up. Jim is visibly disappointed, and at dinner with all the speakers, he blames the turnout on how the climate change conversation has moved away from mitigation and into adaptation—and just human adaptation.

"No one is talking about all the other species, habitats, wilderness—it's just about how humans are going to survive," he says.

"I know," says a petite older woman who looks like Georgia O'Keeffe. "I attended a global warming summit in Taos, and not a single speaker addressed the effects on the natural world. The organizers told me they didn't want to focus on science. Since when did the rest of the world get lumped in with science?"

"Yeah," says another woman, "humans, we're so narrow-minded. That's what will sink us."

"Yes," says WPO's Raleigh-based regional director, "we act as if the Earth is last when instead it's first." He shook his head, dreadlocks tumbling around his shoulders. "If we don't have a habitable home, then nothing else matters—not race relations, not poverty, not who uses which public bathrooms."

"I know!" sighs a young poet from Chicago. "I mean, friends, like, they're always saying, if I make it about nonhumans, people will think I don't care about people. Well," she shrugs, "seeing how awful we are to each other and our home planet, then, like Walt Whitman said, 'I think I could turn and live with animals.'"

Elyse is relieved to get back to her room that night; the poorly attended rally and the dinner talk have deflated her. What if Dan is right? What if she's undermining her artistic integrity, and for something that's not even going to make a difference? So easy, for him, with DWB. So easy to garner respect. Like the poet said, helping people is almost always met with praise. When her boys were in middle school, she'd publicly advocated for education funding and gotten nothing but praise for it. But environmental advocacy work seems to always be ignored or challenged. She sighs, overwhelmed: her paintings pale in comparison to the task at hand for life on Earth.

The dread sticks to her all night. She is standing in the Tropic Room, except all the huge green plants are withered and brown. A giant Venus flytrap dangles over her head, the entire plant dried brown except for the gaping red mouth of the trap. Dan appears, his face carved into red gashes that will never heal. Her boys are there, too, their arms removed, their heads hung low. Only she is whole and healthy and yet unable to heal them. She awakens from the nightmare with a pounding headache and the sheets wrapped around her like a cocoon. If her presentation hadn't been first that morning, she'd have stayed in bed.

But getting up and out helps the dread fade. The conference is filled with so many smart and talented artists, and scores of bright young college students, that she can't help but feel hope renewed. Her presentation goes well, and afterward a line of attendees forms to ask her questions. A tall slender woman waits off to the side, Mona Lisa smile on her face. Once the crowd dissipates, she approaches. "You look like you could use a good strong cup of coffee right about now," she says in a deep southern drawl.

"Oh, yes," says Elyse, "and that's just the start of it." Elyse feels a warmth hearing that southern accent; it always sounds like home, even though it's been decades since she lived in the South.

They wind through the conference crowd to a small coffee shop and tuck into a corner booth.

"So I have to ask," Elyse says, "where are you from? It sounds like the Carolinas, but sometimes I get it wrong and it's Texas."

"Oh, you've got it, girl, I'm from North Carolina. Born and bred. Born in Wilson, live now in Chapel Hill. Didn't migrate too far."

"Wonderful! I grew up in Elizabethtown, at least in my early years. My parents were northerners, though, from Pennsylvania, so I didn't get the accent down very well."

"Oh, well, that explains things. But I thought I saw that Carolina glimmer in your eyes. By the way, I'm Charlotte, Charlotte Muleya."

"Well, very nice to meet you. Are you also an artist?"

And though the conversation turns briefly to art, it also encompasses growing up in the South, and the changes the region is seeing with population growth, development, increased temperatures, rising seas. Elyse brims with questions about North Carolina. Charlotte, however, wants to hear more about Elyse's paintings.

"Oh, well, yes. The one was used by WPO in an ad campaign, you're right. That's where most people know my work. Not that it will get much attention beyond the environmental crowd."

"Oh really?" says Charlotte, drawing out the second word into three syllables, "No interest from galleries for showings yet?"

And so Elyse launches into the Alaska Museum saga—how she'd gotten to yes, only to be put on hold after the WPO ads came out. She's surprised that she's being so open about her failures to this relative stranger; maybe it's that southern accent, she thinks, that has softened her guard.

"I mean, I don't know for certain, it could be a coincidence, but I've just never heard of a show being put on indefinite hold. I think they're just trying to find an easy way of telling me the show's cancelled."

"Well, that's just not right. I can't imagine our museums doing that. But then, we're not an oil state. Even when we were in the throes of the tobacco empire, I can't imagine an artist being silenced. Even now, when we're just about as red as you can get. But maybe they were that way and I just didn't see it ..."

"North Carolina has a long proud tradition of the arts, maybe that helps. Alaska is, well, it's a young state, and you know, what my husband keeps saying," says Elyse, even as she shrinks at bringing him into the conversation, "is that corporate funding of the arts has changed. Now they want something for their donations, like their names on things. Like ads, really. It's no longer about being good corporate citizens; it's just about appearing to be."

"Yeah," says Charlotte, "I see that happen on campuses, too, a building named after the corporation that funded most of it." She cocks her head so that her beaded braids all tumble to one side, "Hey ... if I could get you a show at the Ackland, would you come? It's a long way from home, I know, but we could try to have it in winter, when you might want a little southern sunshine."

"Oh," says Elyse, her face brightening, "yes, wow, thank you! Of course I'd love to. I have fond memories of my parents taking me to the Ackland. And to visit North Carolina again. Maybe go to the Outer Banks."

"Well, you let me see what I can do. I can't make promises, but I do believe this is just the kind of thing they'd love. And," she says, glancing at a clock on the wall, "I've got to go. My session starts soon!"

Charlotte's presentation is an eye-opener for Elyse. Her art, wild and dramatic, is centered on the idea of the world without us, of a return to Eden only to find we're no longer welcome. Elyse recalls the dinner conversation: whether or not we realize it, the Earth is preeminent. Humans can wipe out species, take down forests and mountains, but can't stop the tides and the winds, can't change the flow of basic matter, can't still life's will to endure.

Buoyed by Charlotte's offer and presentation, she spends the rest of the conference listening to talks and wandering the exhibits. One exhibit room is filled with a history of activist artists, from Yoko Ono's anti-fracking exhibit in New York City, to *The Dinner Party* by Judy Chicago, to JR's *Inside Out Project* murals in Atlanta, to Banksy's provocative graffiti. Another exhibits the art of nature—that is, photographs and displays from the natural world. Some are up close, like the precise rows of black-and-white striped cups that are harlequin bug egg cases, and others are far off, like images of river deltas and storm clouds and mountain ranges from space. One section shows the repeating patterns in nature: from the brain's branching to a tree branching to a river delta: the same pattern, beautiful and complex.

All of it gives Elyse a sense of relief, a larger perspective in which to frame her own art, her own life. It's a perspective that had eluded her as she navigated her daily life in Anchorage: that the world is a big place, full of a diversity of people, full of an abundance of nonhuman life, full of beauty and mystery and sheer unstoppable energy.

**

Summertime has, for Astrid, usually been her chance to dive more deeply into her research. As the days heat up, humidity rises, and people move from one air-conditioned space to another, the entire campus moves at a slower pace, reflecting a time when slowing down was the only way to handle the heat. Sashaying, strolling. It's why, she's often thought, that slow southern drawl arose. And it's when Astrid spends more time in her lab, following the dark lines of fossils, tracing the past.

This summer, however, is different. With Sanders's assistants still busy with her collection, the usual summertime quiet is absent. And she is also otherwise occupied—with preparing for India and helping out with Tom Shank's project. She is so occupied that she isn't nearly as bothered this time by Strilay's imminent departure to Churchill.

Or perhaps not so imminent. Forces are conspiring to keep him in the States longer. He's not only continued his speaking engagements but has gotten roped in to the Solutions Project, which outlines how each state can transition to 100 percent clean renewables with existing technology. North Carolina's path is easy, with its solar capacity second only to California's and its offshore wind potential the largest on the Eastern Seaboard. Technologically easy, that is—the politics are another matter entirely, and that's where Strilay's role, as charismatic educator and speaker, is more difficult to replace.

Astrid, meanwhile, has been reading about the jungles of India, especially the epiphytes of the Western Ghats, near Lamont's project area, with its high species counts of orchids. Because orchids have been entirely absent from the fossil record, Astrid knows very little about them; orchids, for her, hold only memories of her mother's passion for them. But that changes when she reads about the recent discovery of a bee in amber with orchid pollen on its back. The extinct bee's pollen payload dates orchids as much older than previously thought.

They're still so very young, orchids, only 80 million years old compared to the 425 million years of lycopods and even the 270 million years of ginkgos, but this is an electrifying reminder of how much remains unknown. It's at the root of what excites Astrid about her work: of the millions of plants and animals thought to have gone extinct over the life of the planet, fossils have been found for only .02 percent of them.

There's so much we don't know. Her mother's voice slips in. How often did Astrid hear Macey say that? Astrid always dismissed it as her mother's very unscientific and mostly wishful thinking, but now she wonders if there was more to her mother than she'd realized.

There's so much we don't know. What if. She gasps. What if lycopods are older than the current fossil record shows? What if she finds in India not only the missing link to the timeline she's spent her career deciphering but also something older, an entirely new branch of the family? Her imagination leaps forward, even as her rational mind pulls back on the reins. Still, she knows that basic science is full of these moments—the blank slate, tabula rasa, rising as a reminder: *there's so much we don't know.*

She stares at the map of India on her wall, examines the marked afforestation project area, the places she wants to search for fossils. Lamont has assured her she'll have time and a driver to do field research, but he warns her that tree-planting is addictive, and she might find it hard to tear herself away. Hardly. He doesn't know how dedicated she is to her decades of research and how close she is to an answer. Work like hers takes patience and tenacity. The tenacity of a ginkgo tree surviving a nuclear blast. The patience of a seed, like the gametophyte of a lycopod taking up to fifteen years to mature, like lodgepole pine cones lying dormant for decades awaiting fire's release.

A few weeks before Strilay leaves for Churchill, Astrid heads to the coast. She's agreed to help Tom Shank once more; she's curious, too, to see how relocation efforts are going. Shank has purchased two properties just inland of the refuge and is working with a hydrologist and an engineer to create the bog-like conditions the plants need. He now has a very able crew of graduate students, and even an undergraduate botany class. Astrid is there primarily for advice and supervision, but she cannot keep from getting her hands in the soil.

Digging up wild plants is nothing like digging up garden plants. In the wild, the roots have grown much more entangled over time, and available space is usually completely used up. So it's difficult to discern where one plant's roots leave off and another's begins. For many sections, Shank has students removing entire blocks of plants, much like a chunk of sod. But where the infrequent lycopod or a few other rare plants are found, he asks Astrid to step in.

On her second afternoon, as she kneels again to gently uproot one of the rare lycopods, she recalls with crystal clarity kneeling in her mother's garden to dig up sweet potatoes. The plants' vines with their heart-shaped leaves tumbled over the dark soil so abundantly that she hated to dig them up; but the first frost had come, and the leaves were already wilting. So she put the small spade into the soil and dug. And the bundle of orange tubers arose, soil falling away like rainwater. There were no other plant roots entangling, pulling, resisting. So very different from the web of connecting roots in this bog, where it is nearly impossible, even with her trained eye and careful hand, to discern where one plant leaves off and another begins. They're all one root web, one community, one organism.

She works slowly, carefully, trying to keep the lycopod as intact as possible while harming as few of their neighbors as possible. She hears her name called, then looks up to see Shank striding across the fields. He has just returned from a donor meeting held on the coast at a resort conference center. He still carries, in his hurried gait and quick speech, the frenetic energy of the boardroom.

"I'll tell you," he says to Astrid, shaking his head, "every time I go to the Outer Banks now, I just get so sad. I just can't stand how those shores have become lined with row after row of cookie-cutter summer mansions, all of them teetering on a sandbar."

"Yes," says Astrid, straightening up and brushing dark loam from her knees. "If only we'd listened to Professor Pilkey back in the '80s."

"Pilkey, yes, took a class from him."

"Remember his book, *The Beaches Are Moving*? It made quite a stir. Almost cost him tenure, if I recall."

"Well, of course he's right. It's just a matter of time before the sand those houses stand on shifts away from underneath them. Pretty soon, I'll reckon, with rising seas and bigger storms. It's gonna be a hard row to hoe for these little coastal communities," he says, sighing. "Sometimes I wonder what this coastline might look like if there'd never been any houses or roads or bridges trying to contain it."

"Yes," says Astrid. "Who knows what seas and sands would have created?"

"Yep," he says, then pauses and looks at the lycopod in Astrid's hand. "Nice job preserving those roots. I sure hope we're doing the right thing."

"Well," she says, turning the plant in her hand, "I do keep thinking about the interconnections between these plants and the soil—all that we can't re-create."

"I know," Shank says, his voice softening, "but it's the best we can think of to do right now. We humans are always making big decisions on incomplete information; we just don't like to admit it."

They stand in silence a moment, looking out over the field, as a light rain arrives like a blessing after the heat of the day. Having been so immersed in the lives of plants, she can almost hear the plants give a sigh of relief. Through the soft patter of raindrops, they hear a clinking sound as three students on the far end gather their tools.

"We'll see you at dinner, then?" says Shank. "I've got to check on those undergrads."

"Sure, see you then."

Shank and the students disappear down the forest trail, the rain squall passes through, and late-afternoon sun sets the stunted forest at the field's edges glistening. Astrid pats the neighboring plants back into the damp ground, then scoops the lycopod into a pot. This plant on its way inland. Strilay on his way to Churchill. She on her way to India. All running off in different directions, like baby rabbits scattering to the four directions when their burrow is disturbed. All she ever wanted to do was to stay rooted in one place, but climate change is making that impossible. Even for this little plant. She looks down at the potted plant she holds in her hands and frowns. Something feels off. Something is missing. The sun glints off her silver wedding ring, and then she sees it: her engagement ring. The opal is gone.

She drops to her knees and sifts through the dark soil. After just a few seconds, she finds it: oval, milky white, threaded with glimmers of blue and green and orange. She holds it up and sighs. Slips it into her shirt pocket, picks up the plants, and trudges off toward the trail. She's been wearing that ring for twenty-eight years, and that stone has never once slipped out. Her thoughts jump from Gareth to Strilay and back again. A sudden chill makes her entire body shudder. It crosses her mind that this is a premonition, the kind her grandmaw used to warn her about, but she shrugs it off quickly: it's just wet clothes from the rain, and perhaps a passing sea breeze.

Chapter 17

On her return flight, Elyse tears up again at the many-fingered Naked Island, long and narrow Harriman Fjord with its glaciers pouring from the Chugach Icefield, the sunlight glinting off snowy peaks spreading in every direction. Her tears are once more a mixture of joy and grief but now with a surge of purpose.

Mornings in her studio, she covers canvasses and sketch pads, working whole days with only walks with the dogs as a break. Even when she hears that Nicolaf will be in Anchorage for a few days in October, even when she hears that Dan will be home around the same time, she does not lose her rhythm. And when she gets the invitation from the Ackland for a show in December, she takes a celebratory hike up Falls Creek, spends the late afternoon dipping in the alpine lake, sharing her lunch with the dogs, and sketching: the ridgelines dotted with Dall sheep; the concentric ripples of the clearwater lake, bubbles rising from the muddy bottom.

She is drawing and painting water—creeks and ponds, rivers and puddles, and the sea. Some are views from just below the surface. She's fascinated by all that's unseen, all that changes with perspective; she's enthralled by the persistent power of water to slowly and imperceptibly alter the landscape. She thinks of her readings in Buddhism—about flowing like water down a stream, and when you come to an obstacle, flow around it, and with time the sharp edges will soften, change, disappear.

In late August she starts in on a painting, working on it into the night even as the days shorten and the stars return, a crescent moon low in the night sky. Her vision of the new painting is so strong that she's impatient with the time it takes one layer to dry before she can paint the next.

She takes the dogs to Kincaid beach. On the sandy bluff, a bald eagle perches on a lone cottonwood, watching the dogs play in surf. Winds shake the leaves of the cottonwood, their rustling melding with the surf's clattering pebbles. The Alaska Range shimmers bright white and palest blue, and a raft of dunlins lifts from the water, a cloud passing in undulating formations. Her thoughts drift—to her painting, to Nicolaf's visit, to Dan's return, to her Ackland show, and to the conference. As each thought arises, it seems to bounce in like a wave and then fan out and be subsumed by the next thought and the next.

By early October she has finished the painting. She loves that feeling of knowing it's done. It's not that it appears perfect to her, but that if she were to brush another stroke, it would detract from what is there. So when she hears from Dan that he'll be home in two weeks, and then from Nicolaf that he's in Anchorage for the next week, she is not surprised by her sense of calm. She makes plans to take a walk with Nicolaf along the coastal trail the day after his talk at the Alaska Federation of Natives annual convention.

The day is blustery, what she used to call a Winnie-the-Pooh day when her boys were young. Wet and windy, even more so along the coast. They meet at Elderberry Park, just down the street from his hotel. It's a joy to see his face again, his compact solid form. But here among spruce and birches, he seems different.

They hug briefly and begin to walk. All but the alder leaves have fallen, and those are a dark brown, dry and dangling. A gust tears them from their branches, sending them skittering down the wet paved trail. The tide is low, exposing the wave-ruffled mudflats. Beyond the sinuous curves of small rivulets flowing to sea is the water, silty gray and whitecapped. The windmills on Fire Island, looking like a giant's flower garden, turn steadily.

"It is so good to see you," says Nicolaf, the words scattered to the winds behind them.

"Yes, and you," she says. "And what do you think of our little village?"

He laughs, and for a moment she's back on the Siberian tundra with him, in that vast rolling sea of land. But just for a moment. That's it, she realizes: he seems smaller here, quieter, less sure of himself.

"It is different," he finally says. "All this forest and building mixed together. Those mountains crowding in close."

"Yes, not what you're used to."

They fall into a familiar silence, with only the sounds of their footsteps and the wind in branches. At a bench along Fish Creek, they sit, gazing out to the mudflats, across the inlet.

"I am hoping to see beluga whales," he says. "I hear they are here."

"Yes, they are, but very few of them now. Their numbers have plummeted, from a combination of human-created threats. You know, pollution, fisheries, habitat loss, oil and gas—see all those rigs out there? I rarely see belugas anymore, but usually in springtime, when the hooligan are running along Turnagain Arm."

"Hooligan?"

"Fish," she says. "Small oily fish, like sardines."

"Fish, yes, fish."

They talk for a while longer, about belugas and harbor seals, about polar bears and walrus, and it feels good to her, talking with someone who speaks about the animals they live around the way most people talk about neighbors or friends. To not have the focus be solely on humans. It feels more to scale, more balanced.

But she does not feel what she had feared: any desire for him as a man. She feels only a friendship, a shared experience and shared view of the world. One that is, for her, rare. One she cherishes. But that is all. It must be all he feels, too, for he does not reach for her hand, does not say or make any movements to indicate otherwise. Perhaps what she desired was who she is reflected in someone so clearly and solidly himself, making her reflection also more clear and true. She tells him about her new painting, about the whole series. She shows him some photos of them.

"I hope they begin to show some of what is at stake," she says. "Some of what I promised you during my residency."

He is quiet as he looks at them, then looks at her with widened eyes, clear and unwavering. A long pause. She checks the impulse to speak.

"They are like dreams," he says, slowly, his voice deepening. "Like my dreams. How can this be?" Another pause. He starts again, his voice changed, brighter, warmer. "I am grateful, my people will be grateful, and the bears and walrus, all of us. This is great gift."

She looks at him carefully. "Well," she says, "I am grateful to you, and your village, and the bears and walrus and tundra, for teaching me so much more than I can ever express in my paintings. But I am so very happy and relieved that you like them."

"Like them? Oh, you misunderstand. But there are no words to explain what I am feeling."

She takes a sharp breath in, again checking her need to speak. She lets his words, her thoughts, settle. They look at each other as another gust pulls alder leaves free, and the whitecaps clatter against the rocks like small drumbeats. It is a long gaze, a long-held gaze, and then a smile, and in silence they both rise to their feet and turn back the way they came.

The next weekend she attends his talk at the Alaska Indigenous Center about how his village protects the walrus haulout, and stays afterward for the reception.

"Wonderful talk," she says. "Everyone loved your story about throwing snowballs into polar bear dens. Here everyone just carries big guns."

"Thank you," he says, softly. "I was nervous. Easier for me to talk when I am on the ice."

"More comfortable, yes, but you did really well."

"I am impressed with how American Indigenous Peoples speak out so freely with their, their concerns. But I don't understand some of things they believe. That sea ice loss is not problem? That polar bears can live on land easy as on ice? This surprise me."

"Yes, me, too, but they are, well, they think their communities benefit from oil extraction, and, too, they don't want anyone telling them they can't hunt polar bears anymore."

"Yes, but true, some of us want to hunt them again too. That I understand. Just not, not seeing how using so much oil is bad for whole planet."

"You want to hunt polar bears?"

"Yes, we would like. We think we should have right to, yes."

"Oh," says Elyse, standing very still. She hasn't put that together until now: It's illegal for Siberian Indigenous Peoples to hunt polar bears; they don't have subsistence rights like Alaska Indigenous Peoples do. So, how much of the Umka Patrol is based on the notion that they can't just use guns and kill them? Why didn't she think of that before? Has she been doing what Dan has accused her of, romanticizing Indigenous cultures? She searches Nicolaf's face to see what she may not have seen there before.

Fortunately, before she can find words, the mayor of Wainwright comes up to Nicolaf, shakes his hand, and Elyse makes her goodbyes, saying she's got to get to the airport to pick up her husband.

Dan arrives jet-lagged and sick with a cold. It's a week before he's well and back on Alaska time enough for them to be awake and alert at the same time. She doesn't push any conversations with him, doesn't bring up their last conversation and the state of their marriage. They move as if in separate worlds through their shared house, exchanging pleasantries and meals, sharing news of each other's lives. He is pleased at her Ackland invitation, but he doesn't ask to come with her and she doesn't invite him. Even their bodies are out of step: each tries, and fails, to initiate lovemaking. It's not that there's a coolness between them but more of a détente. At times she thinks she should wonder what he is thinking, maybe force a conversation, but it's just the echoes of an old habit.

**

Astrid is leaving for India in less than a month and is reeling with all she needs to do. Other than Canada, she's never left the country before. And everyone keeps telling her that India is more different from the U.S. than any other country they've visited.

"Oh," says Ernesto over dinner one night, "it's just magnificent! A sensory feast! But, Astrid, you're going to have to leave all your expectations in your luggage. Don't expect, well, don't expect to have the kind of conveniences we take for granted here."

"Don't worry," she replies, "Lamont assured me I won't be expected to live like the locals. He's got me set up in a small house nearby, with a dedicated driver. It will all be very VIP."

"Yes," Joel nods. "Still. Stay flexible. Things may seem absolutely out of control, but somehow, and how I do not know, they work out. Often in ways that end up better."

"Well," says Astrid, deciding it's best to not to know the story behind that statement, "if I don't like it, I can just return early."

Though overwhelmed with all that needs doing, she still lets Charlotte talk her into going to an exhibit opening at the Ackland. It's by an Alaskan artist who, says Charlotte, grew up in North Carolina, in Elizabethtown.

"Who knows, maybe you'll have some old school friends in common," coaxes Charlotte.

"It's not high on my agenda to play Classmates right now," says Astrid, "but for you, I'll come."

So they all go, Gareth and Charlotte and Astrid. It's a cold December evening, colder than normal. As they walk to the Ackland from Gareth and Astrid's house, their voices are muffled by hats and scarves.

"Too bad Strilay isn't around," says Charlotte. "He'd appreciate these paintings."

"Well, he's not much one for art, you know," says Astrid, "except Appalachian music. He's a fiend for that."

"Well, just you wait, honey. You'll see. I'll bet he'd be pleased as punch with these paintings."

At the door stands a woman with thin blondish hair, a thin frame, long black dress, smiling anxiously. Charlotte walks up to her, gives her a hug, and says, "Gareth, Astrid, meet Elyse Sowka. Elyse, meet Astrid Baldwin, professor of paleobotany, and Gareth Moore, professor of culinary arts. Astrid here grew up in eastern North Carolina too."

Astrid has stopped in the doorway, one foot in and one foot out. She stares at this woman, this Elyse, having known who she was even before Charlotte spoke her name.

"So pleased to meet you," Elyse is saying, holding out her hand. "Thanks for coming to the show. I was wondering, what with this cold, whether many people would show up. I didn't mean to bring Alaska's weather with me too!"

Astrid stands still. As Gareth exchanges pleasantries, Elyse's eyes keep darting back to Astrid, recognition slowly spreading across her face.

"Astrid," she says, "Astrid. I know you. At least, I did. You're—we were childhood friends. I helped you plant your mother's sweet potatoes one time. I was just remembering that, when I was in DC this summer. It *is* you, isn't it? Yes. Wow. This is amazing. All these years, how long has it been? Forty years? Wow. I can't believe I can recognize you. Astrid."

Astrid doesn't speak; she just listens to Elyse's growing excitement. Astrid's mix of emotions is so strong that she doesn't trust what she might say. *Play nice*, she hears her mother say.

"Oh, yes, I think you're right. We did know each other as children. I think we even went to the same preschool together, the only two kids that didn't go to church, as I recall."

"Yes! That's right! And we, well, you know, my parents, they moved us to Oregon, they still live there, just on a houseboat now, with a cat, very simple, easy life for them. And your parents? Siblings, too, if I remember right?"

It's all too much for Astrid, she doesn't want to know this much, share this much. "Oh, you know, so much time has gone by, hasn't it?" she replies, trying to keep her voice light. "Well, I am happy for you, happy that you're doing so well as an artist. Looking forward to seeing this work that Charlotte has been raving about."

"Yes," says Elyse, stepping back. "Of course. Sorry for my rambling.

Just my nerves. This show is my first outside Alaska. Please, come in. But I'd love to find time later to catch up some more, Astrid. I really would."

"Okay," says Astrid, "let's do. But we'll let you get back to greeting your admirers."

As Astrid walks away, she feels a tug on her sleeve.

"What was that?" says Charlotte. "You know her? You look like you've seen Blackbeard's ghost, for chrissakes."

"Oh, it's nothing. Just surprising to see her, and I'm just on edge in my preparations for India."

"Oka-ay," says Charlotte, unconvinced. "Thanks for making that clear as mud."

Fortunately for Astrid, their attention is quickly drawn to the paintings, which are bright and colorful, energetic, and very large. Only one painting to a wall. A total of eight, each a seeming world unto itself, and yet, a progression. Astrid feels as if her eyes are adjusting to a new kind of light. The walrus, the flamingo feathers, mammoth tusk—each such a surprising contrast of light and dark, images, texture. And then she gets to the polar bear image.

She's seen it, of course, seen the ad, anyhow. Charlotte showed it to her. But to see it in person. She feels as if she's entered her kudzu kingdom again, suddenly thrust back into her childhood. She knows it must also be because of seeing Elyse, that unearthing memory, but that's who painted this image, so the memory must be strong in Elyse too. And the bear, the small polar bear, who seems to retain some sense of strength and power, that fearlessness of a top predator, even as he exudes a vulnerability. Astrid can hardly stand to keep looking and yet cannot seem to look away.

"Amazing, isn't it?" says Charlotte, touching her elbow. "The whole series, really powerful. Have you seen the last one yet?"

Astrid hasn't. The room swims as she walks away from the painting and toward the final installment. It is pale in comparison, lacking the color and texture, the raw energy of the others, very smooth and subdued and quiet. It's a broad sand beach, silky salt-and-pepper sand, mostly the wan shades of beige and pale pinks. It's expansive, one wave pouring into the picture and fanning out across the image, the foam just fringing the bottom quadrant of the painting. Awash. The painting is awash. As if cleansing all that the other paintings unleashed.

And at first Astrid can't even see her, the naked form of a woman on the far left edge. Not the modest Venus with her flowing hair and well-placed hands, but a thin, older woman, hands hanging limp on either side of her long torso, breasts sagging with middle age. She kneels on one knee, and one hand is not entirely limp—it seems, at second look, just about to be raised, in prayer or in action, some action just about to begin, or at least the thought of action.

And the sand—it isn't just sand. Beneath sand and wave are the pale outlines of images from the previous paintings—walrus, mammoth tusk, flamingos, skyscrapers, all just barely visible, fading, washed, tumbling to the sand they're becoming. The look on the woman's face is so familiar. A little surprised, a little lost, but also a little—determined. A combination of vulnerability and fearlessness just like, yes, that's it, Astrid realizes, an electric current running through her body, that's why it's familiar—just like the expression on the polar bear's face.

Chapter 18

Elyse absentmindedly smiles, shakes hands, makes small talk with a series of strangers who effuse appreciation for her paintings. Whenever possible, she locates Astrid and watches her look at the paintings. She notices how long Astrid stands before the kudzu painting, notices Charlotte steering her away like a mother shepherding a child. She notices Astrid stepping forward, looking closely at the last painting, then stepping back, sitting down. Astrid moves just as she did as a child: straight back, smooth motions, determined stride. She hardly smiles, just as Elyse remembers.

Elyse remembers so much now. It has all come flooding back at the sight of this woman she has not seen for decades—especially the way in which their friendship ended. It was the first time in her life Elyse had been rejected. And Astrid seems so cool to her that she feels certain nothing has changed: Elyse is still persona non grata.

But to everyone else in this crowded gallery, she is the evening's star. In between furtive glances at Astrid and absentminded conversations with strangers, she notices that the young woman who works at the museum is putting first one, then another, red dot on some of the paintings. She is selling her work.

At some point she notices Astrid has left; Charlotte remains, having made plans to take Elyse to the reception at the vice chancellor's house afterward. With Astrid gone, Elyse relaxes. She turns toward an elderly woman asking about Alaska's winters.

"I've heard it's so dark, and colorless," she says, thin fingers woven together in a loose prayer position. "Is that why you use such bright colors in your paintings?"

"Oh, interesting observation," she says. "I haven't thought of that. You may be right."

The woman beams, nods her head.

Elyse watches the young assistant put a red dot on another painting. She hadn't expected to sell anything, hadn't thought through the process of breaking up the series. It's never bothered her before to sell a painting; it's so rare that usually she just feels as if she's won the lottery. But these are so dependent on each other for meaning that she feels queasy thinking of letting any of them go.

At the vice chancellor's house, Elyse perches on a chair and answers questions about life in Alaska. "No," she says, "there aren't many North Carolinians in Alaska. Yes, winters are long and dark. The snow helps; makes it lighter, and makes for great skiing. Of course," she says, brow furrowing, "we haven't gotten much snow the last few winters. I'm afraid it's a sign of how things will be. Rain and ice instead of snow."

Seeing Elyse's troubled expression, Charlotte sits beside her. "So, y'know, there's something I've been dying to ask you," she says, her voice low so that no one else will hear. "Tell me, how well did you know our Astrid?"

"We were friends when we were very young," says Elyse, "but then my family moved."

"Is that all? Sure sounds to me like there's some backstory."

"Yes," says Gareth, coming up behind Charlotte, "not in all our years together has Astrid ever mentioned you. But she looked like she'd seen a ghost when she saw you."

"Yeah, I don't know," says Elyse, her gaze flickering, "Maybe I remind her of something. Seems I recall her childhood being kind of crazy."

"True," says Gareth. "Her dad was a hard-ass. Then he left the family on shaky ground. Maybe that's all it was. Well, I'm sure she'll want to catch up with you while you're here."

"Yes, I'm sure," says Elyse, not at all sure.

That night, in her hotel room, the noise of the wall heater like an engine roar, Elyse lies in bed wide awake. It wasn't her place to tell Charlotte and Gareth what she now remembers, in a sudden flash flood that unearths memories she'd long ago buried.

They were ten, nearly through fifth grade. Astrid had given Elyse some homemade coupons for Christmas. One was for a sleepover, which Elyse redeemed over Christmas break. Another, the one she was most excited about, was to help Astrid's family plant sweet potatoes that spring. Elyse had helped them harvest sweet potatoes the prior fall and was unconvinced that all those golden tubers really did come from just a small green stem and a few leaves. Having been an admiring friend of Astrid's long enough to adopt her scientific approach to life, Elyse declared that she needed proof. And so, one of the coupons was an invitation to have her own small plot of sweet potatoes, a research test plot, the coupon called it. Elyse would get to plant her own slips, care for them, and harvest them in the fall.

This thrilled Elyse no end. Not only because of the sweet potatoes but also because it meant lots of time at Astrid's house. Elyse loved the chaos of the household, the pesky younger siblings always looking for ways to turn even the most mundane of activities, like eating a bowl of cereal, into some new turbulence. Astrid's mother was nothing like Elyse's, with her quick tongue and frequent laughter, except that both mothers liked sweet sun tea with lots of lemon, so much lemon it made Elyse's mouth pucker just thinking about it. And the father was a completely new creature to Elyse, one whose unpredictability was almost scary. Her own father was steady, serious, calm. Loving, yes, but not demonstrative and always trying to tone down his daughter. At Astrid's, Elyse felt like she was the calm one—besides, of course, Astrid, who always tried to contain or retreat from drama.

It was early March, just when the crocuses started blooming, that Astrid stopped speaking to Elyse. It was in the lunchroom. Elyse joined her friend as always, but when she offered to share her Rice Krispies square, Astrid said nothing. Didn't look at her. Looked right through her.

Elyse tugged on her sleeve, "Hey, what's going on? This a new game?"

Nothing. No response, no eye contact.

"Hey!" said Elyse, louder, leaning forward and sticking her face in Astrid's. "What's going on? You sick or something?"

No response. Not from Astrid. The other kids around them all turned and looked at her, wide-eyed.

"Astrid! What's going on? Why won't you talk to me?" Elyse stood and yelled into Astrid's face.

Nothing. Except Astrid turned to another girl and offered a piece of her pecan pie. Except all the other kids were now watching intently, some of them laughing. Except the lunchroom monitor came over and told Elyse to quiet down, sit down.

Elyse, red-faced and shaking inside, got up, threw out what remained of her lunch, and left. She tried again, several times over several days, more quietly and discreetly in case her outburst in the lunchroom was the cause of Astrid clamming up. In the bathroom when no one else was there. At the water fountain during recess. Maybe Astrid wanted a friend more like her, calm and serious and smart. So Elyse tried to be that. Quiet. Calm. Serious. She asked, she begged Astrid to tell her what was wrong. She promised anything. But nothing worked.

And then Elyse awoke with a stomach ache. It was so bad she stayed home from school—for nearly two weeks, until her mother figured out it wasn't a physical problem. She took her daughter to a therapist, driving all the way to Rocky Mount to find one who treated children. Elyse told the therapist everything about the friendship, spilled it all in a river of tears, and her stomach pains magically ceased.

That's all Elyse remembers. She must have returned to school, must have finished out the year. She knows she never got to harvest her test plot, never went to Astrid's house again. She knows her family spent another year in Elizabethtown before moving to Portland, but that's as far as memory takes her. She lies in bed, air from the wall heater swirling over her, her body suddenly cold, her breath shallow.

"I guess I'll never know," she says aloud. "Sure as hell doesn't matter now. Just another broken promise."

She sits up, punches her pillow a few times to fluff it, and curls up tight under the blankets.

**

Astrid has caved to repeated pleas from both Charlotte and Gareth to attend a dinner party on Elyse's last night in Chapel Hill. It's at Charlotte's house, just a dozen or so friends. She has not, however, caved to their repeated questions about Elyse and her childhood; instead, she's simply answered, with a vague wave of her hand, "I really hardly remember her."

Astrid is irritated with herself for her strong reaction at seeing Elyse again. She's not a child; she is, after all, a fifty-three-year-old woman. She should be more resilient than this. And yet, she is uneasy, in part because she was so moved by the show. She's not usually one for abstract art, but there was something compelling about Elyse's paintings. She's guessing it's just the connections with childhood and with Strilay—the kudzu, the polar bear.

Strilay has been gone three months. She had hoped he'd return after the bears left for winter, but he's written that some bears are sticking around, and he's helping Joe with some grant proposals for new storage containers. He's stepped back from the Solutions Project, and has been fending off requests for speaking engagements, though he's done a few in Canada. He's started to add "eh" to some of his statements and has joked to Astrid that he might change his citizenship. But one thing is clear: he won't be back before she leaves for India.

She's leaving in two weeks. She can scarcely recall now why she decided to do this, but she also can't bring herself to back out. "Just pre-trip jitters," Gareth tells her. "You'll be fine once you're on the plane." Of course he's right, but knowing it and feeling it are two entirely different things. She has wished more than once for a Carolina Coffee Shop lunch with Strilay, complete with one of his rallying speeches to ignite her resolve.

Instead, one sunny afternoon, she meets Charlotte for coffee. Charlotte has just come from another visit to the Ackland. "I just can't get enough of that show," she says, sitting down beside Astrid with a contented sigh. "It's one of the best I've seen in ages. And the crowds there are, well, it's fantastic how popular it is. Gives me hope for the world."

"Hope? How so?"

"Well, y'know, that it's so clearly about climate change, and people aren't shying away but instead gravitating to it. I mean, it's a great example of how art can influence people. Did you see the review in the *News and Observer*? An exciting blend of art and science, they called it. Sublime advocacy for the Earth."

"Science, really? But it's just art. I mean," says Astrid, seeing the look on Charlotte's face, "I guess I missed the scientific aspect."

"Well, honey, no, there were no formulas, no hypotheses, but there was, you can't deny it, an understanding of species extinction, habitat changes . . . didn't you just love how paleontology came into the story? The mastodon, and then the high rises, overshadowing it, but headed for the same fate?"

"Oh, my, perhaps I'd better go see it again, then," says Astrid. "I guess you're right, of course you're right. You know I'm not much of an art critic."

Astrid remembers Charlotte's show at The Last Taco, that idea of the return to Eden. It has haunted Astrid, even crept into some of her thinking about her research. And deepened her admiration for her friend's mind.

"So you will come, then, right, shug?" Charlotte is saying.

"Come?"

"To my dinner party. For Elyse. Tomorrow night."

"Yes, yes, we'll be there," she replies, her thoughts now on Elyse's final painting, the expression on the woman's face.

Charlotte lives in a small stone house just down the hill from campus. "Right in that curve, just past the Limited Sight Visibility sign," she always tells people. "So come prepared to be blinded by what you see here!" Her house sits behind an old stone building that was once a gas station, so there's plenty of parking for parties.

Astrid and Gareth arrive slightly late, unusual for Astrid but, this time, on purpose. She doesn't want to walk into the house and find just Charlotte and Elyse there. Dinner is casual buffet-style, people sitting in the living room and out on the back porch, easy enough for her to avoid alone time with Elyse. Besides, almost everyone there wants to talk to her old childhood friend. Elyse's show has made an impression on the artist community in Chapel Hill. There's even artists from Durham and Raleigh, including an art professor from Duke.

The flaw in her avoidance plan is, however, Gareth. He falls into his usual role as co-host, pouring wine, collecting empty plates, and spontaneously whipping up an excellent sauce for the cheesecake. Astrid is engaged in conversation with the Ackland director about a showing of Coker's herbarium of native flora that will highlight its biodiversity, include some plant fossils, and describe what's known about changes to local flora over time. The director has asked Astrid to be the project's scientific advisor. So she doesn't notice as the other guests reluctantly make their goodbyes. She doesn't notice the house emptying until the director excuses himself, and she finds herself alone with Elyse. Charlotte and Gareth are in the kitchen, cleaning up.

"Well," says Astrid, a slight smile on her lips, "by all accounts, your show was a smashing success. You must be pleased."

"Oh, yes, and surprised. I'm just so thankful to Charlotte for suggesting it."

"Yes, she's very generous."

There's an awkward silence, during which Gareth enters the room, stops, and turns back to the kitchen.

"Anything I can do to help?" Elyse calls after him, beginning to stand.

His head appears in the doorway. "Oh, no, we've got it covered. Y'all just sit and relax."

Elyse sits back on the couch and looks around the room, twirling one strand of hair. Astrid sits stiffly in a chair, her gaze on one of Charlotte's paintings.

"So," says Elyse, "I leave in the morning, first thing."

"Oh, I see," says Astrid.

"So we won't be getting together, you and I."

"No, I suppose not."

"Well, then," says Elyse, taking a deep sigh, "I'll just plow ahead. After I saw you at the museum, I remembered that, when we were about ten, you stopped talking to me. But I never did know why. So I'm just . . . could you tell me why? Or," she continued quickly, feeling suddenly light-headed, "maybe you don't remember, maybe I'm just sounding very silly."

"Oh, well, I . . . yes, childhood, such a long time ago . . . and, you don't recall? That your father fired mine? That after that, Daddy couldn't find another job, and, well, I suppose you wouldn't know this, because y'all moved away soon after, but he never did get back on his feet, as far as we know. He disappeared for good when I was thirteen."

It all comes out in a surprising rush. Astrid had no intention of speaking of any of this again, least of all to Elyse, but she is so taken aback by Elyse claiming not to know what happened that she feels again the full headwinds of betrayal and loss.

"Oh. I had no idea," says Elyse, blushing, voice dropping. "None. My dad never said a thing."

Astrid sits still except for her hands, pressing her nails one by one. Elyse stumbles on, light-headedness turning to queasiness. "I just can't, oh, I am so sorry. I can't believe my dad would do that. I never heard him say an unkind word about your father. Not once. I remember asking him why he was sad, and him telling me it was because his boss asked him to lay something off . . . oh. Layoff."

Elyse glances at Astrid, just once, and then looks down at her own hands, trying to keep them still in her lap, trying to calm the churning inside.

"Well, you know," says Astrid, her voice now calmer, more even, "they called it a layoff, but Daddy was sure yours had it in for him."

"Oh, I . . . well, thank you for telling me, I get it now, why you were mad at me." Her gaze flutters up again to Astrid. "Of course you had to choose your dad over me."

"I thought you knew. I thought you could have, oh, I don't know." Astrid waves her hand, trying to sound nonchalant. "What did I expect of a ten-year-old girl? It was a long time ago. Water under the bridge."

"Yes, it was, but I'm so sad it happened. To your dad, your family, I really liked your family. And to you. So sorry," she says, her voice trailing off as if she is under water.

Just then Gareth walks in. "You two need any more wine?"

"Oh, no," says Elyse, sitting up straighter with a quick forced smile, "I'm all done. I'd better stumble back up the hill to the Carolina Inn."

"We'll give you a ride," says Gareth.

As they drop her off in the parking lot, she turns to Astrid, gives her a long look, a searching look, and then says, "It's been great to see you. And good luck in India. I knew you'd do something big and important with your life."

For the next two weeks, as Astrid packs for India, she's also unpacking childhood memories. She remembers she and Elyse hard at play in the kudzu patch and her mother calling them "two peas in a pod." It was a phrase that stuck, became Macey's name for them both. Macey had liked Elyse, had told Astrid that she was good for her, because Astrid needed someone to make her laugh.

Astrid pulls the small tan roller bag down from the shelf. She wants to travel light, bring few clothes and save most of the space for her fieldwork tools. She hears her father right after he got laid off, yelling after Astrid as she retreated to her room: "Dump her before she dumps you, like her Daddy did me. She's rich, she doesn't know what it's like for folks like us. She doesn't belong here. You'll see, she'll leave without a backward glance."

He was right, Elyse did leave. But then, so did he. Without saying goodbye, without explanation, without ever coming back even just once to check in on her.

She stares at two shirts. What if Elyse's father was simply following orders to lay people off? What if it wasn't personal? Lord knows her father was jealous of those who had it better than he, and his boss, Elyse's college-educated father, would fall into that category.

Lord knows her father was so certain of his rightness that he could have simply decided it was a personal vendetta. Blame is easier than accountability; Astrid had certainly seen that in students, in colleagues, as chair of the department.

She chooses the green shirt, folds and lays it on the pile. Green like Elyse's kudzu painting, all those wild greens on the canvas. Two peas in a pod. Maybe it wasn't personal at all. Maybe Astrid decided to blame Elyse because that was easier than navigating the difficulties of preteen years with an angry father and a friend whose privileged life had begun to rub a raw spot between them.

She rubs her temples, sits on the bed. People. She'll be glad to get in the field, planting trees or digging up fossils, anything other than stumbling around in the wilds of human relationships.

Section 4

Chapter 19

Astrid hates India. From her flight's approach into Mumbai, where she saw the sea of cardboard and tin shacks of the slums, to the dusty roadside café where she shared her rice with a dozen pushy flies, she remains overwhelmed and saddened by India's chaos and crowds. So much suffering and waste, the sidewalks littered with trash so high in places that it looks as if it's been plowed the way she saw snow plowed in Churchill. So many poor people and disfigured street dogs and burdened oxen and clamoring need. Even the colors overwhelm her, clothing and buildings, such gaudiness in the midst of such despair and chaos.

At the Mumbai airport, she is met by Lamont, his pale hands waving crazily like some lost white doves above a sea of bright saris. He herds her through the madding crowds to where her luggage should appear—and though she is convinced it never will, not given the haphazard manner in which everything is done at this airport, still, it does, and Lamont carries it in one hand as his other reaches for hers.

"Let's get out of here," he says, wading through the streaming masses like a fish flailing upstream.

Outside isn't much better. Humid heat and strong odors hit her in the face like a slap. The air is smoky and putrid, a smell she will eventually stop noticing, the same way her childhood friends who lived near a paper mill didn't notice the sickly sweet stink that made her gag. The sounds of dozens of horns endlessly blaring ring in her ears like a belltower gone mad. And the car that Lamont had paid to wait for them—one with air-conditioning—had left with another weary traveler who flashed enough rupees.

"No matter," says Lamont, with forced cheeriness. "We'll get another one."

Even settled in the back seat of a car, air-conditioning on full blast, windows closed tight, inching through traffic, Astrid still does not dare let go her grip on her bag, nor loosen the taut smile pasted on her face.

"It gets better," says Lamont, with a quick, worried glance her way. "At least somewhat, once we get out of Mumbai."

Their destination is much farther south, near Karnataka in the Western Ghats, but rather than fly, they are taking a few days to drive. That way, Lamont says, he'll be able to show her a bit of the countryside while she overcomes jet lag. Once they arrive, he says, she'll be inundated with villagers wanting to meet her, children crowding around, and the demands of the work itself. Lamont also wants to stop at a few temples along the way.

Astrid doesn't much care about the temples, or any cultural sites, for that matter. She has so completely devoted her life to plants, and in particular fossilized plants, that her only connection to culture is through those plants. She's read what she could find of India's history involving plants. There is, of course, the famous Bodhi tree, *Ficus religiosa*, under which the Buddha is said to have attained enlightenment. But it—or one of the many since planted, as successive generations of the tree have been cut down or otherwise died—is in northeast India, far from Lamont's project site. Still, she may yet see it, since she will be heading that way to visit the fossil parks of Madhya Pradesh.

Lamont, on the other hand, revels in the ways people have lived in harmony with their environment—or not, for that matter—throughout the centuries. She had noticed during their time in Churchill his endless curiosity, and now she wonders at his apparent ability to seem at home anywhere in the world. It must be his big personality, his lack of inhibition—like, she now realizes, her father.

They stop in a small town just outside Goa and check into a tiny hotel, the open-air lobby inviting with its bright blue walls, shiny tiled floor, and lush plants. A cluster of large-leaved spotted calla lilies and anthurium bursts from one corner, a blooming vine of bougainvillea spreads bright fuchsia in another. Sweet and familiar scents waft toward her from a dwarf magnolia and pink ylang-ylang whose flowers tumble from clay pots on either side of a wrought-iron table. Astrid sits at the table, grateful for the embrace of fragrances, a thin black cat curling around her legs, while Lamont checks them in. The room is big, with high ceilings, sparse furnishings, and a noisy fan. No air-conditioning. The slatted window opens, letting in a slight breeze and the sounds of the street below: a group of young men walking by, arms hung loosely around each other; two children yelling and chasing each other; a noisy, smoking, muffler-less moped. She sets her suitcase on the stand and drinks down the sweet but cool juice offered upon their arrival.

Astrid is at first bemused by the worn English customs filtering through the shabby remains of the British Empire. The staff waiting for their arrival with a warm washcloth and a cup of sweet juice. The rituals of teatime: small cakes and fragile, flowery teacups. But this sense of decorum is time-worn, teacups often cracked, biscuits somewhat stale, as if nothing has changed since Partition. And it is reserved for guests such as themselves—for those with pale skin and many rupees. She has seen, on her three days of travel by car, with what harshness the less fortunate are treated. This contrast leaves her feeling irritated and ashamed.

The next morning, while Lamont visits another temple site, Astrid chooses instead to just stretch her legs. It's a small enough town that she feels safe walking around alone, but she is still sure to cover her shoulders and knees. Strolling through the quiet neighborhood, the pastel tiny houses, she admires the arching flows of bougainvillea, the intricate decorations above doorways, and the lack, for once, of mounds of trash along the streets. Sunlight warms her shoulders, slows her stride. Then she notices a rectangular piece of paper pinned to a tree trunk. Irritation rises quickly, that someone would so defile a tree; she blazes hot, every cell of her skin awash; she marches over and reaches up to pull it down. But her hand is stopped in midair by the words, in English, which read, *Speaking Tree: He is richest who is content with the least, for contentment is the wealth of nature.*

"Well," she says out loud, "that's nice."

A young Indian woman walking by turns at the sound of her voice, smiles, and continues on her way, blue and white sari flowing around her feet. Astrid smiles back, and softens. As she walks on, the slight breeze made by walking cools her arms. Maybe India isn't such a heartless place after all; maybe there is some charm, and kindness, to be found here.

But the next day, as they drive farther south, she watches a skinny man throw a brick at a cow's head, chasing the cow from the street. "I thought cows were considered sacred," she says to Lamont.

"Right, yes, cows aren't eaten, but that doesn't mean they're cared for, either," he says. "They're mostly just ignored. And there's actually a lot of them dying from starvation after filling their bellies with plastic bags and bottles. They eat whatever they can find, just like the feral dogs, and oftentimes what they find is worse than nothing."

"Oh, well, that's just lovely. Let's see. We've got the sacred cows ignored and dying from trash; the burgeoning population of feral dogs running wild, eating garbage, maimed and diseased; the elephants forced to carry tourists in sweltering heat on gaudy platforms up steep streets. Not to mention how poor people—who comprise most of the population—are treated. And this is the birthplace of ahimsa? Of not harming any living being?"

Lamont gives her a painful smile. "Well, you certainly have been reading up. Yes, yes . . . it's surprising, isn't it? One of those mysteries at which the traveler can only wonder."

That evening, in another small, ornate, and worn hotel, she Skypes with Strilay, wondering again how it's possible for such an idea as ahimsa to have arisen here.

"Perhaps," says Strilay, "the idea originated there because they're so in need of it."

"Well, they most certainly are. But that was thousands of years ago. They obviously haven't learned it."

"Oh, my dear Astrid," Strilay sighs, "the world does not conform to the rational mind. It never has, and it never will. That's the eternal struggle of the scientist."

The tree-planting site is easier for Astrid, but only because it's more rural, with fewer people. It's also, thankfully, off tourism's beaten path. She's grown weary of being treated like a walking rupee note. At a bazaar in a village near Mumbai, she had stopped to ask a wizened old man what the pile of brightly colored herbs and seeds were that he was selling. "Moan-ee," he said, and she repeated it as she took a photo, wondering what the translation was, thinking how Gareth would love to see it. As she strolled off, a small boy followed her, repeating the word *moan-ee*. Her back stiffened as she realized the word was *money*, and they were telling her to pay for taking the photograph. Surprised, afraid, and ashamed that her fear would not allow her to stop and turn and give the boy a few rupees, she quickened her pace and did not look back.

Even at the tree-planting site, she's still the only Western woman everywhere she goes. The younger children, especially, will sometimes stop and stare at her, as if she is an alien with her green eyes and curly hair. "At least," Lamont laughs loudly, "you're not a blonde." But what helps the most is having some purpose other than looking at and buying things, some daily routine.

Her house, though tiny, is all hers and sits next to a small dirt road that is a five-minute walk to the project site. She's grateful to have this space as she sees how most of her neighbors live so crowded together—the way she and her family had lived, all sleeping together in one room, sharing thin mats on the floor. Sometimes she still feels her little brother kicking her in the night during one of his dream chase scenes, those hard bony pummels bruising her awake. Space, her own, is never taken for granted.

She wakes each day to birdsong, songs she's never heard before but are, nonetheless, welcoming. A tribe of macaque monkeys swings through the trees just as she finishes her breakfast. Once at the site, she picks up her tools and heads for the fields. For these first couple of weeks, she's simply working alongside the others planting trees, learning it all. In the evenings, she reads up on the project, talks with Lamont, problem-solves with him. And she stares at maps, plotting routes for fossil-hunting.

The days in the fields planting trees are relaxing. The others, all men, work silently beside her, focusing on the physical labor at hand. She bends to her own work, digging a hole in the warm dark soil, spreading a sapling's roots into it, sprinkling soil around and over the roots, tamping the soil down, creating a lip around the base to keep water from running off.

After a late lunch, she often spends the remaining daylight hours walking the grounds, learning the local flora. There's a giant fig with spreading roots who she visits most afternoons, listing in her note-book which species, from monkeys to orchids, take refuge in the wide limbs and canyoned roots. One afternoon she arrives at the fig to find a group of people—Lamont among them—lying on straw mats on the ground, as if in sleep, but it's a kind of meditation called yoga nidra.

Her walks include the vegetable gardens where food for the project is grown. Often she sees a lovely older woman in the same brilliant blue sari tending the gardens. The woman apparently speaks no English but always looks up and nods at Astrid, who returns the gesture with a slight bow. Each time Astrid stops for longer, and the woman begins to show Astrid the garden, her voice brightening with pleasure in each of her plant charges. She names the plants for Astrid, and then herself, Prisha. Astrid comes to look forward to this time, as, it seems, does Prisha. There is a certain grace in it, a familiarity, tending plants together in quiet.

The familiarity deepens when, one particular afternoon, Astrid finds Prisha singing to the plants and carrying a basket that reminds Astrid of the one her mother used in the garden. It was an old thing, stained and sagging, but still strong enough to carry a full load of potatoes. Sweetgrass, Macey called it, and for the longest time Astrid thought it was just a pet name, same as she gave all her houseplants. Then she learned her grandmaw had made it. Once a year, her grandmaw disappeared for a few days, then returned with sheaves of grasses and bark that she'd hang in a shed to dry. She'd weave them into baskets and sell them on a little table out in front of the house or down the street in front of the gas station, wherever someone would let her set up a table.

As a teen, Astrid never would let friends know that was her grandmother. She shudders now at the memory of her own callousness, realizing it wasn't just the usual teenager embarrassed by her weird family: it was a contempt for her mother's heritage, one stoked by a father who had left years before. Just in case, the teenage Astrid may have thought, just in case he comes back, I want him to be proud of me. But now, standing here in this vegetable garden with a woman who is gentle, composed, content—rooted, deeply and joyfully rooted—just like Astrid's grandmaw and mother, she sees just how wrong that teenager was.

Prisha's song pulls her up. Singing, her grandmaw was always singing, and her mother, singing to the plants. Astrid hasn't thought about her mother's basket, or her grandmaw, for a long time. Yet here in this foreign land these memories rise up clear as bells.

One afternoon, at the rainwater catchment ponds, Astrid sits on a bench, watching a black-crowned night heron stand still as a statue, then in one swift motion, snap up a small insect surfing the water and lift off into the blue sky. From the trees behind her, she hears the now-familiar chattering of monkeys, reacting to the heron's swift takeoff. She laughs. Then sees, striding toward her from the other side of the pond, Lamont in his long white pants and shirt and broad-brimmed hat, looking like some English explorer.

"So," he says, "now you've settled in, it's time you meet our neighbor."

"Yes," she says, leaping up, "I'm looking forward to it."

Their neighbor, Mr. Varma, started planting trees in this area after a flood that drowned dozens of snakes. Just a boy, he'd asked the elders why the snakes had drowned, and in response they gave him a handful of bamboo, and told him to plant where the floodwaters rose. Those elders knew what they were doing: the floods had been caused by deforestation.

Energized by how quickly bamboo grew, and how other plants and insects began to return, the boy kept at it, including more native trees and watering each new sapling by hand every day. It was a life's work, so he built a modest hut in his new forest and lived there, just outside the village, a Thoreauvian life. His forest began to draw elephants who started stealing from villagers' gardens and tigers who made the villagers fear for their livestock and children. Amid their growing threats and anger, he planted bananas and other wild plants for elephant food, and soon the elephants stopped trampling villagers' gardens. And as the forest grew, deer returned, and tigers ignored livestock in favor of their natural prey.

Now there were over a thousand acres of verdant forest, and Mr. Varma had become somewhat of a national hero, and certainly a hero with the international environmental movement for single-handedly re-creating a forest larger than Central Park, where elephants, rhinos, and tigers thrive. Not only was he protecting rare wild animals but he was also doing just what Thomas Lovejoy said would decrease the impacts of climate change: increasing plant biomass so that more carbon is sucked up in photosynthesis.

And all this started because a little boy wanted to keep snakes from drowning. When Astrid first heard the story, she immediately thought of Strilay—how much he'd like such validation of the power of one person's actions. She writes to him that this is why the project is here: to build upon Mr. Varma's work.

The other reason is that plants grow fast in southern India. The global regreening effort is concentrated in those places with the best chances of growing trees as quickly as possible and where there's the willingness of local people, culture, and government; habitat needs for endangered plants and animals; and the possibility of wildlife corridors, like the Yellowstone to Yukon project in North America.

The next afternoon, when they meet with Mr. Varma over tea, Astrid learns that he, too, has embraced this web of reasons for reclaiming forests. "You see," he says, his deep-set eyes looking straight into hers, "we don't usually know all the consequences of our actions, but if we approach each action with a pure heart, then it will bring forth only what is good."

"Yes," Lamont quickly replies, "and likewise, the reverse, right-o?"

"Yes, indeed," says Mr. Varma, taking another sip of tea.

Astrid sits quietly, taking in the small room, windows open wide to forest sounds.

"So," she finally says, "all this," she sweeps her hands wide, "all this forest, you planted it?"

"Yes, indeed, over many years. But of course, I was only working with what already wanted to happen," he says, and in his eyes Astrid glimpses, just for a moment, that same light she saw in her grandmaw's eyes, and sometimes, in her mother's.

They walk the forest, Astrid marveling at the abundant life. Mr. Varma walks as if through a crowd of old friends, stopping to put a hand on a trunk, look up into branches, stoop down and sift through leaves on the ground. Just like her grandmaw. At the foot of one older sandalwood, Astrid sees some painted rocks. She stoops to examine them. Colorful, with miniature scenes of Hindu gods and goddesses, most prominently Ganesha, the elephant-headed god.

"Yes, these," says Mr. Varma, "were painted by my daughter. She says they will help the tree grow faster, but I do not know. I think the tree will make up his own mind about that." And then he laughs, a short, deep belly laugh.

Astrid soon learns that Mr. Varma's daughter isn't the only one applying art to the science of growing trees. On one of her forays to collect fossils, her young driver, Arjun, tells her another tree-planting story, that of Shiva's Robes. The Hindu god Shiva took the form of the sacred mountain Arunachala; the country's largest temple is at the mountain's base, and millions of pilgrims circumnavigate it every year. However, over time, the mountain's lush forests had been cut, and wildlife disappeared. Then, about twenty years ago, a reforestation effort began—and Shiva's Robes are once more becoming vibrant forest. It is, he says, in crisp English, a "remarkable wonder."

"Well," she says, looking out the window at trees zipping by, "it's a very good idea, for the habitat, for wildlife, for water. I imagine it will reap many rewards."

"Yes," he says, "and there is the artistic side. Some people have started to paint some of the rocks around the small saplings, either with Sanskrit sayings or just of flowers, scenes. It's something you should see."

"I would like that, only I hope they aren't harming the trees with this artwork."

"No, they say the trees with painted rocks are growing faster. The trees are responding to the creativity. It's all one, you know, miss? It's all same-same, the science and the art. The trees and rocks and water and people. That is the thing, that is what Shiva wants us to learn from this. As we bend to kiss his robes."

All this talk about art and science and religion makes Astrid uncomfortable. She's not going to argue with her driver, but neither does she believe that painting rocks makes trees grow faster. And yet she can't help but recall what Mr. Varma said: any action we take is merely in cooperation with or resistance to whatever is already happening. She stares out the window, watching oxen standing under the shade of a banyan, two small boys walking hand in hand beside the busy road, a scattering of small birds rising in a field.

Her thoughts roam to Elyse's paintings, to what kind of paintings Elyse would create from Shiva's Robes. A sudden heat floods her body. So strange, to think of her, here and now. It all seems so far away, Astrid's life in Chapel Hill, her childhood memories, the wisp of hurt remaining from that long-ago and faraway childhood event. But Astrid has recalled Elyse's paintings many times since arriving in India. Perhaps it is simply the vibrancy and multitudes of color and patterns adorning this country at every turn.

She has begun to make regular forays to fossil sites. She feels determined to make this more than just a mercy trip; she wants to find samples that might advance her research. She wants to return from sabbatical victorious.

On one outing, Arjun is not available, so she is driven by an older man named Mohammed. The route takes them through a deep forest, and out her window now are large trunks of trees, vines clinging to them. A cool darkness envelops the car, a welcoming one. There's very little of this old-growth native forest left, but what remains no doubt holds great secrets. She taps Mohammed on his arm. "I'd like to stop somewhere in here, to take a look at these trees."

"Oh, no, we cannot stop in Jungle. It is not safe."

"Not safe? But it's the middle of the day. Just for a moment. I want to look at these plants."

"Oh, no, it is not safe. This is Jungle. This is Jungle where Mowgli was found."

"Mowgli?"

"Yes, you know the story, the boy raised by wild animals. He was here, found in here. Many wild animals in here. Not safe to stop."

"Oh, I promise I won't go far from the car."

"I am sorry, miss, but I do not stop in Jungle."

She asks again later, and finally he stops just before they come back out into the open spaces of fields and farmland. He shakes his head as she gets out, keeping his hands firmly on the steering wheel, as if he might just drive off and leave her.

The forest is so dense that a sudden quiet embraces her. The air is humid, heavy like a hand on her shoulder, but cool. Massive trunks rise in great curves, vines climbing and epiphytes nestled in their folds. Scattered spots of sunlight push through the dense canopy to the ground. The soil is dark, a thick humus from accumulated layers of leaves. She hears a quick shushing sound, as if other feet scuffle through the leaves, but sees nothing.

She imagines, just for a moment, the Mowgli story that she read as a child. The fantasy told by a British author who lived here during his country's occupation of India. And here, now, is a grown man who believes it. When she was a girl in her kudzu forest, when she watched rabbits and robins raise their young with such unwavering attention and precise care, she used to imagine being raised by wild animals, thinking it would be better than being part of her crazy family. Such an imagination children have, such belief that anything is possible. She thinks of Elyse, and her paintings, how she still seems to have that imagination—as does her driver. This blurring of the real and imagined, of science and story.

She gazes up into the canopy, a gauze of light wisping down. She hasn't realized how much she'd missed this, time alone with trees. Again she hears a sound, but this time it's familiar, though impossible. It's her grandmaw's voice, her grandmaw who went into the woods alone three times a day, without fail, every time telling Astrid, "Disya 'portun.' Disya who we be."

This here's important. This here's who we be. Astrid leans one hand against a tree trunk, then quickly pulls it away. Ants. Leaf-cutter ants making a line up the trunk. She stares at them, tiny beings dwarfed by their green burdens that rise like sails above their backs. For just the smallest of moments, she imagines the life of a leaf-cutter ant. And then of this tree. Roots splaying in all directions woven with those of neighbors, standing right here day after night after day, season upon season, for hundreds of years. Veil lifts. Boundaries drop. *Disya. Same-same.*

She holds very still, willing it to stay, this strange and wonderful sensation she has felt only a few times in her life. One she has grown to desire. But the very act of willing causes it to dissipate. She shakes her head. It must be this humidity, must be the groundlessness she feels in this culture, so very different from her own. It's unmoored her. Yet she knows, too, and the knowing trails her back to the car like a leafy shadow, that these moments are not just a slip away from reality; they *are* reality.

Back in her small house that night, by the yellow light, she looks back at her pictures and finds, yes, the one of the Speaking Tree. As she reads the note again, she also hears the swish of the woman's sari, and the chiming notes of a bird. She notices, too, now, looking closely at the photograph, how the tree with the note pinned to the trunk is larger than the others lining the road.

She looks up from the photograph and out the window into the dark night, that pitch black of a place where lights aren't left on for no reason, her thoughts turning to Elyse's paintings, to Elyse, to her father. She sees now, staring into true darkness, that she had it all wrong. She had been wrong to defend her father; her father had been wrong to blame his boss. Her father had been wrong so many times, and every time, Astrid had sided with him: against her mother, her grandmaw, her best friend. She sees now that it was she, Astrid, who had abandoned someone: she had abandoned her best friend. It is a terrible admission, one she can only endure because of the utter darkness outside her window, because of the leaf-cutter ants, and the Speaking Tree, because of the moments that ground her, rooted.

The next afternoon, she walks to town on her own, eschewing even the tuk-tuk for a chance to stretch her legs and let the light of day fall upon her revelation. She strides down the hill through the streets lined with stands piled with fruits, vegetables, and mounds of brightly colored spices, and then onto a small backroad to a seamstress who will make her a shalwar kameez, which she has been told will be cooler than her clothes and still cover arms and knees. On that narrow dirt road, she comes upon a man, thin, and clad in a thin cotton robe, with a bare shaved head. He is bent down, sweeping the path before him with a stick to which some palm fronds have been attached. She stops and watches him pass. He raises his head only once, to smile and nod at her. She wonders if he is mentally ill, and says as much at dinner.

"He's a Jain," says Lamont. "It's a type of Buddhist. They're very sincere about the practice of ahimsa. They're not only vegans but will not eat root vegetables, lest there be insects clinging to the roots who are killed when the plant is harvested. He was sweeping the path before him to make sure he didn't step on any insects."

"Oh," she says, "yes, that makes sense. How, how beautiful." She beams, even as Lamont looks up in surprise at her response; she recalls, as if she is there still, the green sails of the leaf-cutter ants and her hand on the tree's dark trunk.

Morning, as usual, she wakes early, hearing the closing chant of meditators on the bluff. Out her open window she sees them returning, a line of people in flowing white, among them Lamont, a foot taller than the rest. She dresses, makes a cup of tea, walks the dirt road to the latest planting area. She passes Prisha in the vegetable patch, bent over from the waist, who rises and flashes a bright smile. Then Astrid reaches the fields of newly planted trees, tiny foot-high saplings planted in the last few days, a mix of banyan, breadfruit, anjily, sandalwood, and cinnamon. A bright blue Indian roller hops among the saplings, seeking insects unearthed in the planting. A butterfly, yellow with golden spots, alights on one anjily, then moves off in search of flowering plants. At the far end of the field she sees several of the planters arriving, tools in one hand, buckets of saplings in the other.

She sighs. It feels good to be part of something so tangible, just as she had been at Tom Shank's site. And this has the benefit, too, of helping those who live here find their way back to a more sustainable way of living. In the month since her arrival, they have planted twenty acres. She is beginning to feel that perhaps this work is worthwhile. She has been rereading scientific papers on the effects of reforestation on climate and biodiversity; she has begun envisioning such projects worldwide.

She hears a high, tinkling laugh and turns to look back down the road. Three women coming toward her, a rainbow of color in their yellow, green, and red saris. On their heads are large bundles, and as they come closer, she sees they are bundles of sticks, firewood for heating and cooking. Each bundle is half again as tall as the women, and yet they walk easily, one hand holding the bundle steady, the other swinging comfortably.

The bundles are so large, it's a wonder they can keep them on their heads. Astrid admires this skill. There's more wood on each head than the saplings a person plants in a day, or two days. Several days. Her mind stops. Stutters. Where are these sticks coming from? What forest is being cut while they are here planting tiny trees? All her sense of accomplishment vanishes like a wisp of smoke. What good is it that they plant these trees when others, likely from natural forests, are being cut? What good is it other than a tree farm? How can it possibly affect world carbon loads? She turns back to the planters, who have now taken their places in the field and are bent over, every one of them bent from the waist, the men in clothes all the shades of brown. She hears the putter of the small truck bringing water for new saplings.

She heaves a sigh, turns back, her cup of tea now empty, and heads down the road, to her house, and to a new set of doubts.

At lunch, she fires questions at Lamont. Where are they cutting for firewood? Has anyone calculated how much biomass is being lost to heating and cooking wood? Is anyone looking for ways to keep deforestation from happening here? A new source of heat and cooking fuel? Solar cookers? Solar heat? Some kind of protections for existing forests? Who owns that land they're cutting on? But Lamont doesn't have answers to calm the flare of her doubts. Instead, he simply says, over and over, Nothing's perfect. We do what we can.

Her sense of futility flames hotter through the long day, and that night, lying in bed, the humidity pushing her down with brute force, she remembers her flight to India. She had a sixteen-hour layover in Singapore and was looking forward to exploring the extravagant Gardens by the Bay as well as all the buildings carpeted with green growing plants. She'd read about this country's commitment to creating green space and knew it's considered perhaps the world's most biophilic city. But the air was so polluted that there was a red alert, warning people to stay inside. Schools were closed, and the government distributed protective masks.

She had nonetheless strapped on the mask provided by her hotel and navigated the haze to two greenhouses, masterful technological feats that harbored examples of the world's diverse ecosystems, from cloud forests to California chaparral. Still, she wondered just what kind of universe she'd dropped into, where the only natural setting to be enjoyed was under glass, protected from the real world outside.

The pollution came from burning peatland forests in Indonesia, most of it illegal burning to clear land for palm oil. Singapore was pursuing legal actions against Indonesian companies, but though Indonesia had arrested hundreds of people over illegal fires, the blazes just kept burning, blazes that were producing more daily emissions than the entire U.S. economy.

There she was making her way to a massive tree-planting effort to stave off climate change, and she found herself in a place literally enshrouded in black carbon from deforestation. It felt, as her mother used to say, like one step forward and two steps back. Or worse: one step forward and one hundred steps back.

Chapter 20

Elyse returns to an Alaska transformed by snow. The forests are blanketed white, the trails soft powder. Campbell Creek is a series of snow-laden ice canyons with patches of open water for one of her favorite overwintering birds, the dipper, to slip beneath its surface. This is a relief, as winter has been, thus far, dismal: either it's been below zero and clear, or above freezing and raining. But now winter is here, and she can feel everyone, from people in the grocery store to birds at her feeder, breathe a sigh of relief. Each morning she brushes off new snow and sprinkles sunflower seeds for the pine grosbeaks who wait in the spruce, red males and cinnamon females perched in green boughs like Christmas ornaments, their breathy love songs threading down to her.

Usually, in the belly of winter, she sleeps more and feels sluggish even when awake, like a bear yanked from hibernation. But now she feels inspired and invigorated. The days are still short but lengthening, the hump of winter solstice behind her. On her skis she can almost feel the Earth thrumming its way back to spring. In her studio she feels that thrum and pours it into drawing and painting. There's no pattern, not yet, but she isn't worried; she just draws, paints scenes, and lets her mind roam.

At the Ackland opening, she'd met someone with connections to a well-known New York gallery, the Venus. Less than a month home, she receives a call from the Venus's owner, inquiring whether Elyse would be interested in a solo show next year. Then, a few weeks later, Aaron from the Alaska Museum calls to say they are now ready to schedule her solo show.

The well-reviewed Ackland show and the grapevine news of her invitation to the Venus have erased anyone's doubts about her artistic integrity. It's a relief, and yet she hesitates, tells Aaron the show she'd planned for the Alaska Museum is now at the Ackland. But Aaron insists that the museum would be happy to display the same show, and will pay to have the work shipped back to Alaska. He asks to meet with her before she decides.

The next week, over a beer at the Rustic Goat, Aaron explains what he couldn't on the phone. "Look," he says, eyes wide behind black-framed glasses, "I never wanted to postpone your show. We fool ourselves to think art can ever be apolitical. When it is, it's just some tame decorations for the walls of a doctor's office. Nothing moves a person like ardor."

"Well," says Elyse, "thank you. Very much. I guess my hunch was right: my show was postponed because of the WPO ad."

"Oh," he says, sitting upright, "oh. Yes, I just assumed. That you knew. Had figured it out. Please excuse my lack of professionalism, but I just wanted to—clear the air."

"You have, thanks. But I'm still reticent, though I can hardly believe I would turn it down. It's just, what if the director postpones it again?"

"Oh," he says, shoulders relaxing, "well, you know we have a new director, and she's shaking things up. And, the board has directed her to make this show happen. They're embarrassed that we let local talent debut Outside."

Then he tells her that the museum is now suffering from the state's single-minded focus on the oil economy. With oil prices dropping, the state budget, and with it, the museum's state and corporate funding, are diminishing. So the museum, he says, is looking to expand their funding base and become less dependent on oil company sponsorship. "So," he says, "we can have broader conversations about things like global warming. And your show would be a perfect signal that we've widened our horizons."

"Okay, yes," says Elyse, feeling delight that her work can be of use. "How can I say no to that?"

As she gets in her car, she turns to the back seat and ruffles Sophie's soft head. "Well, girl, now we've got two shows to get ready for. What do you think of that?"

Sophie licks her hand and stands up, her tail wagging.

"Yes, I'll be busy, but happy-busy. And now it's your turn. Earthquake Park."

Darlene, in the very back, starts to whine as soon as the road narrows and curves. At Point Woronzof, all three burst from the car and down the hill to the beach. The tide is out, the beach a jumble of pancake ice. It's like boulder-hopping, traversing them to the water's edge, where waves lap against ice. Across the inlet, the windmills on Fire Island turn slowly. Beyond, Sleeping Lady is lit pink by winter afternoon sunlight. Elyse spreads her arms wide, then grabs a piece of driftwood and throws it for Darlene.

The next morning, Elyse decides she's got to buckle down and get serious about these shows. Enough doodling; time to at least gather ideas. Though the Alaska Museum would be satisfied with the same show as the Ackland, Elyse would like to add a couple new pieces. But she has no ideas. Fortunately, her phone rings. Mags. Yes, a tea break sounds perfect.

In the following weeks, she gets an increasing number of invitations for lunch or tea or private showings from gallery owners and artist friends. She's fully back in the welcoming bosom of the Alaska arts community. It feels safe and familiar, and she awakens in the morning content. But in her studio she stagnates. Here is it late February; she should be brimming with energy as the sap rises in the trees outside and the longer, stronger sunlight turns the snow to soft kernels that shush when she skis. She wonders if the promise of these two shows has stalled her, that the pressure of having others waiting to see her work has stymied her flow. Perhaps she's just thinking too much about audience.

She'd like to get back to how she felt just after returning from North Carolina. That sense of wide-open freedom. One morning she wakes thinking about Astrid, how it felt to see her again. Surely some of her joyfulness after the trip arose from her relief that, finally, she knew what had happened, and it hadn't been her fault. Nor had it been Astrid's, or anything, really, to do with their friendship. She stretches in bed. Sophie appears, wagging her tail, wanting a morning treat. She ruffles Sophie's fur and wonders why it is that, for her, seeing Astrid felt like reconnecting with a long-lost twin, but for Astrid it seemed, well, painful.

Three days later, she is awakened in the night by the wind driving rain against the windows. Rain, in February. By midday, the snow is nearly gone, the trails and her driveway reduced to ice. She trades her skis for ice grippers and walks the dogs on nearby trails since high winds threaten to topple trees. She looks up at spruce and birch trees she has known for decades, trees who have lived hundreds of years. The winds howl, sudden gusts bending these trees nearly in half.

She hears a loud crack, then sees one of the tallest spruce snap in half and thunder to earth. She gasps, cries out. Her dogs both come running to her side. *You have done this*, she hears, *you have done this*. She swings her head around, but sees no other people. She shakes her head. It's the wind, screaming through the forest, the branches rubbing against each other, the swirl of twigs and needles. That's all. But she still hears it: *You have done this*. Humans, she knows it means, have done this, created this warmer world, this crazy weather. She feels a bone-deep chill and heads for home.

She tries to explain what she's experienced to Dan that night at dinner. Maybe he'll tell her it's just her worries about Justin. Maybe he'll have some scientific explanation to quell the nagging panic. But he's had another long day, the latest in a series of them. The one thing he says only makes her feel worse. "Well, there's no redemptive grieving for the catastrophe of climate change. It's just going to keep getting worse, and we're just going to have to keep suffering loss after loss."

"Oh, Dan," she cries, "that's so dark."

"It is what it is," he replies, then rises from his seat, thanks her for the meal, and heads to the den to watch football. She watches him go, but he doesn't raise his eyes to meet hers.

This is how it is now between them: he's here, but not here. Since his return from Syria, he's been more distant, indifferent, disinterested. He's spending more time in his study, more time at work, at meetings. They rarely have dinner together. And he always comes to bed long after she's asleep. He's nice enough, in some ways more attentive. But it's a surface politeness. Is he avoiding talking about their marriage, where they left it when he went to Syria? Is he angry with her over Justin's choices? She doesn't know, but she also doesn't fret as much as she once would have; she's distracted by her own work, or lack of it right now.

Maybe this is our new normal, she thinks, wiping the table and fixing peppermint tea. Maybe now, with the boys fledged and each of us off on our own careers, we've settled into a separate-but-together phase. Still, she's sad he didn't bother to comfort her. He's right. She knows he is. The grief—and guilt—is not going to be one she can move through, because it will keep happening, losses will keep piling up. But he could have said something kind. He could have offered a hug.

The storm abates, leaving the forest floor cleared of snow, and subzero temperatures set in. On one walk Sophie flushes a snowshoe hare, who pulses through the dark forest in a bolt of white. What of these animals whose fur no longer provides camouflage? Of the smaller mammals who depend on snow for warmth, the plants who survive subzero only because the thick snow protects them? She worries about what spring will bring, whether the tundra, without the winter snow blanket, will remain brown, covered in dead plants. She feels ridiculous being worried for all these small beings, knows she's taking on responsibility beyond what is hers, but then hears again the trees in the storm. *You have done this.* There, in her throat, like a lump of black coal, that haunting knowledge that humans are responsible, directly responsible, refuses to leave her be. There is no refuge in redemptive grief.

It's a gray morning several weeks later when Jim from WPO calls. "I've got bad news," he says. "You'd better sit down."

She thinks it must have to do with the campaign, some new criticisms of her painting. But the ads ran so long ago.

"It's Nicolaf," he says, in a rush. "He's dead. There was a storm in Cape Vankarem, an unusually big storm for this time of year, and with the ice not reaching shore, well, huge storm surges ..."

"What?" says Elyse, gasping into the phone. "What? What? What?"

"He was out with a few other men trying to pull in some boats. A big wave, it took out one of the men, and Nicolaf, being the only one who could swim, went in after him. Neither survived. Big seas, cold waters, they didn't have much of a chance."

"No. No. No."

"I know. It's hard to believe. The walrus beach was hammered, too, and the seawall ruined. They're talking now of just moving the whole town inland."

"I don't . . . I don't believe it. He is . . . so . . . so . . . smart. About things like that. They all are. Were."

"I know, I know. That community is incredibly attuned to the natural world. But things are happening now that none of them have experienced. None of them."

Elyse sits still, praying to awaken from what surely is a nightmare.

"Elyse? Are you still there? Are you okay? I know you two got close during your residency. You really helped Nicolaf overcome his fears of speaking. He was doing so well, too, truly reaching people. We will miss him terribly."

"Yes. We all will. Miss him. I . . . I've got to go, Jim. Thank you for telling me."

She hangs up and stares at the wall. Sits still. Cold, she is shivering, her breath shallow and fast. Then a sudden inbreath fills her, breaks something open. She puts her head in her hands and begins to sob, great big body-shaking sobs, as if the very Earth were being pulled up through her legs and bursting from her chest. Sophie comes over to her, tail between her legs, her soft wet nose touching Elyse's hands. She whines, licks her hand, then settles down beside Elyse, leaning against her legs. Sophie's solid body, her warmth and weight, keeps Elyse tethered to the ground, to the Earth, to this moment and time. As much as she wants to escape it, as much as she wants to flee hard reality crashing in, she also wants to be here, more than ever. Deep down she is sure of that. Even in the depths of unredemptive grief. Her sobs turn to wails turn to heat, to fire. She weeps out all tears. Lowers her hands, looks up. Her eyes fall on a sketch of a tree, a birch, from the windstorm. She is being pushed so hard, this birch, bent sideways, strained, and yet she remains rooted, she holds on.

She has read about the stages of grief. Has learned them, has experienced them. Knows that they come and go and circle back around, that grief is not a linear thing. It's a storm, with surges that surprise every time, that might lessen one day and return the next with renewed ferocity. Over the coming weeks she craves knowing every detail about Nicolaf's death, calling Jim, writing Yurgyev, checking online, looking for every single piece of information. And then she realizes that it doesn't matter; no matter how much she learns, no matter how much she thinks through what could have gone differently, what might have saved him, he is gone, and there's no bringing him back.

She begins to talk to him as she goes about her days, taking him with her on walks, showing him Alaska the way he showed her his corner of the world. She regrets not having had more time with him when he was in Alaska, regrets not telling him how much he meant to her. But what did he mean to her? She never quite understood, not really. It was too caught up in all she feared he might mean to ever know the truth. How quickly a relationship becomes entangled in expectations and fears, how reduced by trying to stuff it into one of society's accepted categories.

She can't sleep. She has no energy. She is lonely. There's no one she can talk to who knew Nicolaf, not well. She can't bear to be around other people, can't pretend she's okay. She cancels a lunch and two coffee dates; she skips a gallery opening. She lets emails and phone calls languish unanswered.

One night as she drifts off to sleep with the help of a sleeping pill, she relives their walk across the tundra, Nicolaf's warm hand in hers as she climbs the lichen-coated outcropping. His hand becomes Justin's hand, as a boy, his small hand slipping from hers as he clambers up a boulder. It becomes the rough trunk of the spruce, stricken down by the storm.

She sits up in bed, startled, suddenly seeing how her grief for Nicolaf is entwined with her worries about Justin and her fears about climate change. It's just all one big mix of fear and grief and a restlessness, too, like an undercurrent. She feels guilty about this at first, thinking she is lessening Nicolaf's value as a human, but then she knows, with absolute certainty, that he would not agree with that. He would, in fact, want it no other way than that she should associate him with place. If only we could love place as much as we love self.

She lies in bed, tracing the spires of the wooly mammoth tusk in the tundra grasses, feeling that wind so strong it brought tears to her eyes. Outside, a gust of wind rattles her window. *You have done this.* Minutes later the wind is a constant roar, and the next few days are aswirl in strong, warming winds that slick back the previous week's thin snow layer to ice.

It's during the windstorm that Dan notices something amiss with her. At dinner he finishes and gets up while she is still eating. This is something that has always annoyed her, as if dinner is just about shoveling food into one's belly and not sharing time together. She's asked him many times if he'd sit until she's done, but though he says okay, he never does. Tonight is no different. So when he notices her eyes are red, his first response is defensive.

"Oh, I suppose you're upset that I got up first? Well, I'm done, and I don't see why, just because you eat more slowly, that I should be made to sit at the table like some child."

"Of course not," she says in a whisper.

"Then what is wrong with you? You've been moping around all evening. Some new drama in the art world?"

"No. It's . . ." She doesn't want to tell him, especially not when he's in such a defensive mood, but it bursts out of her, along with fresh tears.

"So, this was one of the Yup'ik marine mammal hunters in the town? The one you helped with his English?" he says, his voice softening, but only a bit.

"Yes, that was him."

"Well, I'm sorry for your loss," he says, pausing a moment, "but you know, others can fill his shoes. I don't understand why hearing from an Indigenous person is such a big deal anyhow. It'd be better to hear from scientists. The paper just quoted an Alaska Indigenous leader—the mayor of his town—saying that wildfires on the Kenai don't have anything to do with their polar bears and walrus problems. He's just refusing to connect the global warming dots."

Elyse just stares at him. "I've lost a friend, and this is what you think it's about?"

"Okay, okay, I can tell you can't hear this right now, whatever. I'm just saying, something to think about later when you're through grieving."

"You know, Dan, for a doctor, you sure have some piss-poor bedside manners."

"Oh, I didn't realize you were my patient. Sorry!"

"No, but I am your wife. A little compassion wouldn't kill you."

"Yes, you're my wife, so we shouldn't have to play games. Tell me, I'm curious, was there something more between you and this hunter guy? Something you might want to tell me?"

"What are you talking about?"

"I think you know. You're carrying on like you've lost a lover. Is that what's happened?"

"I can't believe you. I haven't been unfaithful to you once, not in twenty-nine years of marriage."

"If you say so, but I do wonder, since we're apart so much. You could have another whole family, for all I know."

"You're the one who leaves, not me. You're the one who could have another whole family somewhere. In Nepal, or Syria. Hell, you could have several families spread across the globe," she says, her tears dried now by anger.

"Yeah, right," he says, laughing. "That's what's going on. You think I'm just over there fucking the local women. You have no idea how hard we work, how desperate the conditions, what hellholes those places are. I'd say it's you who needs a dose of compassion." He stops, glares at her, voice deepening. "So. Sam called me yesterday."

"What?" says Elyse, unnerved by this sudden change in topic. "What did he say?"

"He says your sensitive boy, Justin, has gone and gotten himself thrown in jail."

"He. Has. What?" Elyse whispers, a sudden chill running down her spine.

"He was arrested for turning one of the shut-off valves on the Keystone pipeline. Evidently, that's what his little group is about. Breaking into a secured area and turning off the flow of crude from the Alberta tar sands where it crosses into the States. He was arrested on the spot, all four of them were."

"Wait. Is he in jail right now?" The heat from her anger is doused. Cold, she is cold.

"No. He's already out on bail. Awaiting a trial date. Sam said the group is paying for everything. Said they'd planned for this to happen. Justin knew. He knew he would get arrested. It's all a publicity stunt. Like your artwork used for advertising."

"Is he . . . is he okay?" She doesn't even hear Dan's last sentence, doesn't hear the jab.

"Of course he is. A few hours in a county jail is all. He's fine. He has a record now, though. A college degree just got farther out of reach."

"I . . . I don't know what to say. I need to talk to him. Find out what happened. What he's going to do."

"Yes, you talk to him, that always helps," Dan snorts. "That should fix everything."

And with that, he storms from the room and clomps down to his study, slamming the door. Elyse sits at the kitchen table, her remaining dinner now cold, her hands shaking.

The days, the weeks, they keep marching on, while Elyse stumbles through grief and fear and anger. It takes far too long for Justin to return her calls, and their conversation is stilted. Yes, all that Dan told her is true: he and three others arrested and still awaiting trial. They want it to go to trial because they want to explain their motives; they want to talk about climate change. She listens, she tries not to say something to make him hang up on her.

"Was it, were you the one who turned . . . ?"

"Yes, I turned the wheel, Mom," he says, his voice strong. "It was hard, I had to throw my whole weight into it, hang from it."

"Oh, oh. And did it, I read that the ground, when the oil flow is turned off, it's like an earthquake?"

"Yes," he says, his voice cracking, just a bit, like when he was thirteen and it was changing. "The ground did shudder beneath me when it closed. But we were told to expect that. Still, it was, well, you can't prepare for some things."

"Yes," she says. She can hear what he doesn't say: it was thrilling and terrifying, and much more terrifying than he'd expected. She wants to tell him she'll be right there, she'll help to fix it. She wants to tell him to come home right now, come home where it's safe.

"I just, I want you to be happy," she finally says, quietly. "And I trust you, I trust that you're doing what you think is best. Just know that I love you, and I'm here, if you need anything, anything at all."

"I will, Mom. I'm okay, Mom."

But Elyse is not. The cumulation—Justin, Nicolaf, her stalled work, the fight with Dan, the storm—leaves her lonely, lost, empty. She needs to get out, she finally decides, be around people. She makes herself accept a lunch date with an artist friend. But as she sits in the noisy restaurant, listening to her friend bemoan the grueling application process for an NEA grant, she finds her thoughts drifting to Justin, willing to put his life on the line for something he believes in, then to the tundra outside Cape Vankarem, her standing silently beside Nicolaf. She thinks of all the wasted conversation in this restaurant, all the talking people do that has little substance. Justin doesn't do that; he always says just what's on his mind, no minced words. Nicolaf, too, only spoke when necessary and then with the most precise language.

Back in her studio, the winds still whipping trees outside, she stares at her blank canvas and realizes that what had felt comfortable now feels confining. Her return to the security blanket of the Alaska arts community now feels more like a box she is being stuffed back into, only she no longer fits—and she no longer wants to.

She stares at her wall calendar, all her notations for deadlines, lunch dates, gallery openings. She looks around the studio. She tries to set her mind on the two shows she needs to work toward.

She sighs, calls Justin. He answers, surprisingly. His voice is soft, as if he's just woken up.

"Everything okay?" she says.

"Yeah, fine, just hanging out," he says, yawning.

"Need anything?"

"Naw, I'm good. Listen, Mom," he says, his voice slowing even more.

"Yes?"

"I just want to tell you thanks. Thanks for being such a great mom. And don't worry about me. I'm gonna be fine. This is what I need to do."

"I know. I know. I. I'm proud of you. And inspired. You … you're so fearless. I need to be more like that."

"Oh, Mom, no, you're great!"

"Well, thanks, but still. I could do more. I want to do more."

"Oh, no, you're fine. This kinda stuff, it's easier for me. I'm young, unattached, you know, all that."

"You're right, dear. I know. But still. Just know that I trust you. I'm proud of you. And I'm inspired by you. Don't forget that."

I want to do more. Her words ring in her head as she hangs up. What does she mean? What more does she think she can do? Unsettled, wanting distraction, she turns to her computer. There's an email from Charlotte, with a link to an article in the *Raleigh News and Observer* about the work Astrid is doing in India. About trees. There's a photo of Astrid standing beside the twisted trunk of a sandalwood, and a woman in a bright blue sari standing next to her. Astrid's right arm is around the woman, and her left hand rests on the tree trunk. She is smiling, a rare, genuine smile. The tree spirals up, bends, spreads off to the sky above the women's heads.

The sandalwood looks like the ones Elyse used to draw in high school. Willowy things with leaves dripping off of them like jewels. She drew them around pages in her notebooks, around math problems, on her arms like tattoos. She picks up a pencil and draws one. Then another. She thinks of the sandalwood above Astrid, of the spruce in the forest speaking to her in the wild wind. In the article Astrid describes the "Speaking Trees," how children in the village are now tying small notes to some of the saplings, reminders of compassion and non-harming, little sayings about the value of the natural world. Elyse sketches in some notes, fluttering around the crown of the trees like leaves.

In the weeks to come, she starts to paint again with more direction, more intensity. She paints trees swirling and bending, moving across the canvas, like van Gogh's wild trees, snaking and shaking. Their limbs reach to emit jagged multi-hued curtains of aurora. They spill out into lightning sprites, shattering the bruised sky. Their roots burrow down to Earth's molten core, red lava fire that surges up into the trunks, and limbs, leaves flaming the night sky. The leaves shapeshift: in one they are fire, leaping from branch to sky; in another they are paper missives, misshapen paper airplanes revealing scribbled notes, promises, hopes. The yearning for what could be.

She experiments with the canvas itself, painting on paper grocery bags, on an old torn sheet, on layers of sheet music strewn across the canvas, musical phrases slipping behind a tree trunk, appearing again in the twist of a root below ground. But there is no harmony here, only the discordant sounds of unleashed fury. For these are not comforting trees, they do not exude the safety or complacency of a big shade tree under which to sit, or read, or sleep. They speak, in loud and insistent voices, shattering illusions of a tame and benevolent world that tends to our every need and desire. They tell us, in no uncertain terms, what has always been true: we need nature, but nature does not need us.

Chapter 21

Each day Astrid wakes to the sounds of village life, roosters and children in the streets and the clockwork start of mopeds and motorcycles buzzing by, not a single one with a muffler. Each day brings a new problem to solve, whether it's dealing with a staffing change or finding another source for the water-retention mix they add to each root base. She may have thought she was coming to India to advise about which kind of trees to plant, but all she wants to do is keep her hands in the soil. So every day she plants some trees, and every evening she stops by the community garden to visit Prisha.

Their friendship has grown though they cannot communicate with language. They speak about, and through, plants. The range of vegetables surprises Astrid; many are familiar, many are not. There's a type of radish that's a favorite for the Jains: it doesn't have a tuber, but instead has an edible pod. There's methi, a type of fenugreek, and toor dal, which looks like lentils. And many rows of curry, something Astrid's mother grew one year, just to learn about it, but never did figure out how to use in a dish.

Prisha has an ingenious irrigation system that mimics the water-catchment system set up for the buildings, but hers is made entirely from bamboo. Even the trellises are bamboo. And Prisha has added artistic flourishes. Small glass beads hang from the trellises, catching and reflecting sunlight. Bits of old saris are used to tie up tomatoes, giving each plant a different rainbow of color. It's the kind of thing, thinks Astrid, that Elyse would love. Together, the two women watch as the bees do their necessary pollinating, as tomatoes get plump and ripe, as the Achingapayar's white flowers turn into long, thin pods.

Her fossil-hunting trips sporadically interrupt this routine, though many of the sites are not only difficult to find but very challenging terrain, entirely different from the Pennsylvania hills where she did her graduate work. Still, she does enjoy getting down on hands and knees, pulling out her trowel and brush and dustpan, and slowly, carefully brushing away soil.

She's dropped her desire to return victorious and fallen into simply enjoying the work. Sometimes, another paleobotanist joins her; it helps to have someone who knows the strata, and it's inspiring to work beside someone who shares her fascination with what lies below soil. With their help, and with information from colleagues in Australia and China, she has successfully identified at least two new specimens that will provide good material for a paper, if not the link in her own research. It is just like her mother always said: as soon as she lets go, the answers appear.

Endless days of sunshine and balmy nights give way to slightly rising temperatures, a hint of the liquid heat to come. But the monsoon season is still three months away, and so the saplings must be watered and the gardens irrigated, and the fossil sites are still dry and easy to excavate.

Gareth makes a visit over the university's spring break; he, too, is captivated by the gardens, especially the Achinga payar and karela. Prisha laughs—high and sweet, like birdsong—when Gareth plucks a leaf from a curry plant and takes a bite. And she smiles, questioningly, when he gives her seeds he brought from North Carolina. Astrid had asked him to bring some traditional southern plants that might grow here, just for Prisha. He's brought heritage tomatoes, okra, and a few sweet potato slips he'd hidden carefully in his bags. They visit several area markets, with Gareth entranced by the stalls overflowing with bright vegetables and fruits, the mats spread on the ground displaying heaping piles of ridge gourds and coconuts and palm leaves. But it is at the pyramid-shaped mounds of brilliantly colored spices that he is most engaged. He buys samples of every single one, which he then takes back to Astrid's house and tastes, one by one, being able to name only about a third of them. He then spends the rest of his time finding someone who speaks both languages well enough to name each spice.

"Garam masala. Amchoor. Tamarind. Amazing!" he says. "Learning these could keep me busy for years!"

They visit Mr. Varma's reserve one day, and then on another day go to the one Astrid now calls "Mowgli's Forest." On the way back, they stop at a roadside food stall. This is the kind of place Astrid would never have set foot in before. It's tiny, dirty, and obviously only frequented by locals. But Gareth is insistent. "C'mon, Astrid," he pleads, "I want to dive in and eat some truly local food, not the fancy stuff they're fixing for you at the compound."

"Of course you do, my husband," she says, "but I don't have an iron gut like you. For you, okay, we'll try it."

She has decided she'll just have some chai and won't eat, but once they sit down, the scents wafting toward them are so inviting that her stomach changes her plans. So they both order, she the biryani. While waiting, she goes to the bathroom stall. There's only one, and it's just a toilet, no sink, no water, no way to clean her hands. Nor the hands of the cook, either. She sits back down, smiling thinly. Gareth, meanwhile, has his eyes fixed on the cook, who works over an open-air counter and grill, chopping vegetables, sautéing, flipping them, all so deftly. The man himself is a sight: tall and large and imposing, with a white beard, frizzy white hair, a belly so large it's a wonder he can reach the grill, and an apron over that belly that once upon a time may have been white but now looks like something Jackson Pollock might have worn after a long session of painting.

A slim younger man stands by his side, assisting. The cook scoops up the food onto a plate, and the young man picks it up, but the cooks says something, makes a few gestures. So the young man sets it back down, and then, with his bare hands, pats the pile of vegetables and rice into a triangle shape. Astrid watches, wishing she wasn't, as this plate of food is delivered to her. She stares at it, and at the grimy hands that delivered it, and at the flies that are quickly appearing, but again her stomach makes the decisions, and she begins to eat. It is, she can't help it, one of the most delicious dishes she's had her entire time in India.

Somehow, fortunately, they both survive. Either Astrid is lucky, or she's been there long enough for her digestive system to have adjusted.

When Gareth tells Lamont about it that night, Lamont bursts into laughter. "She's going local on us," he says, elbowing Gareth in the ribs.

Gareth's visit buoys everyone's spirits. The young woman who does the laundry gives him a bright smile one morning, and Astrid says to him, "I have never seen her smile. I've never seen her even look at me, though I always say *namaste* to her in passing, and *shukri-yaa* to thank her. What did you do?"

"Oh, Astrid," he replies, smiling. "It's you they love. They're just happy to meet the lucky man who's your husband."

On one of his last nights in India, after another walk in Mr. Varma's woods, they rush back to her cottage to change for dinner with Lamont. As she's adjusting her dupatta, Gareth touches her shoulder.

"I'll be ready in two minutes, promise," she says, knowing Gareth is looking forward to another evening of Lamont's tales of his world travels.

"You don't get much alone time here, do you?"

"No," she laughs, "I don't. Everything, even driving, is with other people."

"Yes," he says. "And I've been realizing that, well, that you need quiet. Probably more than you get in Chapel Hill, too, being married to such a gregarious guy."

She turns to him, smiles.

"So," he continues, running one finger over her lips, "that's why, well, I'm thinking, why don't we stay in tonight?"

When Gareth leaves, Astrid feels a surprising sweep of loneliness but is quickly put back to work. Still, it lingers, bittersweet, and she wonders if he feels it too. How is it for him, having her gone so long, when they haven't been apart for more than two weeks at a time since marriage? He hasn't expressed anything but support, so perhaps he doesn't mind. Perhaps he's too busy to miss her.

Still, his visit has Astrid thinking of home. She had originally agreed to three months, and that is coming soon to a close. But Lamont—who seems less aggravating after a few months in India, as if the air itself has smoothed his sharp edges—has already been pleading with her to stay longer, and she has been leaning that way. Another month, or two, or three. Maybe stay to see the monsoon season, when everything grows even more lush and green.

She's starting to understand how Strilay was drawn to stay in Churchill. There's something about being so clearly needed that one does not experience often enough, really. At least not in the safe university setting in which she's lived her life. Perhaps this is why people join the Peace Corps or Doctors Without Borders, she thinks, to take a break from the sanitary world of Western patients with their minor ills and dive full-bore into a place where people's lives are constantly at stake, and the means with which to save them are sparse and unpredictable. The challenge of it, and the certainty at day's end, collapsing into bed, of having done something tangible, of having been of use.

For despite her misgivings that this tree-planting effort may not be the most perfect effort to curb climate change, she can see how it affects the lives of those around her—how the opportunity to have a decent-paying job has affected families in this village, how attendance at the school has grown, how the children playing in the streets seem better fed and clothed compared to other villages she's seen on her fossil forays. And Mr. Varma's forest, in which she walks frequently, though always with a tiger guide, reminds her that it is possible to return this land to its wild state, and with benefits far beyond what one might have envisioned. Cleaner air and water, abundant wildlife, more pollinator insects for farms and gardens.

And now, with Mr. Varma's story reaching people around the world, a new source of income has appeared for the village: tourism. Several groups have already come to his forest, birding and looking for wild tigers. There isn't yet anywhere for groups to stay overnight, but that, too, is changing: two developers have come knocking, and the village leaders have been meeting to discuss the options. They invited Lamont to one meeting, and he urged them to go with plans that are more eco-friendly, in keeping with what tourists would want but also to harmonize with the goals of their reforestation work. These plans include water-capture systems, solar panels on every villa, designs to use prevailing breezes to keep dwellings cooler, local and recycled materials, and, of course, local construction crews and staff.

It's on one of her walks in Mr. Varma's forest that she has an idea, one that lingers and grows like the snakebean vines climbing Prisha's trellis. She is standing under one of the largest, and first, of the banyans that Mr. Varma planted, looking up into the spreading boughs and thinking about what a tree is, how it's much more than just one life; how a tree gives, harboring other plants, insects, birds, monkeys.

She thinks about a tree's innate strength and resilience, about the Shukkei-en ginkgo in Japan, surviving the atomic blast. About her ginkgo in Chapel Hill, reduced now to a stump, which, if left alone, will sprout again. About plants, their lives beneath the soil, how they communicate through their root systems, even sharing nutrients with their relatives. How a mature tree will keep offspring in shade so that they grow more slowly, more dense and stout, and therefore better able to withstand winds and storms. She thinks of the lycopods, and all the plants who have lived for nearly 500 million years, continuing to grow on this planet, through all the changes around them.

She is thinking about the longevity of plants, and the importance of that longevity, as she stares up into a tree who's only a few decades old, who could still live for hundreds of years. And what this tree would do in those hundreds of years. The lives this tree would harbor, the carbon this tree would pull from the atmosphere. Yes, she understands that younger trees, with more vigorous growth, take up more carbon than older trees. But there's so much more going on. So much humans have yet to comprehend. Leaving the trees, the forests, the green that remains should be the first line of defense in protecting the planet. Leave a tree. That's her idea. To protect what remains. Forests, ecosystems, and individual trees, everywhere, like her ginkgo, like the oaks lining her long-gone senator's house, like the forests of the Western Ghats.

She thinks of the women carrying firewood past acres of planted saplings. She thinks about the flowering cherry who was cut down at her street corner, for reasons she never did know, and how she misses not just the shade on a hot day but the tree's presence. She thinks of the live oaks her grandmaw sat under, selling baskets, until they were cut down for a parking lot. She thinks of how often trees are cut with little thought to how long they took to reach such size, what other lives depends on them.

It's a small thing, she knows, saving one tree in some parking lot, or a row of trees down a city street. But she's seen how this reforestation project has altered the way people here think about not just the planted trees but all trees. The way it's made them more aware of the plants they live with. She has begun to believe that the act of preventing one tree from being cut down would have ripple effects, waking people up in ways that might affect choices they make the rest of their lives.

This idea, it is so very different for her, so foreign to the way she has thought about the world for most of her life. It doesn't square with who she is back home in Chapel Hill, with who people know her to be, expect her to be—the logical thinker, the science-for-knowledge's-sake researcher. Yet her idea does not shrink but spreads into everything she experiences. Like kudzu, vining its way into everything. But not as nuisance. More like the way the sun's warmth feels after a period of cold. That steady, expansive, relieving warmth. She now feels more content with her time in India, with what they're achieving, and with her fossil searching too. She has a sense, with some larger time scale unfolding, that all of this is related, is leading her to a new—what Strilay would call, and here she smiles broadly—to a new leap.

With this Leave a Tree idea blossoming, even though she does miss Gareth, she finds it hard to think about leaving. But all that shifts when she hears from Joe in Canada again. When she hears his voice, everything falls away, and she feels, for the first time in months, a bone-deep cold. A chilling fear. But it's not that, it's not another heart attack. Instead, it turns out that Strilay, helping Joe repair a bear holding cell, got swiped by a bear in an adjacent cell, so that his arm will be out of commission for a while. He's fine, it's just a nasty scrape, Joe assures her, but still, they want to be safe. Astrid wonders, but not aloud, if they shouldn't have thought of such safety before Strilay helped Joe repair a bear cell. In any case, Strilay is going back to Chapel Hill to recuperate.

And so, she begins to think she might go home. At least for a while. The project here is going well. She's helped them determine the best species to plant at different sites, though mostly that knowledge has come from Mr. Varma. She's visited all the nearby fossil sites several times, collected a dozen good samples from which she can work for at least the next year, and is working with several Indian paleobotanists on a paper. And she's been tinkering with this new idea, one that won't seem to leave her alone; maybe it's time to let it be more than just an idea.

After nearly five months, at the beginning of the monsoons, she leaves. It's not easy, but she assures everyone, especially Prisha, that she'll be back. They give her a big going-away dinner, complete with dancers in traditional dress. Prisha hands her several packets of seeds, tells her, finger raised to lips, not to mention them at the airport. Astrid presses a small fossil into Mr. Varma's weathered hands. Lamont bear-hugs Astrid, tells her he's eternally grateful. And she is off, a driver taking her to Mumbai through a relentless downpour, from which she flies to Bangkok, and then through Anchorage, for a fuel stop.

Chapter 22

In Anchorage there is a mechanical delay, one that puts Astrid on the ground for an extra day. She plans on staying at the nearest airport hotel, but Gareth urges her to contact Elyse instead. Why not? What can it hurt? he says, in his sweetest cajole. And then, after retrieving her luggage, while she's talking with Gareth again, she gets another call. It's an Alaska number. It's Elyse. Gareth has called Charlotte, and Charlotte immediately called Elyse. Elyse says she'll be right there to pick Astrid up, take her to her house where she can rest, sleep, whatever she needs. Astrid, too tired to resist, waits outside baggage claim.

Elyse drives up in a Subaru station wagon with two large dogs. "Sorry," she says, "I'm not allowed to leave these two at home, they just won't have it. But they'll stay in the back, promise."

Bags and dogs. Astrid would, at one time, have been irritated with the idea of dog hair on her clothes and luggage, but after five months in India, and too many hours on a plane across too many time zones, such concerns do not even arise.

At Elyse's she is shown to her guest room. It is light-filled and quiet, the bed inviting with a plump white down cover that looks like a cloud upon which she could drift. Elyse makes her a cup of tea and says she'll be out in her studio if Astrid needs anything. Then she slips out the back door, leaving Astrid in blessed solitude. Astrid lies down, finding the cloud bed even more enfolding than she'd imagined. She feels her weight sink into the bed, feels the noise and commotion of all the airports and airplanes and taxis lift away. The house is so quiet, more quiet than she's experienced in all her time in India. She should get up and take a shower, or be more polite and make conversation with Elyse, but she thinks she'll lie there just a few more minutes before she gets up. She drifts and dreams of snow and polar bears and pale-faced monkeys sunning themselves on boulders. She's on a boat, drifting, and it bumps ashore. She wakes up. It is still light, sun streaming through the window and falling on her legs. But it's dinnertime here. Her belly grumbles. She pulls herself up, finds the bathroom, and splashes cool water on her face.

Elyse calls from downstairs, "There's some food here, if you're hungry."

She descends to find a table laden with biscuits and jelly, yogurt, berries, vegetables, and several kinds of dip, crackers, grapes, a broccoli casserole.

"I wasn't sure what time zone your body's in, whether you'd want breakfast or lunch or dinner, so I made a sort of mashup," says Elyse, setting a glass of lemon water down next to her plate.

They eat, with Elyse talking, nervously, filling the space, about life in Alaska, about weather and seasons and how it compares to North Carolina and Oregon. She asks about Charlotte, then talks awhile about Charlotte's art, how inspiring it is. Then she stops, noticing that Astrid has finished eating. She realizes she's been rambling to a jet-lagged, weary guest, just what she didn't want to do to this long-lost friend. "Well," she says, "I'll head back out to my studio, leave you in peace. Let me know if you need anything." She rises, clears plates from the table.

"Your studio, that's it?" says Astrid, pointing out the window to a small cabin in the woods.

"Yes, it is. Just a little dry cabin; it'd be nice to have running water for cleaning brushes, but a tub and rainwater catchment works pretty well. You're welcome to come see it if you'd like," she says, then catches herself, "but only if you want, I know you're tired."

"Sure," says Astrid.

"It's a mess, I'll warn you," says Elyse as they walk across the sun-lit yard, anxiety growing with each step. "I rarely have visitors."

Sophie and Darlene tag along, tails wagging, Darlene carrying a ball and making a sound like a Wookiee.

"She loves visitors," says Elyse, wishing Darlene wasn't quite so friendly. "She's just showing you her toy, an invitation to play. Not now, Darlene," she says, stroking the dark fur.

Astrid smiles but doesn't reach down to pet either Darlene or Sophie, who brushes her legs like a cat.

Inside, Astrid is struck by color. And movement. Large canvasses lean against every available space, all of them filled with the movement of what look to be trees. Except she's never seen such trees, such vibrant, almost fierce, emotion. Or has she? She gets that feeling again, the one she had in front of the polar bear and kudzu painting at the Ackland, that blurring of past and present, of what's real and what's even more real. She needs to sit. Is dizzy.

Elyse's heart jumps when she sees Astrid's pale face. "Oh, that jet lag," she says. "Maybe you should go lie down again?" She pulls out an upturned crate for Astrid to sit on.

"Oh, no, it's not that. It's just . . ." But she has no words. She is a scientist, not an artist. She doesn't know the language to describe the effect Elyse's work has on her. It's one of those moments again, the ones she wishes would stay but don't, the ones she's learned to heed—just the tiniest moment of boundaries falling away, every-thing suddenly clear, complete. Everything right.

Elyse places a cool glass of water in her hand. "Here, drink this. I'm so sorry. I should have just let you rest." Elyse tries not to let her mind go wild, but she can't help it. Are her new paintings that god-awful? No one else has seen them yet, she realizes with a hot flash, not even Maggie. How could she be so cavalier as to show them to Astrid?

"No, no," Astrid says, closing her eyes, feeling the cool water in her throat. "It's not the jet lag." Behind her eyelids rapid flashes of the women carrying sticks, of the dense smoke air in Singapore, of a sap-ling in her hands dark with soil, of Mr. Varma's tangled jungle. She opens her eyes and, seeing Elyse's worried expression, knows she needs to offer some explanation. So she tells Elyse about the tree-planting in India, the ways the work does and does not seem to be helping, and her sapling of an insight, her Leave a Tree idea. And how Elyse's paintings seem to capture something of this medley of ideas and feelings that still feel new.

It's an outpouring, and when she finally stops, she feels a sudden heat. It's not at all like her. But Elyse is standing before her with a wide grin. Astrid starts to blush. Elyse perches on a stool next to her.

"Oh, Astrid, it is so nice to hear you say these things! And I mean not just praising my work, though I always enjoy that," she grins. "No, it's that what you're saying, well, I get it. Completely. While you were talking I was also remembering when we were kids, sitting in our kudzu kingdom, and—we were talking like this. Two peas in a pod, like your mother called us. I just, well, I am just so happy to hear all this from you."

And then Elyse tells Astrid how she started painting these trees, tells her about the forest walk and windstorm, about the article and photograph of Astrid in India, even about Nicolaf, and her confusion since his death.

"It's just," she says, finding encouragement in Astrid's gaze, "I started feeling this sense of urgency and rootedness all at once. When I began painting these trees. A sense that something was coming through me, I'm just the conduit. As if the trees were . . . well, I can't believe I'm being so open, I mean, we're not little kids in kudzu anymore, but what have I got to lose? The thing is, I've been feeling that, somehow, plants can save us."

Elyse falls quiet. They look at each other, one long deep stare. The room fills with silence, a comforting silence. For Astrid, it's like that moment with Charlotte in the restaurant when she realized there was much more to her friend, only this time there's also a tug of history, of repairing a rift and rekindling a connection. For Elyse that tug of history is also at root, pulling up a deep feeling of wholeness that she hasn't felt for a long time, not since she was a mother holding her baby close.

Darlene sighs, turns around three times, and settles onto the floor near Astrid's feet. Astrid smiles, pets her, and begins again to talk, her voice clear and steady. She describes the scene in Singapore, tells Elyse about the falling of her ginkgo and the Shukkei-en, about the simultaneous tree-planting and tree-cutting in India. She confesses to a deep undercurrent of futility that she tries to but cannot keep at bay. Elyse listens, nods, remains silent until Astrid stops. There is another long and comfortable pause, and then Elyse starts to speak, seamlessly picking up where Astrid left off. She tells Astrid about Nicolaf's town, the polar bears, the walrus, and the storms. Then Astrid picks up, tells Elyse about Strilay and Churchill and Joe. Elyse talks about Justin and the valve-turners. Astrid talks about Prisha and Macey, her heritage. They weave a single blanket from their separate experiences, experiences that resonate and overlap. Meanwhile the sun keeps sliding sideways, the golden glow deepening.

"Oh, if you're waiting for the sun to set, don't bother, it won't until sometime in the middle of the night," laughs Elyse. "Come, let's go find some more food, and wine."

"Okay," says Astrid, "yes. But one more thing: I want to apologize. For abandoning you. When we were girls. I was wrong about your father, about you."

"Oh," says Elyse, drawing in a sharp breath, "I . . . thank you. It's okay. We were kids. He was your dad. But thank you for saying that. It's . . . I . . . I've missed you."

"I've missed you, too," says Astrid, "and I didn't even realize it."

They talk long into the night, long enough to finally see summer's brief darkness descend. At some point, Dan comes home and spends a short time with them. Astrid is curious about DWB, and her questions set him off into a long-winded story that Elyse has heard dozens of times, but that, through Astrid's eyes, reminds Elyse of the amazing work her husband does in the world.

On a walk the next morning, climbing through cottonwoods to a bluff along the streaming gray mudflats of Turnagain Arm, Astrid impulsively—for her—invites Elyse to Chapel Hill. "Perhaps," she says, "You could come as artist-in-residence for a month or so.

There's a small cottage for the artist. Families are allowed, so I'm guessing you could bring your dogs. What do you think?"

"Oh, wow, that sounds . . . great! I mean, I'd love to! But, well, it's a lot to think about. Let me . . . thank you so much!"

Astrid smiles at Elyse's enthusiasm, the same kind of childlike excitement she remembers from their childhood. It's still there, that bubbly wonder. They walk over a small bridge. A clear creek chatters its way down the mountainside, threading among aspen and cottonwood, bouncing beside the unfurling palms of devil's club, blueberry, and kinnikinnick, skipping and leaping all the way to the sea.

"I'll bring it up with the Ackland director, then. I'm sure they'll be interested, given the success of your show and how they're doing more collaborative ventures with other departments. This would be, well, certainly something the environmental studies program will be excited about."

"That sounds so great! Thanks!" Elyse says, hoping her enthusiasm hides a sudden upwelling of anxiety. Living in Chapel Hill, even for a few weeks, how would that affect her already rocky marriage?

"And maybe we can talk more, then, about the Leave a Tree idea," says Astrid.

"Yes, I've been thinking . . ." says Elyse, words tumbling out as fast as she can think them, "maybe I could paint portraits of some of the trees that are threatened, highlight their uniqueness, their history, their personality. You know, a kind of—portrait gallery."

Sophie, off in the woods, lets out a yip, and a snowshoe hare dashes in front of them across the trail. The two women stop and watch the flash of brown dart and dodge and effortlessly bound into an alder thicket, disappearing into the forest tapestry. The dogs appear, wet and muddy and long-tongued with joy. A passing breeze sends the newly opened aspen leaves to shaking, a high soft clapping filling the air around them.

Chapter 23

Home, Astrid walks across a quiet, sun-soaked campus to her office. It, too, is quiet. Sanders's project is finished, his graduate students no longer rooting around in her collection. His conclusions were, unsurprisingly, exactly what ExxonMobil wanted: plants like lycopods had survived similar warming periods with little negative effect, and thus would survive this one as well, whether or not it was caused by humans. In fact, he'd gone a step further and postulated that, by providing more carbon dioxide, warming is good for plants and may benefit agriculture. The oil corporation had been so pleased that Sanders received more funding for an even larger follow-up project. He'd outgrown Astrid's collection and had moved to Yale, where he'd been given a position at the prestigious Peabody Museum. So her lab is once more hers alone, and she can return to her own work uninterrupted.

She sits at her desk, carefully opening one of the boxes containing samples she collected in India. She's excited to begin working on these, looking for the missing links to the lycopod family tree. At least she thinks she is. After about fifteen minutes, she sighs, gets up, and paces the room. She runs one hand across the top of a cabinet, stoops and stares in at her collection. During her entire time in India, she was never really alone, except in bed at night. She always had someone with her—a driver, a tiger guide, a colleague, other tree-planters, Lamont, Prisha—every waking hour. Even walking to town by herself, there were always other people in the streets, in their gardens, buzzing by on mopeds. Now, as much as she craved solitude during all those months in India, she feels uneasy being alone.

After a few more minutes of pacing and staring out the window, she sets the fossil back in its wrapping and heads out the door, home to Gareth.

Elyse, in her studio, stares at her wild forest. The work, she knows, is becoming more abstract—which might make it harder to do something collaborative with Astrid. Still, the idea thrills her. She rereads Kandinsky's *The Art of Spiritual Harmony* and imagines the tree portraits being entirely abstract—about feeling rather than representation. Like their own music, the language of trees. She has talked to Dan about Astrid's offer, and he was very nonchalant about her leaving, and taking the dogs, for a couple of months. Surprisingly nonchalant. She actually wishes he had protested, just a little. Crazy, she knows, given how much she'd have appreciated such support, or at least a lack of resistance, when she was going to Cape Vankarem. What does she really want from him, from this marriage? It feels like constantly shifting sands.

She puts down her sketchpad and walks to the house. Starts preparing dinner. Dan comes in the door an hour later, pecks her on the cheek, and they sit to their meal. Silence spreads across the table, so Elyse attempts a jump-start. "Tell me, what have you heard from your colleagues in Syria? Are things improving there yet?" she asks.

"Not much," he says, not bothering to stop eating.

"You know," she tries again, "when Astrid was here, and you two were talking about DWB, I, well, I was reminded of how proud I am of you. Of the work you do. I just wanted you to know that."

"Thanks, yeah, it's challenging, but you know me, I like a good challenge," he replies, finally looking up with a quick, bright smile.

There, in his eyes, she sees that man she'd fallen in love with. The man who loves adventure, the man who was such a fun father all those years to her—their—two boys. Desperate to make that version stay, she soldiers on, "Oh, yes, and what great stories you bring back from them. Remember telling the boys your stories at nighttime? And trying to keep out the scary parts, the dangerous parts?"

"Yeah," he smiles again. "Yeah. Wonder if I shouldn't have, though." He puts down his fork. "I mean, look at Justin. Maybe he'd be more careful. I think now that some things are best left unfiltered." Then he looks up at her with an expression she doesn't recognize, some mixture of sorrow and—and what? some other emotion—as if he wants to say something else, but doesn't.

Astrid takes the long way home, wanting to see what's become of her ginkgo. Before going to India, she'd lobbied to have the stump left, to let the tree sprout back from its roots. It's gone, though, the stump dug up by the grounds crew; there was no way they'd leave an unsightly stump right in front of the entrance to the psychology building. It's been replaced by a new ginkgo, a sapling whose trunk is no thicker than her wrist. She stands for a moment before this new tree and feels a turbulence of sorrow and happiness—a turbulence that has grown familiar and carries with it a new kind of calm, a grounding in the midst of groundlessness. In a sudden passing breeze, clusters of green leaves wave like small hands.

The arboretum embraces her with flowers, bees humming happily in the wisteria. She perches on the bench under the pergola, just for a moment, letting the sticky heat of summer settle onto her skin. Her homecoming has been uneventful. Gareth had picked her up last night, cheerily as usual, which reminded her of Elyse. They'd had a nice long conversation over a glass of wine before he went off to bed. She, meanwhile, jet-lagged, had stayed up several hours. He'd had a plant waiting for her, of course: a lemon tree in a bright blue pot. She is—well, she'd hoped it would have somehow been obvious to her that he had truly missed her. Such a strange feeling, for her to even be thinking about this. And yet, here it is, leaving her feeling all—she hears her mother's voice—all catawampus.

The house is empty when she arrives, and Gareth shows up just in time to change and head back out the door, to the welcome-home dinner at Ernesto and Joel's. Their house is large, light-filled, and decorated in shades of white and mauve. So big, thinks Astrid; in India twelve people would live here. The living room is filled with Astrid's favorite people. Strilay finds her first, envelops her in a big hug, his thin arms surprisingly strong. Charlotte is there with a new girlfriend, Morgan. Astrid, upon meeting Morgan, feels that small worry in her chest, the one about Charlotte and Gareth, dissipate like mist. Morgan is a chemist with one of the labs in Research Triangle Park; she's very quiet and serious, very reserved in her gray suit and sensible shoes, very much not like Charlotte. Dean Thorn is there, too, and confides in her how disappointed he is that Sanders has not only left the university but has poached some of their graduate students. He bemoans Sanders's lack of loyalty until Strilay appears, steering the conversation toward her India trip. But she's not yet ready to tell Strilay about it, at least not everything.

After the party, as Astrid steps into their small, quiet house, she lets out a long sigh and says, "Ah, what a wonderful home to come home to."

"That's music to my ears," says Gareth. "The place feels much better to me, now that you're back."

"Does it?" she says, turning to him, watching his brown eyes carefully, "Are you glad to have me home? I mean—are you really? I've been gone awhile; maybe you've gotten used to things without me."

"No, no, not at all. Whyever would you say that?"

"You seem, well, you seem to have gotten on just fine without me, and you didn't exactly beg me to come home."

"Of course not. Astrid," he says, his hands on both her shoulders, "look. I want you here. I wouldn't mind if you were *more* here. If you were more interested in us, in being with me. I just try hard not to smother you with too much togetherness, since you're so daggum independent. But believe you me, I'd love to do a little smothering!"

"Oh, okay, I think," she says, her smile strong and almost involuntary, like the first time they met. "Yes. More of it. I missed you. Missed us. I don't want to, but I think I was taking you for granted. I don't want you to have to turn to anyone else for—companionship."

"Oh, hell's bells," he says with a gap-tooth smile. "Whatever has been going on in that big brain of yours?" He pauses, begins again, his voice deeper, his gaze unwavering. "I'm not turning to anyone else. You're it. You're stuck with me, like it or not. I'm not going anywhere."

Conflicted about her marriage, wondering what Dan is thinking, confused about what she wants, Elyse does what has become a habitual response whenever anything has her stumped: she takes the dogs on a long walk and then visits Binky. She knows, midsummer, the zoo will be crowded and the bear won't be in need of any company. She may not even be able to get a good view. But as she walks the familiar trail toward her enclosure, dodging stroller wheels and catching one small boy, running fast and looking behind him, before he trips just outside the llama enclosure, she notices that there are no crowds around Binky's enclosure. No one at all, in fact. Just a sign on the fence: This exhibit temporarily closed. She scans the entire enclosure; there's no bear in there.

Her heart beats faster, her palms sweat. She rushes back down the trail toward the entrance, her tolerance for children and strollers dissipated. Ticket agents are busy, so she bursts into the gift shop and asks the first employee she sees, but the young man knows nothing, only that the polar bear exhibit is closed indefinitely. She races back out, looks around for someone, anyone, who works at the zoo—and then remembers she has Beverly's number in her phone.

"Where's Binky?" Elyse asks as soon as Beverly picks up. "I'm at the zoo, and she's not here. The exhibit is closed. Did something happen?"

"Oh," says Beverly, "yeah . . . Binky is sick. I don't think they know what it is yet, and so they're just, well, taking precautions, in case it's contagious, and also, you know, trying not to stress her. She's there, just in the back. Doing lots of sleeping."

"Okay, okay," says Elyse. "Well, how could I find out, who could I talk to, to see what's wrong with her?"

"The bear veterinarian. His name's . . . tell you what, I'll give him your number. He can call you."

"Okay, okay, thanks, Beverly. Wow, such a shock not to see her in there . . ."

"Yeah, weird, huh? Well . . . gotta go . . . studying for an exam . . ."

Two days go by, and the veterinarian doesn't call, so she calls Beverly again. And learns what's wrong with Binky. Binky is depressed. It's common among zoo animals, especially bears and other predators; their lives in zoos cannot replicate even a fraction of what their wild lives would be. Even just in space alone: most bear enclosures at zoos are about one-millionth the size of a wild bear's territory. So zoo animals suffer a form of madness caused by confinement that's so prevalent it's been given its own name: *zoochosis*. The zoo veterinarian is trying to figure out what medication—antidepressants, antipsychotics—will work for Binky.

"But you can't tell anyone I told you," says Beverly. "Zoos don't want visitors knowing animals are medicated just to keep them from acting weird."

"Is this why," says Elyse, her voice hushed and halting, "is this why she sleeps all the time?"

"Yeah, partly. She's bored. And she gets stressed by all the visitors, especially when they try to make her wake up and do something. And she can't do anything about them, can't chase them, can't eat them." Beverly laughs, but stops quickly. "Sorry. Look, it's just the deal. She's a zoo animal. This is the life she's stuck living. So we try to make it as comfortable as possible."

For days afterward, Elyse feels lost. She should have known that Binky was suffering. She had certainly guessed as much. She feels stupid, indulgent, for thinking that going to see Binky was helpful to the polar bear. One of the many delusions humans live with, she thinks, so that they can justify their cruelty. Finally, she decides that the only way for her to face this reality is to go to the zoo again.

What she finds, though, is another polar bear in Binky's enclosure, a very small one, a cub, little white puffball with black button eyes and nose, rolling about on the concrete, all alone. A sign replacing the closed one says this cub was just orphaned when his mother was shot and killed in defense of property by an Utqiagvik resident.

Elyse stands still, feeling another round of shock, just as Beverly appears around the corner.

"What is this about, this orphaned cub? Do you know what happened?"

"Oh," says Beverly. "Yeah, I do. It was my cousin who shot the mom. He told us that bear was going after his muktuk in the shed next to his house."

"And he shot her, even though she had a cub?"

"He says he didn't know there was a cub until after he shot the sow, and the cub came running out from behind a fuel barrel, running straight to the dead mom. The cub climbed on her, and so was super easy to catch."

"Oh!" says Elyse. "Why couldn't he have just chased them off instead of shooting?"

"Yeah, he's kinda gun-happy, unfortunately," says Beverly, shaking her head. "I don't like him much; I kinda avoid him when I go visit. He is a good whale hunter, though, people say he has very good aim."

"Well," says Elyse, pointing to the cub, "here's proof of that."

"I know," Beverly says. "It sucks. People at home are always telling me, I guess 'cause I work at the zoo and they know I like animals, they always are telling me that our people have been hunting polar bears for thousands of years and they haven't gone extinct, so we should keep getting to hunt them as much as we want. My grandma, though," Beverly's voice softens, "she says guns have made it too easy. She says snowmachines and guns have messed things up. She says we can't even hear what the animals and the wind and ice are trying to tell us with those engines blaring so loud."

"Oh," says Elyse, "your grandmother, she sounds wise."

"Yeah, but no one listens to her. Except me."

Astrid's days are bright since she and Gareth cleared the air. And busy. She and Gareth have been working with Lamont and Solar Cooking International to donate solar cookers and hold cooking classes in Karnataka. Lamont sent her a photo of Prisha showing her daughter how to use one, cooking okra from the seeds Gareth brought. And she's approached the Ackland director about inviting Elyse to be an artist-in-residence. He agreed, quickly and enthusiastically, especially when the art department and the environmental studies department signed on to co-sponsor. She and Elyse have decided on next April and May for her visit. Eight months from now.

Enough time, Astrid hopes, for her to have a better handle on these India samples, so that she'll feel fine about stepping away from them to work with Elyse.

She sits now at her desk, staring at one of the samples, trying to recall what she had noticed about it in the field, or what the paleobotanist from Jaipur had said about it. She flips through her field notebook. There's a knock on her open door, and she turns to see a young woman, one of Dr. Sanders's graduate students, the one Astrid had surprised that day she'd come to her office after hours. The one who jumped up and left at her arrival, as if she'd been caught doing something wrong. One who had, evidently, not abandoned UNC for Yale.

"Yes?"

"Dr. Baldwin, do you have a minute?"

"Yes, yes, I do," says Astrid, marking the page in her field notebook before setting it down.

"I've . . . my name is Aisha Moire. . . . I was working with Dr. Sanders . . ."

"Yes, I recall seeing you here, going through my collection."

"Yes! Yes, that was me. And so I, well, I'm looking for a new research project, now that Dr. Sanders has left, and Dean Thorn suggested I talk to you. He told me about your work in India, and that sounds so interesting, I've always wanted to go there, I have a great-aunt in New Delhi . . ."

"Oh, well, yes, I don't have the funds, really, for . . ."

"I know. Dean Thorn told me. But he said, he thought, that the university, well, that they could find funding for me, if you agreed to have an assistant."

Astrid looks at the samples from India. She'd always envisioned doing this work alone. Had actually looked forward to it. But she has been struggling to make any progress. An assistant could speed things up, free her for other things.

"I already have office space in the grad student study room," Aisha says hurriedly, "and my schedule is very flexible so I can do my work in here when you're not here, to stay out of your way . . ."

And so Aisha comes to work for Astrid. It works out so well that more grads flock to Astrid, some also left stranded by Sanders. She works with Lamont and her Indian colleagues to set up a work-study program: students go to India for a semester, volunteer with Lamont's project, and help with fieldwork at fossil sites. "An academic mashup," one student called it as Astrid cringed. But even she, who still requires all of them to have a strong foundation in basic research, acknowledges that there's no telling what the future will require of these students, only that it will demand they think about and do things differently.

It's on a late night, when she's thinking how the future will require something different, that she comes across the pile of papers and newspaper clippings Gareth has given her over the years on her probable ancestors, the Gullah Geechee. Sleepless, she sifts through them. One article describes their ritual of going into the woods three times a day to commune with the natural world. Just what her grandmaw did. Astrid stares at the words. Drops the paper, gets online, finds out more, listens to recordings of the language, of songs, one that's exactly what her grandmaw used to sing. Exactly. Suddenly she's under the old oak with her grandmaw, beside the bean trellis with Prisha, leaning against the tree with leaf-cutter ants, standing before Elyse's tree painting. Desire and joy spring up in her like a fountain that has been dry for ages. And from that wellspring flows renewed courage, banishing the last of her doubts about her own knowing, which is, she finally sees, beyond all scientific learning. *Disya who we be.*

Astrid shrugs off old assumptions. She seeks answers where she hasn't before. Working with Aisha, learning more about Sanders's project, Astrid finds, in a disagreement with one of his basic assumptions, a key to her own research. She's delving into Strilay's work on linear time, much to his eternal delight, and linking her test plot findings to the fossils from India. Asked by a reporter for the *Daily Tar Heel* to explain what she's focused on now, she says it's just like studying history, except in reverse: she's studying today's lycopodium to get insights into the ones from the past, but with one difference: a shift in time's linearity since the Industrial Age began.

She tells the reporter about being in Churchill, standing over that small, and now endangered, lycopod. About wondering if her work in paleobotany was irrelevant and even a waste of time—if she was just fiddling while the barn's burning—trying to weave together the past while the present is unraveling—and how that moment was the beginning, really, of her seeing how it all connects.

"As a paleobotanist," she tells the reporter, "I spend my time studying species that have gone extinct, many from changes to climate. So I look at the species around today, the survivors, the adaptors, and I can see their place, and the place of humanity, in the larger continuum of life. That's why climate change is so terrifying. I know what mass extinction means."

Astrid smiles as the reporter can't think of anything to say but "Continue, please." She knows this work seems far from paleo-botany, but she can no longer stay quiet about what is happening to the plants that still root the Earth in place.

"Many plants are, now, because of human development, stuck on an ecological island," she says, "so they can't even migrate in response to a changing climate. They've run out of room. Just like the plants and animals of the far north: from polar bears to lichens, there's no more north for them to move to. It's all, well, it's a mess. So—I'm using my knowledge of the past to show what may happen in the future. If we don't wake up very soon."

Chapter 24

Wolverine Peak rises 4,500 feet above the Anchorage bowl. It's one of the most prominent and recognizable peaks of the Chugach Mountains' front range. All winter long, whenever Elyse sees the mountain, from her car or a trail or out a high-rise window downtown, she looks forward to climbing to the peak again. And now she is, finally. Late August, and the trail is snow-free to the top, though any day now termination dust may appear. Tinges of yellow and orange already thread summer's welcoming green.

She's thankful, in the midst of so much going on, to find this window of a blue-sky day to climb the mountain. Justin is still awaiting a trial date, but they have a good lawyer and high hopes. And he's calling and texting her often, as is Sam. They're both coming to visit in a week and have plans to backpack Crow Pass. She feels connected to both sons again, which alone puts her at ease. Binky's health has improved, not so much because of the medications but because of the cub, who Binky seems to have adopted. With the good news from the Ackland, she's also been making plans to go, and take the dogs with her, for at least two months next spring. It's a long way off, but she's coordinating it with preparations for the shows at the Alaska Museum and the Venus Gallery. It's a continual amazement, how well her art career is going—even as her marriage has deteriorated. She and Dan have had a few sessions with a marriage counselor, but they haven't done much good. At the last session, a few days ago, Dan made it clear he was done.

Elyse stops, sits on a boulder, takes a long drink from her water bottle. Sophie and Darlene are off in the alder below her; they've hiked above the treeline now, almost done with the alder patches, tundra stretching above and around her. It's a steep climb in this section, but she loves this moment of breaking through alder to a wide-open view. Below her spreads the city, the gray arms of Turnagain Arm and Cook Inlet curving around it like a liquid protection; beyond rises Sleeping Lady and the Alaska Range, the saw-toothed mountains jutting above icefields, the conical peaks of the volcanoes—Spurr, Redoubt, Iliamna, Augustine—spiraling into blue sky. All this beauty, mixed with all the sorrow she's feeling. A bittersweetness pervades the very air. Just as she was finding her way back to loving Dan, he is giving up.

What he'd said, at the counselor's, was not as chilling as the way he said it. Calm, clear, clinical. As if he were preparing relatives for the impending death of a patient whose heart transplant was failing. Practiced, and distant. "I'm just done," he said, or something like that. She was too much in shock to remember much now, all she remembers is how it felt, how her body had grown cold, her head so light she felt dizzy, her legs turned to lead.

"It feels liberating, really," he'd said, then turned to her. "We've had a good long run. Raised two fine young men, had lots of great adventures. I don't regret a minute of it. But, face it, Elyse, we're traveling different paths now."

"Wait," she said, "are you saying we're one of those couples who split as soon as the kids fledge? Have you been sticking it out for them?"

"I'm just tired," he said, "of the friction between us. You're changing in ways that are good for you, I'm sure, but they're not, well, it's just not working for me. And you don't need me anymore, not really," he continued, as she sat still, gripping the armchair. "We're mostly just two ships passing in the night. I doubt you'll even miss me."

She had stumbled through some response about them supporting each other's growth, about how together they each have the most freedom to grow, how that's what marriage was about. But he didn't hear her. He was done. All that was left, in his mind, was some paperwork.

She should have known. A few nights earlier, when he'd slipped into bed hours after her, she woke and turned toward him, her nose to his neck, finding that spot just under his ear where she could always smell his unique scent. She breathed it in and, desire rising, curved her arms around his chest, the familiar softness of his skin against her palm. But he'd said, without even turning to look at her, "Not now. I'm tired."

And so they are separating. Give it a year, the counselor suggested, before deciding whether or not to divorce. I still want to try, Elyse said. Dan had then laid out his plans: he was moving to Geneva to take a position at DWB headquarters. He already had one foot out the door.

Elyse has almost reached the summit. The ridgeline she now follows drops off on one side into a nearly vertical cliff, one she doesn't like to approach too closely. At least, not on just two feet. Mostly she keeps her gaze focused on the other side, which curves down into a bowl laced red and yellow and threaded with silver rivulets from a multitude of springs. Then she stops, drops to hands and knees, crawls to the edge, and peers over the steep side. Sophie and Darlene are already standing at the edge, staring down, ears perked up, tails waving.

Liberating. Dan said it was liberating. The word has been ringing in Elyse's head like an insistent tune that won't be silenced. Like a bell ringing, one she has been hearing for longer than she knew, until now. It's all clear now. She looks over and down into the vertical maze of dark rock spires where small patches of green cling to scree. Down, and down, and there, among the turrets, lying on a larger patch of green, chewing their cud, are three Dall sheep.

She stares at them, awed at how impossibly comfortable they seem on such a sheer drop. She sits back and gazes all around at the shimmering lakes and streams coursing through emerald valleys, the complex notes of rocky ridgelines dancing off in all directions, and feels, just for a fleeting moment, as if she is falling through herself, and all that remains is a beautiful emptiness, that whoever she has become, has always been, is all this, these mountains and valleys and streams and sky.

The day Astrid's profile in the *Daily Tar Heel* appears, Strilay calls and says they must have lunch together right away. As she walks to the Carolina Coffee Shop, she wonders what he has to tell her now. She knows his arm has healed, although it's still somewhat weak, and so perhaps he'll announce plans to return to Churchill again. But no. As soon as she finds him, sitting in the booth that might as well have his name inscribed on it, he begins to clap.

"Bravo!" he says. "Bravo, Astrid! Music to my ears, m'dear, music to my ears!"

"Why, thank you, but for what?"

"Your interview! You've connected the dots, and you've gone beyond even my wildest dreams. Oh, I'm so very delighted. Beyond delighted."

"Thanks," she says, chuckling, "Does this mean I'll pass your ethics course, then, Dr. Strilay?"

"Pass it? My dear Astrid, you're passing me! You're up there with the likes of Dr. Leakey now."

"Oh, I don't think—no, mentioning him and me in the same sentence, no. But thanks."

"So, what's next? What new worlds to conquer? Or shall I rephrase: what new worlds to save?"

"Oh, well, why don't you tell me what you're up to, first?"

And so he does. He's increasingly involved in the Solutions Project, has a winter full of speaking engagements around the country, and a ticket to go to Churchill in one month. "But just for three weeks," he says, "so don't get that worried look. Just to see the bears head out onto the ice. It does my heart good."

"Okay, just three weeks, and no heavy labor near penned polar bears, right?"

"Right. Joe is under strict orders from his boss. They were simply terrified I was going to sue. But Astrid, back to you, what's next for you?"

"Well," she says, lowering her voice, "I had this idea in India, but I just don't know . . ."

She tells him, hesitantly, about the Leave a Tree idea. How it sprang from what he'd told her about black carbon, from Lovejoy's theory, from watching people cut forests for heat and cooking while also seeing the benefits of the tree-planting project for communities.

"And Elyse's paintings," she says. "I'm not sure how they fit, but her work is powerful. . . . I don't know. I'm worried, the longer I'm home, that this project could harm . . . could make it hard for me to get funding, to continue my research . . ."

Strilay leans in, bushy brows raised. But he waits for her to finish.

"I might be jumping off the deep end here. I'm thinking I should back up a bit. Maybe not include the art, since that might undermine the credibility of the science," she trails off with a sigh.

"Oh, no, do not scale it back," says Strilay, his voice firm. "The potential in reducing black carbon is only good news if we act on it. And the art, cross-discipline work is needed now more than ever. People aren't making decisions based on science, Astrid. Just look at this project I'm working on: North Carolina could get to 100 percent alternatives tomorrow, if only we had the political will. Which depends on people's perceptions."

He sits back, his voice taking on a weary tone. "There's a solar farm project near Elizabethtown that's on the rocks because of some of the worst misinformation I've ever heard. At the town council meeting, one resident said that solar farms cause cancer; another said the solar array would suck up all the energy from the sun, not leaving enough for surrounding crops."

Astrid laughs, but stops quickly at the look on his face.

"I wish I was joking," he says, "but even more terrifying is that this was from a retired science teacher. Science! Imagine what kind of education she gave her students."

"Surely no one believed her?"

"Oh, Astrid," he says, "we've got to disabuse ourselves of the assumption that humans are rational creatures."

He sighs, takes a sip of coffee. The coffee shop is filling with the lunchtime crowd, and outside, the sun blazes down a noonday heat that amplifies a muggy September day, as summer's heat lingers into the fall.

"All the science in the world will not change people's minds, and that," he says, "is where art comes in. It reaches us on another level. We make decisions now from our echo chambers, especially with something as complex and intangible as climate change. But art can break through all that. It can slip in like light waves."

He raises both arms, palms to the sky. "Things are always changing, that's simply the nature of matter and energy. And that means people's minds are constantly changing too. They're not responding to fact alone, but they are responding. So we've got to slip in through art. The power of images and story and a certain, well, alchemy."

Astrid sits, listens, leans forward. This time, as the sparks leap and ignite, she sees what they reveal, and welcomes them.

Elyse sits at her kitchen table, the map of North Carolina spread out before her. She is days away from leaving for Chapel Hill. Everything is ready for her departure. The house, simplified now with Dan's belongings mostly gone, will be in Beverly's care. Elyse visited Binky yesterday; the bear was on her back, great paws in the air, rolling and swatting and playing with the cub, who climbed all over Binky as if she were a giant jungle gym. Binky didn't seem to notice Elyse was even there. Her last conversation with the zoo administrators was encouraging: because Binky, rather than humans, has been caring for the cub, the cub may be eligible to be released back into the wild. And they are in conversation with wildlife authorities and Polar Bear International about Binky being a surrogate mother for other orphaned polar bear cubs from around the world. It's not a Disney ending; polar bear cubs are still being orphaned, and animals like Binky are still doomed to a half-life in a zoo.

Elyse stares at the map, glad that she'll be escaping her home territory for a couple months. It's been a hard winter with Dan gone. She traces the lines of the Outer Banks with one finger. Astrid has told her they'll get to visit Dr. Shank's project at the coast and spend a couple of days at the Outer Banks too. Elyse was last there years ago, when her boys were little. It was just the three of them; Dan was off on some trip somewhere, she can't recall where, and Elyse had decided to take the boys to beaches she remembered from her childhood. They'd had a grand time, building sandcastles, watching the sunset from Jockey's Ridge, dressing as pirates and telling Blackbeard stories.

Last month, on their Crow Pass backpacking trip, it was just the three of them again, plus, of course, Sophie and Darlene. The boys were great; Sam so even-keeled as always, and Justin so self-assured that she's grown even more at ease with his path. So many times it's been just the three of them; so much of her married life she's spent without Dan. Ships passing in the night. If that.

She looks at her finger, stopped on the point that marks Cape Lookout. The lines of the Outer Banks look oddly familiar. They look like—the mammoth tusk on the tundra near Cape Vankarem. Those same arcs, points, curves, lines. The movement, like a song, or a dance. There's something out of time about these shapes, a kind of language being spoken. Time, the passage of time. Time's arrow is not so straight; it's full of curves and points and gaps. Her sons, now grown. Nicolaf, now gone from the world. The complexity of his culture, how little she knows, how complicated things seem, but at root, she knows this to be true, all living beings want the same thing—to endure. Nicolaf's community, the walrus, Binky, polar bears, her sons: all thrum with the will to endure. The tusks, their lines, reminders of all the life that has lived on this planet, all the beautiful beings gone. And all the beauty that remains.

Astrid and Elyse are walking into town from campus. Elyse has now been in Chapel Hill for a month, but in the last week the town has changed. Finals are over, students have dispersed for the summer, and the town has grown more quiet even as the days warm. They're heading to the Carolina Coffee Shop for lunch with Strilay and are talking about the aversion people are developing to discussing climate change, and about *solastalgia*, a new term that psychologists have coined to refer to the particular type of distress caused when the natural world around a person changes for the worse.

Elyse feels it deeply, a sense of panic, of being overwhelmed, one that she's sure fuels others' choices to simply ignore, or try to ignore, what's happening. Until, of course, they can't; until their very home is at risk from rising seas or hurricanes or fires. Yes, Astrid feels it, too, has felt it for some time, that unnamed sorrow pulling her down the underground river. But now, she feels also a lightness, a hope rooted in action. So she reassures Elyse with her mother's wisdom—do what you can, release the outcome—and with the story of Mr. Varma, who didn't have anything in mind except planting bamboo to save a few snakes.

They walk slowly, on a circuitous route that takes them into the arboretum where the wisteria is newly blooming, their sweet grape scent trailing them like a shadow, and then by the ginkgo sapling with his thin yet promising branches. Elyse, seeing a flicker of sorrow cross Astrid's face, suddenly recalls, and speaks, an age-old saying: plant trees whose shade you will never sit under. Astrid smiles, and nods.

They fall silent. The sun shines bright overhead, and the paved sidewalk shimmers heat waves up before them. They veer off to a narrow footpath and follow a cracked sidewalk through a vacant, scrubby, wooded lot. Dandelions give way to honeysuckle vines who yield to a mix of saplings and shrubs and then a deeper, darker green. They come to three cement steps, moss-laced and angled downhill, with just enough room for two to sit. The shade is soothing after the brilliant sunshine, soothing and calming. It's a shade not from trees, but from kudzu. Kudzu has transformed the abandoned lot, has covered old buildings and telephone poles and other, unidentifiable objects—all of it—creating a green sea that spreads over everything. The two women sit on the cool steps and let out long, deep sighs. Then they both lean back on their hands. They gaze up into the vibrant emerald kudzu. A light wind rises, scattering sunlight like a prism, wedding the tangle of leaf to the blue sky beyond.

Acknowledgments

From the Kudzu maze I retreated to behind our first house in Asheville, to the polar bears I watched scavenging the whale-bone pile in Kaktovik, the other-than-human world inspired every word of this story. I'm forever grateful to them, forever in love and awe. I'm also thankful for other writers, especially Anne Pancake, Linda Hogan, and Barbara Kingsolver, who've shown me what fiction can do with big intangible subjects that extend beyond humans. Thanks to those who provided insights on early drafts, and those who inspired and encouraged me, including Antonia Fowler, Mei Mei Evans, Carol Hult, Alyson Pytte, Gretchen Primack, Martha Amore, Wanda Moser, Carlo Laertini, and Lisa Couturier. Many thanks to Peggy Shumaker and the team at University of Alaska Press for making this book a reality. Gratitude to my son, James Holleman, for his love and support. Bottomless thanks to my husband, Rick Steiner, for cheerfully and lovingly enduring all the angst that comes with writing a novel. And finally, to (and for) my dad, Andrew Albert Scotchie (1931–2017)—whose advice to his kids was so often spot-on—for asking me, after my first nonfiction book came out, "Why don't you write a novel?"

About the Author

MARYBETH HOLLEMAN was raised by North Carolina's Great Smoky Mountains and lives in the embrace of Alaska's Chugach Mountains. She's author of *tender gravity: poems*, *The Heart of the Sound*, co-author of *Among Wolves*, and co-editor of *Crosscurrents North*, among others. She's also co-editor of the forthcoming *Alaska Literary Field Guide*. Her award-winning work appears in over 50 venues including *Orion*, *Christian Science Monitor*, *Sierra*, *North American Review*, *zoomorphic*, and *The Guardian*. She's held artist residencies in such diverse places as Hedgebrook, Mesa Refuge, Ninfa, Denali National Park, and Tracy Arm Ford's Terror Wilderness. She transplanted to Alaska after falling head over heels for Prince William Sound just two years before the oil spill. When she's not kayaking those beloved fjords, she's following her wild huskies up and down Alaska's mountains.